THE
Soul Keys

Alan D. McNarie

for Cathy.

Enjoy!

Alan D. Mc Narie

The Larry Czerwonka Company, LLC
Hilo, Hawai‘i

First Edition — November 2015

This book is set in 12-point Garamond

Published by The Larry Czerwonka Company, LLC
czerwonkapublishing.com

Printed in the United States of America

ISBN: 069249667X
ISBN-13: 978-0692496671

In loving memory of
Auntie Margaret "Be" Wright Jones,
nurturer of waifs, artists and other lost souls.

Contents

WARNING

All butterflies are insane.

It starts in larvahood. A caterpillar is born a slow, ugly orphan, easy pickings for any bird, mantis, spider or wasp that comes along. Easy pickings, not easy death. A mantis seizes you and just starts chewing while you're still alive. A spider injects poison to paralyze you, then wraps you up to wait until it's hungry—at which time it injects another poison to liquefy your insides, then sucks you up like a soft drink.

But wasps are worst of all. A wasp stings you to paralyze you, hauls you off to its nest, injects its eggs into you and walls you up in a cell, where you wait helplessly while the eggs hatch and the wasp's larvae slowly eat you up from the inside. The lifestyle of wasps is a powerful argument against a merciful Creator.

The caterpillar has only about 200,000 brain cells, and most of those are devoted to insecurity. It overeats to compensate.

Meanwhile, an oedipal-like crisis is developing. For all the caterpillar's life, plants have fed and sheltered it. Plants are like the parents it never had. And it's chewing the hell out of them.

Finally the caterpillar can't take it anymore. It walls itself off in a cocoon and hides from the world.

Inside that woven prison, that do-it-yourself rubber room, the tiniest of keys turns in the tiniest of locks—a few neurons fire, a few molecules trade places on a filament of protein—and everything changes.

When the former larva emerges, it's skinny, beautiful, and completely mad. It spends its adult life giving oral sex to flowers. It's as gaudy as a flower, itself. In its insectish way, it probably thinks it *is* a flower.

Then, one day, a flower turns out to be another butterfly of the opposite sex.

They can't handle the shock. The male flies off and dies. The female lays her eggs and dies.

The eggs start it all again.

This book was a figment of the author's imagination. It's becoming a figment of yours. As you read this, it's slipping into your brain, like a tiny mite crawling into a pore in your skin, to emerge someday, perhaps, as an invisible butterfly.

(A mite would have to be insane to want to be a butterfly.)

Or it might be a wasp larva.

If this makes you at all nervous, please close the book and put it down. Do it now. Do not turn the page. This is your final notice.

TOO LATE . . .

I

Babe in Armor

Sander Keynes knew he was in trouble when he saw the armadillo in the bathtub.

"How the hell did you get in there?" he asked, though usually he didn't curse, much less talk to animals.

He'd taken an unscheduled afternoon nap, and was still half in a dream he'd been having about a woman in a bathing suit and a white rat in a window. Otherwise, he probably wouldn't have addressed the armadillo. Had the beast merely been in the bathroom, he still wouldn't have lapsed into conversation. He'd have just retreated and looked for a broom, mop or other armadillo-herding device. But the armadillo was in the tub. Sander wouldn't even have noticed it, half-hidden behind the shower curtain, if he hadn't heard the scratching of its claws on the yellow plastic pseudo-porcelain. Its football-sized body didn't seem to be designed for climbing even minor barriers.

"How the hell did you get in there?" he repeated.

"Damned if I know," the armadillo replied.

Sander shrieked and retreated, slamming the bathroom door.

"God! Jenny'll be here in twenty minutes," he muttered frantically. A nice girl. Some strain on the relationship already, thanks to yesterday's events. And now he was talking to hallucinatory animals.

It wasn't merely the armadillo in the bathtub, or even the talking armadillo. Half a dozen things had just happened that never happened to Sander Keynes. Shrieking. Slamming a door. Hallucinating anything. Inviting a nice girl to his apartment.

Well, that last had happened before. But not very often.

One thing changes, he thought, *and the whole world goes to pieces.*

In the living room, the TV blared. *Who turned the TV on? Oh, right, I did.*

"What does it all mean?" asked Charles Kuralt. "We've all dreamed of this moment—have envisioned the hatch of the flying saucer opening, have pictured green Martians or little gray aliens with huge eyes. But who would have imagined that the hatch would open, and we'd find—no one?"

Maybe the alien is an armadillo who beamed into my bathtub, Sander thought. Then a little bit of the usual Sander asserted itself. *Interesting thought, but it doesn't solve the immediate problem. You can deal with what's in the bathtub or with Jenny—but don't try both at once.*

He ran to the bedroom for his pocket calendar, leafed frantically back to the phone numbers, grabbed the phone, misdialed, dialed again.

"Hello?" came a slightly out-of-breath voice, after the fourth ring.

"Hello, Jenny? It's Sander. Listen, I think we should postpone tonight. I'm coming down with something."

"Something?"

"Yeah, I think it might be food poisoning, or stomach flu, or something. Suddenly I'm feeling really rotten." *Great. Now she has an image in her head of me throwing up.*

"Gee, that's too bad. I was looking forward to dinner. We need to talk about yesterday. Can I bring you something?"

"No, that's okay, I sure wouldn't want you to catch this. But I was looking forward to tonight, too. Can I call you in a couple of days?"

"Yeah, sure, I guess. I'll just throw a burger on and watch the UFO news. As soon as I finish drying off. I'm afraid you caught me in the shower."

Images of Jenny, wet and naked. *Damn it. Showers. Bathtubs. Armadillos.* "Yeah, that sounds like a good idea. I'll just lie down and watch the news, too."

"Okay. See ya."

Damn, damn, damn, damn. Of all the nights to have a nervous breakdown. Open the bathroom door. Maybe it will be gone.

He cautiously opened the door a crack, and peaked in. Then slammed it again.

"It's okay. I'm decent," called the high-pitched, reedy voice—the sort of voice that might occur if living lips were stuck on the bottom end of an oboe. "Well, actually, I'm naked, but I think that's normal for me. . . ."

Sander tried to recall what he knew about armadillos. Almost nothing. Just an occasional roadside sighting—usually after one of the beasties had already encountered a pickup truck. There hadn't used to be armadillos in southern Missouri at all—a by-product of global warming, maybe. Sander remembered reading that they had a sort of spring reflex—instead of running from danger, they popped upward and rolled into a ball. Great defense against coyotes, maybe, but not against motor vehicles. He also remembered reading that armadillos could carry leprosy. There had been an armadillo-wrestling fad in Texas, until wrestlers' fingers had started falling off.

"You don't have leprosy, do you?" he called.

"I hope not."

Face your fears, dammit, he thought, and pushed the door open a few inches.

"You're not from a flying saucer, are you?" He asked.

"A what?"

"A flying saucer. A UFO."

"Look, I just said I didn't know how I got in this room. Why would I know if I was from a flying saucer?"

"Great," Sander muttered. "A talking armadillo with amnesia."

"Is that unusual?" asked the armadillo.

"You're not being very helpful."

"Neither are you," the armadillo said pointedly.

"Why should I help you?" Sander said, starting to get angry. "You invaded my apartment. You ruined my date."

"Sorry. Didn't mean to. Don't know how it happened. Look, just help me out of this tub, and I'll leave."

Sander shook his head vigorously. "You might have leprosy. I don't want my fingers falling off."

The armadillo raised its naturally downward-pointing face to peer at its host. "Face your fears," it said.

Sander hesitated. "I'll go get a broom," he said, and shut the door. "Better yet, the shovel."

"Violence isn't necessary," came the armadillo's muffled voice, plaintively.

When Sander was in college, he'd shared an old farmhouse with five other students. They'd had a big backyard garden. The others had abandoned it when they discovered how tedious weeding was. But Sander had kept at it: had grown cantaloupes until the borers got them, lettuce until the rabbits got it, tomatoes until the frost got them. Then he'd graduated, gotten a job and moved to an apartment. But he still had his spade: a big, awkward memento—maybe a promise, a little dream. There'd be another garden someday; another round against the rabbits.

Forget the rabbits. You've got an armadillo to deal with.

He extracted the shovel from a flurry of flapping shirts and returned to the bathroom and opened the door.

The armadillo backed against the rear of the tub.

"Roll up in a ball," Sander said.

"No," said the armadillo in a tremulous voice. "I'm gonna face my executioner. If you're gonna crack me open with that thing, you've gotta do it with me looking at you."

"I'm not going to kill you," Sander said exasperatedly. "I'm just going to use the spade to scoop you out of the tub."

He started to lower the shovel. Despite its brave words, the armadillo panicked, reared and scrabbled against the back of the tub, accidentally hitting the shower valve knob. Cold water spouted from the showerhead. Startled, the creature popped backward and landed with a loud *thunk!* that sent Sander on a hasty retreat. Being a North American armadillo, the beast couldn't roll into a complete ball, but it curled up as much as it could as it bounced and rolled, then rocked to a halt.

"Okay," it squeaked. "Scoop me out or kill me. Please, just make it quick."

"It's a good thing I'm not a Mack truck," Sander said disgustedly from the hallway. He advanced again into a bathroom reeking with the musk of armadillo fear, slipped the shovel blade under the surprisingly heavy ball of mammal, then grunted and heaved. The armadillo cleared the tub rim, thudded to the floor and rolled under the sink. Sander scrambled to avoid it.

Cautiously, bit by bit, the armored huddle unfurled. "Thank you," it sighed. "I'm going now. You can put the shovel away."

"I'll do it later," Sander said. Still clutching his spade, he backed away from the bathroom door.

His guest approached the doorway cautiously, poked its nose out and sniffed. "Uh, which way is out?"

Sander gestured with the spade. "Turn left, out the hallway, across the living room. Stay out of the kitchenette."

"Hmm. That brings up an interesting question. What do I eat?" the creature muttered, and scuttled down the hallway.

Good question. What do they eat? Sander wondered. He watched the creature hesitate, sniff, then start across the living room. *It only seems to know what I know about armadillos. It does what I know they can do, like the pop-up trick. Maybe this is still a dream. But if it is, it's got some fine, fine detail . . .*

On the TV, a talking head with a general's stars on its shoulders was droning in the wake of the top story. "As you know, we first learned of this event through an anonymous phone call," it said. "It's imperative that we locate that caller. He may have knowledge of the vehicle's missing occupants. He may have been in contact with alien diseases. He may even be a hostage. We have to prepare for every contingency . . ."

The armadillo stopped at the apartment door. "Uh . . . I can't reach the knob," it said.

With a sigh, Sander crossed the living room, stepping well clear of his guest. He undid the bolt and opened the door. "There." *Maybe now I'll wake up.*

But his level of consciousness didn't change. Nor did the armadillo move.

"Well, go on," Sander urged it.

"I can't," it said, its voice quavering.

"Why not?"

"I don't know what's out there. What if there's an elevator?"

"There is an elevator. I tell you what. I'll walk you to the elevator, let you in and punch the ground floor button. But I'm not riding down with you. You'll have to wait until someone gets in, then bolt for it. I'm not being seen in an elevator with a hallucinatory armadillo."

The animal shifted nervously from paw to paw, a little armadillo dance. But it still made no move toward the door.

"Well?" Sander asked impatiently.

"This place is all I remember. What if I *am* a hallucination? If I step out of your sight, will I suddenly cease to exist?"

"That would solve a lot of problems for me, wouldn't it?" snorted Sander.

"Would it? If I walk out this door, *you* won't know where I came from either—or if I'll be back."

His host considered.

"What makes you think I'm a hallucination?" pressed the armadillo. "You said a while ago I might be from a—a 'flying saucer.' Which is more likely?"

"Neither of them is likely! *You're* not likely!"

"Would you stop it!"

Armadillos weren't well equipped to show emotion, so this one exercised one of its few options: it popped into a half-ball again. Sander leapt back as it thumped to the floor. More thumping followed. The neighbor below was pounding angrily on the ceiling.

The armadillo slowly uncurled. "You think you've got problems. I don't know who I am, what I'm doing here. . . ."

"That sounds just like the rest of us," Sander pointed out.

"Reactions to the incredible events near this sleepy Ozark town range from stunned denial to calls for military action," reported a fatigue-jacketed Adriana Dias, in the field. "Texas Senator Ted Cruz has called for the immediate mobilization. . . ."

Sander punched the TV's "off" button irritably. That wasn't like him either. He *liked* listening to the news.

". . . and the only person I've met thinks I'm either a space alien or I don't exist!" continued the armadillo, bitterly. "Aren't there any other alternatives?"

"Well, you could really be a talking armadillo," said Sander. "But I majored in biology, and I don't see how that's possible at all. You don't have the brains . . ."

"Gee, thanks. You're *so* supportive."

". . . or the larynx, or the jaws, or the lips, despite what I'm hearing. I feel like I'm watching a Narnia movie, or—what was that movie with the talking pig? *Babe*. . . ."

"Let's approach this logically, before I go nuts with fear and pop internal again," said the armadillo, prancing nervously. "Possibility Number One: I'm a hallucination. . . ."

Sander had a sudden flash of insight. "But if we really can approach this logically, we can eliminate that possibility! The subconscious isn't logical! Hallucinations don't make sense!"

"Very good. That leaves the other one—the saucer thingy. Why do you think I came from a flying saucer?"

"I—it's all over the news. I—they found one up near Waynesville, on a sandbar of the Big Piney River. It—uh, Charles Kuralt said it was empty when they found it. . . ."

"Wait a minute," his companion interrupted. "Isn't Charles Kuralt dead?"

"You're right," said Sander wonderingly.

"Uh-oh. Score one for the hallucination."

"It must've been Scott Pelley," Sander amended. *But it's not like me to make that type of mistake*, he thought. He'd been a sort of fan of network correspondents, ever since he'd learned his mother had named him after Sander Vanocur. "Wait a minute. How did you know Charles Kuralt was dead?"

The armadillo shuddered his plates—perhaps the armadillo version of a shrug. "Beats me. How do I know English? We've got too many questions. Can we take them one at a time? How far away is Waynesville?"

"Maybe an hour and a half up I-44, depending on the traffic."

"So lots of things must've happened within a 90 minute drive of here. Why pick out the UFO?"

"Because I—dammit, nothing else that strange has happened in the last 24 hours."

"So if I'm a saucer-related phenomenon, why didn't I show up in a bathtub in Waynesville, instead of Springfield?"

"I don't know, dammit!"

"Uh-oh. Logic is melting back into blind intuition. Not good," muttered the armadillo. "But it's the only lead we have. I guess we'll have to go to Waynesville."

"Waynesville? Why?"

"Because that's where the saucer is, dammit! Aw, look, now you've got *me* cursing."

"Well, I'm not prone to cussing myself, normally. But . . ."

"Look, if I'm somehow connected to that saucer, the only place I can think of to find some answers is the saucer itself."

"But the place will be crawling—media, government officials, the military. They're not going to let us near it!"

"Maybe not you—but who's going to suspect an armadillo?"

"Well—well, go," said Sander. "But why should I go off with *any* stranger that I've surprised in my own bathroom, armadillo or otherwise?"

"Because I can't get down the elevator alone. And I gather armadillos have real bad luck on Interstates."

"But that's why *you* need me to go. Why should *I*?" Sander persisted, stubbornly.

"Don't give me that!" The creature's little nostrils flared. "You need to know why I'm here as badly as I do!"

"But . . ."

The armadillo lowered its ears, looking somehow wise.

"Face your fears," it said.

"I don't want to go back there," Sander whispered.

II
Toyota Billiards

"Shit," muttered Jennifer Duenckel-Chillingworth (soon to be just Jennifer Duenckel again, any day now). "Shit, goddammit, shit, shit, shit, SHIT!"

First the flying saucer. Now Sander "coming down with something." Antarean Flu, maybe? The Betelguesean chilblains? And the Feds looking for them. They'd get put in some sort of quarantine ward, at the very least. She pictured interrogators in isolation suits, doctors with very large needles . . .

"Shit, shit, shit, shit, SHIT!"

Something brushed her leg. Jenny looked down. "Well, Pumpkin, what do we do?" she said. "Should Mommy turn herself in? Should she go hide somewhere? Or just pretend it never happened?"

Pumpkin looked up at her. "Mrow?" Pumpkin said. (Talking with animals was not unusual for Jennifer at all.)

Sensing that something was distressing Mommy, Pumpkin jumped into her lap to remind her of what was really important. He nearly pulled Jennifer's towel off in the process.

"Oh, Pumpkin," she said, scratching the cat's ears. "Mommy can't turn herself in. They'd shut her up in some kind of hospital, and then who'd take care of you?"

10

What could she do? She wracked her brain for useful precedents, without luck. She'd been in high stress situations before, but nothing remotely like this. She'd never even gotten a traffic ticket. The only time she'd ever been in court was for the restraining order and divorce hearings. She'd never been wanted urgently by anyone, except Harlan, goddamn him.

(She'd never used to curse at all, much less use the S-word. That was one of Harlan Chillingworth's legacies.)

"First the divorce, and now this! Shit, shit, SHIT!" She set Pumpkin down and paced to the bedroom and back, trying to think and not lose her towel at the same time. She made the same trip several times before pausing long enough to put on clothes. Then she stopped in the middle of doing that to go into the bathroom and take her own temperature, in case *she* was coming down with the Antarean Flu. Then she remembered to finish dressing. By then, she'd only thought of one alternative.

When Pumpkin's Mommy had a problem, she usually talked to her own Mommy. But Mom lived clear up in farmhouse outside Brazito, near Jefferson City. She couldn't be reached by phone in the evenings because she was busy tending her website, and cable had never reached the farm, and she'd never bought a cell phone. "Shit!"

Jenny packed some essentials into the old blue travel bag she'd had since her brief college stay, then went through the kitchen cupboards to find a three-day aquarium feeder block, then filled the tank of the old Purina Cat Chow weekender she'd found at a garage sale. Pumpkin plastered his orange-yellow bulk against her legs. "Mngeeeeew," he said intently. She didn't totally trust the weekender to trickle down cat food as Pumpkin ate it, so she set out an extra bowl of food and an extra bowl of water.

Pumpkin's face was still in the food bowl when Jenny and her suitcase went out the door.

Driving though Springfield on the Kansas Expressway (which, if you stayed on it, actually took you north to Iowa), she considered her route. Brazito was about 130 miles away, and there was no good road. She could go up I-44, then take winding US 63 along the Ozark ridge-tops through Vienna and Westphalia. Or she could take US 65 up to US 54, and crawl through the stoplights of Tourist Hell around Lake of the Ozarks. But at least the tourist traps would be closed by the time she went through . . .

I haven't had dinner yet, she suddenly remembered. *Blasted Antarean Flu.*

It would be past 9:30 before she even got out of the city. She wouldn't arrive at her mom's house before midnight, when the door would be firmly locked. She'd probably end up at a Jefferson City motel for the night.

She found a fast food place, grabbed a chicken sandwich at the drive-through window, then pulled her aged Civic back onto the road. The I-44 turnoff loomed ahead. Her mind was still boiling as she turned onto the Interstate. *Why didn't I stop him from calling that TV station?* she wondered for the thousandth time.

She was wondering it for the thousand-and-fifth, when she realized that she was nearly on top of the US 65 exit. Still gripping the half-eaten sandwich in one hand (the mayo-slathered breast fillet trying desperately to slip out and escape), she started to pull into the exit lane. A truck horn blared. She swerved back just as a semi charged alongside, cutting her off.

"Well, I guess we take 63 after all," she told the night in general. "Shit, shit, SHIT!" She wished all UFOs and their absent owners a long stay in hell, then instantly regretted the thought. It sounded like something Harlan would think.

The first good day I'd had in years, she thought, *and we had to find a flying saucer.*

It had been a gorgeous day. The Big Piney River flowing clear and green under the canoe. Turtles arranged like emerald brooches on protruding snags in the river; herons taking leisurely flight as the canoe approached. Rapids fast enough for whoops of delight, but not screams of terror; long, slow, lazy stretches where dragonflies hummed in the spring silence, interrupted once or twice by the mysterious low booming of artillery practice at Fort Leonard Wood, a few miles downstream. Sander in the bow, the endearing little thinning hair patch on the back of his head peeking out through the gap in the back of a faded blue Kansas City Royals baseball cap. Surprising muscles standing out on his arms, as he leaned over to draw the canoe away from some rock or snag that had just been abandoned by a small explosion of turtles. Their canoe had just cleared a section where the river forked around an island—a narrow, swift passage fraught with overhanging trees. Then, on the gravel bar below the island, a silvery-gray shape that wasn't natural at all. . . .

"Shit, shit, SHIT!"

What was Mom going to say when her daughter drove in and said, "Mom, I've met a very nice man. He doesn't hit. He's got a regular job. But he found a flying saucer, and now he's got some kind of disease. . . ."

Well, Mom will handle it better than most moms, she thought.

First, though, she had to get there. An hour later, she was astonished to find herself in the middle of a late-night traffic jam: red taillights and flashing brake lights twinkling like a gargantuan string of Christmas lights for as far as the eye could see in the rain-soaked night. The opposite lanes held no head-lights at all.

"Must be an awful accident," she muttered. She turned on the radio and scanned until she found a newscast.

"And in our top story," droned a woman's voice, "US Army regulars and National Guardsmen continue their alien hunt in the Mark Twain National Forest. An object alleged to be a empty flying saucer was found Thursday near Fort Leonard Wood, which is believed to house several nuclear ICBM sites. Roadblocks have been set up restricting access to the area, while thousands of soldiers comb a 400-square-mile stretch of Ozark forest. . . ."

"Shit shit shit shit SHIT!"

The next exit loomed. She made a snap decision and pulled off, passing through the hamlet of Lacquey in a few seconds.

". . . are seeking anyone who may have had contact with the object," continued the radio. "Quarantine facilities have been set up at the Army School of Chemical Warfare in Fort Leonard Wood to examine them for possible alien organisms. . . ."

"SHIT!" Jenny hated doctors. She'd seen too many of them in the past five years. They'd generated fat bills out of her bruises and broken bones, then sent her home to the disease. . . .

A southbound connecting road led to Missouri 17. *How ironic,* she thought. *South on 17. Sander's shortcut to the Big Piney River.* But State 17 also led northeast, then crossed under the Interstate and wound northward. She started to turn that way, then braked. A sign ahead read:

ROAD CLOSED
MILITARY TRAFFIC ONLY

"SHIT!"

I've gotta think, she thought. *Maybe I can take 17 south, then angle over to 63 at Licking.* She turned south and drove two or three miles, past a few houses, then saw another ROAD CLOSED sign ahead. She pulled off on the narrow shoulder, stared at the sign, voiced a single "SHIT," then opened the glove compartment to look for a map.

Meanwhile, unknown to Jenny, Reserve Pfcs. Mickey Ryan and Walter Berger of the Missouri National Guard were barreling south on State Route 17, their Humvee loaded with communications equipment for what had already been dubbed "the Great Martian Bug Hunt." They also had three six-packs of non-regulation beverage on board.

"You sure we're not gonna get in trouble for this, Berg?" Ryan asked uncertainly, as he popped the lid on another can.

"Hey, it was bought already," said Berger. "If we don't drink it now, we're not gonna get to. Besides, it's all a fucking farce anyway." Berger was already a can ahead. He cranked up the volume on his iPod.

"No, I'm serious, Berg," Ryan yelled over Black Crows in Berger's ears and the Barenaked Ladies in his own. "This could be serious shit, drinking on duty."

"It's a farce, man! There ain't no friggin' Martians! They ditched some sorta stealth plane, and don't wanna admit it exists! So they leak this cock'n'bullshit about a UFO! Even the Old Man was grinning! How can it be dereliction to have a brewski or two while looking for somethin' that don't even goddamn exist? What are we gonna do, *miss it?*"

"I don't know, Berg," repeated Ryan, knocking back a swallow of Old Milwaukee.

"Besides, this might not be a bad time to get thrown in the brig for a few days," drawled Berg. "I mean, we might miss our deployment."

"Aw, Berg, just shut up," said Ryan. "Shit. Our last weekend in the states, and we have to spend it hunting Martians in the goddamn rain."

"Hey, enjoy it while you can," Berg said. "Ain't no rain where we're going."

Taillights loomed ahead, blurred into red fuzz-balls by the curtains of rain. For a few crucial seconds, Ryan didn't notice that the lights weren't moving. He started to align himself behind them. His right tires crunched on gravel.

"SHIT!" he screamed, and jammed on the brakes.

To his credit, the Humvee was only going 16 miles an hour by the time it hit the left rear of Jenny's Toyota. But the mass-to-mass ratio of a Humvee to a Yaris is so lop-sided that the former can impart tremendous momentum to the latter, even at low speed. The little Yaris spun off like a croquet ball.

"What happened, man?" said Berg, who'd been caught in mid-swallow. Foam was dribbling from his chin down on his fatigues.

"SHIT!" said Ryan. "Aw, man, SHIT!" He sat shaking for a moment, leaned out of the Humvee to puke, then peered through the windshield. There was no longer another vehicle in the field of his headlights. "I hit a car, I think."

Berg squinted into the rainy night. "I don't see a car. I bet you just hit a, a whatsit, an armadillo, or maybe a deer."

"I 'dunno, Berg." He jammed the Humvee into gear again. He didn't notice the patch of light in the woods to the right.

By the time they reached the trailhead, Ryan had convinced himself that he'd fallen asleep at the wheel, that it was a bad dream, that it hadn't happened. Berg would back him up. Berg hadn't seen a car. And if it really had happened, maybe they'd accept that he'd sincerely believed it hadn't. Private Ryan's chief concern, conscious and subconscious, was saving Private Ryan.

Jenny moaned slowly back to consciousness, and heard an engine grumbling nearby. A man was approaching with a flashlight. He leaned over to peer in the window. The flashlight's reflected glow revealed a broad, homely, vaguely familiar face: vanishing hairline, large friendly mouth, twinkling eyes, bushy brows. Groggily, Jenny rolled the window down.

"Hi. You might want to turn off the ignition, in case there's a fuel leak," the man said.

Jenny saw her hand move to the car key, as if in a dream.

"That's good," said the man. He had a deep, friendly baritone voice: the sort that reassured you, just hearing it.

"Do I know you?" she asked.

"Oh, you may have seen me on the road somewhere," he said. "You'll be all right. Just stay in the car."

"Look, could I get a ride back to the highway?"

He shook his head, still smiling. "Sorry. You don't need a ride in the Winnebago this time. Just sit tight. He'll be by before too long."

"I'm going to be all right," she said, and believed it. She dreamily watched the man walk away. A large vehicle lumbered back onto the road and rumbled away into the rainy darkness.

"Funny," she murmured. "He looked just like that old newsman . . . Charles . . . whazizname . . ."

Her woozy head should have been exuding a ring of stars or tweety birds—or was it her neck that really hurt? She leaned back gingerly against the headrest and drifted into unconsciousness again.

It was still dark when she awoke with a start. Ignoring the pain in her neck, wincing only slightly at the bruised welt on her ribs from the shoulder harness, she jerked the door handle. It didn't open. But a rising crescendo of panic-amplified kicks persuaded the passenger side door to cooperate. She scrambled out of the car.

"Oh God, my poor little car! SHIT!"

In the rainy night, she had to explore the damage mostly by feel. The front end had incorporated a couple of saplings, the trunk was crushed in, and the entire car was canted at a crazy angle. It wasn't going anywhere under its own power.

Then she heard a low rumbling from the direction of the highway—not the hum of fast-moving tires, but the authoritative rumbly whine of large engines, many engines, moving slowly. It was an instinctively ominous sound—the sort of noise that you'd expect to hear in a horror movie, just before the twelve-foot-long killer bees came into sight. Or in a war movie. . . .

Troop convoy, she realized. She saw the flicker of headlights through the trees, then turned and ran.

III

The Smell of Sex and Death

"I never really liked this city," remarked Sander, as they cruised down Sunshine Street in the darkness.

"Well, I can't see much of it so I'll have to take your word," said the armadillo, crouched on the passenger side floorboard. Sander, still afraid of leprosy, hadn't offered to help it clamber up on the seat. "So why are you here?" the creature asked.

"Let's not get into that existentialist garbage again."

"I'm not. I meant, why are you in this town—what's it called?"

"Springfield, Missouri."

"Why are you living in Springfield, Missouri, if you don't even like it?"

Sander shrugged. "There was a woman."

They rolled through the green light at the Campbell Street intersection, past the Valhalla-sized hunting lodge that housed Bass Pro's "Wonders of Wildlife" museum/zooquarium. The streets were nearly deserted, which was according to plan. Sander had insisted that they wait until after midnight before leaving the apartment.

"If you're real, my building doesn't allow pets," he had told the armadillo. "If you're not real, I don't want my neighbors to see me talking to thin air."

Now, as he drove, he kept an eye out for anything else abnormal: a green elephant ambling outside St. John's Medical Center, or a brigade of Union ghosts marching up Glenstone Avenue from the national cemetery, or maybe some stray dogs shooting craps in a gas station parking lot—some further sign that this really was all a dream. But alas, any green elephants stayed safely camouflaged in the shrubbery. Aside from the usual eerie we-hours transformation of a bustling city into a vast emptiness, and the argon streetlights transforming his Mediterranean Blue Honda Fit into a ghastly shade of brownish black, the only thing extraordinary remained the armadillo sitting on the passenger side floorboard.

"A woman. It figures," mused the recalcitrantly surreal mammal. "Is she worth it?"

"No, she *wasn't*," said Sander, then softened his tone. "She was okay, I guess. We met in Biology Club up at Northwest Missouri State in Maryville. She moved down here for a job at St. John's, and started her RN courses, and I followed. But this is another university town. They've got biology majors up the wazoo. I finally got a job at Bass Pro. . . ."

"You sell fishing lures?"

"I'm Assistant Aquarium Keeper. Bass Pro's got several big aquaria. I measure out the fishes' rations, keep the pH balanced, work with the vet. . . ."

"Sounds like a lifetime dream come true," said the armadillo.

"It beats being a hallucination," Sander retorted.

"I'm real enough to *me*." The armadillo stared moodily into the shadows under the dashboard. "You said there *was* a girl. What happened?"

"She got her RN, and got crankier and crankier, and had less and less time. Taking second priority to bedpans is not fun."

"I can imagine."

"You can? That's boggling."

"What's so boggling about it?"

"Well, either a figment of my imagination is imagining what I feel, or an armored rodent is relating to my love life."

"Would you stop that? How do you think it feels to be reminded every other minute that I might go *poof* and disappear, if somebody just stops thinking about me? And I'm *not* a rodent. You should know that, Mr. Biology Major."

"I should know a lot of things. I should know that you can't talk."

"Look, let's get back to what we were talking about before," said the armadillo, a tad desperately. "So you and Ms. Bedpans split up, and you were left in a town you don't like doing a job you didn't plan on. Why didn't you leave?"

"It just never happened," Sander said glumly. "I was going to go back to school after Greta finished her RN training."

"What were you going to study?" the armadillo asked softly.

"Paleoanthropology. I wanted to go to Africa and finally discover the Missing Link. But we spent all our money on Greta's courses, then we split up, and there was no money. And then tuition went up and student aid dried up, and the recession happened and never stopped for anybody but CEOs. So I'm still feeding fish, and Johanson and Tim White and the Ethiopians are over there, discovering so many missing links that we don't even know which chain we fit in anymore."

The armadillo mulled this over. "Well, you've got them all beat. None of them has ever discovered conclusive evidence of extraterrestrial intelligence. Not to mention a whole new sentient species that looks like a talking armadillo."

"None of them has to worry about men with straightjackets coming for them if they announce their discoveries."

"But they're *looking* for you!" pointed out the armadillo. "Not the men with the straightjackets. The ones who write news stories. They *want* to find the man who found the saucer. All you have to do is step forward, and you're in history books!"

"Yeah, right," replied Sander, savagely. "I'll just walk up and say, 'Hi. I'm the guy who found the UFO. And oh, by the way, there's a talking armadillo in my car.' And they're going to say, 'Uh-huh, sure.' And then they're going to whisper, 'Roger, we got another one. Call the guys in the white coats.'"

They swung onto US 65 and arrowed northward toward I-44. A moody silence prevailed for two exits.

"Uh, by the way, what's your name?" the armadillo finally asked.

"You're grilling me on my love life, and you don't even know my name?"

"Uh, well, no. Somehow that hadn't come up yet."

"Sander Keynes."

"Sander?"

"Don't even ask."

It started to rain. Sander switched on the wipers and stared grimly at the pavement ahead, stretching like an endless glistening salamander skin under the jaundiced streetlights. "So what's yours?" he asked.

"What's—oh, my name? I don't know. I don't think armadillos usually have them."

"Armadillos don't usually hitch rides in my car. If you're not going to go 'poof' any time soon, I ought to call you something besides 'Hey, Armadillo!'"

The Division Street exit split off, as if the giant salamander skin was being flensed in strips to make leather belts. But the salamander skin was just a simile, not a hallucination. One more exit before the Interstate. . . .

"I'm going to call you 'Dick,' Sander said.

"Gee, thanks. How Freudian," remarked the armadillo. "You know, I make a really weird-shaped phallic symbol."

"Nah. There was a Congressman from Texas who retired a few years back. His name, believe it or not, was Dick Armey. I'm naming you for him. Dick Armeydillo."

"Yeesh," said the armadillo. "First I'm a penis, then I'm a politician. I think I prefer the penis."

"Hey, it's perfect. He was from Texas. So are you guys."

The Kearny Street exit split away. The Interstate loomed ahead. Sander switched lanes and peeled off. The little Fit churned around the curved ramp, then accelerated.

"Why do you assume we're from Texas?" Dick asked. "Aren't there any Missouri armadillos?"

"There weren't when I was a kid. Then for some reason you guys started spreading northward, and we started seeing armadillo carcasses along the road. . . ."

"Ugh. Do you torture all your figments this way?" Dick appeared to study the floorboard—an easy impression to give, since his nose naturally pointed downward. "I don't think I'm really an armadillo, Texas or otherwise. You're right, there isn't enough room in this little skull for all of me. It's like I'm somewhere outside, looking *through* the armadillo."

"Yecch. You see through the whole armadillo, entrails and all? Or just the eyes?"

"Eyes, nose, ears, the usual. Right now, I'm sensing a lot of hunger. Are you sure you don't know what armadillos eat?"

"My best guess is insects."

"Yum. But you know, I think you're right. Stop the car."

"Why?"

"I want to find an ant hill."

"Are you kidding? We just got on the Interstate! Can you wait until we're out in the country, at least?"

"Oh, all right. But don't wait too long. Not only am I hungry—I don't think I'm housebroken."

They drove on in silence for a few miles.

"Sander?" the armadillo said, finally.

"What?"

"I really am hungry. Really, really hungry."

"Can you be really, really hungry for a while longer? We're just getting started."

"And I have to pee."

"Oh, all right!'

He pulled off on the shoulder and reached across to open the passenger door, which swung outward with a horror-movie groan. Dick scrambled over the lip of the door well, fell out, and tumbled into the darkness for quite some distance.

"Are you okay?" Sander called.

There was a moment of silence. "Fine," came Dick's voice from somewhere below. "I roll really well."

Sander sighed, then felt in the glove compartment for his flashlight, found it and flicked it on. It worked, but the batteries were weak. He got out, walked around to the passenger's side, and surveyed the terrain by the light of a beam that flickered occasionally. Briefly, he caught a flash of red: the armadillo's eye.

"Hey, you don't have to watch," Dick said.

"Right," Sander sat down on the guard rail, felt its dampness creeping into the seat of his pants, and wondered how soon before the rain resumed. As if on cue, droplets began falling.

"How'd you manage to roll right under this guard rail?" he asked.

"If you walk over by the car door, you'll see that the bank is eroded out from under the rail," came his companion's voice. "'Good thing I'm armored."

"I bet armadillos think that a lot," replied Sander. A semi rolled by in a blast of dirty spray. "Look, can you really find ants down there in the dark?"

"It's not so dark for me. Besides, I can smell 'em. And these ears work really well." There was rustling below, and the muffled snap of wet breaking branches. "You're right. I eat ants. Yum." A moment later, he added. "Worms, too."

"Well, hurry up down there."

"Hey, I haven't been here long enough for you to eat a Big Mac. It's gonna take a lot of ants to fill up an armadillo."

That's right. I never had dinner. Damn. "I'm getting back in the car. It's wet out here." He started back around the car, then noticed headlights pulling off the road behind the Fit. The second car rolled to a halt six feet from his rear bumper. The gumball machine on its roof lit up, transforming the roadside into a wild nightclub of boogying lights and shadows. Sander's flashlight, completely outclassed, hung its head in shame.

"Oh, wonderful," Sander breathed.

The officer got out. A flashlight beam in the prime of its youth raked Sander from eyes to feet and back. "Are you all right, sir?"

"Uh, sure, officer. I just got out to stretch my legs for a moment."

"Pretty dangerous place to stretch your legs, mister. You should have stopped at a gas station."

"Well, to tell the truth—I couldn't wait that long."

"I see. Sir, would you mind stepping this way? This is a field sobriety test. Please hold your arm out straight, like this, then touch your nose with your index finger. . . ."

"I haven't been drinking!"

"Sir, just do as you're told."

It was Sander's first field sobriety test. He almost tripped out of nervousness when the officer made him walk along the shoulder line amid the riot of police car lights.

"Okay, sir," he heard at the end of the ordeal. "Next time, try to hold it until the next filling station. This is an Interstate. Emergency stopping only. It's a good thing you were zipped up, or you'd have been facing lewd conduct and indecent exposure. I suggest you get on down the road, now."

"But . . . yes, officer."

Sander got in the car, took his time starting the engine, and then pulled carefully onto the road. *I could just leave him here,* he thought. *That'd solve a lot of problems.*

But even as he thought it, he was frantically looking for a mileage marker. He finally spotted one a few hundred yards up the road, and drove on, staying 5 mph under the speed limit, until the patrol car passed him and shot ahead. He thought hard all the way to the next exit and nearly went on past.

If I leave him there, I'll never know . . .

He jerked the car onto the off ramp, crossed over, started back toward Springfield, turned around again at the next exit, and began watching for the mileage marker again. He was watching so intently that it slowed his reaction time when a small shape scuttled onto the road ahead.

"Look out!" Sander screamed, slamming on the breaks.

Instead of running, the thing crouched, looking like a king-sized pill bug. When it tried to pop up, it was already under the car. It bounced or rolled most of the length of the undercarriage, then crunched under the skidding right rear tire.

"Oh, God! Oh no!" Sander fought the car back under control, braked to the shoulder, and ran back to where the armadillo lay in the right lane. Its skull and the front half of its shell were crushed. The hind legs were still quivering.

"Oh, God! Oh, Dick!" he sobbed. Bracing himself internally, he grabbed a hind leg and dragged the ruined creature off on the road shoulder, then crouched beside it. "Oh, Dick, I'm sorry."

"I am, too."

Sander sprang backward with a shriek, and nearly fell over the guardrail.

"I'm back here."

Sander twisted around and saw another armadillo. "I tried to talk to her," it said, its voice quavering. "She ran onto the highway. I guess other armadillos really don't talk."

"Dick?" Sander said.

"Nah, it's my twin brother, Rick." But Dick's heart obviously wasn't in the sarcasm. "This is my fault. She's dead because of me."

"Uh, how did you know it was a she?"

"Good God, you ask something like that now?" Dick hesitated. "I smelled it. She was in heat. I'm going to be sick."

Sander shook his head. "Let's get out of here, Dick."

"We ought to bury her or something. . . . No, I guess that's not appropriate. Armadillos don't practice burial."

Sander opened the passenger door. The armadillo scrambled in with some difficulty.

"You know, you could help me," he said. "You've already got armadillo on your hands, now. I can smell it, dammit." But by the time Sander had processed this through his shocked brain, the armadillo was in the car. The human shut the door without comment, then walked around and got in himself.

If he has so much difficulty climbing over things, how was he going to mount her? he caught himself wondering, then recoiled in horror at his own thought.

Miles passed wordlessly. Finally Dick broke the silence. "I hope you can stop somewhere and wash your hands. You don't know what it's like, smelling death and sex together, with the intensity that I smell things."

"I can't even imagine," Sander said, boggled. "But I want to wash my hands, too. And we need some gas." He didn't mention that he was also hungry. He didn't want to think about hunger and crushed armadillos at the same time.

But few gas stations along this route remained open all night. They passed one exit, then another.

"Damn," remarked the armadillo softly. "I'm still hungry."

Well, he brought it up. "You couldn't find enough ants?"

"Or worms. I'm beginning to see how this armadillo thing works. Bugs are high protein, but I need an awful lot of them. I bet most armadillos spend all night eating. That's why we've got all that body armor. We can't spend time or calories running away."

"That makes sense."

"Big problem, though, if you're a sentient critter. I've got important stuff to do, like finding that saucer. But I'm going to starve to death if I spend too much time doing it."

"Hmm. I think I know a solution, if you can last till morning."

They drove on, past intersection after intersection without an open gas station. . . .

IV

Unidentified Floating Object

If Captain Donovan Agrewsky hadn't had a regulation crew cut, he'd have pulled all his hair out by now. It was two a.m. in the goddamned morning, nearly 27 hours after Operation Celestial Freedom had commenced. The river was rising, and the Object still stood on the sand bar. Fortunately it wasn't resting on the spindly legs that movie flying saucers used, or it would have keeled over in the soft sand. Instead, it simply sat on its curved bottom, or appeared to—how much was buried in the sand was anyone's guess. He'd love to find out. A Sky Crane chopper had been put on standby, the engineers had rigged a sling, and the Old Man had even put in a request for Navy SEALS to help if the operation had to be completed underwater.

But then the Brass had started arriving. Not just Army. Everybody's Brass. The Corps of Engineers had recommended building a cofferdam to divert the river, then cutting a road and moving the Object out on a crawler. Then a Forest Service official showed up to claim jurisdiction, saying the Object was on National Forest land. She had promptly gotten into a five-way debate with the Corps, the EPA man and the State Department of Fish and Wildlife man, regarding unpermitted dams and road excavation in a National Forest. Then the State

Archeologist and the Smithsonian team had arrived, both asking if the Army could prove the Object had just landed, or if the river had excavated it; if the latter, this was an archeological site and had to be surveyed and mapped before it was disturbed. Then a US senator had shown up, demanding that the site be fully photographed for his subcommittee investigation before anything was moved. Then the NDIA had requested that the operation be turned over to a special civilian contract team flying in from the Skunk Works. Then an Air Transport officer had called, demanding to know the *weight* of the Object before he could release the Sky Crane.

Now the sandbar had disappeared, water was lapping closer to the Object's open portal, and another helicopter had just lowered another rope ladder for yet another official. Accompanied by an armed private, the newcomer, in a civilian raincoat, approached along the floodlit river bank.

"Captain Agrewsky?" called the new visitor.

"That's me," Agrewsky said warily.

The newcomer flashed a badge. "Senior Special Agent Warner Lickenstein, FBI Special Investigations. I'm here to assume jurisdiction over this operation. National Security priority."

"Sorry, Agent—was it Lickstein?" said Agrewsky, as evenly as possible. "You're not in my chain of command. I need authorization from my base commander before I can take orders from you. And he's still arguing with Interior, the NSA, the NDIA and CIA."

"The CIA's here?" said the agent, looking agitated.

Damn. Was I authorized to say that? "I'm not at liberty to discuss that, sir," Agrewsky said hastily.

"But CIA's clearly out of its jurisdiction! This is an *internal* national security matter!"

"Sorry, sir," Agrewsky said. "You'll have to take that up with someone else." He turned to the nervous guard. "Private, please escort this gentleman to the ops center. Tell Jacobs I said to copy his credentials and give him one phone call, as soon as Security clears it."

"Yes, sir," the escort snapped a salute. "This way, Mr. Lickenstein."

The protesting agent was led away. *If he does turn out to be the one in charge, I'm in deep shit,* thought Agrewsky, turning back to the river. The Object was rocking gently in the current. *I'm in deep shit anyway. That thing's going to roll off the bar any minute, and I'm the man on site. I'm going to be the scapegoat.*

He felt a joy-buzzer-like sensation on his thigh: the Advanced Field Telephone's silent-ringing system. He checked the scrambler setting, then answered. "Agrewsky."

"Status?" came the Old Man's voice.

"Water's still rising, sir. It's about a foot from that hatchway or whatever it is."

"Is there any way we can seal it?"

"We don't know how, sir." *Hell, there might be a switch right inside the door, but we can't get authorization to look.* "We tried using 0x-22 sealant and sheet plastic. The sealant just slipped off. That hull's slicker than Teflon, sir."

"Listen, Agrewsky, if that thing starts to come off the sandbar, I want you to destroy it, on my own authorization."

"Sir? Confirm, sir?"

"Destroy it. My first duty is to protect this Army base. If that thing goes downriver, it'll float right through here."

"I understand, sir. I am unable to comply at this time."

"Why the hell not, Captain?"

"No available means, sir. We're off-road. No ordinance here larger than small arms. We can't get a tank in through the trees.

We didn't bring C-4, because we didn't know how this thing would affect it and vice versa. You'd have to authorize an air strike. We'd need half an hour to evacuate, with all these civvy officials. In my opinion, we don't have that much time, sir."

"Damn."

"Sir? We might be able to fly some charges in. But what if this thing's nuclear?"

"You're monitoring for radiation?"

"Faint background, sir. NASA said we could expect that, if this thing's actually been out in space with cosmic rays. But it could be shielded. We don't know."

"Thank you, Agrewsky. Continue present operations, pending further instructions."

"Yes sir," he said, as the AFT clicked off. "Damn." The water was now less than a foot below the Object's gaping portal.

"Captain?"

"What, sergeant?"

"Sir, what's our evac plan if the river goes over its banks?"

"Have Jolson call Air Cav and tell them to have six Black Hawks stand by, just in case. And tell Simpson to plot a land escape route. If the Old Man gets itchy, we may have to run in a hurry, even if the creek don't ri—"

He was interrupted by a sudden crescendo of shouting and cursing from the men along the riverbank. The Object had suddenly floated free.

"Squads Able and Bravo, downstream!" screamed the captain. "Night travel, arms only! Keep that thing in sight!"

But the thing had already disappeared. Not sunk. Not disappeared down the river. Just vanished.

They're going to need a scapegoat, Agrewsky thought, sickened. *And I'm right here.*

V

From Cedars to Lebanon

False dawn: a little smudge of bluish-gray, making the sky just lopsided enough to show which way was east, more or less. Thick mist hung like the cigar smoke from God's all-night poker party, obscuring the abyss below the rim of a bluff, a foot from the tree where Jenny Duenckel-Chillingworth had been clinging, afraid to move, since she'd nearly stepped to her death in the dark. Somewhere beneath the mist, a river chuckled.

It must be the Gasconade, Jenny thought. *I was completely turned around. God, why did I run so far from the car?*

She wasn't sure how long she'd been clinging to the tree. She was cold beyond shivering, all the way to shuddering.

Well, you can see, now, she thought. *Get moving, before the soldiers show up.* She began working her way numbly back through the brush, toward dawn and the road.

As the sky lightened, the struggle became fiercer. Sometimes the cedar thickets were simply too dense to fight through, and she had to retrace her steps, her neck spasming like an electric shock each time she had to duck a branch.

You escaped Harlan Chillingworth, she told herself. *You can get out of this.*

"Damn you, trees!" she shouted. "Out of my way!"

Had Sander been there, he might have observed that the human body, with its upright form and maximum of branch-catching vertical area, was evolved for the African veldt, not juniper thickets; had it evolved for the latter, we would all look like pigs. But Jenny simply did what humans had been doing for eons: she improvised with the body she had. Her dexterous human hands bent or broke smaller branches; against the larger ones, she used her legs and torso like a small bulldozer.

Sunlight—the real, shiny stuff, not the diluted, insipid pred-awn mix that arrived like watered beer at the retina—began to shaft through the branches. Encouraged by the promise of real sun on her goose-bumped skin, Jenny attacked the thicket with a reserve of energy she hadn't known she had. She tripped and entangled herself in the rusty remnants of a barbed wire fence, lost fabric and skin clawing herself free, forged onward—and broke through to the roadside.

She stood a moment, shaking, then collapsed to sit huddled on the wet grass. She felt horribly exposed, but too utterly drained to will herself to stand up again. The April sunlight tried to warm her, but simply wasn't up to the task.

"Shit," she muttered, but the word no longer held any power. This had gone far beyond shit.

She thought suddenly: *He's coming, Charles-whatever-his-name-was had said. But who is coming? Did I miss him?*

As if in answer, she heard the approaching *shoosh* of tires on wet pavement. It didn't sound like a Humvee.

A deep blue Honda Fit rounded the curve into view.

"It can't be . . . ," she muttered, then stood and waved frantically.

The Fit swerved off the road and screeched to a halt. The driver got out and stared.

"Jenny?"

"Sander?"

"I must be hallucinating," they both muttered at once, as Sander trotted toward his erstwhile canoe partner.

"Jenny, what are you doing out here?" he asked.

"Sander, how did you find me?" she asked, simultaneously.

"I-I didn't know you were here! I thought you were home in Springfield!"

"I had a car accident. I got hit and went off the road, and then I got lost. . . ."

Then Sander made maybe the best decision of his life: he reached out and hugged the dirty, bedraggled, soaking-wet woman. And Jenny let him hug her, despite the bruised ribs and spasming neck, and the welts the branches had left on her breasts, and her previous resolution not to let him get this close until at least the fourth date, and even despite Harlan Chillingworth.

Then Sander made a mistake. He started asking questions.

"What were you doing out here, Jenny?"

"I was . . . I was driving up to see Mother. I was upset about the saucer. . . ."

"How'd you get down here, south of the Interstate?"

"There was a roadblock, and-and I pulled off to read a map, and then after the accident this troop convoy came through, so I ran into the woods, but I got lost. . . ." It had been pure instinct, the primal fear of a lone woman facing a horde of soldiers. But more than that . "I had this vision of a man in a white isolation suit, saying 'What were you doing in a restricted zone?' And behind him, doctors with long needles. . . . Sander, they're looking for us. They think we could have alien diseases—wait a minute. What are *you* doing here? I thought you were sick."

"No, I'm okay. Though I may have been exposed to leprosy."

Another mistake. Even Sander knew it, the moment it spouted out.

"What?" Jenny jerked back.

"I-I hit an armadillo. I dragged it off the road afterward. It's been quite a night. We ran out of gas. . . ."

" 'We'?"

"I mean, *I*. I mean, me and the car."

"I don't want to think about this," said Jenny, which was not a mistake. "Can you take me somewhere warm, with coffee?" She turned painfully to go to his car.

"I'm taking you to the nearest emergency room, Jenny!" stated Sander emphatically. "You've been in an accident. You've spent the night out in the rain. You're probably hypothermic."

"I'm all—I'm all right. My neck just hurts, and I'm cold. I want to go someplace and get warm." She kept walking.

"Jenny, wait!"

She opened the passenger door and got in.

"So I *was* hallucinating," breathed Sander. Both relief and sadness flooded through him at once. Then anxiety. "I've been hallucinating. . . ." he muttered again.

Then Jenny screamed. The door flew open and she tumbled out into the ditch.

"Jenny!" He rushed to her aid.

Jenny scrambled away on all fours and sat in the wet grass, staring wildly at the open car door.

"Something against my legs," she gasped. "Something hard and bristly like a—like a giant beetle."

I'm not hallucinating! Sander thought. *Or I'm hallucinating that Jenny's here, too.*

"Sorry," came Dick's voice.

"Who said that?" Jenny gasped. "Sander, what's happening?"

"Uh, that's Dick," Sander said.

"Who's Dick? Sander, I don't see anyone."

"Right here. I'm the armadillo."

"Armadillo? Sander, I don't see any armadillo!"

"You don't? But you can hear him?"

"Well, that's different, anyway," said Dick.

"I'm hallucinating. I've got to be. Sander, you can't be here. You didn't know where I was."

"You're right, I didn't. I was astonished to see you here."

"But you said you hit an armadillo. That's why I'm hearing a voice that says it's an armadillo. I'm free-associating."

"I look like more than just a voice, to me," the voice complained.

"Dick, just shut up a moment, would you?" snapped Sander. "Look, Jenny, please calm down. Craziness is happening, and I don't know why. Dick thinks it's because of the saucer somehow. I can hear him, too, and I can see him. He really does look like an armadillo. We both can't be hallucinating the same thing."

"But I can be hallucinating both you and . . . and . . . Dick. For God's sake, that's gotta be Freudian. Sander, I saw Charles—whatshisname—shit! I can't think of it. I don't think I've seen him in years. . . . A newsman. . . .

"Charles Kuralt? You saw Charles Kuralt, too? But Charles Kuralt is dead."

"What?" Jenny continued staring at the empty passenger compartment. "Maybe I'm dead, too. Maybe—maybe death isn't nothingness. Maybe it's just craziness, all the rules breaking down." She got up, wincing. "I've got to find my poor car. I've got to see if my body's in there."

She felt Sander's hands on her shoulders, turning her around. Out of habit, she ducked and turned her head to protect her nose. But no blow came. *Wait, this is Sander.* She let out a strained giggle. "Well, I know it's not hell. If it were hell, you'd be Harlan." She looked at him in wonder. "Charles Kuralt said you were coming. . . ."

"Jenny, listen," said Sander. "I don't know—maybe I'm hallucinating you hallucinating me. . . ."

"But I'm hallucinating you!" she protested.

"Whatever. I think there's a good chance that all this is in somebody's head. I've been waiting for something else weird to happen ever since Dick showed up, and this wild a coincidence just about fits the bill. But you look real, and feel real, and act real, and even smell real."

"I smell?" she said, her lip quivering.

"Just like your usual perfume, plus crushed cedar," Sander lied politely. "But Jenny, if there's any chance this is actually happening, we need to get you to an ER."

"Okay. Okay. I'll go along," she said, shuddering again.

"Let's get you in the car and get the heater going. Dick, I'm sorry, but we're going to have to put you in back."

"But we have to find that UFO!" Dick's voice protested.

"Dick, it's too late. It's daylight. The army's all over the place. They've probably already hauled the saucer off to some secret base in Roswell, New Mexico, and they're locking up people who saw it, and Jenny needs our help. Now get out for a minute, please. I'll put the rear seats down, so you can have the whole back deck."

"Oh, all right, but I'm *not* giving up. We're going to find that saucer." There was a scuffling noise and a startled grunt, then something rolled into Jenny's shins. She shrieked and sat down hard in the ditch again.

"Sorry." came Dick's voice, from her feet.

"Are you two okay?" queried Sander anxiously.

"No, I'm not okay!" Jenny shrieked. "What's happening to me?"

"Dick took a tumble getting out of the car, and rolled into you. Dick, please, just wait by the tailgate, and I'll lift you in. Jenny, can you get up?"

"I'm okay, too, said Dick's voice, pointedly.

Sander helped Jenny to her feet and steered her to the car, then opened the tailgate, dropped the rear seats and heaved an unseen object into the back. Something shuffled about, then settled. "If we aren't going after the saucer, could I at least get some breakfast?" Dick's voice asked.

"Sure," said Sander, "Excuse me, Jenny." He reached under her legs and retrieved what looked like two cardboard Chinese food cartons. "Night crawlers or mealy worms, Dick?"

"Well, night crawlers are a little rich for breakfast—but what the hey."

"Night crawlers it is." Sander opened the bait carton and set it on the rear deck. "Oh, Dick, do me a favor and don't pee on those life vests, okay?" He closed the hatchback, then got in and started the car. "Next stop, ER," he said, gunning the car back onto the road. "Lebanon has a hospital, doesn't it?"

"I left the scene of an accident," Jenny said, wonderingly.

"That's the least of our worries," said Sander, turning up the heater. Warm air surged like liquid sunlight around Jenny's face. "I stopped to buy some bait for Dick at Wild Wilhelm's Wilderness Outfitters," her rescuer continued. "You know, where we rented the canoe? They said the FBI had been there, asking who was on the river Thursday. So had the Highway Patrol, the Forest Service, and two guys with corporate calling cards. And the *Kansas City Star,* and ABC and CNN and the *National Enquirer* and a guy from the Huffington Post. And somebody with a French accent."

"Oh, God," Jenny moaned. "Sander, let's just skip the ER, okay? I mean, what if they've already broadcast our names, and the doctor calls the police?"

"What have we done wrong?" Sander asked.

"It's not a matter of doing something wrong. If we walk into that ER and start talking about invisible armadillos, do you think they're going to let us out again?"

Sander shook his head as if to clear it. "One thing at a time. Let's find out if they're broadcasting our names." He turned on the radio and located a newscast.

". . . Last seen floating down the Big Piney River toward Fort Leonard Wood. Calls for a Congressional investigation have already begun. Meanwhile, civil and army authorities are seeking anyone who may have seen the object on the river Thursday. Five canoeists have come forward so far, but the identity of the caller who first alerted the world about the object remains unknown. A White House spokesman said that while the object does not appear radioactive, those exposed have reported a range of undisclosed symptoms. Special examination facilities have been set up at the School of Chemical Warfare at Fort Leonard Wood. Anyone who saw or touched the object should call 911, or contact the Fort Leonard Wood facility at. . . ."

"God, Jenny," said Sander. "Maybe it wasn't a UFO. Maybe it was some sort of chemical weapons container."

"I don't care!" declared Jenny. "We're not calling in!"

"But you've got to admit, something seems wrong with us."

"Nothing's wrong with you!" interjected Dick. "Except maybe that Jenny can't see me! *I'm* the one with something wrong. I really am stuck inside an armadillo!"

"So do *you* want to go to the fort, Dick?" Sander asked.

"No!" said Dick emphatically. "If there's really a chemical that turns people into armadillos, I'm not putting myself in the power of people who were twisted enough to think it up!"

"Ditto for people who'd invent something that makes people think talking armadillos are real!" exclaimed Jenny.

"Hey!" these worms aren't disappearing into thin air, back here!" remonstrated Dick's voice.

Slowly, painfully, Jenny turned to peer back at the deck, then slowly, painfully faced forward again. "Yes, they are," she said, her voice carefully expressionless.

"Either way, who else would have an antidote?" Sander asked.

"God, would they use it, if they had one?" Jenny wondered aloud. "Its existence is probably classified. They could just keep mum and have some free test subjects."

"They wouldn't do that," protested Sander. "This is America. They . . ."

"Did you ever read about what happened during the nuclear tests in the Forties and Fifties?" interrupted Jenny. She'd been a history major, before she'd dropped out to marry Harlan.

"But that was back in the Cold War."

"Yeah, right. What about Guantanamo?" *My god*, she thought, *I'm arguing with a man. And he's not threatening me.*

"Okay, okay," conceded Sander. "But Jenny, you could still have real hypothermia or whiplash or internal injuries. How about if we go to the ER and just not mention armadillos?"

Jenny forced her befuddled brain to consider. "All right," she said, finally.

"Okay by the armadillo, too," said Dick, after a moment.

"Okay, we head for Lebanon, and hope whatever's happening isn't contagious," Sander said, then had another thought.

"Oh, God. Maybe it is. Maybe there's already a plague. Did you ever see an armadillo in Missouri until the last few years?"

"No. No, they're *not* like me," Dick stated flatly. "They can't talk. I tried, remember? I think she could smell me, maybe even hear me a little. She reacted like she'd seen a ghost. But I couldn't even warn her not to run into the road."

"Maybe after a while, they forget they were human," suggested Sander.

"Uh-oh. I already don't know who I was before I was an armadillo," observed Dick. "This is almost making sense."

"No, it isn't," said Jenny. "Even if the army were making people into armadillos, which is absurd, it still wouldn't explain why Sander can see you and I can't."

That stumped them all into silence, which lasted for most of the rest of the journey back to Lebanon, Missouri.

VI
Flying the River

When 200 or so square miles of raindrops get behind it, even a small river like the Big Piney becomes an awesome force. Had a canoe ventured out the morning after the Object drifted free, the river's surging brown waters would have pretzeled it around a snag within minutes.

The Object, however, had resources that a canoe lacked.

Some of those resources were actually absences. A canoe is designed to go somewhere; it must travel a little faster than the water, or the river will grab its bow and stern, turn it broadside and wrap it around a rock. But the Object had no bow, no stern, and no particular destination; it moved as the river moved, flowed where it flowed.

The Object was, in this way, actually practicing a very advanced form of Aikido, a martial art based on harmonizing with one's opponent. The Object harmonized so perfectly with the river's *ki* that the river never even saw it as an opponent.

The Object also had some proactive features going for it. Its slicker-than-Teflon (and much tougher) skin shed rocks and snags as if they were raindrops. The alien guidance system kept the object as perfectly balanced as an Aikido *sensei*. And of course, when it moved, it disappeared.

(This is the problem with all those 20th Century saucer sightings. Klingons notwithstanding, humans assumed UFOs would appear on radar or float before peoples' eyes. But star-hopping species would have stealth technologies light years in advance, literally, of a B-2's. Either all those sightings were bogus, or the visitors *wanted* to be seen.)

The Object was as inconspicuous as an Arab browsing the river's bazaar. The Blackhawks and Hueys and surveillance drones prowling overhead saw only roiling water and snags, floating logs and old tires, and the occasional crumpled canoe.

One might draw parallels between the armed forces' inability to see the Object and Jenny's inability to see Dick the Armadillo. But such analogies could be misleading. It's unwise to mistake the messenger for the message.

VII
Familiarity Breeds a Puppy

Apollonasia Brechtlein Duenckel was a good mother and a take-charge sort of person. But she had another important qualification for dealing with her daughter's current problem. Appy Duenckel believed in ghosts.

Also vampires, demons, rakshashi, angels, manitou, djinn, nixies and fairies, among others. Appy was an equal-opportunity believer. She believed in many levels of reality, and figured they all must be as richly populated as the natural world.

That went for philosophy, too. "Some folks think life has no purpose," she'd been telling people for more than four decades. "That's poppycock. The problem is that there are too many purposes, a lot of which we don't care to notice."

At age 18, when she was already supporting herself as a belly dancer at county and state fairs, she'd spent the night on the State Fairground in Springfield, Illinois (no relation to Springfield, Missouri), listening to the scurryings and rustlings after the marks had all gone home. The next day, she'd bought a small composition book. On the first page, she'd penned, very neatly:

The purpose of humanity is to feed and shelter rats.

Thus began her life's work, her magnum opus: *The Book of Purposes*. On the April morning after the flooding of the Big Piney River, Appy had finished her morning chores and had just started Volume 98. She did most of her writing on the computer these days, but continued to hand write this project in composition books, just for consistency. She plunged into the first page, riding a tide of inspiration:

> The purpose of Argon street lamps is to accustom us to the lighting of Hell.
> The purpose of computers is to provide a warm hiding place for certain species of ants.
> The purpose of paleontology is to give God a better hiding place.
> The purpose of astronomy is to give God a better hiding place.
> The purpose of geology is to give God a better hiding place.
> The purpose of physics is to give God a better hiding place.
> The purpose of God is to hide from humanity.

Of course, she'd recorded many other purposes for God, over the years. An infinite God could have infinite purposes. She forged onward:

> The purpose of Hell is to discourage humans from dying prematurely.
> The purpose of Heaven is to free the gene pool more rapidly of people who can't stand the idea of dying.

The purpose of burial is to keep things that eat
the dead from accidentally eating the living.

She was interrupted by the sound of gravel crunching in the
driveway, and stepped into the front dining room to look out
the window. An older but well-kept blue Honda hatchback had
pulled up. Doors popped open. The driver emerged: male,
slightly balding, sandy-haired, late-30s or early-40s. Then Appy's
youngest daughter got out, wearing a man's windbreaker
draped over disposable hospital scrubs. The blue paper "fabric"
around her bra and panty lines was crinkled and discolored, as
if it had been wet. A fat white support collar hid her neck. Red
welts and scratches stood out on her face and arms.

Appy went and got her .22-caliber Favorite varmint rifle
from its rack over the back porch doorway, then went back to
the front door and opened it.

"Hi, Hon," she called to Jenny. Then, cradling the gun cas-
ually, she turned to the man. "Hello, there. You don't really
look like an abuser. But they usually don't, and I've sort of had
it. So I'll let Jenny explain why she's been in a hospital, and
then I'll shoot you if she says so."

"No, Mom, don't!" her daughter exclaimed.

"It's okay, Jenny. I'll just tell them I thought it was a rob-
ber. Nobody's going to put a little, wispy 63-year-old woman in
jail for protecting herself."

"No, Mom, please! This is Sander Keynes. He's a nice
man."

"I've heard that one before."

"No, I mean it, Mom! I got in an accident, and Sander took
me to the emergency room."

"I've heard *that* one before, too."

Sander stood where he was, frozen. He'd been about to say, "Hello, Ms. Duenckel. I'm glad to meet you." His mouth was still half-open, in a slight smile, though his eyes had widened.

"No, Mom, really!" said Jenny, frantically. "I totaled the Yaris! Somebody hit me—I mean, hit the car. . . ."

Sander unfroze enough to say, "Honest, Ms. Duenckel. I wouldn't hurt a mouse. Literally. I use live traps. I'd never hit a woman, and I certainly wouldn't hurt Jenny. . . ."

"I've heard *that* before, as well," Appy said. "But I'd like to believe it. So Jenny, what are you doing here, why the paper suit, and why does it look like you peed your pants and milked your bra?" Another suspicion raced through her mind. Had she lost a grandchild before she knew one was coming?

"I got out of the car and got lost, Mom," said Jenny. "My clothes were wet. The ER gave me these to wear."

"The hospital wanted to admit her, but she wouldn't stay," offered Sander.

"Mom, we're in trouble," her daughter said. "It's not Sander's fault. Well, not much, and he didn't mean it—I mean, it's got nothing to do with me getting beat up—I mean, because I *didn't* get beat up. Not since Harlan. It's something different this time, and I did get in a car accident, and Sander rescued me, but he called the police and the TV station before that and—can we come in and explain?"

"I don't know," said her mother. "Can you do it any better inside than you're doing out here?"

"I-I . . ."

"Well, come in anyway. There's still some of your old clothes up in your room. I don't know if they fit anymore, but they'll fit better than anything of mine would."

"Thanks, Mom." She walked stiffly up on the porch.

"You can come, too, I guess," Appy told her daughter's male companion. "But if you don't mind, I'll keep the .22 with me a bit longer. I always wanted to shoot a real varmint with it."

"Uh, okay. That reminds me—I'll be there in just a moment."

Appy halfway expected him to get in the Honda and drive off. Instead, he opened the tailgate and pulled out a soggy-looking pink blouse and a wet pair of jeans. But he didn't close the hatchback again. "Stay here for now, okay?" he said softly to someone inside, paused, then added, "Well, when that cop came and I had to leave you by the roadside, you didn't go 'pffffft' and disappear then, did you?"

Appy, who read lips very well—a useful skill from her "theatrical days," as she called them—noted this one-sided conversation without comment.

"Here's Jenny's clothes," Sander said lamely, approaching the porch. "Honestly, Ms. Duenckel, I wouldn't hurt Jenny for anything. She's a sweet girl."

"That hasn't kept other people from hurting her," Appy noted, watching the car as she took the soggy evidence of Jenny's story. "Well, after you. Living room's through the dining room and to the right. Hon, you find anything wearable?"

"I think so, Mom!" Jenny called down from her bedroom. "I'll be down in a minute."

Her male guest had perched himself nervously in the living room's least comfortable armchair.

"Want some lemonade?" Appy asked him, without smiling.

"Uh, yes, please, that'd be nice, thanks," said Sander.

Appy dropped the wet clothes off on the back porch, then went to the kitchen and returned, walking with the easy glide of veteran waitress, a plastic pitcher in one hand, three glasses in the other, and the .22 cradled in her left elbow. She set the glasses and pitcher down on the ring stained coffee table, then settled in the recliner. "Help yourself," she said. " 'Fraid it's not real lemonade, just that instant stuff."

"Uh, thank you," said Sander. "Shall I pour some for you?"

"Sure."

A few moments later, Jenny joined them. She'd found an old Missouri State sweatshirt and squeezed her lower half into a pair of faded, uncomplimentarily tight jeans.

"So, what have you two been talking about?" she said brightly, settling on the corner of the couch nearest to Sander.

"We haven't yet," said Appy. "Now, you were saying about trouble?"

"Lemonade, Jenny?" asked Sander, pouring.

"Sure. Uh, Mom, you know about that UFO they found in the Big Piney?"

"Sure. I *do* check the news sites sometimes," said Appy.

"Well, we found it first."

"Huh," said Appy. "Well, tell it."

"We went canoeing Thursday. We were the first ones on the water, and it was a weekday and early in the season, so we pretty much had the river to ourselves. . . ."

"Wait. How'd you come to be free to go canoeing on a weekday?"

"Sander had some vacation coming, and I'd covered for another employee last weekend. I didn't get fired again, Mom."

"We figured Bass Pro could do without me for one day," added Sander.

"Wait another minute, Sander," interrupted Appy again. "How can a man who can't bear to set a mouse trap work for Bass Pro?"

"Mom!" ejaculated Jenny, embarrassed. "They sell lots of things, not just guns and fishing rods. Hiking boots, canoes, camping gear. There's even a restaurant."

"I maintain the aquariums, Ms. Duenckel," said Sander. "I *preserve* life." Staring at the .22 still resting in Appy's lap, he thought of the fish that he sometimes found floating when he went to work. He gulped and added, "I try my best to keep them alive, anyway."

Appy grunted. "I got no quarrel with selling hunting gear, per se. One purpose of life is to die and feed things. I was just curious as to how you reconciled yourself to it. Well, go on about the saucer, Jenny."

"At any rate, we came around an island, and there was the saucer. The door was open, but Sander looked in and said nobody was inside. So we floated down to our takeout, and Sander called the police. Then, for some reason, he called the TV station. . . ."

"I just figured that if we told only the authorities, we might never hear about it again," Sander interjected.

Appy leaned back and considered. "So you're the ones they're looking for, eh?"

"Yeah, I'm afraid so, Mom. And if they catch us, they're gonna lock us up in the School of Chemical Warfare. . . ."

"What?"

"We heard it on the radio. They're taking anyone there who saw the UFO to Fort Leonard Wood. But that's not the worst of it, Mom. That saucer—we think it may have done something to us."

"Done what?"

Sander cleared his throat. "We may be seeing things."

"Or hearing things," added Jenny.

"What sort of things?"

Sander shifted uncomfortably. "A talking armadillo."

"And Charles Kuralt," added Jenny.

"Didn't he pass away sometime back?" her mother asked.

Sander nodded. "I'm afraid so."

"And this aardvark. . . ." began Appy.

"Armadillo," corrected Sander.

"This armadillo. What sort of things does he say?"

"Uh, mostly that he's hungry," said Sander.

"He's sort of sarcastic," added Jenny.

"Speaks good English, eh?"

Just then, the phone rang. "I'll be right back," said Appy, and went into the dining room to take the call.

"So how are we doing, do you think?" asked Sander softly.

"Well, she hasn't shot you yet."

Appy returned. "Now, this armadillo—is he out in the car?"

"I told him to wait there," said Sander.

Appy nodded. "Let's go see him."

"Uh, Ms. Duenckel?" said Sander as they followed her out onto the porch.

"Oh, call me Appy," she said.

"Uh, Appy, if you can see the armadillo—you're not going to shoot him, are you?"

Appy glanced down at the gun, still cradled in her elbow. "Nah. The only varmint I planned to plug, maybe, was you. But I guess I owe you an apology, Sander. That was Sheriff Schmidt on the phone. He said there'd been a car accident down in Pulaski County. He asked if I'd seen Jenny. I said I hadn't."

"Oh God," Jenny moaned. "They've found the car. You can bet they're going to check with the emergency rooms. . . ."

"And they've got my name from the outfitter," groaned Sander.

"Who's 'they'?" asked Appy.

"Everyone," said Sander. "The FBI, the Forest Service, the media . . ."

". . . and somebody with a French accent," added Jenny.

"Hmm," said Appy, and continued her march down to the Honda. She peered into the open hatch. "So, where's this armadillo?"

"He should be there in the back," said Sander. "There he is. Dick? You awake? This is Appy Duenckel, Jenny's mother."

"You folks haven't been fishing, have you?" Appy asked.

"No," said Sander. "We've been fleeing. Why?"

Appy shook her head. "Well, I don't see any armadillo."

"I actually can't see him, either," said Jenny. "I just hear him, and sometimes feel him. Sander says he's an armadillo, and so does Dick, so I have to take their word for it."

"I can't hear any armadillo, either," said Appy.

"Oh great," moaned Jenny. "So we *are* hallucinating."

"I didn't say that," said Appy. "I just said I couldn't hear nor see him. But I think he exists."

"Why?" asked Sander, almost dumbfounded.

"Well, either he's there, or one of you two was eating worms, and left a couple of wriggly bits behind." Appy considered the situation. "Is Dick housebroken?"

"Uh, not exactly, but he tells me when he has to go."

"Then we'd better invite him in. You hadn't ought to leave an animal in the car. It could get heat stroke."

"Okay. Come on, Dick. What? Sorry." Sander turned to the others. "He's a little grumpy about being woken up. Armadillos are nocturnal, you know."

He leaned over, picked up something invisible but moderately heavy, and lowered it gently to the ground.

"He'd make a hell of a prop for a mime act," remarked Appy. "Let's go up on the front porch. It's a beautiful spring day, and your critter can do his business whenever he feels the need. 'Good thing I haven't replaced old Abdullah yet."

"Abdullah was the farm dog," Jenny explained. "He died last winter."

"Uh, could I wash my hands?" asked Sander. "Armadillos can carry...."

"Sure. Through the dining room, first door to the right. I'll put the gun up and fetch another chair."

As she did so, Appy rapidly leafed through her mental catalogue of supernatural possibilities.

"What does this armadillo say about himself?" she asked, after they've all reconvened.

"Uh, he doesn't seem to know much about himself," said Sander. "He claims he has no memories from before I found him in the bathtub."

"Well, that rules out a pookah," said Appy. "Pookahs *know* who they are." She sipped her lemonade and considered a moment longer. "I suspect your armadillo friend is a familiar."

"A what?" said Sander.

"A familiar. Now, I'm no witch, but I've known a few and studied a little. A familiar's a critter that becomes a witch's psychic companion. Traditionally it's a cat, or maybe a bat or a toad, but it can be just about anything. A lot of witches today use white rats, I understand. More portable."

"But why can't you and I see him?" Jenny asked.

"So what's the connection between witches and UFOs?" Sander asked, almost simultaneously. It said something about his changing mental state that he hadn't just snorted in disbelief.

"Sometimes other people *can't* see the familiar," Appy said. "I suppose it's a spell or something. I haven't been initiated, so I wouldn't know the mechanics. Anyway, I see two possibilities.

Either Dick's a spy, sent by some witch who's gotten interested in Sander and the saucer . . ."

Sander winced and stared at a spot on the porch floor. "Dick's denying that pretty emphatically."

". . . or else Sander has the makings of a pretty powerful warlock and doesn't realize it. Maybe the saucer freed up something in him, and he summoned Dick subconsciously."

Sander thought for moment. "But that's not really an answer," he said. "It just puts a pat name on the mystery. How did I summon him? How can he talk? How'd he get in my bathtub, and why can't he remember anything before he got there?"

"Hey, that's how science works," snorted Appy. "Witchcraft, too, I suspect. You don't solve any mystery, really. You just give it a name, describe its behavior and put it to use. We don't really know what gravity is—just what it does."

"Huh. So what does an invisible armadillo do for you, Sander?" asked Jenny.

"I don't know. Mostly what any armadillo does, I guess. Eats bugs, poops, sleeps all day. Criticizes my life choices."

"You made choices? That's unusual," remarked Appy.

"Well, not many, I guess," Sander admitted.

"He's asleep again, now?" asked Jenny.

"Curled up like bowling ball in the corner of the porch."

"It's not his purposes as an armadillo that count for you, I think," said Appy. "It's his purposes as a familiar. Familiars go where witches can't, and find out things."

"He offered to do that," said Sander wonderingly. "He wanted to check out the saucer. He said the army wasn't going to notice an armadillo. We were headed there when we found Jenny."

"My, now, that was a huge coincidence, wasn't it, Jenny? Were you going back there, too?" asked Appy.

"No! I was coming home to see you. But there was a traffic jam, so I got off the Interstate to find a way around, but somebody hit me from behind—hit my car, that is, and . . ."

"I see, I see," said Appy. "Hmm. If I remember right, a witch sends his or her spirit into a familiar to use it. The talking part of the armadillo may be part of you, Sander. Anyway, something's trying awful hard to get you both back to that UFO. Maybe it's something inside you, maybe something outside. But it does seem your purpose to go back to it."

"Well, if that's our purpose, we bollixed it royally," said Sander. "The radio said the saucer was somewhere at the bottom of the river. We'd have to evade the whole Armed Forces just to look for it."

"Maybe not," said Appy. "Maybe not." This talk of psychic familiars had reminded her of someone. . . .

"I'm too tired to go looking for flying saucers," said Jenny despairingly.

Sander nodded. "The doctor said to take you home and put you to bed."

"Well, she's home now," said her mother. "Her bed's right where she left it when she went off to college. And I imagine you're tired, yourself, young man, after being up all night talking to animals and rescuing my daughter. You could borrow my oldest son's room. Why don't you both make like your invisible friend and hibernate for a bit?"

They didn't require much persuasion. Appy waited until she heard satisfactory sleeping noises, then got on the phone to make a call before someone bugged her line, if they hadn't already. After all, the purpose of telephones was to let people talk without seeing whom they were talking to.

"Hello, Gilroy?"

"I know," said the phone. "Stop by. We'll work on it."

"Thanks." She hung up, got the .22 down again and went out to the porch swing. *As soon as Dick's gone, I should look into getting a puppy,* she thought. *Maybe a Rottweiler this time.*

At about 4 p.m., the FBI called—followed by CBS, CNN, Fox News, the *Kansas City Star,* the *New York Post,* the *St. Louis Globe-Democrat,* Al Jazeera, a man with a French accent and Harlan Chillingworth—the last in violation of two different restraining orders.

Appy denied everything.

VIII

Harlan Loves Jennifer

Terrence Harlan Chillingworth sat in Quonset Hut Raphael of the Ozark Compound of the Church of the Children of Yahweh the Immaculate White Father, trimming his toenails with a clipper that was enameled matte black so light glinting off it didn't give the owner away in combat situations. The evening news was on.

"... continues near Waynesville, Missouri, for the alleged flying saucer that washed down the Big Piney River on Friday. In what may be the best-documented UFO case ever, the saucer was discovered by canoeists on Thursday, and filmed shortly afterward by a helicopter television crew sent to cover a nearby traffic accident. Tonight, Fox News has an exclusive interview with Senator Mike Huckabay on the threat these extraterrestrials pose to our freedom. . . ."

Click

"... the so-called 'saucer lady.' Officials believe Jenny Duenckel-Chillingworth and her companion, Sander David Keynes, were the first people to . . ."

"Her *companion*," muttered Harlan. "Shit. Blaspheming the sanctity of my marriage. I'll kill him. Oughta kill her."

"... car found wrecked and abandoned in Mark Twain National Forest. Sander Keynes's voice has been identified by co-workers as that on television station and 911 tapes of the first calls reporting the saucer sighting. . . ."

"Play the damn tapes," growled Harlan. "Just let *me* hear his voice." *Snick, snick, snick*, went the toenail clippers.

The phone rang. Harlan hit the TV mute button. "Yeah."

"Hello, Brother Harlan. This is Brother David. The Reverend sends his deepest thanks for the generous contribution from yourself and that newspaper—what was it called?"

"I forget." *Snick, snick.*

"Well, anyway, the Reverend said the money will be put to very good use finishing Quonset Hut Gabriel. By the way, could you take guard duty in sector 12 at Oh-24-hundred hours?"

"Sure. But I may have to leave soon. I feel that God is about to give me a message, that I'll be given a divine mission to fulfill." *Snick. Snick.*

"Uh, hallelujah, Brother Harlan. But you can do Sector Twelve at Oh-24-hundred?"

"Sure. Praise the Lord."

"Very good, Brother. Praise the Lord. Separation Forever."

"Separation Forever. Bye." *Snick, Snick.* The toenail shavings fell to entangle themselves in the weave of the dirty gold carpet, where he forgot them. [1]

---

[1] (He could forget the clippings, and not get stabbed in the feet by their sharp little corners later, because of an undocumented species of carpet mite whose body has adapted to secrete a special enzyme that reduces the keratin in finger-and-toenail shavings to a digestible gelatin. The same enzyme works on dog, cat, and human hairs but not as well. So the little mite has developed a secure niche for itself, subsisting on hair between occasional feasts of nail-parings.

Nature abhors a vacuum. So do carpet mites. But if it weren't for vacuums, they'd overpopulate. The purpose of vacuum cleaners is to keep carpet mites in ecological balance.)

Snick, snick, went the clippers in the silence of the hut. Then Harlan remembered the remote.

Click.

"And in other news, Former House Speaker Newt Gingrich announced today that he was running . . ."

Click.

Ah. Nancy Grace. He always clicked to Nancy Grace last.

Harlan had a secret. Harlan was the only person alive who knew Nancy Grace was the Messenger of God. Only Harlan knew that the Black Box was the key to decoding God's Message.

"The trial began today for . . ."

Click.

Harlan waited a moment, then aimed at the Black Box again.

Click "Kill" *Click*

Click "Killer" *Click*

Click "Kill" *Click* said Nancy Grace.

Nah.

Try this figment instead:

Harlan roused himself from his daydream. The copy of *Gun and Knife Trader* he'd been reading slid off his thigh, as he twisted to grab the beer on the floor beside the couch. He eyed the trailer's darkened interior. *Tomorrow,* he thought, *I'll hunt for a better place. Maybe even rent the duplex again. Our duplex . . .*

A wave of pain and guilt drove him off the couch. He went in to the kitchenette table, sat down, and stared at the yellow pad that Legal Aid had given him during the divorce. The letter he'd been writing on it lay half-finished: the letter that would justify it all, make it right again, if only she'd get to see it, if she weren't dead already or worse at the hand of that Sander scumbag.

What sort of a name was "Sander" anyway? Polish, maybe?
Slavic, he bet. He read what he'd written so far:

> . . . I know it looks aweful in those papers but, my
> love Jenny, it was the only thing I could do to hep
> you. If that Sander kidnaped you and is hiding you
> somewhere they'l fined you because now
> everybody knows you look like that, you look so
> beiutaful they'll all want to hep you. I'm sorry it's
> blond and your not blond anymore but you should
> be, you half a blond soul like an angel. And now we
> half money so when they find you, you can come
> back I can treat you better because I half over sixty
> thousand dollars thats how much all the magazines
> and TV shoes paid me, Jenny.
>
> Jenny Id do anything fore you, you know that,
> don't you?

Harlan grabbed the ball-point pen from the table and began
writing again:

> I know it wood be different now Jenny because
> we'd half money if you came back. I wouldn't be so
> strest out you know that I only hit you becase of the
> stress, trying to be everthing you needed in a man,
> so you wouldn't half to go be a waitress like your
> worthless mother, so you wouldn't ever think of
> playing around, cause your so beautiful my love
> Jenny everyone would love you but you don't half
> any sense about that. Your so innocent. Don't you
> see I'm only alive for you and your only alive for
> me, but when you left you had to go be a counter

girl again in that stupid red uniform. You shouldn't be on display like that in those stupid uniforms, you won't half to be on display ever again, only a few days in those stupid magazines so thay can fined you. I don't really think saucer men got you that was just for the papers. If that Sander has laid a hand on you I'll kill him, that's how much I love you. So if they fined you and you see I've finally provided for you and don't half to be stresst out anymore and you still dont come back, I'll kill myself, that's how much I love you, Jenny. I'd even kill you if you turned into a hore like your mother, you know what God says about hores Jenny, don't be a Jezzabelle. That's how much I love you, I'd save you from that anyway I know how. I couldn't stand it if you were raped but I wood forgive you, I'd take you back even then, that's how much I love you. I hope your safe. If your reading this in heavin, please forgive me and know God forgives me and I'll be with you soon and I'll only be the good part of me then, God will wash us both clean, that woodn't be so bad, wood it, because we'd never half to be afraid again. God knows how much I love you, he couldn't refuse anybody who loved so much from coming to heavin.

I love you Jenny I love you I love you I love you.

— Harlan

He stared at the letter a long time, tore it off the pad and folded it, then realized he had no new envelopes. He couldn't mail it anyway. He'd found out where her new apartment was, but if he sent it there, even if she weren't missing, the police would get it and give him another warning, and show it to him in court so he'd know it wasn't even opened.

He put the letter in an envelope that a water bill had come in, and stuck it on the refrigerator under a magnet shaped like an apple pie with a crosshatched crust. One of her magnets. She'd left three behind: the apple pie, a cherry pie, and a little plastic sailfish with its bill broken off.

Looking at the sailfish, he felt his eyes burning again. He went back to the living room, turned on a lamp, and unwrapped the brown grocery-bag paper from the first thing he'd bought with his new money: a hunting rifle, a thirty-aught-six with a beautiful blued barrel, gleaming black scope and gleaming walnut stock. *How can it be so dark and shine so?* he thought, then thought, *that's like poetry. I'll have to remember it. Maybe I can tell it to Jenny sometime.* He'd bought the gun from a friend at the garage, so there'd been no background check.

Harlan had washed out of boot camp before he'd learned how to field-strip an M-16. He didn't know much about hunting rifles, either—just what he'd read in the gun magazine. But he stared at the beautiful gun and felt one fact deep in his soul: this gun was going to kill someone.

Maybe it would be that Sander Keynes. Maybe Harlan Chillingworth. Maybe even Jenny, or maybe all three of them. He prayed to the Lord, with all the sincerity he'd ever prayed anything, that when the time came he'd choose the right person.

IX

Of Fish Tanks and Fishbowls

We briefly interrupt this narrative to bring you an alternate viewpoint. Many people do not share Sander Keynes' unfavorable opinion of Springfield, Missouri. Springfield is, in fact, a very pleasant and livable city. On a scale of Springfields, from Springfield, Massachusetts to the Springfield inhabited by Homer Simpson's family, Springfield, Missouri, probably ranks number three or four.

Springfield is called the Gateway to the Ozarks: that modestly beautiful plateau, riven by deep, forested canyons, clear-flowing rivers, razor-backed erosion ridges and a couple of mini-mountain ranges, that constitutes the highest region between the Appalachians and the Rockies. That means a whole lot, if you live in Kansas, Illinois, Oklahoma, Iowa or Northeastern Texas. Springfield is also the Gateway to Branson, Missouri, but collectively is considerably more intelligent than the latter, as Springfield is home to three colleges and has never had a theater dedicated to Andy Williams.

Springfield has a fine small zoo, a decent art museum, an interesting little Civil War museum, a Civil War battlefield, and a good regional fair (where Apollonasia Duenckel, then known as Asfura the Blonde Egyptian, once shimmied her then-much-younger belly, but where family entertainment is now the rule—not that Asfura ever considered her belly dancing unfit for children, mind you. She'd done some other things occasionally—but not in Springfield). The Springfield area also boasts the beautiful Crystal Cave, as well as Fantastic Caverns, the world's only drive-through commercial cave.

And of course, Springfield is home to Bass Pro Outdoor World, that incredible bait shop made good, where this figment alleges Sander and Jenny to have met. Outdoor World—and to paraphrase Dave Barry, we aren't making this up—houses the world's largest hunting and fishing supply store, plus a taxidermy shop, a fishing tackle repair shop, a wildlife art gallery, the Tall Tales Barber Shop (where they'll tie a clipping of your hair into a trout fly for you) and Hemingway's Blue Water Restaurant, where customers can dine on alligator tail filets with lemon cream sauce. The complex's National Fish and Wildlife Museum, known on tourist billboards as "The Wonders of Wildlife," features a reconstructed indoor Ozark forest with real tree trunks sporting fake leaves; a concrete-and-glass artificial river where giant, primeval sturgeon and paddlefish stare at the people staring at them; a tank of otters, carefully separated from the fish; a saltwater tank with live sharks and a little triggerfish that circles the tank endlessly, looking for a way back to its lost Hawaiian reef; and a concrete den full of very bored bobcats. There are also dozens of exhibits featuring taxidermied dead animals, including rows of deer heads, a mounted and stuffed elk with stuffed and mounted wolf slashing at its throat, and a stuffed mountain lion affectionately nuzzling her two adorable stuffed and mounted cubs. There are banks of hunting and fishing video games, signs explaining the role of hunters and fishermen in maintaining wildlife populations, and a "Conservation Hall of Fame" featuring John James Audubon,

Teddy Roosevelt and other wildlife advocates whose inscribed lists of accomplishments all include the word, "hunter."

"They oughta call that place 'The Wonders of Wildlife and the Joys of Killing It,'" remarked Appy, once. But that, of course, was only her personal opinion.

But it was the 30,000 gallon saltwater tank behind the bar in Hemingway's that had enthralled Appy's youngest daughter. She'd begun making monthly pilgrimages, ascending the stairway over the meandering concrete trout stream and under the rickety rope bridge where a giant stuffed black bear toyed with a foolishly unarmed backpacker-mannequin, and entering the restaurant to order a seafood pasta she couldn't afford and to stare through the fish tank's glass wall. For Jenny, raised in a Midwestern world of muddy green catfish and grayish bass, the realm of brilliant yellow tangs, graceful stingrays and puffy porcupine fish seemed something akin to the Land of Oz.

A waitress there, stumped by one of Jenny's myriad, rapidly bubbled questions, had pointed out Sander to her. Happy that someone had taken an interest, he'd answered her graciously and patiently, acting so completely unlike Harlan that Jenny had suddenly taken notice of something besides the fish.

But the fish had seized her imagination in a way Sander hadn't. She'd bought a tropical reef fish calendar, rented National Geographic documentaries about them, gazed longingly at saltwater aquariums in pet stores. . . .

The fish were swimming through her dreams—blue-neon-striped wriggly little cleaner wrasses; orange spotted tangs like tuxedoed diplomats, parrotfish as brilliantly plumaged as their avian namesakes—when her mother gently shook her awake.

"Ow!" she squeaked.

"Are you actually supposed to sleep in that thing?" Appy wondered dubiously, eyeing the fat white neck brace.

"I don't know, Mom. I was supposed to ask my regular doctor when it should come off. But I can't go back there now. I can't go to work tomorrow. . . ."

"It *is* tomorrow, Hon. You've been out for about 18 hours."

She groaned. "I'm going to lose my job. Again." It wasn't much of a job—passing out burgers at a fast food place—but she'd kept it longer than any job she'd had in years. It had helped that she hadn't been coming in with unappealing facial bruises, recovering from injuries, or just having to quit because Harlan told her to.

She groaned. "It's Monday?"

Appy nodded.

"Jeez, I can't believe this." Then she had another horrifying thought. "Ohmygod! Pumpkin! My fish!"

"Don't you worry. We'll make sure Pumpkin and your fish get taken care of," Appy said soothingly. "But you need to get up now. I just got a phone call from a tabloid. They offered me $5,000 for exclusive photos and interview rights for 'My Daughter was Abducted by Aliens.' We've got to get a move on."

Sander was already up, sipping coffee at the dining table, reading the Sunday *Columbia Daily Herald Tribune*. A stack of other papers lay on the table at his elbow. He looked up as she entered, pleasure and concern mixed on his face. "Hi, Jenny. How are you feeling?"

I must look awful, Jenny thought. "Okay. My neck hurts." She sat down across the table opposite him: sweet, deferent, slightly balding Sander, keeper of the fish of Oz, dreamer of ancient skeletal man-apes. *Is this my true love?*

Well, if he isn't, I'm sort of stuck with him for now, anyway. She shocked herself with the thought, but realized, grimly, that it was true. Sander wasn't going back to being a fish keeper any time soon, not with half the world's government agencies chasing both of them and an invisible talking armadillo trailing him around. Maybe that aquarium wasn't the career he'd wanted, but it was a better job than hers. . . .

God, she thought. *Did that flying saucer marry us?*

"Your mom went into town and got the papers," said the object of her contemplation. "All the papers. The Columbia and Jeff City locals, the *St. Louis Globe Democrat,* the *Kansas City Star,* the tabloids. Brace yourself."

Her hands went up to the white collar. "Already braced," she said, smiling brightly.

He returned the smile, briefly, then looked grim as he shoved the stack toward her. The first paper, a tabloid, had been turned face down. She flipped it over. SAUCER NABS WOMAN, blared the headline, over a slightly blurry photo of a smiling young blonde lounging in a slightly racy one-piece swimsuit. She chuckled, then peered more closely at the picture of the girl. Then stood up with a yelp.

"Where'd they get this?" she half-shrieked.

"Probably the same place they got this one," Sander said, and flipped the next tabloid over. I MARRIED SAUCER WOMAN, the headline screamed, over a photo of her walking up a pier toward the camera, with an obviously pasted-in UFO hovering behind her.

"Harlan! That bastard! He took these pictures at Table Rock Lake on our honeymoon!" She choked back a sob.

"Your mom says the pictures are all over the Net, too," added Sander.

"You don't want to read all of what's inside," said Appy, entering the room with a cup of tea for her. "But I think you oughta be aware of how it ends, Honey." Her mother picked up the tabloid and opened it, then read aloud: "I will never rest until I find my true love again. I don't care what the aliens have done to her. I will not rest until I get her back."

"That bastard! I'll kill him! I'll kill him!" She'd held up through it all until now. But now something inside her whispered, *It's okay. You've had enough.* She burst into tears.

"Jenny . . . ." Sander rose, started around the table toward her. But her mother beat him there. "It's okay, Hon," she said, wrapping her skinny arms around her daughter.

"I swore I'd never let him make me cry again, Mom," she sobbed. "You know the worst of it? He thinks he's going to heaven for what he's doing. He's got this speech about how he knows he's a sinner, but he's gonna go to Heaven because of his love for me. He's just gonna keep coming and coming, because he thinks his salvation depends on it."

"That's one sick man," said Sander. "It's no wonder you were ready to plug me, Appy, if you thought I was like him."

"The women of this family have notoriously bad judgment when it comes to picking men," Appy told him. "But I do have some hope that you'll be the exception to that rule."

"Mom, we're just dating!" Jenny sobbed. "We *were* . . ."

"Well, you're sort of in this together for now," her mother said. "Let's all make the best of it. It seems like overkill, but I'm going to go watch the morning news." She released her daughter. "Now drink your tea. We've got lots to do."

Sander slipped around the table and took her mother's place. "Jenny, I know we haven't known each other very long, but your mom's right. I'll stick by you in this, if you'll stick by me."

"Sounds okay to me," she half-chuckled through her sobs, and slowly regained control. "Where's Dick? Is he asleep?"

Sander nodded. "He spent the night out grubbing for grubs, then went under the porch to sleep. He said he felt more secure with dirt under his belly."

"You know, this is the first time he hasn't been right there with you, since you found me by the roadside."

"Yeah. I think he's getting more confident of his own existence. When I first discovered him, he was afraid he was going to go *poof* into thin air at any moment."

"Sander, you'd better get in here," came Appy's voice from the living room.

They went to the living room together.

". . . sought as a person of interest in the disappearance of Jenny Louise Duenckel-Chillingworth, whose wrecked Toyota Yaris was found near the alleged flying saucer landing site in Mark Twain National Forest," said the local newscaster. "Duenckel-Chillingworth's husband, Terrence Harlan Chillingworth, says he suspects foul play."

The camera cut to footage of Harlan's raven-haired, weather-beaten face, blinking in the sun outside their former duplex. "Jenny's a cautious girl," he told the camera. "She'd never have been out on a country road by herself. She musta been lured out there, or kidnapped. . . ."

Cut to the reporter: "Duenckel-Chillingworth and Keynes are believed to have discovered the alleged UFO while canoeing on the Big Piney River on Friday. Duenckel-Chillingworth is described as five-foot six, approximately 155 pounds, with reddish blonde . . ."

"I am not! That's 15 pounds heavier than I really am!" Jenny erupted. "No, really. I'm *not* lying. And I'm *not* reddish blonde. I'm a redhead."

"You're blonde in those tabloid pictures," Sander noted.

"Harlan made me bleach my hair."

". . . Keynes is in his mid-thirties, approximately five foot eleven, 175 pounds, with sandy, thinning hair. . . ."

"They've got me dead on, anyway. Wonderful," muttered Sander.

"Great, just great. We're all over the tabloids and the TV. Harlan's got the whole country working for him." She felt her eyes tearing up again.

"You know, that isolation ward at Ft. Leonard Wood is maybe looking less bad, suddenly," said Sander. "At least *they* couldn't get at us." He nodded toward the TV.

"Don't even think it, Sander," said Jenny. "I hate doctors. I wish we hadn't gone to that ER. And I don't trust a batch of generals. They'll be fighting over us like a piece of meat." *Harlan was ex-military,* she thought to herself.

Appy nodded. "I agree. If you turn yourselves in, we'll never see you again. There's too much at stake. If the courts can't protect Jenny from one lousy ex-husband, how will they ever preserve you from men with real power?" She paced back and forth, thinking hard, then went to the shelf and tore some blank pages from Volume 98. "You two need to get away from here. I want you each to make a list of everything you'd need to do before a long vacation. Meanwhile, I'm going to borrow your car, Sander, if you don't mind."

"Sure," said Sander. He handed her his keys.

"Okay. I'll be gone a while. I've pulled the curtains. Stay inside. There's Tofu Scramblers in the fridge for breakfast, and lots of salad fixin's for lunch."

"Once a dancer, always a dancer," sighed Jenny. "Could you bring us back some real eggs, Mom?"

"Why Jenny," her mother said. "People around here know my habits. If I went out and bought eggs, it'd be suspicious." She grinned. "They know there's a whole henhouse out back. I raise 'em to sell, you twit. There's twelve dozen eggs in the 'fridge in the cellar. Just duck down when you cross the screen porch to get to the cellar door, so nobody can see you."

"You didn't know your own mother kept chickens?" Sander said incredulously as the Fit roared out of the driveway.

Jenny shrugged. "Last year she had rabbits back there. She's got a lot of nerve, questioning you about Bass Pro when she's peddling cholesterol."

They sat down to make out their lists of errands.

"What exactly does she want us to do with these?" asked Sander. "Do we put down stuff like 'go to the bank,' when we obviously don't dare?"

"Knowing Mom, she's got all that figured out already," said Jenny, with an odd note of peevishness in her voice. "Mom's always known what to do. It's been the bane of my existence."

"Even what to do with Harlan?" Sander asked gently.

"Yeah, she did. But I wouldn't listen." She paused, then said, "Maybe not with Harlan. She knew I had to get away. But she once told me, 'When a man goes really bad on you, there's finally not much you can do but shoot him. And then you get to entertain prison guards.'" She stared out the window, her face pale and tense. "Sander, you're a very nice man. But I wish you'd never gotten involved with me. Because Harlan's going to keep coming for me, and you're not mean enough to stop him."

"Oh, Jenny." Sander wanted desperately to reply, but could think of nothing to say. And something in her eyes stopped his impulse to rush over and hug her. "Jenny . . ." he repeated.

"Well, we should get back to this," said Jenny.

They made separate lists but consulted freely, trying to think of all the things one always remembered two hours down the Interstate.

"So where are we going on this vacation?" Jenny joked. "Baja? A Caribbean cruise?"

Sander sat back and stared at imaginary horizons. "A month-long canoe expedition," he said. "Start on the Current, as high up as the spring flood allows. Float down to the Black River, then the White and the Arkansas, then bayous and cypress country all the way down the Mississippi to New Orleans. Start with trout flies. End up hand lining for hundred pound catfish."

She smiled. "I thought you didn't kill things."

"Catch and release, Jenny. Catch and release."

She chuckled. "I've got a better idea. A two week, all-expense-paid tour of the Solar System, courtesy of Saucer Air!"

"See the Camouflaged Canals of Mars!" elaborated Sander. "Dine by candlelight to the magnificent view of Saturn's rings! Dance to the Music of the Spheres!"

Jenny chuckled. "Even Harlan couldn't find us there," she joked. Or maybe half-joked.

They had finished their lists by eight a.m., and breakfast by nine—Sander turned out to be a good cook, conjuring the health-food-prone contents of Appy's refrigerator [with some help from the cellar] into French toast with nutmeg syrup and some imaginative but tasty omelets.

When they were done, Appy still wasn't back. They washed the dishes. Jenny tried watching TV, but her neck hurt, and daytime television, like cola, doesn't taste that good when you've gotten out of the habit. So she went back to bed. Prowling the living room, Sander noticed the shelf filled with composition books. *Jenny's old schoolwork?* he thought. He pulled one out at random, and read:

The purpose of agriculture is to kill everything that isn't a soybean.

The purpose of soybeans is to grow people to help them propagate.

The purpose of ranching is to raise people to help cows propagate.

The purpose of feedlots is to increase the need for soybeans.

Ten o'clock came and went. The old mantle clock in the dining room struck the half hour, then crawled toward eleven. Sander opened an earlier volume:

The purpose of Mott the Hoople is to make people wonder what a Hoople is.

The purpose of miniskirts is to offer possibilities.

The purpose of pubic hair is to make us think when we buy bikinis.

The purpose of bra-burning is foreplay.

When Jenny awoke around noon, Appy still wasn't back. Nervously, the two fugitives made tahini-butter sandwiches, then tried the TV again, but shut it off when they heard a vehicle coming up the driveway. It was not the sound of a Honda Fit.

"Damn," said Sander. "What do we do—hide in the hen-house?"

"The cellar!" said Jenny. "Quick!"

They ducked out on the screen porch. Sander helped Jenny heave open the trapdoor, followed her down and lowered it after them. She flicked on the light, and pointed to several seven-foot logs propped against the far wall, as if Huck Finn had stored his raft there and walked off for some private time in the woods with Slave Jim.

"Get under that tornado lean-to," Jenny hissed. "I'll turn the light out after us."

Sander ran to the little shelter and crawled inside, collecting damp spider webs as he went. The room went black. Then he heard Jenny stumble against the ties.

"Shit!" she whispered, and crawled in to join him under the moldy-smelling wood. They heard the muffled sound of the front door opening and closing. Then the egg refrigerator's compressor rumbled to life, drowning out all other sounds. When it shut off, they heard a muffled voice call, "Jenny? Sander?"

"That's Mom," Jenny said, and started to scramble out.

Sander laid a hand on her shoulder. "What if she's not alone?" he whispered forcefully.

She froze, then sat down again slowly. "Please don't touch me without my permission," she whispered.

"Sorry," he whispered back.

A single set of footfalls crossed the floor above. The trapdoor groaned. Light washed around their hiding place.

"Are you two down there?" Appy asked.

"Yeah, Mom," Jenny replied. They crawled out.

"She always hid down here when she was a kid, too," remarked Appy. "Made her easy to find. Here's your keys." She tossed Sander a set of car keys as they emerged from the cellar.

"Wait. These aren't my keys," said Sander. "They're not even Honda keys."

"Nope. Dodge Power Ram 50 pickup. Mitsubishi product. Four-wheel drive, camper top, engine just overhauled. A little rust, but not bad. Brand new tires. Should be good for at least 30,000 more miles."

"But what happened to my car?"

"I've still got friends on both sides of the tracks," she said. "I sold your car to a fence I know. It'll leave the state in pieces, with the serial numbers filed off. He's helping me with fake IDs, too. They'll be ready in a couple of days."

"They cut up my car?" Sander sputtered in disbelief, as Appy led them to the dining table, where a couple of large shopping bags awaited. She slapped down two envelopes.

"Two thousand, cash, for each of you," she said. "Don't stash it all together. I recommend a big bill or two in each shoe." She upended a large Wal-Mart bag. "Clothes. I had to guesstimate your sizes, but they should work. I had your police descriptions to go on, after all."

"But where'd this all come from, Mom?" breathed Jenny.

Appy grinned. "Part of it's the difference between what I got for Sander's car and what I paid for the truck. But most of it's your inheritance, girl. Spend it wisely. I'm afraid I gotta change my will, now—only fair to the other kids."

"Uh, Appy, this truck isn't, uh, hot, is it?" Sander asked.

"Nah. It's legal. I bought it off Jenny's brother Bill. But you don't have to file the title until your current, er, problems are resolved."

"Hmmm. Where are my other keys?" Sander asked. "I gave you my whole key ring, didn't I?"

"I've still got 'em," said Appy. "I may need 'em when I run down to Springfield on your errands. Better give me your keys, too, Jenny, so's I can get Pumpkin and take care of the fish. Good. Now stow that cash while I go fix me a salad. We've got lots to do, and a visit to pay to someone, once it's dark."

"Who's that?"

She smiled mysteriously. "Someone who just might be able to find a sunken UFO without a shitload of helicopters."

X

The Wet Toothpick of the Mind

A Dodge Ram Power 50 is not a Sport Utility Vehicle. Its Mitsubishi-built cab holds no Moroccan leather ergonometric bucket seats; the dash has no standard AM-FM stereo with CD player and woofers and tweeters. The tires aren't six feet tall; the paneling isn't walnut burl; there are no crew cab, external roll bar with a row of lights across the top, yellow fog lights, 5-liter V-8, or "Trucker Girl" mud flaps. The windows crank up and down by hand. The only concessions to convenience are a four-wheel drive mechanism that doesn't require getting out of the truck to lock the hubs—and a sliding rear window panel, which comes in very handy if you have a talking armadillo riding in back. The Power Ram 50 is all utility, with none of that "sport" nonsense: the clean essence of small truck.

Of course, they don't make it anymore.

"I like it," said Sander. "I've always wanted a truck."

"Well, just remember, it's my inheritance," sniffed Jenny.

"But I have to have a share in it, too, after what your mom did to my Fit."

"Oh, God, joint property. This is moving too fast, Sander."

"There she is."

Appy's little red Subaru was pulled off on the roadside ahead of them. She'd left fifteen minutes earlier to check adjacent lanes for parked cars or tire tracks ("They may be able to hide their own bodies in the bushes," she'd said, "but you can bet they didn't walk out here from Jeff City"). Then she'd driven by her driveway and honked twice. At her insistence, they'd waited two minutes to see if another car passed before they had set out, in case Appy herself was being followed.

Appy pulled out and led them to US 54 and Jefferson City. They drove downtown, past the gleaming marble State Capitol (an architectural duplicate of the US Capitol building; Missouri is not a state particularly known for originality) then on into Jeff City's rather run-down business district.

"This place stinks," noted Dick, hunkering down in a plastic tub that Appy had filled with Osage River sand for his comfort.

Sander sniffed. "No worse than any small city. How did you ever stand Springfield?"

"I didn't, for long."

"Oh, hush, you two," scolded Jenny. "Springfield's a nice town."

"It still stinks," said the armadillo. "Car exhaust and pigeon poop, dogs and doggie do, people feet and people armpits and cat pee and drunk pee. But there's something else nasty here, like car exhaust, only stinkier."

"Probably diesel fumes from the railroad tracks. They're only a couple of blocks away. Look, she's stopping."

"Good. Can armadillos get car sick?"

"Gad, I hope not," said Sander. "Here's a parking space."

Sander parallel parked the truck—no mean accomplishment, after years in a subcompact.

"Do you think we should bring Dick along?" he asked

"Just try to leave me here," huffed the armadillo.

"That'd be easy," replied Sander. "I just wouldn't open the camper door."

"Sander, don't be mean," said Jenny.

"Okay, I won't. But what if he isn't invisible to everybody else? The only people we've tried him on are your mom and us."

"Please don't leave me back here," piped the armadillo, plaintively. "Those nasty fumes are mixing with the smells of all this wonderful live bait Appy bought. It's inhumane. If I don't get sick, I'll probably eat this stuff all at once, and poop on your sleeping bags."

Sander glared back at him. "You wouldn't."

"Better your sleeping bags than my sandbox."

"I thought that was why Appy put that tub of sand in there."

"Well, where do you expect me to sleep, then?"

"There doesn't seem to be anybody around," Jenny noted.

"Let's hope not," said Sander. "It *is* 7 p.m. on a weekday, and we're two blocks from the nearest bar."

They waited until Appy flashed her headlights to signal "all clear," then got out and unloaded the armadillo without incident. Appy met them outside a small, grimy brick business building. Three golden spheres had been painted rather crudely on one of the shop windows. A CLOSED sign hung in the door.

"A pawn shop?" asked Sander incredulously.

"Not really," Appy said, knocking on the shop door. "Hardly anything in here's true pawn. They're his prizes."

"Prizes?" asked her daughter.

"Yep. How do you *think* a real psychic would make his living?"

"Prizes?" echoed Sander.

"Psychic?" said Jenny.

The door creaked open. A craggy, beard-fringed face peered out.

"Ah, Asfura. Long time, no see. I've been expecting you."

"Of course you have. You're a psychic. Besides, I called ahead."

"True. Hello, Sander. Hello, Jenny."

"Uncle Gilroy? You're a *real* psychic?" said Jenny in disbelief.

"Let's talk about it inside," the man said, with a smile and a wave of his hand. Then he cocked his head, as if puzzled. "Er, you too, Dick."

"Thank you," said Dick suspiciously. He trotted through the door, past the feet of Uncle Gilroy, who frowned, though not in a hostile way.

"That's odd," he said absently.

"You can see him?" asked Sander.

"No. But I don't doubt that he's there. Something's definitely there." He scratched his beard. "Well, why don't you folks come on up to the parlor, and I'll get some sodas."

He led them through the shop, which was crammed to the rafters with fishing rods and bowling balls, stuffed animals and televisions, Igloo coolers and weight training machines and a lot of things with the Pepsi logo on them. They entered a stock room filled with an even vaster array of miscellany, then climbed a circular steel staircase (Sander carried Dick) into a sumptuously furnished but somewhat messy apartment that appeared to take up the entire second story. Most of the internal walls had been knocked out; in their place, tapestries and carpets hung from the rafters, dividing a large living-room-like area in the back from other spaces toward the front. Some hangings appeared aged and dingy, others new—all colorful to the edge of gaudiness, full of scarlets and golds and blues.

Thick layers of rugs underfoot yielded as luxuriously as a giant teddy bear's stomach.

Sander put Dick down on a splendid oriental carpet. "You be sure and let me know if you need to go," he said. "Uh, could I wash my hands somewhere?"

"Toward the front, first door on the left," said their host. "Heck, it's the *only* door." Gilroy himself disappeared behind a glittering tapestry of a fancifully depicted lion hunt.

Appy seated herself in a parlor chair before a velvet tableau of card-playing dogs, while Jenny lowered herself stiffly to a pile of enormous red plush cushions. "Prizes?" she asked again.

"Of course," Appy said. "He knows which sodas have winning bottle caps before he opens them. He knows the right moment to stuff his slip of paper into the contest entry box. He can guess the weight of any pumpkin, and knows which lakeshore development will honor its giveaways and which will try to stiff you."

"Gee, he must make a killing at the Lotto."

"Uh-uh. Too dangerous," said their host, emerging with four cans of soda. "Let's see, Sprite for you, Jenny, and Diet Dr. Pepper for your mom, and a Mountain Dew for Sander when he gets back—no, silly me, it's after four. He'll have a ginger ale. See, I *do* make mistakes." He bustled back after a different can.

"Too dangerous?" Jenny repeated. She was still looking a bit stunned.

"Yep," he called from the kitchen. "If you ever crawled under a lottery office, you'd see more wires than a telephone exchange. Phone taps, supermikes, digital descramblers. Bugs. The moment you win big, you're on the list of every con artist and racketeer in the country—and that's if the Mob hasn't infiltrated the game itself. Even a psychic can't beat a fixed game, and he knows what they'll do to him if he tries. Much better to go after the little stuff, the random stuff you can sell. It's a decent life. It keeps me busy, and beats the hell out of holding séances." [1]

Sander had returned from the bathroom by then. "Uncle Gilroy, this is Sander. Sander, Uncle Gilroy," said Jenny. "Well, he's not really my uncle, but I always called him that."

"I'm her spiritual uncle," Gilroy said. "More than that, actually. I'm her godfather." He grinned a beaming but somehow saturnine grin, full of gold-capped teeth. He was a tall, bony man, made taller by a shock of stiff hair that was still mostly black, though his beard had long since gone gray.

"Uncle Gilroy used to come by whenever a fair was open in central Missouri," continued Jenny. "He was a magician. He always brought me stuffed animals from the midway, and he did the neatest tricks. I didn't know his tricks were real. . . ."

"Isn't it amazing how easily we accept that they *are* real, now that there's an invisible armadillo in our lives?" Sander mused.

Gilroy grinned, seating himself cross-legged in a pile of cushions with surprising grace for a man of his age and height. "Most people don't accept it," he said. "That's why I haven't been lynched. But to your problem: there's an armadillo in your lives. Do you want him out?"

"Hey!" said Dick. "Watch how you answer that! You might get what you want!"

---

[1] Author's note: the reader should be reminded, here, that this work is a figment, and the opinions and allegations of the characters are not necessarily true. The author has not crawled under a lottery office to verify Uncle Gilroy's suspicions. Monster centipedes might get the author if he tried that.

"I just want to know where he came from," said Sander. "I want to know why he's here."

"Not asking too much, are you?" snorted Gilroy. "You can't even answer those questions about yourself. All right, you think the armadillo has something to do with that UFO you found."

"I don't know that it's a UFO," said Sander. "We never saw it fly. It may have been some sort of nerve gas container from Fort Leonard Wood."

Gilroy smiled again, as if savoring some private joke. "What happened when you encountered the UFO?"

"Uh . . . I don't remember," Sander asked wonderingly. "Not exactly. . . ."

"Periods of amnesia are common when people get too close to those things," said Gilroy understandingly. "That's how all those abduction stories get started."

"I remember looking inside, but not seeing much. There was a sort of setback all around the walls, like a circular dashboard or something, but I don't remember seeing any controls."

"Jenny, do you remember what happened?" Gilroy asked. "Did Sander enter the saucer?"

"Uh, no, I don't think so," said Jenny. "He just kind of leaned in and looked. I remember . . . there was a little flash or flicker, as if something had just shorted, only I never heard any crackle or fizzle or anything."

"Hmm." Gilroy leaned back in his cushion and looked into space. "I think the saucer may have given you a gift, Sander."

"A gift? What sort of gift?"

"Well, the sort that lets you see talking armadillos, for starters. What else it does, remains to be seen."

"How does it 'let' me see talking armadillos?"

"I don't know."

"Thanks."

"Hey, I don't know how I see what I see, either," said Gilroy. "I don't even know how I see the stuff my eyeballs see, once it gets into my brain. There was an idiot named Skinner who described the mind as a 'black box,' because nobody could see into it directly. He wrote a book called *Beyond Freedom and Dignity,* claiming that since *freedom* and *dignity* were abstract ideas, and we couldn't see inside our heads, then those abstractions didn't really exist. 'Big mistake to think what you don't know is the same as nothing. There are all sorts of things we don't know. Some of them can run over us from behind."

"Ask him if you think it's a coincidence that you don't know what happened in the saucer, and *I* don't know what happened before I landed in your tub," pressed Dick.

"Uh, the armadillo has amnesia, too," said Sander. "Only his is more extensive. Could that be related to the saucer, too?"

Gilroy chuckled. "Everything's related somehow. Catherine Zeta-Jones and a rat both have teeth. The Empire State Building and walruses both contain water."

"I mean a *causal* relationship," persisted Sander.

"Rat teeth and Catherine Zeta-Jones's teeth both cause food to disappear."

"No, I mean . . . I mean . . ."

The psychic grinned. "Could the UFO have caused both your amnesia and Dick's? Maybe. I know a lot of things, but I don't know that for sure. Amnesia's a black box inside a black box. If *you* can't reach it, I certainly can't."

"Ask him if finding the saucer would help," prompted Dick.

"Would finding the saucer help?"

"Maybe. Maybe not."

"Aw, come on, Uncle Gilroy," said Jenny. "I've seen you pick aces from unmarked decks, tell fat ladies their weight to the half-pound—all kinds of neat things. You can't help us with this?"

"Cards and bathroom scales are specific things. Whether or not something's 'helpful,' isn't," replied Gilroy. "Things can be helpful or unhelpful in a lot of different ways at once."

"Just like they can have a lot of different purposes," chimed in Appy.

"Exactly. Something can cure cancer *and* make your hair fall out, for instance. Good for your life, bad for your sex appeal."

"Hey. Bald guys can be plenty sexy. Just look at Jean-Luc Piccard and Vin Diesel," Sander pointed out, indignantly.

"True, true," said Gilroy, smiling like the Cheshire Cat—which was a little unnerving for Jenny, who'd seen Gilroy disappear before.

"So what *can* you tell us that could be useful for solving amnesia?" she asked.

"I can tell you the name of a good head-doctor," Gilroy said. "Unfortunately, he's not all that good at brains. Should've stuck with ear, nose and throat. Or I could maybe tell you where the flying saucer is."

"I see," said Sander, suddenly suspicious. "And what would your fee be?"

"No fee," said Gilroy. "Asfura's an old and dear friend."

"Asfura?"

"An old stage name," explained Appy. "I got tired of 'Apollonasia'."

"No fees. No obligations?" persisted Sander.

"I like this guy," Gilroy told Appy. "He's a sharp mark. No, Sander, no obligations to *you*. This is a family matter; you're thrown in for free. Family has its obligations—Uncle by blood or by naming, doesn't matter. Besides, Carnies are family."

"Bunk," said Appy. "Carnies cheat each other all the time."

"Hey, no family's perfect," said Gilroy. "So, do you want me to find the saucer? No obligation now—just someday, a family member may need *your* help. Maybe me, maybe somebody else."

"Of course," piped up Jenny. "Let's get on with it."

"All right, then. Let me get my maps and a toothpick."

"A toothpick?" Sander asked, as their host bustled off.

"He's going to map-dowse," said Appy, as if that explained everything.

Gilroy returned with a clutch of rolled USGS topographic maps under one arm, a garbage bag in one hand, and a toothpick dangling like a cigarette from his mouth.

"All right, let's get down to work. Anybody with a live can of soda should pick it up." He cleared a dozen or so empty cans off a large, low table and into the bag, then dragged the table to the center of the room, amid a bow wave of carpets.

"Okay, gather round. Dim the lights a little, Asfura, just for old times' sake—but not so much that we can't read the maps. Ever seen dowsing done, you kids?"

"You mean like water witching?" Jenny asked.

"Precisely. People don't know why it works, but it does. Certain folk can go out with a forked willow or peach switch or a pair of copper rods, and tell you exactly where a vein of underground water is. And it doesn't have to be water. A good dowser can find just about anything, from car keys to lost cows. Map dowsing's similar, but instead of walking all over, you use maps. Grab four books from that corner shelf, would you, Jenny?"

"Which ones?"

"Doesn't matter. I just need something to hold down the map corners." He unrolled a map and pinned it in place with *Tristram Shandy, The Satanic Verses, Memnoch the Devil* and an old *Lasser: Your Income Tax*. Sander recognized the Big Piney River, wandering blue among the map's curling nests of pale green elevation lines.

"So where's the peach switch?" Sander asked.

"A peach switch is sort of crude for this scale," said the psychic. "I use a toothpick. For some reason, it seems to work better if it's soaked in saliva." He plucked the aforenamed item from his mouth. "Now, Sander, you got anything on you that you were wearing when you looked into that saucer?"

"Uh, nothing except my wallet."

"Could you loan it to me for a minute?"

Sander started to pull out his wallet, then hesitated.

Gilroy grinned. "Or something from it. A library card, a photo, anything."

"Uh, okay."

"Sander, wait a minute!" said Jenny. "You weren't wearing your wallet, remember? You stashed it in that ammo can, in case we upset the canoe."

"Rats. You're right."

"What about your pocketknife?" Jenny suggested. "I remember you had it that day, because you demonstrated the saw blade to me. Do you still have it?"

"You're right!" He fumbled in his pocket, then pulled out a Victorinox Swiss Army Knife, Huntsman model, its red handle dulled by years of abrasive pocket grit. "My mother gave me this knife when I was sixteen," he said, lovingly.

"Hmm. Lots of memories. Tough to sort out," muttered Gilroy. "Could help a little, maybe." He turned the knife over in his hand, then seemed to remember his guests. "No psychic is 100 percent sure of anything, but I've got about a 75 percent chance of finding things with this method. It goes up to around 80, if I've got something that's been in close proximity to what I'm dowsing for."

Grasping the pocketknife in his right hand, he clutched the wet end of the toothpick delicately between the thumb and forefinger of his left hand and began sweeping it slowly across the map, advancing an inch or so with each sweep.

"I think I'll mosey up front and watch out the window," said Appy. "I know what *my* next job is, already."

Back and forth the toothpick swept. Gilroy paused, popped the toothpick back in his mouth for a minute, then resumed. The toothpick approached the map's upper edge, made a final sweep . . .

"Nothing," breathed Gilroy. He laid out another map.

"Damn," Appy cursed softly from the front room. A moment later, she slipped wordlessly back through the apartment, giving Gilroy a wide berth, and peered out a window at the building's rear. Then she passed through again, going to the front. Sander started to ask what was wrong, but she brought her finger to her lips, then pointed at the concentrating Gilroy and shook her head. Then she was gone again, gliding quietly in her no-nonsense waitress shoes.

The toothpick waved its way across a third map, then a fourth. Two more times, Appy slipped silently through.

About midway across the fifth map, the toothpick suddenly quivered, then jerked downward so violently it seemed to nearly pull itself out of Gilroy's fingers. He lowered the toothpick to rest like a little wooden bridge across a band of blue ink.

"There it is," Gilroy said, "clear down on the Gasconade. You kids mark that spot. The map's yours. You have to decide what to do with it."

"You're going to go find it, aren't you?" said Dick. "The saucer, I mean."

"We need to try," said Jenny. "Right, Sander?"

"People float the Gasconade all the time," said Sander. "They'll find it again, long before we can get there. I don't know why somebody hasn't already reported it." Then he took a breath and squared his shoulders. "But yes. We need to try."

"You found it?" called Appy softly, from the front room.

"I believe so. Virtually certain so," said Gilroy.

"Good, because we've got company."

"Porkers?"

"Tan Ford full-sized sedan. Federal plates. You're the psychic. You tell me."

XI
When Words Fail, Try Micro-Cameras

English is one of the most versatile and adaptable languages in the world. Thanks to its bastard parentage—its prissy French whore mother and stolid Anglo-Saxon peasant father—or more accurately, its dandified French father and stolid, gloomy Anglo-Saxon milkmaid mother, since it was the French who pretty much screwed the English back then—English has a huge repertoire of vocabulary and syntax, high and low words, frontal assaults and Byzantine stratagems. There are few things you can't say in English, if you try long enough.

That said, the Mother Tongue still has a number of topics that she stumbles over: things that other languages say in a word or two, but English must call out siege engines and secret agents to tackle. The Thai language, for instance, has a myriad of two-word phrases containing the word *jai* (heart), which enable its speakers to describe their emotional states with incredible accuracy. One such two-syllable phrase denotes what one feels when faced with a companion who has caused pain, in a situation where one cannot show that pain openly. (Look how many words English required just to say that.)

English is also horrible for describing smells and tastes (again, Thai, for instance, has separate words for the blandness of milk, potatoes and rice), and the mother tongue of Shakespeare is pretty imprecise when it comes to discussing philosophy (as any German will tell you. But then, precise philosophical terminology didn't prevent *Mein Kampf*). And in English, one poor word often has to bear far too many burdens.

There are many kinds of *tired*, for instance. There is the fatigue of honest hard labor: the go-home-fall-instantly-asleep sensation that a Third World farmer feels after spending all day behind a team of oxen. There is mental tiredness, the "brain-fried" sensation after cramming for an exam. There is the desperate, self-feeding fatigue of insomnia. There is the strain of mindless concentration, felt by factory workers and clerk-typists the world around. There is the fatigue of anxious waiting:, the poisons of accumulated frustration and maybe fear, which build up in the blood of a prospective father during a difficult labor or in loved ones waiting at the airport for a plane that's long overdue. And then there are compound tirednesses, such as the maddening mixture of forced concentration, boredom, and frustration that FBI Special Agent Warner Harvey Lickenstein was feeling in the snoop van outside Sander Keynes's Springfield apartment complex, 46 sleepless hours after watching helplessly as the UFO disappeared down the Big Piney River.

Now he was stuck here, watching empty apartments, while all the real action was happening around Fort Leonard Wood. National security at stake, the woods full of top foreign and industrial operatives—it would be a counterintelligence goldmine just to ride the back roads up there with a long-lens camera and a high-gain mike. And this was his territory, dammit. Or was, until that damned Army captain had ushered him off and lost the damn UFO, and all the Washington teams had moved in. . . .

And all he could say was, "God, I'm tired. You got any more coffee?"

The van was the command center for surveillance of Sander Keynes's and Jenny Duenckel-Chillingworth's apartments and related targets. Both main stakeouts were officially external— no court-approved wiretaps. These days, though, it hardly mattered; you could watch just about anywhere, listen in on almost any conversation, and it was all perfectly legal. They'd already installed micro-video cameras, hallway mikes, directional mikes, permissioned feeds from building security cams, digital audio enhancement programs and white noise filters, all without entering the apartments. They had a chip cam impersonating a fly speck in the dot of the "i" in the stairway Exit sign outside Jenny Duenckel-Chillingworth's apartment, and a lipstick cam in the crotch of a tree overlooking Sander Keynes's bedroom window. They had infrared scanners that could literally detect the heat of passion through a brick wall. And since the Agency wasn't worried about getting convictions in this case, they could use gray and black ops devices: e-mail traps, wireless phone descramblers, and digitally filtered conduction mikes that could listen in a heating conduit and separate a dozen conversations occurring in various apartments along the conduit's path.

Thanks to the miracle of electronic parts produced with cheap Asian labor, all these devices together amortized out at less than one agent's salary. A round-the-clock operation like this one, which once would have required a dozen or more agents, now needed only three two-man shifts to maintain a much higher surveillance level. Like most older FBI agents, Lickenstein was a trained accountant, so he appreciated those numbers—especially since nobody got fired—they just got to surveil more people.

In this case, even with everyone important out in the woods, Lickenstein still had an immediate team of five agents, plus secure links to the agents that the Jefferson City and Kansas City offices had finally assigned to check on Duenckel-Chillingworth's and Keynes's parents. The Jeff City team had gotten organized less than an hour ago; he was still waiting for KC to check in. Information might move at the speed of light, but the chain of command was considerably slower.

Special Agent Walter J. "Wally" Sutherland was manning the van's hot seat at the moment. He wasn't happy, either.

"I don't know why we needed the van for this," he groused. "We could've watched from the office, and been a lot more comfortable."

"We gotta use the van once in a while, or they delete it from inventory," Lickenstein said tiredly. "Speaking of security—what are the spooks doing right now?"

"Our spooks, or everybody else's?"

"Well, start with ours."

Sutherland pointed and clicked. "The DIA guys just changed shifts. They haven't found our bug on their van, or else they're pretending they haven't. The Chinese are watching the DIA. The Iranian is poking through Keynes's dumpster. The Brit's on his cell phone in his hotel room, recounting what the DIA told him. The Russian's off at his usual bar, harassing his usual waitress. Man, if we had a wire on her left titty, we'd hear everything."

"Nothing I'd want to hear. I listened in on enough drunken Russkies pitching woo to last me a lifetime and a half, back in Chicago. How about the Israeli?"

"He had to write a mid-term paper tonight. That's the trouble with exchange student sleeper agents. The Japs and Germans went outdoors as soon as word got out that the army'd lost the Object. My guess is they're surveilling the river."

"My guess, too," sighed Lickenstein.

"Same with the industrial agents, except that one Frenchman. He's still tracking down all of Keynes's e-mail recipients." Sutherland point-clicked from ISPY to 5THESTATE, then gave a little whistle. "Okay, War, we got something to fix, maybe."

"What've you got?"

"We've got a dummy layout from the *MorningStar*. One of the tabloids. Won't be on the newsstands or the Net for two days yet."

"What the hey. Put it on."

Sutherland hit a key. Lickenstein's own monitor flashed a front page with the garish headline: HUBBY TO SAUCER LADY: I FORGIVE YOU.

"We know about him already. We've got the divorce papers."

"Yeah, but somebody entered his name in our search systems as 'Harley.' This story calls him 'Harlan.'"

"Hmm. Ex named Harlan, boy friend named Sander. Maybe this lady's got a fried chicken fetish. . . . But we're talking *tabloid* here. It's not like they're known for their proofreading."

"Neither is our help at the office. Better check, hadn't we? If nothing else, log the possible AKA. That's SOP."

"Oh, all right." Lickenstein pulled up the Jenny Duenckel-Chillingworth's Temporary Restraining Order. He frowned, then clicked up a couple of other documents. "Damn. You're right. We didn't catch it, because there's a *Harley* Chillingworth in town, too. Criminal record and everything. We've been staking out the wrong guy. This'll take days to straighten out."

"Damn. Well, should we get started?"

"Right," said Lickenstein. "We," in this case, meant him, since Sutherland was at the monitors. Lickenstein reluctantly cut orders to uninstall surveillance from Harley Chillingworth's house. The man had been promising. A joy-riding conviction at 19; cruised Internet "snuff" sex sites. Had visited Waco, Texas, ostensibly to attend a sauce-maker's convention—he owned a small company that produced Chilly's Hot Chili Barbecue Sauce. Cheated on his taxes. *I could nail him on that,* Lickenstein thought, *if I could pitch it to a DA who's a Democrat.*

He saved Harley's file to a flash drive, wiped it from the hard drive, then opened a new one, "Chillingworth, Harlan," and entered known data. The searchbot began gathering tax, credit, driver's license and gun registration records, traffic abstracts, commercial mailing lists and confiscated hacker e-mail files to filter for the most current URLs, P.O. Box(es) and street address. Meanwhile, another part of the multitasking processor trolled the police nets for dossiers, fingerprints and outstanding warrants.

A billion dollar federal software program to do all this was still in bug-riddled limbo—but they'd easily equipped this van and its ilk with unregistered software confiscated from hackers, terrorists, drug cartels and porn rings. Zero-budget items—no oversight, no publicity. Most of the bad guys didn't know they had it. Neither did Congress. Congress hadn't thought to ask.

Lickenstein let the programs work while he finished his coffee, then checked the results so far. Checkered employment and driving records. Court-ordered attendance, Alternatives to Violence and AA; checkered compliance record. No outstandings, but several priors: mostly domestic violence and public disturbance. A felony assault reduced to deferred plea. Current

TROs on behalf of Jenny Marie Duenckel (a.k.a. Jenny Duenckel-Chillingworth) and Apollonasia Brechtlein (a.k.a. "Appy," a.k.a. "Asfura") Duenckel. (The 'bot auto-linked to Appy Duenckel's FBI file—Jeff City's domain. He snuck a quick peek anyway, and whistled. "Hey, Wally," he said, "check out her mom's file sometime. Juicy.") Recent subscriptions to *Knife and Gun* and *Soldier of Fortune*. Promising.

He logged the most likely current addresses and typed up surveillance orders: strictly lily-white this time; they might find something they wanted to prosecute. You had to treat known criminals more carefully than innocent civvies.

"Activity in Jeff City," broke in Sutherland.

"Finally. What've they got?"

"They located the mother's car." Sutherland grinned. "Charley Stokes says they lucked out. They were on their way out to the farm, and spotted the car a few blocks from Jeff City HQ. Female subject's mom is believed close by."

"Great."

"Okay, they spotted her. Upper story window over a pawn shop."

"What's the name of the shop?"

"Middle Earth Pawn. Want to check business records?"

"Why not?" He typed in the name and launched a 'bot. "Got'em. Owner's one Gilroy John Leonard. Cross-checking for other records . . . hmmph. No priors, but he's under investigation. The local authorities think he might be fencing. Lots of his merchandise comes by mail, no pawn slips. File's open but inactive. Former carnie. A.k.a. Leonardo the Magnificent. Hmm. Subject's mom used to work the fair circuit."

Sutherland sighed. "Probably just a tryst. But Jeff City's planting a cam surveilling the entrance, anyway."

* * *

"Someday I'm going to write a book about the sex life of old broads," said Special Agent Carl Brinkley. "The hours I've spent listening in on seventy-year-old mobsters talking dirty to their sixty-year-old mistresses. . . . If we really wanted to wipe out the Mafia, we'd just play the tapes back to their wives."

"I've heard my share of old wives talking dirty, too," said Stokes. "Usually to their husbands, though. I guess if you marry a hit man, you think twice about cheating. But either way, it gives me the creeps—old skinny people making love. Yecch."

"You think that's bad. Just think about old fat people. Doesn't it just make you quiver all over?"[1]

"Ye-h-h-h-hch." Stokes shuddered. "I hope we don't get authorized for a tap on this place."

"That's the worst thing about this case," said Brinkley. "I don't know what we *are* authorized for. This lady's got a rap sheet, but it's all ancient. What's she supposed to be doing now that's illegal? Even those two other subjects that we're supposed to watch for. I know—if we find them, observe and report. But what are we looking for? What're our grounds?"

"National security, connected to that UFO," said Stokes.

"Of course it is, El Braino. But so they saw a flying saucer. What's the federal violation?"

"Well, the guy's wanted for questioning in the disappearance of the lady," suggested Stokes.

"And if the lady shows up, too?"

"She could be a hostage."

"Suspicion of kidnapping. We could go with that," Brinkley said. "Hell of a lawsuit, though, if she isn't. And that CDC

---

[1] Again, we emphasize that opinions expressed here are those of Special Agents Stokes and Brinkley, and do not represent the author's own views on sex, aging, or adipose tissue. They don't know what they're talking about.

doctor, wanting to know if the suspects show 'aberrant behavior.' What the hell's 'aberrant behavior'?"

Stokes shrugged. "If somebody's acting psycho and endangering, we apprehend, observing full AIDS protocol. Otherwise, observe and report."

"What, they've got some sort of alien brain bug?"

"Maybe. Maybe."

"Observe and report," repeated Brinkley, nervously. "Observe and report. Safest to do just—"

"Here she comes," interrupted Stokes.

A petite, sixtyish woman had emerged from the pawnshop. Her gaze seemed to linger a moment on the agents' car. Then she walked to the red Subaru and unlocked the door.

"You know, I bet she was a looker, thirty years ago," said Stokes. "I bet she was a blonde bombshell."

"Could be, could be," said Brinkley. Get ready to move."

The woman entered her vehicle. Stokes reached for the ignition key.

The Subaru peeled out, tires squealing. The odor of burnt rubber wafted through the air.

"Go, go, go!" shouted Brinkley. "We've got grounds, now!"

"We aren't traffic cops, you moron!" said Stokes, gunning the big Ford onto the street. "*Observe and report.* I'll observe. You report!"

After they had sped off in (discreet) pursuit of the rubber-burning granny, a Lincolnesque man in his late sixties emerged from the pawnshop. He paused, listening to the fading sounds of the chase. The microcam Stokes had planted in a knothole on a light pole across the street recorded him walking away, then a blurry hand planting a wad of chewing gum over its lens.

Off camera, Uncle Gilroy entered the blue Dodge pickup a half-block away, then drove back into the alley behind the building. A few minutes later, the pickup drove off again.

A lovingly restored metal-flake-cherry-red Volkswagon Karmann Ghia pulled into the street and dropped back to follow the pickup at a discreet distance, as it threaded Jefferson City's back streets to US 50, then headed for US 63 and a stretch of the Gasconade River between Vienna (pronounce VAI-ENNA) and Vichy.

The microcam had failed. But the paparazzi, at this stage of the hunt, were relying on eyeballs.

XII
Armadillo Eyes

When Dick had remarked that he had "the usual" senses, that didn't mean his senses were the same as a human's. Life looks a lot different from an armored shell a few inches above ground level. As the armadillo made his way along the banks of the Gasconade River, the surrounding night was a world of vivid but soft-focused grays. Trees were not silhouettes but textured, moving creatures, rustling gently in the night wind; stars beamed like the tiny suns they really were, expanded to blurry Van Gogh proportions.

I've got a bad case of astigmatism, he told himself, then thought for the umpteenth time, *Gee, if I know that that is, I must have been human once.* But the blurry stars seemed perfectly normal, now.

As he scrambled along the riverbank, the hickory trees and understory flowed like a distorted ocean around his almost-360-degree vision. Only very close up were things very clear to his myopic eyes. In place of depth judgment, he had a cruder gauge of distance: anything not within striking range of his tongue was a vague blur (unless it was moving, in which case it became a very vivid blur).

That was okay, because he had other, much more finely tuned senses. His big ears flicked back and forth, precisely locating the construction noises of ants in their burrows and the rustlings of crickets under soggy leaves. And the *smells* each air current carried to his nose! The tangy, acidic scent of ants, the mucky, vaguely decayed odor of earthworm castings, the precise odors of varying degrees and kinds of wet and dry rot, the pungency of old leaves crushed underfoot, the heady perfumes of night-blooming flowers, the sweet greenness of moving foliage, the great panic of odors from disturbed earth. . . . *Humans must be barely alive, not to know all this!* Dick thought exuberantly.

The problem was how all this sensory equipment, so marvelously adapted to the task of filling an insectivore's stomach, was going to be of any use in detecting a flying saucer.

Especially when his hypersensitive ears were being played like a bass drum by the noise of helicopter rotors.

Dick crouched against the earth, experiencing one of those rare transcendental moments when one sense flows over to become another—in this case, sound into pain. *Go away, please go away,* he thought desperately at the chopper.

And it did—not because Dick had psychokinetic powers, but because helicopters usually went away after passing overhead.

Unless. . . .

The throbbing blades faded downstream—then stopped fading.

The damned thing's hovering, thought Dick. *Either it's found a big patch of Gasconade Gold, or . . .*

A marijuana bust seemed unlikely at this hour. Dick scuttled forward as fast as his armadillo legs could scuttle, despite the throbbing of his battered eardrums.

The Gasconade is one of the crookedest rivers in the world. There is one stretch where canoeists can paddle for an entire day, camp overnight, and take out the next morning only a half-mile from where they started. Fortunately, Dick was not walking alongside that stretch. But by the time the armadillo reached the spot where the helicopter had been hovering, the stars were fading into a misty false dawn. The chopper had left by then; continuous suspension in mid-air over a single point is an unnatural state even for a helicopter. By then, however, Dick could easily follow the noise of the trucks and Humvees ahead.

He stayed inside the belt of trees and underbrush that lined the bank, to avoid having his shell rearranged by the traffic in the adjoining soybean field. He didn't encounter humans on foot until he was almost on top of the activity.

". . . Full compensation for my soybeans!" someone was shouting over the general, painful hubbub.

Dick swiveled his ears, homing in. Had that farmer found someone in actual authority, or was he remonstrating with some bored private on guard?

"I'll see that you have the proper forms to fill out, Mr. Ziegler. We're fully authorized under the Emergency Military Powers Act of—"

"The hell with your authorization! Did the American People authorize you to come in and trample my soybeans and take away my flying saucer?"

"*Your* saucer?"

"Damn right. It's on my property, isn't it?"

"So if an airplane crashed on your property, it'd be yours? Besides, it's in the river, not on your land."

"That's part of the bank!"

"Gravel bars aren't part of the bank."

"But that's an old bar! There's trees growing on it!" The farmer's voice was drowned out for a moment in the roar of a Humvee. By the time the vehicle had pulled away, Dick was almost on top of the two disputants.

"... *need* this saucer." Obviously the farmer was taking a different tack.

"*Need* it?" The officer sounded slightly amused. "You're going to plow fields with it, or herd cows, or something?"

"Look, I've been a hardscrabble farmer all my life," the farmer pleaded. "But the government keeps taking away my ability to make a living! I had to stop selling milk back in the seventies, when they passed this new rule saying a dairy had to have a concrete floor and running water. Running water for a barn! Then we was selling eggs to restaurants for two-fifty a dozen last year, but the local produce dealer wants to buy them for sixty cents, so he turns us in for not having a proper license! A *license* to sell eggs! Then the egg inspector tells us we have to candle every single egg we sell!"

"Cap'n Browman?" another soldier intruded. "We got the Sky Crane. It's coming at oh-seven-hundred."

"Good! Thanks, Sergeant!"

"Shall I call C of E and cancel the 'dozers?"

"No way! *This* time we keep our backup plan in motion!" Browman told him, and turned back to the farmer. "Look, mister, I don't have time to ...."

"You ever try to hold every single egg out of forty dozen up to a light every night, just to see if there's an embryo or a blood spot? And this, when we gather the eggs twice a day, every day! 'Ain't time for no embryos to grow! And our equity got wiped out in the crash of '08, and the bank doesn't want to lend us any more money. Then I heard this saucer was down here, and I thought, we're saved. We got a tourist attraction as good as Meramec Caverns—and now you come in and want to just take the saucer, and ruin my soybeans, too!"

"We'll take care of your soybeans. Just fill out the ...."

"Well, by God, we fought a war once, because the British was puttin' troops in our homes and taking our property. Maybe we'll fight a war again! Maybe I'll just call the folks over at that damn compound, that Church-of-Jesus-Patriot or whatever, and join 'em. Maybe we'll just have another Revolution!"

Bowman's voice suddenly went steely. "Sergeant Holly! Arrest this man!" he barked.

"Yes, sir!" said another soldier, grimly.

"Arrest? What the hell are you talking about?"

"You've just threatened sedition against the United States Government, Mister, and referred to a known terrorist group. Sergeant, put this man in a truck and assign a guard."

"Yes, sir."

"But—goddammit!"

By then, Dick had moved on. He knew where the saucer was. He couldn't see it yet, but he could *smell* it.

It didn't smell like a human machine at all—no odors of oil or hot metal or friction or exhaust. If anything earthly, it smelled vaguely like eucalyptus.

Maybe it's a giant cough drop, thought Dick. *No wonder no one can find the aliens. They're the Smith Brothers.*

Along the bank ahead, he could hear the voices and clumsy crashing about of dozens of men. Still a little unsure as to how completely invisible he was to the general populace, Dick decided to avoid that route if possible.

Without much soil to cut down through, Ozark rivers tend to have either shallow gravel banks or high stone bluffs. Fortunately for Dick, the bluff at this point was on the far side of the river. Even so, reaching the water wasn't easy. He finally found a game path to the water's edge, stopped to lick some larvae from an old deer turd, then started down.

And promptly slipped.

Losing his balance, he popped into a defensive ball, bounced down the rest of the bank and hit the water with an Armadillo Cannonball.

"What was that?" he heard Captain Browman say, as the armadillo bobbed to the surface. He unrolled, filling his snout with water in the process, and sneezed.

"I'll check it out, sir!"

Armadillos are unlikely-looking swimmers, but they're actually not bad at it. Dick instinctively gulped air into his stomach to add buoyancy to his heavy body, and paddled behind a fallen tree, just in case he wasn't invisible to someone.

"Don't see anything, sir," called a soldier's voice after a short time. "Probably just a beaver or something."

I've got to get there before that big chopper comes, the armadillo thought. He decided to risk it, and struck out, scrambling his clawed feet frantically to gain steerage against the cold spring current. The saucer-smell drifted and eddied across the water's surface, but generally grew stronger until the scent was overpowering (to an armadillo nose). His legs touched gravel. He dragged himself out, and felt the sudden, overwhelming urge to get rid of the air he'd swallowed. Fortunately, the roar of Humvees covered the resulting belch.

Something neither rock nor tree loomed above him— something smooth and regular and vaguely shiny, and drawing a lot of attention from blurry human figures.

The soldiers apparently didn't see him as he skirted past, following the saucer's perimeter. The gravel bar's backbone was crowned by a few sycamore and willow saplings. The saucer had lodged among them, but remained remarkably level. As best Dick could tell, soldiers were rigging some sort of sling under it.

The armadillo wondered what would happen if he walked into a human who couldn't detect him. Would they simply pass through each other?

But they heard the splash when I fell, he thought. *Now's no time to experiment.*

Ahead, something leaned against the saucer's side. It proved to be a set of metal steps—Dick guessed it normally was used to put pilots into fighter planes or something. It definitely was *not* designed to help armadillos enter flying saucers.

To say the next few minutes weren't easy would be like saying pro wrestling isn't quite realistic or childbirth is maybe just a little painful. Dick finally developed a system of locomotion that worked, but only very laboriously, fighting metal, gravity and fear of discovery with each aluminum step. Each step was barely one armadillo wide and just under an armadillo tall. Standing as diagonally as possible on one step, Dick had to rear back, use his tail for a backstop, and hook one paw over the next step, then slowly work his way over until he was perpendicular enough to get his other front paw up. Then he had to spring with his hind legs, curl his shell and drag himself diagonally forward, all at the same time, until just enough of his body was above the step's edge to tip him forward onto it. This all made a horrible amount of noise. Fortunately, a bulldozer was being backed off its trailer just then, making an exponentially *more* horrible amount of noise.

One Step. Two Steps. Three. Four. . . .

He reached the lip of the last step, reared himself up . . .

The bulldozer cut its engine.

"Who goes there?" a voice very nearby shouted.

"What is it, Mick?"

"I heard something!"

"What? Where?"

"Up on the steps!"

"There's no one there."

"Maybe he got inside. Cover me, Murphy."

"Cowley, you know we're not supposed to go in there. You're gonna get in trouble."

"Hell, nobody's been *able* to go in there. But we're in *real* trouble if somebody got past us unauthorized. Cover me!"

Dick froze. Private Cowley's footsteps paused at the base of the ladder. Dick heard his heavy, frightened breathing; heard a little *snick!* that might have been a toenail clipper, but more likely was the safety catch of an assault rifle.

I guess I'm going to find out whether his foot passes right through me or not, thought the armadillo.

The guard hesitantly mounted the first step, then the second.

Maybe he'll stop when he's high enough to look in.

Fourth step. . . .

Brace for impact.

Then, inexplicably, Pvt. Cowley's foot came down on empty air to the right of the step (and Dick).

"Shiiiit!" screamed the soldier. He landed with a thump, a short burst from his M-16, and a moan.

"Man down! Man down! Medic!" screamed Murphy.

Naturally, everyone assumed the man was "down" from a bullet, and hit the dirt themselves.

Dick took advantage of the confusion to lever himself over the rim of the last step and scramble through the portal beyond.

The dim interior was as Sander had described it: circular, with a featureless shelf/panel running around the perimeter. At least, featureless as far as Dick's eyes could make out.

Outside, pandemonium had erupted. "No! He heard something on the steps!" Dick heard Murphy shout. "Up there!"

Dick crouched in fear, at any moment expecting an avalanche of soldiers and M-16s to tumble through the portal. "What am I doing here?" he asked, under his breath.

Faint lights suddenly flickered around the room's perimeter. "Oh." said Dick. "Hmm."

Footsteps rattled up the aluminum steps outside.

As the first soldier's helmet appeared in the portal, the opening disappeared, as silently and thoroughly as if it had never been.

XIII

The Dragonfly King

Sander was power-dreaming, big time.

He was cooking barbecue on a desert cliff top when Sarah Palin and her entourage came up.

"How'd you like some extra sauce?" Sarah said, giving her body a lascivious twist.

"No thanks," he replied. "Who knows where that's been?"

Sarah marched away in a huff.

"Well done," remarked Robert Heinlein from a nearby rock. A brassiere was draped like military epaulettes across his shoulders. "I salute you," he said, and did so.

Sander returned the salute, then turned to watch the spectacle below. The cliff overlooked a huge, humpbacked black hill of solid iron ore, which had become magnetized and thus attracted repeated meteor strikes. Another meteor was expected. Glenn Beck and a host of evangelicals sat on the summit, challenging the meteor to end the world.

Festive crowds had gathered on the cliff to watch. On the ledge below Sander, Mott the Hoople tuned their instruments.

"Let's let Sander sing with us," one of them said. "He's got a good voice."

"Sounds good. What shall we play?"

"What the hell, let's play surf music."

They struck up the chords, and Sander began singing amid
a welter of Beach Boy harmonies, and the words of the song
conjured the scene from desert into beach, like a bad karaoke
video:

When you talk of love,
I see a woman standing in the summer sun
When you talk of love,
I see her watching for the man who won't come home.

Well, the surge rolls in and the surge rolls out
And the breakers keep on breaking and
The searchers, they would all long since have gone
But her eyes keep them out on the waves
And the surf ski riders brave the spray
Trying to find a body for her to take home.

When you talk of love,
I see her walking on that beach on summer days
When you talk of love,
She's trying to conjure up his image from the rainbow
spray.

Well, she's had two kids with another man,
And she doesn't think he'd understand
So she's never told him why they're always here.
She walks along the sand alone
And her kids ride skim boards in the sun
And he sits under an umbrella and has another beer.

And her body's not so perfect now,
It was never perfect anyhow,

But a few of us who see her cry inside,
For the moment that defined her
In the eyes of thirty searchers
Is still frozen in the stare of those green eyes.

Well, the surge rolls in and the surge rolls out. . . .

The song faded out. The beach scene faded into the stip-plings of dew on a truck windshield. Sander stretched stiff legs, but couldn't stretch them very far; shrugged stiff shoulders, but not very much. Dodge Power Ram 50s are good for many purposes, but the cab is not good for sleeping.

The valley of the Gasconade was filled with pre-dawn mist. Sander fumbled with the glove compartment handle, hoping . . . yes, Appy had transferred the glove compartment stuff from his Fit to the truck. He groped through the contents, fished out a pen and a battered notepad, and feverishly wrote down the lyrics that still rolled through his head. They were so weirdly clear that he wondered if he'd heard the song somewhere before. He stared at the words in puzzlement—what was a "skim board," anyway?

But more than that, the image of the woman still haunted him. She was no music video actress: 40-ish, beginning to spread a bit at the middle; moderately short brunette hair, high cheekbones and slightly gaunt face. And those startling green eyes, staring seaward with more than sadness in them: a terrible mixture of pain and longing and abstract concentration. . . .

He glanced in the back. It had been a cold spring night. Jenny was curled in a tight ball in her red sleeping bag, with nothing but her newly-dark-auburn hair showing. No, Jenny wasn't the inspiration for this vision.

He wondered if Dick was back. Then he noticed a low rumbling, somewhere out in the mist. Heavy machinery. . . .

He jerked the door of the truck open and rolled out, nearly losing his footing on the dew-slick grass. They'd parked for the night just off a gravel farm road, in the pull-off to a farmer's field bordering the river. The fog, brewed of April rain and distilled by the sharp cool of a clear night, shocked the senses like good Bourbon: essence of spring. Sander flapped his arms for warmth and circled the truck. "Dick?" he called softly.

No answering call, no scuffle and rattle of armadillo armor moving through the tall grass.

"Dick? Dii-iick . . ."

A new mechanical noise was drifted through the mists. A low throbbing, growing louder.

Helicopter.

He banged on the camper door. "Get up, Jenny! We may have to move fast!"

"Wha . . . ?" came the sleepy response from inside. But a few moments later the tailgate crashed open and Jenny crawled out. "What's happening? Where's Dick?"

"He's not back yet. Jenny, there's a helicopter out there somewhere, a big one. Gotta be military."

"Oh, God. We've gotta get under cover." She started to run to the cab's passenger door, then ran back. "What about Dick?"

The helicopter throbbed by, hidden by the fog but so close that the ground vibrated. The sound—if "sound" could describe such an aural pounding—moved upstream, then seemed to hover.

"Get in the truck and get out of here!" Sander shouted over the mechanical thunder. "I'll hide in the trees by the river until

Dick comes back, then walk out and hitch a ride. I'll meet you at—uh—at that big Catholic church in Vienna!"

"Sander, how are you going to hitchhike with an armadillo?"

Just then, the *thrub-thrub*-ing of the chopper rotors seemed to accelerate toward them. They had no time to do anything but rush into each other's arms, before the thing loomed out of the mist: a Sikorsky Sky Crane, an enormous primeval spraddle-legged dragonfly, a giant flying helicopter skeleton, a bellowing demon-king of the air. And suspended below it was the silvery saucer, fading to invisibility as they watched. The super-chopper and its burden roared directly overhead, knocking them to the ground with a sheer barrage of noise, then disappeared into the mists.

XIV
A Blatant Foreshadowing

Meanwhile, on the slopes of Mauna Kea on the Big Island of Hawai'i, a koa log lay rotting.

Listen. This is important.

Before humans and their allied creatures arrived, Hawai'i held no grazing animals bigger than bugs and no predators larger than a small hawk. The rainforest was full of strange and luxurious plants, from 20-foot-tall primeval tree ferns to juicy giant *akala* raspberries, for whom thorns were about as useful as an appendix. It was all one big, happy family, with nobody killing each other any more than absolutely necessary. Even the insects were so laid back that many had lost their wings.

When Polynesian voyagers first arrived, they wiped out several species of birds. But pretty soon the Polynesians learned to fit in, too, and became Hawaiians, and happily practiced survival of the fattest. Literally. The plumpest woman was the preferred mate. Screw you, Darwin. *Aloha*.

Presiding over this Edenic jungle was the great koa, one of the weirdest and most beautiful trees on earth. Young koa look like thornless locust trees. But as they mature, the little locust-like leaves are replaced by big sickle-shaped "leaves" that are actually elongated, flattened petioles—the little stems that normally connect leaves to twigs. Koa is the caterpillar-butterfly of the tree world. It gives a whole new meaning to the phrase, "turn over a new leaf."

Youthful koa grow tall and straight in big groves that are mostly the same root system with many trunks. If a trunk falls, knocking down the underbrush, the koa roots sense the sunlight warming the soil of the new-made clearing, and saplings sprout from the roots. As the grove matures, though, fewer trunks survive. They grow into enormous, mossy, twisted grandmothers, like giant bonsais, and produce thousands of seeds in long, curling, wonderfully rattly pods. The seeds fall to earth, where they can lie for years, awaiting the trigger of sunlight on bare soil.

One day, Captain Cook arrived in Eden with a shipload of cannons, horny sailors and VD. Soon another captain decided it would be a great idea to drop off some cattle. The cows thought it was pretty great, too. They ate all those juicy, thornless understory plants like ice cream.

The koa roots felt sunlight on the denuded, cow-trampled soil, and obligingly sent up little green koa shoots. The seeds felt the warmth, and popped their little shells. Millions of tender green seedlings and rootlings shot up all at once.

Yum, thought the cows.

Soon nothing was left in most places but old trees, their roots trampled and muddy, their children eaten. The cows started losing weight. So ranchers brought in Kikuyu grass, which had evolved on the African veldt, where it had learned to grow really fast, to make up for all the wildebeests and elephants, elands and zebras, cape buffaloes and kudus that were chewing on it. Kikuyu grass was so virulent that it grew on top of fence posts.

Spreading over the ravaged forest floor, the grass grew so thick that sunlight never touched the soil again. One by one, the grandmother koas grew old and died. Soon Mauna Kea's middle slopes held a vast koa graveyard, where only broken gray trunks poked up through the grass.

Koa can be beautiful even in death. When polished, the rich, golden-brown wood seems to glow with an inner light, a treasure for furniture-makers. But there was plenty of dead wood to salvage, without probing under the turf.

So the log slowly changed into termites, hidden under the grass that had smothered its children. There was little *aloha* left in it. It was not murderous—it was a log, after all—but it was perfectly capable of abetting a murder.

Remember it, lest you stumble.

XV
The Soggy Pinhole to Heaven

Grey Eagle Marsden lowered his digital Nikon with its 180-1000 mm. auto lens and moaned in frustration. The shot of the century wasn't going to come out. The mystery saucer couple, standing directly beneath an actual flying saucer! (Okay, so it was hanging beneath a helicopter. It was a saucer, and it was flying.) Damn fog. The damn saucer had just seemed to disappear. And he couldn't frame all three elements—saucer (or ring of cable net outlining an invisible saucer), couple and chopper—or even any two of them in the same frame, without reducing them to ant-size.

"You got that? You got it?" Worley McDermont was shouting.

"Yeah, sure," said Grey Eagle. "Maybe."

"Never mind," said McDermont. "We've faked that shot so many times nobody would believe it anyway. Get in the Karmann. Let's go flush those birds."

Grey Eagle ran to the car, lifted the hood (A Karmann Ghia, for the uninitiated, is a vintage VW Beetle in Italian sports car drag, with the engine in back and trunk up front) and laid his camera, tripod and all, into its plastic foam bed. Then he crammed his six-foot-three-inch frame into the passenger seat while McDermont slipped behind the wheel.

"Time to get up close and personal!" McDermont cackled.

The Karmann's souped-up Volkswagen engine roared like a giant lawnmower. They peeled out of their blind in a copse of cedar, sped 85 yards down the reddish farm road and slid to a halt in a spray of gravel, directly across the mouth of a farmer's pullout where the blue pickup was parked. Their quarry had just stood up from the wet, helicopter-disheveled grass.

"Got'em!" McDermont cackled. He leapt from the car to keep the "birds" busy while Grey Eagle extracted himself. Cursing, for the umpteenth time, his partner's penchant for antique subcompacts, the photographer dragged his backup camera from behind the seat.

"Mr. Keynes! Ms. Duenckel-Chillingworth!" McDermont was saying. "Nice hair jobs, I must say! Worley McDermont, from the *Star*. Could I ask you about what just happened?"

"What?" said the man by the truck. "Sorry, I can't hear you. That helicopter. My ears . . ."

"I said, I'm Worley McDermont from the *Star*. Could I . . ."

Grey Eagle zoomed in on dazed faces, hair bedraggled and clothes mussed from chopper downwash or diving to the ground or just sleeping in a truck. They looked like disaster victims. The Nikon's shutter reeled off a series of clicks.

The woman realized what he was doing. "Stop that!" she shrieked. "Please, no pictures!"

"Sorry, Ms. Duenckel-Chillingworth, can't do that. Freedom of the press, obligation to our readers," said McDermont smoothly. He saw the man clenching his fists, and added, "And Grey Eagle here's mighty attached to his cameras; he wouldn't take kindly to your tampering with them."

"Get in the truck, Jenny," Keynes said. The woman's hearing had recovered enough to understand him, or else she'd decided on that course of action independently. She ran for the passenger-side door. Grey Eagle paralleled her, took a through-the-window shot from the driver's side, then circled around the front, his camera clicking away. *Damn. Dew on the windshield.* He swiped the little cold jewels off with his shirt sleeve, and went back to work. *Clickclickclickclickclick.* Somewhere in this roll would be the magic combination: no glare, no backlight, a woman's panic-stricken face. Pulitzer stuff, except he worked for the wrong rag for that.

But the woman had dived into the car headfirst, kept her head down as she slammed the door shut, then buried her face in the seat. This seemed a little beyond the don't-shoot-me-my-hair's-mussed type of camera shyness. He shrugged, and ran around the pickup to where McDermont had their male subject cornered. Keynes was trying to step around the reporter and get to the driver's side door. McDermont was expertly blocking his path.

"Be reasonable, Mr. Keynes. After all, you *called* the press that first night. Don't you *want* this story to be told?"

Grey Eagle moved up beside his partner, adding 250 lbs. of $^1/_8$th-Pawnee warrior to the line of scrimmage. He'd been a professional bouncer and avid amateur photographer, before discovering that the reverse combination paid better.

"I didn't know the *Kansas City Star* resorted to stuff like this," Keynes said, maneuvering. "Wait a minute. Which *Star* are you?"

McDermont changed tactics. "Look, you're just a working shmuck like us," he wheedled. "But we could change that. *MorningStar* will pay big bucks for an exclusive."

Keynes tried to circle around them. They countered by swinging like a gate on a hinge, ending up directly in front of the driver's side door. McDermont kept up the assault. "Look, you want some privacy till this blows over? We could arrange that. Maybe a three-star hotel for a week. Just tell your story. We'll take care of you like newborn babes."

Keynes suddenly made a break—for the *back* of the truck. He dove into the camper and slammed the tailgates behind him.

Undaunted, McDermont rushed around to the cab, with Grey Eagle close behind, and banged on the passenger window. "Ma'am? I've got a message for you from your husband. He forgives you, he loves you, he wants you back. We can arrange a meeting. . . ."

The woman shot him a horrified stare, then ducked her head again. Keynes shouted something from inside the camper. Grey Eagle thought he heard the woman say something like "What about Dick?" or maybe "What a dick!" Then she scrambled across to the driver's side, and tugged at the seat belt with one hand while awkwardly trying to shield her face with the other.

"Watchit, Eagle, they're gonna try something!" yelled McDermont.

The Ram 50 roared to life, then shuddered as the 4-wheel-drive engaged. It backed up five feet, then lurched to the right, leaving the pullout and twisting at a crazy angle as the wheels crossed the roadside ditch on the slant. It reached the road, backed again, then spun a hail of gravel.

"Get in the car!" McDermont yelled needlessly. Grey Eagle already had the door open, and was cramming himself in.

"We'll just have to circle back and get Dick, after we've lost them," said Sander, through the sliding window, as the truck turned back onto US 63 at Vienna.

"They're right on our tails," said Jenny, staring at the side mirror. "They're not even trying to be discreet."

"They don't want to be," said Sander. "They're trying to intimidate us."

"How are we going to lose them, Sander?" asked Jenny, her voice cracking. "They're in a damned sports car."

"Well, it looks like a sports car," said Sander. "My mom's best friend had one of those when I was a kid. It's really just an old VW bug in a hot body, unless they've souped it up. We're getting chased by a car that's even older than this truck. But we're not going to play their game. Stay under the speed limit, and be careful. There's one little town along this stretch that has a speed limit sign mounted on a trailer. They roll it to different places along the road to catch tourists. The last thing we need is a cop on our tail, too."

"I know. But what are we going to *do?* Did you hear what they said about Harlan? He's using those paparazzi for a personal search party—and I can't even report it to the court if we don't want to wind up in Fort Leonard Wood."

"Relax, honey," Sander said, the pet-word slipping out unconsciously. "How's our gas?"

She glanced at the gauge. "About half a tank."

"Okay. When we get to Rolla, head into the nearest filling station anyway. Pull in and stop like you're going to get gas, then shift to the passenger seat. I'm going to sprint around and get in, so I can drive. I'll risk one more encounter with those scuzzballs. They've already got pictures of us anyway."

They rolled through Vichy, came down off the ridge into the long straightaway just before Rolla.

"They're still tailgating us," said Jenny. "God, now Harlan's going to know what we look like and what we're driving again."

"Not to mention the FBI and God knows who else," Sander added.

"What color am I going to have to change my hair to, now?" Jenny moaned. (She had a true aesthetic problem there. With help from Appy and Miss Clairol, her hair was now a deep reddish-auburn. But most hair tints, added to her freckled complexion, would have looked instantly fake.)

"One thing at a time," said Sander. "First, we've got to lose these jerks. There's a filling station right up ahead, just the other side of the I-44 overpass."

"Sander, I've got an idea," said Jenny. "Stay put the first time I stop. I'm gonna fake 'em out."

She pulled up to the pumps, waited for the Karmann Ghia's occupants to get out and start toward them, then gunned the engine and sped around behind the station. But the paparazzi recovered quickly. They pulled around the building and honked as Sander clambered into the cab.

"So what now?" asked Jenny.

"Like you said, they're driving a sports car. *We* have a pickup. Let's go where the deer and the pickup trucks play."

They wove through downtown Rolla and got on US 63 southbound, with the Karmann Ghia still in blatant pursuit. Soon a brown wooden sign proclaimed, "Entering Mark Twain National Forest." Sander drove on till he saw a logging road, then braked suddenly and pulled down it. The little red sports car followed, eating a cloud of dust, and skidded up behind them when Sander stopped to engage the four-wheel drive. He backed up to lock the drive in, causing their pursuers to spin their wheels in a hasty retreat. Then onward. . . .

The gravel road soon degenerated into a maze of water-filled potholes. Sander took them at just under ramming speed. The paparazzi followed, dodging holes as best as they could. Shoals of solid rock loomed up through the dirt, then disappeared with a jolt beneath their wheels. They slalomed through a huge puddle. Jenny whooped.

"This is like shooting a rapids on land!" she shouted.

An intersection with another logging road loomed. Sander jammed on the brakes. Gravel roared behind them as their pursuers also braked frantically. Sander cranked the wheel left, clearing the crossroads moments before the Karmann would have rear-ended them. It re-oriented itself and followed.

They were headed south now, with their pursuers following at a slightly safer distance. Another big puddle loomed, then another. The truck threw walls of spray to either side. The Karmann slowed to drive around the puddle rims, two wheels in the water and two out. The Dodge was gaining ground. They braked a little to round a sharp curve, then began a steep descent into a forested little valley. The road narrowed, hairpinned again and continued downward. With less room to dodge potholes, the Karmann fell still further behind.

Then Sander slammed on the brakes again. Just ahead, the road curved into a stream boiling with spring runoff. A low standing wave of water humped itself over the concrete ford.

"Can we make it across that?" asked Jenny.

"I think so," Sander said. He suppressed his doubts, jammed the four-wheel-drive into low, backed, then started forward. The truck gained speed and hit the water. A roar of spray erupted, splashing across the windshield in a solid, blinding sheet.

"Watch out!" cried Jenny, unnecessarily. Sander managed to slow a little, reducing the bow wave to manageable proportions, and hit the windshield wiper switch. He forged onward, carefully keeping the truck in the middle of the hump of water that marked the ford. The water rose higher and higher . . .

. . . then began to recede. "We're gonna make it!" cried Jenny, gleefully.

The pickup roared out onto the far bank. Both Sander and Jenny were laughing and whooping. "Let's see that little sports car wannabe try *that!*" shouted Sander. Then he glanced in the rearview mirror. "Ohmygod . . ."

"What?" said Jenny.

"Those idiots *are* trying it!"

The original Volkswagen Beetle was renowned, among other things, for its ability to float. In Australia there was even an annual race pitting Beetles fitted with exhaust snorkels in a "drive" across a small bay. [1] The Karmann Ghia shared its famous cousin's aquatic abilities just enough, in this case, to lead to disaster. The little car hit the water with a tremendous splash—then floated right off the concrete slab of the ford.

Sander saw this in the rearview mirror. He braked in horror, then threw the transmission into neutral.

"Sander, what are you doing? Let's get out of here!" exclaimed Jenny.

"They're in trouble, Jenny!"

"Good! They deserve to be! Let's go, while they're distracted!"

Sander shoved the stick into first, started to take his foot off the clutch, hesitated, and then killed the engine.

"Sander! Please!"

"You want us to leave the scene of another accident?"

"But it isn't *our* accident!" Jenny pleaded desperately.

"Jenny, so far in this mess, I haven't actually done anything wrong," her companion said. "Those guys are pond scum, but I don't want their deaths on my conscience." He set the hand brake, got out and ran to the back of the truck.

---

[1] (The Aussies also reputedly invented the "Australian bug haul," in which teams of twelve husky college students carried Beetles 100 meters, then crammed themselves inside to drive back to the starting line. Which events, along with dwarf-tossing and Australian Rules Football, have only contributed to the world's impression that Australians just don't have enough to do.)

The canoeing gear from Sander's deceased Fit was in the back of the pickup. Sander found his life vest at the head of Jenny's sleeping bag, where she'd used it for a pillow. Some frantic rummaging produced the rope that had tied down the canoe.

McDermont's beloved, custom-restored Karmann Ghia floated downstream, fetched up broadside against a submerged tree, groaned, twisted and flipped. Water poured in through the open windows. The snag broke. The car whirled around a whirlpool, then settled into deep water in a bend of the creek.

McDermont got out the moment the water pressure equalized, but Grey Eagle's door had jammed when the car hit the tree. He twisted and pounded futilely on it as the car tipped on its left side and struck bottom, shoving the driver's door shut again. Grey Eagle frantically tried to squeeze his big frame through the passenger side window, which was about the size of a 1950 TV screen. He'd gotten halfway out when the camera dangling from his neck caught on something. He was still corseted in German steel when his diaphragm muscles rebelled, sucking water in to quench the fire in his burning lungs.

He twisted for one last look at the sun shining dimly through the muddy water above, as his vision slowly contracted to a single pinhole. Then he was moving, sliding effortlessly along a long tunnel toward the point of light.

I'm having a near-death experience, he thought, *just like the ones the ones McDermont writes about. . . .*

Suddenly he was free, floating in a world of light: a stream much like the one he'd just left, only clear as aquarium glass and awash with sun-sparkles. A heavyset, balding man stood, fly rod in hand, in the glittering shallows. He looked up and smiled with his broad mouth, homely and reassuring.

"Are you God?" Grey Eagle asked wonderingly.

The man chuckled. "Hardly. But not the other guy, either." He reeled in his fly and flicked it outward again, a perfect cast. Then he remarked, "The Chinese have an ancient story about a man who dreamed he was a butterfly, then awoke and wondered if he was a butterfly dreaming he was a man. But he asked the wrong question, I think. He should have asked, 'Is a dream manning the butterfly?'" The fisherman reeled in his fly again. "Well, time to go. Look for a new job. The one you have pays well, but it's bad for your soul."

Grey Eagle felt himself being sucked back into the hole, as if a giant whirlpool had caught his feet. *Heaven is going down the drain*, he thought, and laughed hysterically, filling his lungs with water. He coughed, choked, coughed again. . . .

Then the universe bloomed like a Big Bang into a partly cloudy sky and pine trees and a creek bank. McDermont and Keynes were both peering anxiously down at him.

"Hey, buddy, you okay?" said McDermont.

"I'm . . ." Grey Eagle rolled over and retched another spray of water from his lungs. Some went up his sinuses, which was not as bad as where it had just been. Someone pounded on his back.

Finally he managed to cough his vocal chords clear of water. "I'm all right, I think. What happened?"

"You got stuck," said Keynes. "I had to cut your camera straps to pull you free."

"My cameras . . ."

". . . Are still at the bottom of the creek," said his rescuer. "I lost my pocketknife, too. My folks gave me that knife. . . ."

"My cameras . . ."

"Cameras, hell. That's my car out there!" McDermont erupted, then subsided. "Never mind. I'll find another one. I

127

don't suppose we could salvage pics off a drowned memory chip?"

"No, you won't," said Keynes, grimly.

"Look, we're very grateful," said McDermont, "but we've gotta earn a living. You understand."

"Look yourself, scuzzbag," said Keynes. "That woman in the truck wasn't abducted by a UFO. She's fleeing her ex-husband, who beat her up and threatened to kill her. When you delivered that message from him, you violated a restraining order."

"Really? Hey, this just gets juicier."

"If you print photos, he'll know what she looks like again, and what we're driving. You're threatening her life."

"Aw, that's being just a little melodramatic, isn't it?"

"We're not publishing the photos, even if we can salvage them, which I doubt," coughed Grey Eagle.

"The hell you say!" reacted McDermont. "Those photos are exclusive property of the paper!"

"You forget I'm an independent contractor," said Grey Eagle. "The paper didn't want to pay me health benefits. All you've got is first rights. No first publication, no damn rights."

"You are in such trouble," breathed McDermont.

"So are you. Harassment, terroristic threatening, violation of a restraining order . . ." said Sander Keynes.

"Your word against ours."

"Their word against yours," interjected Grey Eagle.

". . . And a long, long way to walk," added Keynes.

McDermont paused, considering. "Okay," he conceded. "We protect her identity. We can make something up. But let me give you my card, in case you change your mind."

Keynes sighed, then nodded. "Let's get your friend to the truck. I seem to be making a career of rescuing accident victims."

XVI

Meanwhile, Back at the Brass

Walter Baker, Chair of the Special Task Force on the Big Piney Incident, thrummed his fingers on the table with one hand and combed a lock of thinning, grizzled hair off his forehead with the other. Neither motion was particularly worth noting, except that both happened so often. Michael Dupres and Jerry Karpov had a running wager on which mannerism Baker would perform more often at any given meeting. For this one, Karpov had finger-thrumming and Dupres had hair-combing. At the moment, Karpov was ahead.

"So what's the Facility got for us?" asked Baker. "Bill?"

Brigadier General Tyler Williams III, a.k.a. "Buffalo Bill" Williams, thrummed his own fingers. "Highly advanced stealth technology. Highly advanced," he said. "We're working on the tech side of it."

"In other words, you don't know how it works yet?" said Baker.

"We're working on it," repeated Buffalo Bill.

"Well, what *can* you tell us?" Baker pressed. He hadn't risen through bureaucratic ranks to his current NSC[1] position by taking "We're working on it" for an answer.

"Results are inconclusive as yet," said Buffalo Bill, "but we're working on it."

"Bill, would you please be a little more specific?" said Baker, fingers thrumming. "Just exactly *how* are you working on it? What tests are you running?"

"Inferospectroscopy. Passive infrared, electromagnetic and radioactive emissions monitoring. Radar footprint. Sonar scanning. Wind tunnel tests. We haven't tried X-ray or CT, for fear of interfering with its electronics."

"And what are these tests telling you?"

"Data's incomplete as yet. I'd rather not draw conclusions."

"Bill, are you learning anything at all?"

Buffalo Bill smiled tensely. "I must say with all due respect, Walter, that I have to resent the tone of that remark a little. We're treating this thing just like we'd have treated a captured MIG of a type we'd never seen before. Only this MIG is so radical we don't even know what it's supposed to do. Whether it's armed. Whether it's booby-trapped."

"Well, it hasn't exploded yet."

"It did something to those canoeists, and to three of our soldiers."

"We'll get to that. Right now, I want to know what *your* team's found. What'd you learn from wind tunnel tests?"

"Uh, I haven't got the exact figures in front of me, Walter."

---

[1] National Security Council. The President's personal intelligence organization. Traditional training ground for future Secretaries of State with ambiguous morals and inflated egos. Graduates include Henry Kissinger, Al Haig and Condaleeza Rice.

"Bill, this is a *joint* Special Task Force. We've been ordered to share all data—*ordered*—by the President."

For a long moment, silence reigned, except for a furious finger-thrumming match between the general and Baker.

When you have a team of rivals, thrumming matches happen, thought Dupres philosophically, as Karpov's bet turned into a sure thing.

"You know the problem I have," Williams said finally, in a voice as taut as a condom on the nose of an ICBM. "Some people in this room don't have clearance to read the specs on our *own* stealth planes." He shot a glare at Dupres.

"And the General doesn't have the psycholinguistic expertise to interpret a first contact from outer space," said Dupres, the SETI[2] representative, with a slight smile.

"Our psy-war people are working on that," said Buffalo Bill.

"What if the aliens came in peace?" Dupres asked.

"Then where are they?" Buffalo Bill snapped. "If I came in peace, I'd study the language, let everyone know I was coming, then plunk down someplace very public and wave my diplomatic credentials. I wouldn't set down on a sandbar just outside a major military base, then disappear."

"Bill, what happened in the wind tunnel?" demanded Baker.

Williams glared at the lot of them. Then his shoulders slumped ever so slightly. "We don't know," he said.

"What do you mean, you don't know?" Baker whipped back a lock of hair. "What were the test results?"

"We know the results, but we don't know what they mean."

---

[2] Search for Extra-Terrestrial Intelligence. Former government project, now privately funded, that scans for signals from alien civilizations.

"Then tell us the damn results! Maybe we can help you figure them out."

The general scowled, then surrendered. "Here's all we know. If the wind rises over 5 mph or the thing rocks off horizontal by two degrees or more, its stealth systems go on. I.e., when we turn on the fans, it *disappears*."

"But the *air* doesn't disappear," pointed out Lacey Hatfield, the CIA rep, who had spent 20 years flying Blackbirds and U-2s on covert reconnaissance. "What turbulence did you measure?"

Buffalo Bill shook his head. "It's got an extremely low drag coefficient."

"How low?" asked Baker. "In layman's terms, if you can. Not just a number. "

"All right," said the general. "In layman's terms. This thing creates about as much air disturbance as a paper wasp."

Hatfield whistled. "They've done for air drag what the B-2 did for radar profile. But how the hell does the thing stay in the air? Certainly not by creating lift."

"That shouldn't be much of a problem," said the general, "given that they seem to have done for gravity what they did for air drag. A single man could lift this thing, if he could find a way to grab onto it."

"Of course, we don't know that it *does* stay in the air," observed Karpov, who held posts with NASA [3] and a think tank

---

[3] Officially, National Aeronautics and Space Administration. Unofficially, National Aerospace Subsidy Administration; Not Always Savvy Administration; Nearly Always Silly Administration; Navy-Air Force-Scientist Alliance; Never Actually Solves Anything; National Association for Spending Advancement; Nuts And Screws Aloft, etc. Not to be confused with the Northern Alien Spaceship Advocacy.

at MIT[4] and had PhDs in psychology, biochemistry, linguistics and theoretical physics. His specialty, if such a word applied to him, was the nature of consciousness. But since exobiology was, so far, a science with no data, a general theoretician like Karpov had been a natural choice to head the project's civilian research team.

"Just because it *looks* like a UFO, we've assumed that's what it is," he noted. "But we haven't seen it fly. We don't even know if UFOs really exist, or if they're a folk myth."

Baker thrummed his fingers. "Bill, tell them. They may not have your clearance rating, but the FBI's vetted everybody here, and they're all sworn to confidentiality."

Buffalo Bill shifted uncomfortably, then drew himself up. "Walter, I do this under protest," he said stiffly. "There are 371 reported incidents for which Occam's Razor cuts to a genuine extraterrestrial technology. No, not Roswell—Roswell *was* a folk myth, a real classic example, where stories about a balloon accident and a test drop of crash dummies merged in the collective consciousness as one event. See, Doc, I *do* know something about sociodynamics," he smiled condescendingly at Dupres. "The incidents I'm referring to were culled from military records, not some FBI investigation of crackpots. Sworn affidavits of military personnel, backed up by electronic detection systems data—AWACS[5] and NORAD[6] fixes, satellite

---

[4] Massachusetts Institute of Technology, though they haven't institutionalized technicians there in years. Actually a pretty cool place. Noam Chomsky used to hang there, and there's a room where some of the planet's best minds design tiny robots that behave like insects. So far, the mosquitobot has not escaped.

[5] Airborne Warning And Control System. Those big Air Force jets with the mushrooms growing out of their backs.

[6] North American Aerospace Defense Command—though just how, exactly, they got NORAD out of that, the author is unsure.

photos, attempted fighter interceptions, naval and airbase radar logs. We have two sightings from NASA manned spacecraft—and three from Blackbird pilots, Lacey."

Hatfield nodded. "I'd heard stories."

"You weren't supposed to," said the general.

"Not from the pilots," said Hatfield. "From administrative personnel."

"Shit," breathed Buffalo Bill. "I want to talk to you about that later, Lacey."

"Get my bosses' permission first," said Hatfield.

"Wait a minute," said Dupres. I've read all the military reports you guys would declassify—BLUEBOOK, GRUDGE, SIGN, all the way back to SAUCER.[7] They always pooh-poohed the existence of anything extraordinary."

"Hey, we were *ordered* to," snapped Buffalo Bill. "You remember that Brookings Institute study—the one that said civilization as we know it would collapse if confronted with a genuine alien culture? Besides, we weren't sure it wasn't the Russians, launching some sort of secret weapon to foul up NORAD. So we kept all the good stuff out of the official studies."

"At any rate, UFOs aren't just folk tales," said Baker.

"But that doesn't mean *this* is a UFO—or if it is—that it landed where we found it," said Karpov. "If I were to set a spaceship down near a military base, the last thing I'd do would be to leave it on an exposed sand bar and turn its cloaking devices off. Though of course, a real UFO pilot might think some other way entirely."

---

[7] Code names for actual Air Force task forces, projects and studies re UFO sightings, starting with SAUCER in 1948. SAUCER, quickly renamed SIGN, was followed by GRUDGE, then BLUEBOOK, which Jack Webb made into a Dragnet-like TV series (*Just the facts, Mr. Gorshwakslx*).

"Hmm. Maybe this thing's a decoy," said the general. "Maybe it's there to distract our attention from somewhere else."

"More likely, they didn't put it down there at all," said Dupres. "The site had no evidence of blast scarring or abnormal radiation—nothing to indicate a landing. The river probably brought it there. And given how well it's resisted the military's best efforts with hardly a scratch"—He gave Buffalo Bill an infuriating wink—"there's no reason to think this thing hasn't been on earth for years, even centuries. That would certainly explain why we can't find the occupants."

"If there *were* any occupants," said Karpov.

"You think this thing was a drone?" asked Baker.

"That's one possibility," said Karpov. "This thing's smaller than the space shuttle was. Unless they've found a way to go faster than light, I wouldn't consider the Object big enough to provide viable living space for an interstellar voyage."

"Then why does it have a cabin at all?" asked Hatfield.

Karpov shrugged. "Maybe it *is* a shuttle, and there's a mother ship out there somewhere, a la *Independence Day*. Maybe they *have* broken the speed of light. Or maybe the 'cabin' isn't really a cabin."

"You know, Doc, you're scaring the hell out of me," said Williams. "A vehicle that's invisible to radar—hell, to just about any detection technology—and virtually frictionless—hell, bullets would probably just slide off. And either there's a big mother ship with more of them, or they can hop between stars in no time at all, so a whole invasion fleet could be anywhere in a second or two? I'm wondering if maybe we ought to go up to DEFCON 4." [8]

Baker thrummed his fingers. "That's the President's decision, Bill. I'll take your recommendation to him, if you want. It sounds to me, though, like there's not much we could do if they did decide to attack tomorrow."

"And it's not just aliens I'm worried about," said Williams "If word gets out on what this thing can do, there's not a country nor a defense contractor on earth that can afford not to try to get this technology. Just think what would happen if Iran or North Korea acquired one of these things."

"I'll try to scare up more money for more security measures," said Baker. "But it's equally important to keep our best minds fully informed, so we can crack this thing ASAP. What if China digs up another saucer tomorrow? What if they already have?"

"Meanwhile, back to the data we have," suggested Hatfield. "If that space inside the Object is not a cabin, what is it?"

"Who knows? A cargo bay, a classroom," said Karpov. "Maybe even an illusion."

"I'm beginning to wonder about that," said the general. "If we get closer than six centimeters to that hatchway, it *disappears*. We can't even find evidence that there *was* an opening—no seams, nothing. I thought maybe it was a holographic projection or something. But we fired a laser into it and recorded the

---

[8] The highest level of military alertness. Picture Chill Wills and his crew approaching the Point of No Return, worried silo commanders fingering the keys to the safes where they keep their launch codes, and millions of schoolchildren about to be told, at any minute, to hide under their desks, where a nuclear blast will take exactly .000000154 more seconds to reach them.

bounce-back, just as if the beams had crossed an open space inside the hull."

"Let me get this straight," said Dupres. "You're scared to use X-rays on the thing, but you fired a laser at it?"

"It was a very low-energy laser," said the general.

Baker's fingers thrummed again, once, then stopped. "Can we use the laser to map the interior?"

"We're working on that," said Buffalo Bill. "But it'll probably just confirm what we've detected optically. There seems to be a raised band around the equator of interior wall, but no other discernable features."

"Well, it sounds like we won't know what it's for until we can find a way to get in," said Baker, "if then."

"Maybe that's its purpose," speculated Dupres. "Maybe it's a puzzle. You find your way in, you win the prize."

"Or if you find your way in, it proves you're dangerous enough that they have to wipe you out," said Buffalo Bill.

"Could that be what happened to those canoeists?" asked Baker, brushing back a lock of hair. "Harry?"

Harrison Grubb, M.D., of the CDC&P,[9] had been waiting silently, as usual ("He's rehearsing his next speech to himself so he can enjoy his own imaginary words," Dupres had once whispered to Karpov). He looked like a 50-year-old Antonio Banderas, but was actually 60; he had preserved his face from wrinkling by never changing his faintly benign expression.

---

[9] Centers for Disease Control and Prevention. If you're having trouble keeping this cast of characters and agencies straight, think of it this way. Grubb is the doctor in the movie *Outbreak*. Baker is Harrison Ford's character in *A Clear and Present Danger*. Dupres is Jody Foster in *Contact*. Williams is Gen. Jack Ripper in *Dr. Strangelove*. And Karpov is Dr. Strangelove himself, only sans wheelchair, less evil, more sane and more appreciative of irony.

"We've accounted for everyone on the river that day, except Keynes and Duenckel-Chillingworth," he said. "None of the subjects reported getting inside the cabin. Six who looked in the portal have reported hallucinatory experiences. We're holding them for observation at the Chemical Weapons School in Ft. Leonard Wood. We had to send the rest home. I'd have kept them all in quarantine, but we had no solid epidemiological evidence. Their families were threatening lawsuits."

"I'd have *found* some evidence," growled Buffalo Bill.

"Just like you found in the wind tunnel?" Dupres couldn't resist remarking.

"Nobody was less anxious to send those people home than I was," said Grubb. "I hope we haven't just missed the chance to nip an epidemic in the bud. But to declare a medical emergency, we have to demonstrate a clear public danger. We've run every possible test on the canoeists. No bacterial agents, no viruses we could detect—but that doesn't mean there aren't any. No consistent physiological symptoms. No evidence of contagion."

"So you have no idea what's causing the psychological symptoms?" said Baker.

Grubb shook his head. "Some victims reported seeing flashing lights within the portal. Flashing lights have been known to trigger epileptic fits and posthypnotic suggestions."

"Hmm. Could this be a phenomenon related to that Japanese killer cartoon?" asked Baker.

"That what—oh, I know—that *Pokemon* episode that gave all those kids headaches and seizures?" said Dupres.

Grubb nodded noncommittally. "The timing of the light flashes in that cartoon *may* have induced adverse neural activity patterns in the viewers. Those children had no hallucinations, but maybe—*maybe*—something similar happened with our Big

Piney victims. Our best guess is that if the Object was involved, it may have been as a trigger, rather than a source of disease."

"Is there any sort of discernible pattern for these hallucination victims?" asked Baker.

Grubb shook his head again. "Some have symptoms resembling paranoid schizophrenic delusions. One subject reported that an invisible dragon followed him around until it accidentally incinerated itself. Another says she sees ghosts that rush around, brushing dandruff off some people's shoulders and sprinkling it on others. But the other pathologies for schizophrenia aren't there—neither behavioral nor physiological. They're not acting schizophrenic—just behaving like normal people confronted by abnormal experiences."

"Chemically induced, maybe?" asked Buffalo Bill. "This sounds a lot like an LSD derivative to me. Or maybe TH3CA[10]—never mind."

"We're aware of the Army's studies of combat applications for hallucinogens," said Grubb, dryly. "We've consulted with the CBS [11] experts at Leonard Wood; the pathologies don't match up with any known chemical agent. We've found no traces of such agents in the victims, the Object or its immediate environment. Blood chemistry in some subjects was off a bit, but in ways attributable to stress and excitement. We're very fortunate to have had USACMLS's [12] *full cooperation* on these tests." When he said *"full cooperation,"* everyone heard the italics.

---

[10] Never mind.

[11] Chemical/Biological/Smoke, not Columbia Broadcasting System. One might argue that smoke consists of chemicals. But hey, if you want to explain about redundancy to guys with gas grenades, go right ahead.

[12] US Army Chemical School. A Strictly Defensive Organization.

"I should interject that the studies Harry referred to were purely defensive in nature," said Buffalo Bill, nervously. "The Chemical Corps' entire efforts are directed at protecting our own boys."

Baker nodded. "Yeah, yeah. What about the Facility, Bill? Any new cases among personnel?"

The general shook his head. "None confirmed. We've taken precautions. Nobody looks directly into the portal; we use mechanical monitors and robotic guidance. No injuries since the Gasconade site, when that private slipped and fell while challenging an imaginary intruder." He thrummed his fingers. "I don't know if I should even mention this. The only thing out of the ordinary since the saucer arrived . . ."

"What?" said Baker.

Buffalo Bill shifted embarrassedly. "Uh, people are reporting a poltergeist."

XVII
Pandora's E-Mail Box

The essence of the Gasconade River is slow beauty: a stately, ancient current cut deep into bend after hairpin bend: sparkling shallows, sunbaked bluffs, deep shade, deep pools. Go to the St. Francis River for white water; the Gasconade is for deep gray-blues and lush greens. Go to the Current River for trout. The Gasconade holds sturdier, more powerful quarry.

Standing in the shallows above one of those deep pools, a heavy-set man with a wide, contented smile was stalking that quarry. He flicked the rod back and forth, reeling out a spider-thread of line that gleamed in midair, catching the sunlight of the spring morning. The glittering spoon lure at the end finally sailed into the deep pool, almost against the bank. He trolled it slowly back, making the spoon jerk and flicker like a silvery minnow in distress.

A second man, older in appearance, slighter of build and much more antiquated of dress, was making his way downstream along the bank as the spoon made its glittering journey upstream. The spoon emerged from the water, flinging sparkling droplets, just as the older man got into comfortable talking distance.

"Any luck?" the older man asked.

The fisherman shook his head, grinning ruefully. "There's a big bass hanging out in the shade of that snag over there," he said. "But he appears to be smarter than I am."

The older man grinned in return. "Oh, well. So did Dan Rather. And guess where *he's* going."

"Why, Brother Kit," chuckled the fisherman. "That wasn't very charitable."

"Hey, I don't have to be a saint full-time anymore," said his companion. "The Vatican's decided I'm just a legend. And I've got good help, these days."

The fisherman shrugged, as the spoon did its wounded-minnow-dance upstream again. "I figured there'd be some room for changes like that," he said. "The problem with most people's idea of Heaven is that it *doesn't* change. I think Huck Finn had it right, when he allowed that if all he was going to do was sit around and strum harps and sing all day, he was going to aim for the other place."

The older man nodded. "True. I have it on good authority that in fact, anything that lasts an eternity changes into hell. In the farthest depths of hell, below the chambers of fire and ice and feces, there are rooms where people are condemned to do the things they loved most in life, until they are bored sick of them and hate them with a bitterness beyond belief. The most common chambers hold husbands and wives, pent up forever with nothing but each other. They're followed closely by the chocolate and ice cream caves. And then there's one big chamber where they keep all the lovers of Mexican food. Now, that's *real* hell."

The fisherman chuckled. "Be very careful what you love," he observed. "Consider whether or not it contains beans."

Kit found a comfortable stump along the bank and sat down to light his pipe. "That's why hardly anyone really enjoys church services, you know," he said. "No matter how beautiful the choir is or how lovely the stained glass. Church services are just too damned long. . . . So where is he?"

"Just around the bend," said the fisherman. "He spent the night over in those cottonwoods." The spoon lure emerged from the water again, and sailed once more in a beautiful, glittering ark toward the pool and its indifferent denizen. "Ah, the beautiful, curling, slow-moving Gasconade," the fisherman intoned, "that stately queen of minor rivers, sovereign of morning mists and leaping fish, her snags bejeweled with thousands of scarlet-flecked emerald turtles, her sandbars spangled with pearly fresh water mussel shells, with yellow agates and chalcedonies pocked with quartz crystals, the overhanging trees of her verdant banks flecked with the patient blues of kingfishers and the flashing scarlet of cardinals and red-winged blackbirds, her shallows ornamented with great blue and lesser herons, her deep pools paddled by teals and ducks and haunted by great green catfish, her . . . bored with this, yet?"

"Yes," chuckled Kit.

"Multiply it by three days and nights, add mosquitoes, and you begin to picture *his* state of mind," said the fisherman, as the silver spoon emerged glittering from the water again. "I imagine he'll call it quits today. There's cold beer in the Winnebago. Want one?"

Three days of trespassing, haunting the river's banks, hiding from the occasional farm truck that plied the road; three days of brooding about the 30,000-gallon aquarium and its bright fish that he'd probably never get to feed again. And on the morning of the fourth day, still no Dick.

Sander Keynes arose shivering from his dew-soaked campsite among the cottonwoods, packed his camping gear, and hiked out to watch for the Ram 50. Soon it appeared, though it was a little hard to recognize at first. It had been repainted a rather uneven gray by means of spray cans from three different hardware stores, then tinted reddish brown with Ozark road dust, then striped with runoff from the heavy morning dew. But the driver's side window rolled down to reveal a familiar face.

"Hi, Jenny," Sander said.

"Hi. No Dick?" she asked.

"No Dick," he said. "I'm beginning to wonder, again, if there ever was a Dick."

"There was a Dick," she said firmly. "Look, you can't give up hope, because if you do, he really is lost, because no one else can see him. You have to believe in Dick."

"Yeah, I know," he said. "But we've gotta face it. If Dick were coming back, he'd have made it by now. Maybe a coyote got him, or he fell into the river and drowned, or maybe he just got lost. Or the military got him. Or he was inside the saucer when they took off, which also means the military got him."

"Maybe he just forgot the rest of himself, and became a regular armadillo. But if he hasn't, I'm sure he's survived. He's pretty smart, for an armadillo."

"That's a freaking understatement. Anyway, I don't think we're gonna find him here. I'm coming with you." He threw his pack into the back of the truck, then got in beside her.

They drove in silence for a few minutes, if silence was what you could call the roar of truck tires crunching red gravel on an Ozark country road. Maybe Sander and Jenny were brooding. Or maybe the tire noise and road dust discouraged the opening of mouths—which may have provided conditions conducive to brooding. Neither of them noticed a tan Ford sedan parked under the trees as they passed it by. (Fortunately, the sedan's driver and passenger were down on the river, covertly surveilling a Belgian industrial spy as he poked around the saucer retrieval site.) At any rate, neither spoke until they had reached the blacktop, which in the Ozarks is also often more red than black. Then the truck tires were screaming on the rough macadam surface, but at least the dust was behind them, except for that residual burnt-limestone smell that hangs in the cabs of all country vehicles in the Ozarks.

"What are you going to do now?" Jenny asked.

"I don't know," said Sander. "I guess I lived without Dick before."

"But you didn't have half the government and all the tabloids looking for you. By the way, our friends from the *MorningStar* have struck again. It's under your seat. I didn't want it staring at me while I drove."

"Oh, God, what now?" Sander fished under the seat and extracted two McDonalds coffee cups, a Double Cheeseburger wrapper, an empty Mountain Dew can ("Jeez, remarked Jenny, "How can you actually drink that stuff?") and the offending tabloid. "It's been keeping appropriate company, "Sander remarked. He shook it gingerly and looked at the front page.

"MURDEROUS HUSBAND STALKS SAUCER WOMAN," screamed the headline. Below it was a picture, taken through a windshield, of a woman hiding her face.

"Damn them. They just keep coming on," Sander said angrily.

"Sander, look at that picture again," Jenny said.

He glanced irritably at it again, then stared. "You're a blonde."

Jenny nodded. "I've got hair just like that honeymoon picture Harlan took. And it's not even me. That windshield line looks more like a sedan's. That photographer kept his word, and still got the front cover. And the story's barely about me at all. It's about Harlan—his criminal record, his alcoholism, the TRO, even his dishonorable discharge. They're giving Harlan a taste of his own medicine!"

"Good."

"Maybe, maybe not." said Jenny, considering. "Harlan'll be furious. He may go after that reporter—what's his name?"

"I can't think of it right now. I've got his card, though."

"Or he may try to take it out on me. Or Mom." She suddenly looked stricken. The Ram 50 accelerated, driven by the unconscious pressure of her tensed foot. "Sander, Harlan knows where Mom lives. We've got to warn her!"

"How?" Sander asked. "Jenny, please calm down and slow down. We can't go barging back there. We know she's being watched. And we can bet her phone's been bugged by now."

"Yeah, but will any of those guys come to her aid if Harlan shows up? " she asked bitterly.

"And besides, Jenny. . ."

"What? What?"

"If Harlan really does go there, and you show up, you'll be playing right into his hands. And I—well, I just couldn't stand to let that happen to you."

"Sander, don't," said Jenny, after a moment. "Please don't ever think you have to protect me. Most of the things Harlan did to me, he said he did because he had to protect me."

That led to a long moment of silence, while Sander tried to digest Jenny's statement, but found no way for it to go down that didn't hurt worse than a dozen burritos. What sort of a relationship could they have where he didn't want to protect this woman?

It might have been comforting to know that Jenny was pondering the same scary territory.

Unable to make any headway, Sander turned back to the original problem and thought furiously.

"Your mom's computer . . . ," he said. "Is she online a lot?"

Jenny nodded. "That's how she pays a lot of her bills. She has her own website—astrological forecasts, advice to the lovelorn, cyber-matchmaking. She practically sleeps with it." Jenny's giggle had a slightly hysterical edge. "She says it's more intimate than a man, and it doesn't leave hairs all over the bathroom."

Sander decided to let that one slide. "Okay, I've got a plan. Let's head into Jeff City. . . ."

Since they were traveling without cell phones to avoid being tracked, they had to find a computer at the Missouri River Regional Library. There was an anxious moment when Sander handed the librarian his fake ID, kept in a frequent flyer ID holder so the plastic window would obscure the card's lack of holographic anti-counterfeiting film. But the librarian barely glanced at it before issuing Sander a temporary library card. Sander and Jenny had discussed their strategy on the way to town, but he paused for a few moments to review in his head one more time before logging on to pull up Appy's Web page.

MADAME ASFURA'S
CONSTELLATION OF THE HEART

proclaimed large scarlet letters, over a zodiac wheel that rotated around a starry facsimile of a nude couple whose starry golden hands met over an outline of a Valentine heart made from a constellation of red giant stars. Sander scrolled down the directory, ignored the horoscope and dating sections, resisted the temptation to browse a page called "The Best of the Book of Purposes," and clicked on the advice section. A gaudy JPEG of two beautiful, naked cupids appeared—not little baby cupids, but mature, fully endowed ones: a blonde female with very pink skin and male apparently of African extraction—holding the ends of a scarlet banner with ornate gold letters that read:

MADAME ASFURA'S ADVICE OF THE HEART.

Beneath it lay a BBS window, with the instructions:

The purpose of relationships is to generate all sorts of emotions, not just happiness. But if your relationship is creating too much pain, tell Madame Asfura about it in the window below, and then select, type, and confirm your password in the slots beneath it. Please limit your request to 40 words or less.

Madame Asfura's reply will appear in the magic chest below. You can open the chest by typing your personal password in the slot beneath. Sometimes Madame's answer appears immediately; sometimes you may have to wait up to 72 hours. The spirits work in mysterious ways.

While you're waiting, please check out the marvelous sites below. Your patronage of them keeps Madame Asfura's advice free to all.

After thinking carefully, Sander typed:

Dear Madame Asfura,

My girlfriend's violent ex is very angry at her, but can't find her. But he knows where her mother is, and my girlfriend's very worried because her mom lives alone in an isolated place and could be vulnerable. What can we do?

Sincerely,

Lost My Heart in Armadillo, TX.

Sander turned to Jenny. "So, do you think that will do it?"

She nodded. "She'll figure that out easy. I just hope whoever's eavesdropping doesn't."

"Okay." He typed "ArmadilloAZ1" in the "Password" and "Confirm Password" slots and pressed "Enter." The BBS window went black, appeared to catch fire, and shriveled away.

"All right, let's get out of here," he said.

"Sander, shouldn't we wait for a reply from Mom?" Jenny protested.

"Jenny, we know the FBI's in town," said Sander quietly. "If they trace that message, they could be on top of us any minute."

She nodded and shut up. They logged out and left. "We are going to check for replies," Sander said, as they reached the truck. "But it'll have to wait for 30 miles."

They got onto US 54 and headed north, crossing the big green Missouri River bridge just as, unbeknownst to them, a tan Ford sedan pulled up to the Missouri River Regional Library . . .

The FBI hadn't traced their internet session—but a library clerk, a regular *MorningStar* reader, had heard Jenny use Sander's name.

Thirty-five minutes later, the Power Ram 50 entered Columbia, home of the University of Missouri's main campus and of computers galore. But with no university ID, the two fugitives had to use the downtown Kinko's to log in. Sander pulled up Madam Asfura's website and typed in the password. The treasure chest creaked open. Ashes swirled out, which magically

un-burned into a peacock-like phoenix, which coughed up a
scroll that opened to read:

> Dear Lost,
>   Your girl friend's mother sounds like a tough
> old bird. A word to the wise should be sufficient.
> She'll make arrangements, I'm sure. By . . .

"She's okay!" exclaimed Jenny joyfully, drawing stares from
a couple of users at nearby stations.

"Wait, there's more," Sander said. He scrolled down:

> . . . the way, you have a message from Dick on the
> Big Island of Hawai'i. He says:
>   "You hold the keys to unlock the soul and end
> the world. Weather's fine. Wish you were here."

XVIII
Stonehenge Revisited

Missouri is a state of marvelously surreal place names. In Missouri, you can drive from Vichy to Vienna in 15 minutes, and then be in Taos within an hour. In another hour or two you can pass through Lebanon on your way to Carthage. Without leaving the state, you can drive to Macon or Farmington or Memphis, Nevada or Washington or even Belgrade, then drive north to Mexico. In Missouri, Lexington hosted a *Civil* War battle.

And then there are town names that are simply peculiar: Tightwad and Licking, Cowgill and Blue Eye, Knob Noster and Braggadocio and Stet (so named when a Postal Service bureaucrat misunderstood a common correction symbol on a town charter application) and, of course, Peculiar.

So it would only seem proper for Jenny and Sander to arrange a meeting with Worley McDermont at Stonehenge.

Stonehenge wasn't a town, however. Stonehenge was Stonehenge. It was erected by engineering students from the University of Missouri at Rolla's famous School of Mines and duplicated exactly the proportions and positions of the inner circle of stones in the English original, except Rolla's stones looked less crude. (Future mining engineers couldn't appear to do sloppy work, after all.)

Worley McDermont sat on the Altar Stone, eating Spicy Pork Rinds and enjoying the sunset. "I gotta remember this place," he murmured. He knew a commune of devil worshippers about an hour and a half south of Rolla. He'd tip them off about this locale. Maybe they'd give him and Grey Eagle an exclusive on a sacrifice. Probably not human. A bloody calf would do, its genitals maybe removed with surgical precision, to tie it in with saucers and cattle mutilations.

Maybe if the magazine paid her enough, Jennifer Duenckel would stretch out on this stone and pretend to be a virgin.

But first she had to show up. He glanced anxiously at his watch, then at the sun, setting not far off the Heelstone Lintel. Fantastic shadows tiger-striped the ground and stones. An elderly woman tourist, the only other person on the site, was framing the sunset between two stones for a photograph. "Damn. If they stood me up. . . ." McDermont muttered.

"Oh, they haven't," said the tourist, snapping her photo. She straightened up, looking suddenly less old and frail. "Worley McDermont, I presume?"

"If you're Jennifer Duenckel, that's a great disguise," said McDermont, recovering quickly.

"Sorry to disappoint you," said the woman. "I'm her mother, and for the moment, her agent."

"Hey, I didn't agree to talk to any agents."

"You didn't say you wouldn't," said Appy. "I don't suppose Tonto or one of his brethren is lurking out there somewhere?"

"Hey, he'd be real upset if he heard that. He's only part Pawnee—but if he was full-blooded, he'd hate it even more."

"I know. I figured if he was in earshot, then that might flush him out."

"Bad lighting conditions right now," said McDermont. "We'll get photos later, if we can make a deal. You'd better start bargaining fast, though, because this story's aging by the minute."

"Oh, I think we can revive it. How about some inside poop on other saucer witnesses being held against their will at a *germ warfare facility?* Plus, I drop my lawsuit over your magazine's plagiarism of my astrology cyber-column."

"And how much might you be wanting for these favors?" McDermont said, smiling.

"These terms are not negotiable, so write them down carefully," said Appy. "First, in all photos published, Jenny remains a blonde."

"No problem," said McDermont, jotting a note. "It would only confuse the public if we changed her image now."

"Second, no more borrowing of anything on my website without my written consent. If you want to use my stuff, we can negotiate a separate contract."

"Hey, your stuff's kinky enough that my editors just might go for it. Let's sit down over that later. Right now, the mosquitoes are chewing the hell outa me."

"Third, the interview's to be held in complete privacy, and the location of the interview is to be divulged to *no one.*"

"Hmm. I can't guarantee what happens if we get a subpoena— but other than that, sure. We set up safe houses for interviews all the time."

"Forth, absolutely *no contact* of any sort between any of us and Harlan Chillingworth."

Rats, thought McDermont. *There goes the ambush.* He sighed. "All right. He's mad at us right now, anyway. 'Sun's going down. Can we get to the cash?"

"All right. Three thousand each for Jenny and Sander, plus 500 for me. I need to buy a good guard dog."

"Okay," he agreed readily. He'd been authorized to pay more. The conglomerate that owned *MorningStar* could feed the story to its papers in London, Antwerp, Bonn, Sydney, and Quebec. The traditional newspaper industry was shrinking, but the tabloids were doing just fine, thank you.

"I'm not quite done," said Appy.

"Aw, c'mon."

"Just one more item. An all-expense-paid trip, including air-fare, rental car, and beach house for one month on the Big Island of Hawai'i."

XIX

Where the Fish Came From

The beach house in Kapoho Vacationlands wasn't deluxe. The roof was metal; the plywood walls were painted flaking pale green outside and uniform pink inside. The furniture was rattan recycled from a local resort. Water came from a rain catchment tank and had to be boiled before drinking. Over the john, a charmingly hand-lettered sign proclaimed:

HERE ON THE COAST WHERE SUN MEETS SEA,
FRESH WATER ISN'T HAULED FOR FREE.
PLEASE HELP OUR WATER TANK MAKE DO
AND ONLY FLUSH FOR NUMBER TWO

A lava flow had long since claimed Kapoho Village itself. The nearest town was Pāhoa, but the beach house owner hadn't recommended it.

"It's probably better to drive to Hilo," she'd said. "Pāhoa's kinda wild."

But the house also had its charms. It was set on the edge of an old lava flow that had thrust its black tongue into the ocean, creating a narrow cove. The stark black stone and white sand of the "yard" made the bright greens of palm trees and low-growing *naupaka* vines even more startling—and the pink-and-magenta bougainvillea blossoms downright shocking. And at the edge of all this vividness, crumbling lava-and-concrete steps led down to another world of azure water, pink and yellow corals and multi-hued, surprisingly familiar fish. She was staying on the edge of the World's Largest Saltwater Aquarium.

Or at least, she was coming back there to sleep, after the airport closed.

"There's not nearly as many fish as there used to be," the landlady had told her sadly. "Part of it's the economy, that's making people fish for food—but a big part's that awful aquarium trade. They ship out thousands of fish a month. You seldom see a yellow tang any more, and there used to be clouds of them. And a lot of the fish get injured when they're captured, or die of decompression or pH or temperature shock on the plane. The rest get stuck in little aquariums with no cleaner wrasses to remove their parasites, no coral polyps and anemones to filter the water, no tides and seaweed to oxygenate it properly. Some family just got the aquarium because they think fish *look* neat, and they don't know the first thing about taking care of a living creature that's ripped out of a whole web of living creatures. So the poor things die, and the dealers come out here to net even more. . . ."

Does Sander know about all this? Jenny wondered.

The landlady, a cheerfully leathery 46-year-old grandmother named Sara (blondes age fast in the tropics), had met their plane to give them keys and directions.

"So you work for a magazine, Ms. Kinny?" she'd asked, stirring her coffee in the little airport lounge.

"Uh, not really. But I did some work for them. And my name isn't Kinny, by the way. It's, uh, Dingle."

"Oh, sorry, I just got your reservation and assumed. So you kept your maiden name, then?"

"Uh, no, we're not married," said Jenny nervously.

"Oh. I see," said Sara. "Well, I pretty much follow scripture myself, but I know about not casting stones. And hey, here I am, divorced myself. What's your significant other do?"

"Uh, he's a biologist."

"Oh, we've got lots of those on the island, working with all the endangered species." She looked about. "So when's he coming?"

Jenny shook her head. "I don't know. We got to Los Angeles okay, but then he missed the plane. He went to get us a snack and just disappeared."

"Well, people get lost at LAX all the time. He'll probably come in on the next flight. Enjoy your stay, Hon. *Aloha.*"

But the next flight had arrived, and the next. Jenny had dragged her old overnighter to the rental car agency, picked up her subcompact and driven it to the public parking lot (airport security forbade anyone from parking at curbside for more than a few seconds), then walked back to stand in the sweet soup of canned Hawaiian music at the base of the escalator that all arriving passengers descended at Hilo International Airport (which actually received no international flights). She'd watched residents drape fragrant leis over returning loved ones and vacation-mooching relatives; watched tearful reunions and solitary tired homecomings, bedraggled parents carrying sleeping children, local families picking up Igloo coolers in lieu of luggage. And Sander hadn't come.

Finally a woman security guard had approached.

"Ma'am?" the guard said.

"Y-yes?"

"Sorry, yeah? But da airport going close now."

"But my-my friend—he missed our flight, and I've got the directions and phone number for where we're staying! If I leave, he can't find me again!"

"But no can stay heah. Call tomorrow, yeah?"

So Jenny had set out for Kapoho, gotten lost, and driven until the road abruptly disappeared under a wall of cooled black lava. She'd stood for a few minutes with a cluster of tourists atop the flow, and looked in awe at the distant orange and white steam plume where molten lava was entering the ocean. But none of the tourists had known where Kapoho was, so she'd driven back 25 miles to a gas station and gotten directions in half-understood Pidgin. Following them, she'd gotten as far as the Pāhoa bypass, but then couldn't find any road called "Makai." [1]

Finally, long after midnight, she'd spotted a faded sign for "Kapoho Vacationlands," and followed a rough road to a clump of oceanside houses—then had gotten lost in a tangle of looping, potholed drives, and ended up in a field of scrub brush.

---

[1] *Makai* means "ocean-ward" in Hawaiian. Nobody in Hawai'i uses compass directions; instead, they speak in terms of *mauka* (mountain-ward) or *makai* and the next district down the coast. Ask even a *haole* (white person) how to get to Kapoho, and he/she will say something like, "Go Puna on Volcano Highway to Kea'au bypass, take it to Pāhoa bypass and turn on the second *makai* road after the first Pāhoa exit, go to the Y-intersection, turn Hilo, drive past the big *pu'u*, turn Ka'u at the crossroads and watch for the sign on the makai side." And this is in English. We won't even go into how it's done in Pidgin.

Unlike New Englanders, Hawai'i residents don't, as a rule, deliberately lead tourists astray. But this directional system may be an example of linguistic natural selection. Lost tourists help the local economy by stopping at local places along the way, instead of driving straight to their multinational-corporation-owned resort. And they see more of Hawai'i—which is why they came, isn't it?

Too tired even to cry, she'd rolled down the windows to admit the lulling roar of the ocean, and slept the exhausted sleep of the jet lagged and despairing, which even an Aveo's cramped seat and the tiny shrill whines of mosquitoes cannot finally prevent.

The next morning, she'd found the beach house. But she still had no idea how she was going to find Sander, if Sander was still at large.

XX

A Hell of a Day at the Office

Worley McDermott was fond of old sports cars, for reasons partly economic, partly romantic. Sports cars were chick magnets, but new ones were out of his salary range—especially when you figured in insurance. Vintage sports cars were chick magnets, too, and cost much less. A Karmann Ghia looked like a sports car, anyway, and Uma Thurman had driven one in *Kill Bill: Vol. 2*, so it had to be sexy. He'd actually picked up a lady once, in his old Karmann. She'd gotten off at the next truck stop, but it had reinforced his theory.

Now Worley was on the hunt again, cautiously nosing his rented Chevy compact down the red gravel road.

"I better not mess up the damn paint on this thing," he muttered. He hoped he had the directions right. The voice on the phone had been hard to make out, as if the man were speaking through a rag. He'd sounded vaguely familiar, but all these hillbillies sounded alike.

There were very few Karmanns left on the road. Worley had found only two in the local craigslist. The first had proved to be cancerous with rust, as riddled with holes as a stockbroker's guaranty. This was his last chance anywhere close to Springfield.

First driveway. Second driveway. "This must be it," he muttered, and turned into a long, semi-graveled farm lane, easing the Chevy over the washouts. A farmhouse appeared ahead, its tin roof a solid rust-brown, its white paint mostly peeled off. The place didn't even look lived in. "Jeez, this 'billy doesn't even cut his front yard," muttered McDermont. "Maybe I can trade him a lawnmower for the car."

The drive widened into an irregular turnaround that served the house, an equally decrepit barn and a rusty, open steel shed. Parked in the shed was a cherry-red Karmann Ghia convertible, its custom metal-flake paint glittering in the late afternoon light.

"Hot damn," breathed McDermont. He whipped the rental car around and slammed it to a halt in front of the shed, then bolted out for a closer look. The Karmann's top was down. The seats had been reupholstered in cream-colored vinyl. A Blaupunkt stereo gleamed in the dashboard.

"Whoa, baby," McDermont said softly. "You are a beaut."

"She is, ain't she?" said a semi-familiar voice. "I bought her with some of your blood money. Your thirty pieces of silver."

Harlan Chillingworth stepped around the corner of the shed, into view. His right arm cradled a large hunting rifle.

McDermont froze.

"Why'd you tell those lies about me, Worley?" Chillingworth asked. He shifted the rifle awkwardly to a readier position and thumbed the safety off.

"Uh, we didn't lie, Harley," said McDermont, woodenly. "We just quoted our sources, told both sides of the story. . . ."

"Dammit, don't call me 'Harley'! I'm not some motorcycle freak! I'm a good, patriotic American citizen!"

"Sorry, Harlan."

"Why'd you try to ruin my life, Worley? I trusted you."

"Harlan, your life isn't ruined," said McDermont plaintively. "You've got lots of money now, a good car . . ."

"You helped steal my wife away from me. That makes you an adulterer, sure as that Keynes is."

"How do you f-figure that, Harlan?"

"She woulda come back to me, now I had money to take care of her," said Harlan. "Sure as day, she woulda quit that counter-girl job and come back. But then you give her a batch of money and print big, screaming headlines that I'm out to kill her. Worley, the Bible says, 'Thou shalt not commit adultery.' It says 'Thou shalt not lie.' And it says, 'Thou shalt not covet thy neighbor's wife.' Were you coveting my Jenny, Worley? Is that why you scared her away?"

The little black hole at the end of the rifle barrel stared at the reporter's chest. Embarrassed at its gaze, his chest muscles pulled so tight he had difficulty speaking. "I-I didn't covet your wife, Harlan," he said. "It was just business. We paid her for her side of the story, is all."

"Uh-huh. Worley, she wouldn't've said those things about me. I might correct her some, but I love Jenny with all my heart and all my soul and all my strength. I'd do anything to protect her. I'd kill you to protect her. That's how much I love her. Don't you understand that?"

"You love Jenny. Right, I understand. Uh, you don't need the gun to explain that."

"No, I don't need the gun to explain that. I need it to get some true facts out of your lying mouth, Worley. Lie down in the dirt there. Do it now."

Worley reluctantly knelt.

"All the way down! I want your face in the dirt, you shit-eating liar!"

Worley obeyed, pressing his cheek gingerly against the shed's dirt floor, his nose inches from a dried cow pie. From this viewpoint, the cow pie was mountainous, and the little Karmann's red door towered up out of vision.

Harlan's knee landed in the small of McDermont's back so hard that it knocked the wind out of him.

"Worley, where's Jenny at?" drawled his captor. Something hard and cold jammed down against the base of his neck.

"Uh, I-I dunno, for sure," gasped McDermont.

There was the double-click of a round being levered into the rifle's firing chamber.

"Where, Worley?"

"Hawai'i, somewhere. The Big Island. The magazine rented 'em a beach house, someplace called 'Kapoha' or 'Kapoho.'"

"You wouldn't be lying again, would you, Worley?"

"No, I swear to God!"

"You know what, Worley?" said Harlan. "I believe you."

McDermont heard the *snick* of the safety going on. The cold metal withdrew from the back of his neck.

"I believe you, because you wouldn't try to protect her, if it meant your own hide," Harlan continued. "You'd sell her out like Judas. Don't you move, now, Worley."

Silence, for a moment. Then the gunstock slammed into McDermont's neck. The cow patty mountain seemed to bounce up and down as his head bucked against the dirt. The wet crunch of his own vertebrae mixed with Harlan's voice:

"You're never (*crunch*) going (*crunch*) to hurt Jenny (*crunch*) again!"

"Damn—it's just like Grey Eagle said!" exclaimed McDermont, as the tunnel walls whizzed past. Ahead, the pinhole grew into a dazzling disk, then opened outward. Sunlight sparkled on a clear Ozark stream. A heavyset man was fishing. He looked up, then smiled sadly.

"Sorry," he said.

Then the world collapsed, and he was sliding down the tunnel again, faster and faster. A new pinhole appeared, glowing an ugly, orangish yellow. It swept open, engulfed him . . .

To his left was a vast maze of cubicles; to his right, a row of cramped, dingy sound studios. A tobacco haze hung so thick that it burned the eyes and clung, malodorous and oily, to the skin. A deafening cacophony of chattering computer keyboards, typewriters and teletypes and ringing telephones shook the stinking air. An argon-yellow glow oozed down from somewhere in the cavernous haze above, transforming McDermont's blue sports shirt to an ugly greenish-gray.

Through the open studio door beside him, he saw a gray-haired man scribbling notes at a ratty wooden desk, with a telegraph key and a heavy, old-fashioned radio microphone arranged before him. A sweat-stained black fedora was squashed down on his sloping forehead; his once-white shirt, the sleeves rolled up above his elbows, was grayed with tobacco smoke, tinted yellow by the lighting and heavily stained about the armpits.

"Hello, McDermont," he said, looking up. "I've been expecting you. Winchell's the name. You've heard of me? No?" He scowled his disappointment. "Let me show you your cubicle."

He led McDermont down the smoky row of work stations—some occupied, some littered with construction debris. One tiny radio studio held an empty, steel-reinforced swivel chair. A sign hung from the microphone: RESERVED FOR RUSH DELIVERY. The next studio was festooned with hundreds of already-smoke-begrimed bras. A sign on the chair seat said PARK STERN HERE. Another, festooned with American flags and swastikas, bore the sign:

AT BECK'S CALL

Finally they stopped at a 6' by 6' cubicle. Gray walls, stained brownish by the smoke and browner by the light, held dozens of yellowed black-and-white pictures from *Screw Magazine* and *Big-Assed Mamas*, plus a fuzzy shot of Princess Di inside the wrecked Mercedes. A gray generic 386 PC with a non-ergonometric keyboard sat beside a grimy white landline telephone on the battered desk. McDermont glanced at the PC's black-and-yellow screen.

"Is that Windows?" he said.

"Version 1.0," said Winchell, gruffly. "Have a seat."

McDermont sat down. The non-adjustable, cushionless wooden swivel chair screeched in complaint.

"You'll be unable to get up again," said Winchell. "Free will doesn't operate down here. Likewise, you'll find you can't turn down your assignment, which is to interview all our new clients about their sex lives: how many, where, what positions, which diseases, whether size really mattered. Not just the babes. The middle-aged men, the fat teenagers who died in botched abortions, the hairy transvestites, the Baptists, the Mormons. For all eternity." He started to leave.

"You're the Devil?" McDermont asked.

Winchell paused. "Naw, just your spiritual forefather, dirtball. That's why *I'm* down here."

The phone rang.

"That's your first call," said Winchell, and walked away.

165

McDermont watched helplessly as his hand reached toward the ringing phone. Over the machine clatter, he heard Winchell's voice enunciating, broadcast-style: "Hello, Mr. and Mrs. North and South Hell and all the ships at sea! Let's go to press!"

XXI
A Moment of LAXity

At this point we face somewhat of a dilemma. Which question is most pressing:

1. Why did Sander miss the plane?
2. Will Harlan catch up with Jenny, and if so, will he destroy her in order to save her?

   or

3. How on earth did a nearsighted armadillo manage to send Appy a message from Hawai'i?

For centuries, it has been the author's prerogative (subject, of course, to the editor's whim, which is subject to the publisher's whim, which is subject to the whim of the marketplace, which is subject to the whim of whatever censoring bodies and pressure groups happen to be active at the moment), to dictate what the reader will read next. For centuries, readers have rebelled by skipping ahead, and authors have punished them by plugging in plot twists, so the "cheater" who turns to the end discovers that he/she doesn't know how he/she has gotten there.

This current work, however, is a democratic, equal opportunity figment. Question #3 is addressed in Chapter XXVI. Question #2 begins to be answered in Chapter XXVII. You, the reader, are free to read them in whichever order you choose. It's the author's whim to pursue Question #1 first. If you want to be a mindless sheep [1] (or a highly intelligent, superbly rational being who, naturally, *chooses* the same path as the author), please feel free to come along.

It didn't start out as an attempted hijacking.

Sander folded up the copies he'd made from the *Atlas of Hawai'i* that he'd found at the Columbia Public Library. "If we're gonna be here another hour, I'm going to get us some food," he said.

"Okay, but don't go too far," said Jenny.

Leaving the drum-shaped terminal room, Sander headed down the straight corridor. Sander, surprisingly, had never flown before. (Although when you live in Missouri on an assistant fish-feeder's income and your parents are only a hundred or so miles away, maybe that's not so surprising after all). But he and Jenny had already overcome several challenges. When it came to airports, they'd learned, being clean-cut, White and

---

[1] The author here apologizes for a blatantly specist, inaccurate stereotype and a gratuitous slur on all sheep everywhere. Of course sheep have minds. Otherwise, we wouldn't need border collies to change their minds for them. Border collies are widely believed to be the most intelligent of all dogs, which suggests that it actually requires considerable brainpower to out-think a sheep.

Further evidence: when the author was young, he heard that some schoolmates of his had fed a lamb three bottles of beer, after which it (the lamb, not the beer—or, to be perfectly accurate, the lamb with the beer inside) climbed a ladder. This again suggests that sheep actually have far more mental and physical dexterity than we give them credit for; they're just really, really inhibited.

Consider what it must be like to be imprisoned in a body that another species has turned into a wool-making machine, and to watch your children being hauled off for sacrifice to bloodthirsty gods or snobbish gourmands. If you had a mind trapped in such a horrid situation, wouldn't you devote most of your brainpower to the task of trying not to think about it?

Midwestern had distinct advantages. The TSA guards at Lambert Field in St. Louis had barely glanced at their fake IDs. They'd gotten the same treatment at O'Hare in Chicago, where the couple had successfully found and navigated the inter-terminal rolling walkway, with its long corridor of avant-garde lights and tinkly New Age music, just in time to catch their next flight.

So Sander set out into LAX with 45 spare minutes, a false sense of confidence and a blissful ignorance of airport food.

He was also near exhaustion, as well as somewhat distracted. He'd gone open-eyed for the past 14 hours, and had gotten very little sleep since their trip to the library in Columbia. A little treasure chest kept opening over and over in his mind, and the scroll kept unrolling to the same words:

YOU HOLD THE KEYS TO UNLOCK THE SOUL AND END THE WORLD.

What keys? he asked himself for the 2,376th time as he walked down the corridor. He found a fast food place and a restaurant whose entrees looked memorable only for their prices. He didn't mind hamburgers, but deep instincts nagged inside his tired body: the same instincts that had told prehistoric hunters it was okay to bring fresh rabbits home to your mate, but if you're still courting, you'd better kill a bear.

"There's gotta be something better," he muttered.

What keys?

He stopped at a kiosk and bought a box of chocolates with a fancy Italian name, in case no bear was in the offing. Then he stopped to use a restroom, and washed up at a basin next to a man who was shaving.

What keys?

As he straightened, he heard the thin clatter of metal, and saw a pair of fingernail clippers on the floor by the waste bin.

The man who'd been shaving was just stepping out the door.

"Hey, mister!" Sander called. "You forgot something!" He rushed out the door, saw the man passing through another door and followed him, but lost him in the crowd outside.

"I'd better get back," he told himself. Absentmindedly dropping the clippers in his pocket, he set out at a trot.

Then he realized that he'd passed beyond a security checkpoint. He'd have to go back through it to return.

You idiot, thought Sander. *You're risking identification for a box of chocolates.*

Kim Yung was bored. This was not uncommon for a TSA guard. But he'd gotten fast-tracked for citizenship in the Bush era by reporting two fellow Korean students for remarks suggesting possible terrorist activities; he knew the value of keeping his eyes open. When he got bored, his eyes opened wider.

They opened very wide when a nervous-looking brown-haired man with gray eyes plunked a small, silvery object into the basket along with his spare change, then stepped through the metal detector. Kim stopped the man for a pat down, then dangled the nail clippers before the suspect's face.

"This is contraband," Kim Yung said.

"But I just found it inside the terminal," the man protested.

"This is contraband," Kim Yung repeated. "Not allowed inside."

"I'm going to hijack an airplane with nail clippers?" the suspect replied.

In Korean, each word has a different meaning, depending on whether it's pronounced with a high, low, rising or falling tone. In English, tones apply to whole sentences. Kim Yung may not have realized that the rise at the end of Sander's sentence denoted an incredulous question, not a statement—or maybe he knew he could repeat the man's words without that rising tone.

"He said, 'I going to hijack plane with nail clippers,'" Kim told his superiors afterward. "He resisted arrest."

Kim Yung didn't know English all that well. But unfortunately for Sander, he did know Taekwondo.

XXII

If Only They'd Watched the News

Winston "Jaguar" Bertram was in his element. A deliberately ugly room. Ugly chipped beige paint, with a smelly urine stain on one wall. Ugly beat up gray table. No windows. Bare light bulb in a dirty porcelain ceiling fixture. Ugly unpadded straight-backed chair parked under his victim's squirming rump. More comfortable folding chairs for him and Billy Cartman, who was seated, playing "good cop." Bertram wasn't using his chair. He stood, emphasizing his height and bulk, and stared fiercely down at the man across the table. All standard stuff. He'd been doing it since his MP days—had taught it to South American officers at Fort Benning and to Central Americans in Panama, so they wouldn't have to torture people so often to get simple answers. (They hadn't needed ugliness lessons; their jails were already ugly.) If he hadn't left the Army before Iraq happened, he might have saved his country some grief.

He was rather contemptuous of the mules and wetbacks he'd dealt with since he'd joined Immigration. After the military hard cases he'd handled, these civvy perps were usually no challenge. But this guy across the table was different. They hadn't even ID'd him yet. He hadn't spoken a single word. But he was no wetback, that was certain. He didn't look like a trained pro, but Jaguar had seen Al Qaida's training tapes. Those guys knew how to *not* look like pros.

He didn't look Muslim either. But some Afghans and Chechens had gray eyes. Or he might be Russian mafia.

They'd e-mailed out his fingerprints. No matches yet. But the FBI always had a few million prints they hadn't digitized yet. If this guy lawyered up or somebody produced a writ of habeas corpus, the government's case right now was too flimsy to deny bail. Then his friends at the TSA would have a brutality lawsuit and a batch of bad publicity on their hands. He had to get this perp to talk, damn it. Maybe not a confession yet. He'd settle for a couple of words. He had to hear that voice, hear if there was any accent. *Anything* this guy said would reveal *something*.

"Let's try again," Jaguar said. "Let's start with what we know." He tossed the driver's license down on the table. "We know this license number belongs to a 65-year-old church secretary in Potosi, Missouri. We know there was nothing else in your wallet but cash. No credit cards, free frozen yogurt cards, no pictures of your wife and kids. Nothing that says you're a human being. We know your brown hair is starting to grow blond roots, and a security officer heard you say you were going to hijack a plane. We know we already got you for falsifying the driver's license, and we're gonna get you for something worse, because you wouldn't fake an ID and dye your hair for no reason. If you cooperate, maybe we limit the damage here. If you don't, maybe we do a lot of damage."

"Look," pleaded Cartman, "you gotta have family somewhere that's worried about you. Just give us your name. Let us call them. Wouldn't you like to tell them you're all right?"

The man said nothing.

"Who says he's all right?" said Jaguar. "Either he's done something he shouldn't have, or he was planning something worse. And he'd better hope his buddies don't do it without him, because this crud's gonna pay, whether we catch his buddies or not. The question is, just how much is he gonna pay?"

Silence.

"Look," said Cartman, "I don't know if you're running or planning. But either way, it's gotta end here, or it'll only get worse. You gotta let us help you."

The man just stared at the table with his right eye. His left eye was swollen shut, courtesy of Kim Yung.

If only we could do waterboarding, Jaguar thought. He upped the stakes, moving around the table so it was no longer a protective barrier. That was a risk. The guy was cuffed, but with his hands in front; he might try something. But if a freaking airport guard could do the perp that much damage, then Bertram was a lot bigger threat to the perp than the perp was to him.

"Look, you fuckin' idiot," Jaguar said. "Billy over there's being nice, but he's FBI, and you're charged with fucking attempted hijacking. And I'm friggin' Immigration, and I don't even know you're an American. So you've got *no* rights with me. You'd better goddamn speak up now and tell us who you are. Right now, we don't even have a fuckin' next of kin to notify."

Silence.

Jaguar moved around behind the man: the position of maximum vulnerability for the suspect, short of putting him down on the floor. "Okay, one more thing we know," the agent said, and threw the suspect's boarding pass down on the table before him. "You left St. Louis on the redeye, changed planes at O'Hare, debarked at LAX. Final destination: Hawai'i." He bent over, so his voice was next to the suspect's ear. "A lot of military targets there, aren't there? Schofield, Kaneohe . . . and Pearl Harbor. That would be nice and symbolic, wouldn't it?"

The suspect picked up the ticket with his handcuffed hands, stared at it—then crumpled it and shoved it into his mouth.

"Shit!" Jaguar said. "Drop that, you son of a bitch!" He grabbed the perp's head, tried to pry his jaws open. The man kept chewing. Jaguar dug his fingers into the man's cheeks.

"Jag! For god's sake!" said Cartman. "Let the man finish his meal. We've got the electronic ticket record."

Jaguar let go. "Okay, now we got you for destroying evidence," he snarled. "You're gonna be in a long time, after your trial. If you ever get a trial. I mean, if you don't say who you are, we can't tell anybody you're here, can we? 'Cause we don't fuckin' know who to tell!" He started for the door. "Let's put this fish back in the tank awhile, Billy. I'm gonna go find him a few big, smelly cellmates with big dicks."

He stormed out, then went behind the one-way mirror to watch Billy work. "Good job," whispered Corcoran, his boss.

"You know what?" said Billy. "I think that guard is full of bullshit about you saying you were going to hijack a plane. I bet he was covering his ass for overreacting. Nobody says he's gonna hijack a plane with a nail clippers, then just clams up. Am I right? 'You done chewing on that paper?"

The man shook his head, then swallowed.

"Come on, Mister, help me out here," wheedled Billy. "Jaguar's not kidding. He'll bury you. You gotta at least tell me who you are, if you want me to help you."

The man's shoulders shook.

"Shit, he's choking!" shouted Billy. "He's turning blue!"

Jaguar rushed back into the room. By then, Billy was already around the table, seizing the man in a Heimlich maneuver. . . .

XXIII
Oh. Rats.

"They get me as I was go to work," said Chow Yun Hoon. "I wear my Pizza Hut Uniform and no Green Card. My parents don't know expense it has here. I cannot live with allowance they give. I went all my classes. . . ."

"At least you knew you weren't playing by the rules, working with no Green Card," said Willy Kishimoto, from the bunk below him. "My folks came here when I was two. How was I to know they never took out citizenship papers for me?" He shook his head. "Now those idiots keep asking what I know about Ahm Shinryo, or however it's pronounced. . . ."

"Ahm Shinryo?" asked Chow Yun Hoon.

"Some suicide cult in Japan. They did something with nerve gas a couple of decades ago. Jeez, I shoulda known this would happen. My people have been through this before." Willy laughed bitterly. "I thought America was over the Yellow Peril."

"I did nothing wrong. Nothing at all," chimed in Kim Song Soon. "I went to an anti-government rally in Seoul once. They don't understand. If you're a student in Korea, you *have* to go to anti-government rallies."

"It is obvious for me," said Achmed Rajul. "I am Pakistani. I have been here ten years. I do research in microbiology. So of course I am a bioterrorist. Of course I'm not a doctor."

"How about you on the floor?" Willy asked.

Lying on his foam pad, Sander Keynes considered. Silence hadn't worked that well with the two cops. Not that he'd meant to keep silent. He'd just been paralyzed, unable to think. . . .

He was still paralyzed.

"No answer? Have we a real terrorist here?" said Achmed.

"Sorry. I just don't want to talk about it," Sander mumbled.

"Woooo," said Willy.

Could quarantine be worse than this? Sander thought. But if he told his captors who he was, they'd probably guess that Jenny had been with him. And then there was Dick's message. If the Feds got access to his head, they might figure out what was in there before he did. So far, he'd met no one in government whom he cared to entrust with a new way to end the world.

"Ah, c'mon, down there," said Willy. "You sound just like an American. You must've been here a long time."

"Maybe he lies there to spy on us," said Achmed.

"Hey, any of us could be an informant," said Willy.

"You'd make an excellent candidate yourself, Achmed," noted Kim. "Who would suspect an Arab of spying for the Americans?"

"I'm *Pakastani*, not Arab!" protested Achmed. "I spit on the Arabs!" He followed thought with action. Unfortunately, the person on the floor below was not an Arab.

An uneasy silence ensued. Sander wiped Pakistani spit off his cheek, adjusted his one blanket, and tried to sleep.

It wasn't easy, even exhausted as he was. He'd never been in a cell before, much less on a cell floor. A lumpy stainless steel combination toilet-sink-drinking fountain towered over his head. At the base of the john's bulging underside clung a small colony of slime mold or algae or something, watered by condensation droplets that occasionally broke loose and raced in tiny upside-down rivulets down the bowl's underside. At Sander's feet rose a steel slab door, broken only by a food tray slot and a little window of heavy steel mesh.

"Hey, you down there," said Willy. "I'm sorry, but I gotta use the crapper. Watch your face."

He climbed down, carefully planted his feet on either side of Sander's head, dropped his pants, and sat. Sander rolled on his side and scrunched to avoid direct hits on his eyes by any splash droplets, and tried not to think about the smells and plops and gurgles emanating from immediately above.

His new view wasn't much better. A shiny black spider busily repaired a web under the bunk. Beyond it, in the shadows, was an air duct grate: the cobweb-befuzzed stuff of escape movies. But this particular grate was too small to be an escape route for anything larger than a rat.

What keys?

"You know, if they turn me loose, I'm going to visit Japan anyway," said Willy. "I want to find out what I'm being persecuted for. But I hear the Japanese don't accept Nisei, either. That's the trouble with Americans. We're all displaced persons. We don't fit anywhere."

What keys? Sander thought, drifting off despite himself. . . .

"Airplanes aren't safe," said Willy as they boarded Amtrak's gleaming *Japan Chief.* They climbed a spiral stair to the car's upper deck and took their seats, which were huge and luxurious.

"Isn't this the way to travel?" sighed Willy, reclining. Not just two inches back. *Reclining.*

But something was troubling Sander, as the train lumbered into the air, sluggish with the weight of enough fuel to cross the Pacific.

What keys?

"Trains don't fly," he said.

So it didn't.

Amid wreckage and roaring flames, he came upon a blackened jet window. A white rat peered out at him. Beyond it, he glimpsed Jennifer Duenckel's terrified face. *"Jenny!"* he roared, and smashed the window with his bare fist, which was also a rock. But Jenny's image shattered along with the pane.

The rat hopped out. "The first key," it said, with a Japanese accent, "opens the door between dreams and reality."

Slowly the message sank into Sander's sleep-mind. *If that's true, then, oh no . . .*

Sander panicked awake, banged his head on the toilet bowl and fell back, stunned and disoriented. Slowly, he remembered where he was. The john's black mass loomed above his face. Somewhere in the dark above, two men were snoring.

I have to get out of here, he thought. Light beckoned through the door's food tray slot and small window.

The first key opens the door between dreams and reality. Sure, you can escape from here, he thought bitterly. *In your dreams.*

He tried envisioning a dream-key turning in the cell lock. But this side of the door had no keyhole. *What the heck, envision one.* He pictured an imaginary key turning in an imaginary hole. *How phallic,* he thought with a half-smile.

But the door was a very solidly built prison door. Phallic images didn't work on it. It was not a door to be screwed with.

He tried to picture the door as a woman, but that was just too much of a stretch for his Midwestern mind.

I conjured up an armadillo once, he thought. *Maybe I can dream a rhinoceros to knock the door down.* But that dream was too damn big. Trapped in a cell with an imaginary rampaging rhinoceros with a very phallic horn. . . . This unpleasant reverie was interrupted by a scuttling noise in the air duct. He recognized the sound from his college days in the old farmhouse. *Great,* he thought. *This place has rats.*

The scuttling grew louder. By the light that struck the floor from the cell door's window, he could dimly see a rat nose poke itself through the grate.

A *white* nose.

"*Konichiwa,*" it squeaked. Or something like that.

Startled, Sander tried to jerk upright. His head collided with the john again. The rat nose disappeared. He heard its owner scuttling rapidly away down the shaft.

"Wait!" he whispered between his teeth.

The scuttling paused, then very tentatively approached again. The nose reappeared.

"I don't suppose you speak English?" Sander whispered.

"Yes." The rat squeezed through the grate, then sat back on its haunches. "They are coming, Papa-san," it said. "I don't like them. If you go with them, do not trust them."

Someone stirred in one of the bunks above them.

"Keep your voice down, please!" Sander whispered. "Trust who?"

"I don't know their names. I'm just a rat."

Sander remembered Appy's explanation about Dick. "Are you a witch's familiar or something?"

He could swear the little thing shook its head.

"Then what are you?"

"A rat!"

"But how can you talk?"

"I don't know. *You* dreamed me." The rat dropped back on all fours. "They are coming!" it squeaked, looking wildly around. "Please hold still," it said, and scurried up Sander's pant leg.

"Hey!" squealed Sander, jerking and hitting his head again.

"What the . . ." said Willy sleepily

"Quiet, please, Papa-san!" pleaded the rat's muffled voice, from midway up Sander's left calf. "I won't bite!"

Sander froze, then lay back hastily. Voices and footsteps were coming up the hall. They stopped at his cell door. Two faces took turns peering through the cell window. Then the door swung open. Sander squinted in the sudden, painful light.

The two men in the doorway—one Afro-American, one Caucasian—wore blue surgical scrubs bulked out by the business suits beneath. Surgical masks and plastic bonnets partially hid their faces. Behind them stood nervous guards in similar garb.

"'Changed his hair color," the Caucasian remarked. "Cute."

"Hello, Mr. Keynes," said the Afro-American. "'Long way from Springfield, Missouri, eh?"

"Who are you?" Sander asked.

"CIA, Mr. Keynes," said the Caucasian. "Please come with us."

XXIV

Live from Tau Ceti . . .

Jerry Karpov smiled when his computer beeped, signaling the conference call.

"This should be a good one," he murmured.

He clicked on the "Accept" icon. The other participants' images popped up like the Brady Bunch on the divided screen: Baker, of course, and Dupres; Mark Wozniofsky from Caltech, Jim Bob Masterson from the University of Hawaii-Mānoa, and Harrison Grubb, M.D. (Karpov had learned that Grubb disliked being called "Harry," since some wags at CDC had started calling him "Caterpillar"). Karpov made the introductions, then let Baker assert his official authority.

"Drs. Wozniofsky and Masterson, welcome aboard," Baker said. "Jerry's recommended you both highly. I know the FBI's briefed you, but I want to quickly review security rules. Open sharing among committee members, but *nothing* to anyone outside the committee and staff. All communications *re* this business must be in person or via approved secure channels. Is that understood and agreed to?"

Both the newcomers gave their assent.

"All right, Jerry, what have you got?"

"Just another odd question," said Karpov. "As you've said, we need to investigate all avenues so we can eliminate them, if nothing else."

"So what do we need to eliminate today?"

"Regarding the 'missing alien' problem," said Karpov. "What if it isn't missing?"

"You think the alien's somebody in custody?" asked Baker. "Nah. We screened all the canoeists' DNA. Even Keynes, once they nabbed him in L.A. If he's not human, he's such a good copy that he could marry your daughter and give you grandkids."

"Not likely," chuckled Karpov, who was 42, single and mostly celibate. He generally preferred ideas of women to the real thing. "But I'm not referring to human-looking aliens."

Baker raised an eyebrow. "Inhuman-looking aliens?"

"Even more opposite than that," said Karpov. "Most of our tests on the Object have assumed that it's a spaceship designed to carry creatures that are at least roughly like us. But what if it isn't?"

Brief silence.

"It isn't a spaceship? Or it isn't designed to carry aliens like us?" asked Dupres.

"Good. You caught the complex question and split it up," smiled Karpov. "But we can still split those two questions into a few more. What if it's alien, but not a spaceship? What if it's an alien spaceship, but isn't designed to carry aliens? What if it's a spaceship, but isn't alien?"

"Well, we know *we* didn't create it, anyway," said Baker. "And I can't imagine anyone else being that advanced—though the Russians threw us a few big surprises in their day."

"What if it's not technology?" said Karpov.

Baker's fingers gave an exasperated thrum. "What else could it be?"

Karpov shrugged. "It could be biology. Or biotech. Maybe it's its own passenger. There are all kinds of examples of space-faring critters in science fiction."

Baker's image leaned back in its video chair and ran its video fingers through its thinning video hair. "Any evidence to support that?"

Karpov shrugged again. "The thing sheds x-rays, so we don't know what's inside. Spectroscopic and visual evidence suggest an outer shell of interlaced carbon filaments bonded with a complex organic compound. That could describe a biologically-formed substance—or a graphite tennis racket."

"Wait a minute," said Mike Dupres. "What about the poltergeist reports? If the Object's the alien, who shifted those boxes in my office?"

"Probably *menehune*, Mike," said Baker dryly.

"Who?"

"Little Hawaiian gnomes. That, or some fellow scientist who wants to make that crackpot SETI guy look *really* silly."

"So these incidents are all practical jokes? You're starting to sound like a BLUEBOOK investigator."

Baker's fingers thrummed. "Don't pull an Agent Mulder on us, Mike. You're too valuable."

"I'm not saying the Object *is* alive," said Karpov, "just that we need to examine the possibility. We don't even know whether it's animal, vegetable or mineral. I've enlisted Mark and Jim Bob to help us figure that out. Jim Bob's an evolutionary zoologist; he's published on everything from fruit flies to coral colonies, and helped design life-detection experiments for NASA's Mars probes. Mark's a botanist specializing in "fringe species"—the types that survive in extremely hostile or transitional environments. That gives us coverage on plants and animals, though if this thing's really alive, it may more closely resemble some other terrestrial life form such as bacteria, fungi or *archaea*. Jim Bob, do the data you've examined preclude the Object from being an animal?"

One of Jim Bob's great vices, and virtues, was that he never stopped thinking. He'd known this question was coming, but he still hesitated, giving it one last think-through.

"The big objection is its conjectured origin," he said, finally. "I can't picture any known form of animal tissue surviving a journey of interstellar distances—not to mention atmospheric entry. Maybe an encysted microbe or spore inside a meteorite, but nothing as complex as an animal."

"Could someone on this planet have bio-engineered it?" asked Baker. "The Iranians, say, with enough hired Russian scientists?"

Jim Bob shook his head. "UH-Mānoa's on the cutting edge of biotech, and *we* are nowhere close to this sophisticated a project. But then, nature routinely evolves creatures 'way more adaptable than our best machines. If *we* can create a spaceship, why couldn't nature?

"And the thing does display some animal-like traits. In fact, it shows some striking similarities to a specific group of earth creatures."

Jim Bob's image reached for its mouse. The participants' windows rearranged themselves, leaving a blue square in the screen's lower left corner. The words LOADING FILE flashed in the new window, followed by an image: what seemed at first to be a large eye staring from a clump of red coral. Then something moved. The eye had mottled red tentacles attached.

"Higher cephalopods such as octopi can alter skin cells called chromatophores to duplicate their surroundings," said Jim Bob. "They put a B-2's stealth capabilities to shame."

The octopus took off across a sandy ocean bottom, instantly became sand-colored, then settled under a yellow coral head and faded into yellow obscurity.

"But these are dumb animals," said Baker. "If the Object *is* alive, is there any evidence that it's intelligent?"

"Those animals aren't as dumb as you think," said Jim Bob. "Cephalopods have the largest brains of any invertebrates. Check this out." Another file loaded: blackness suddenly broken by multihued lights, rippling along torpedo-shaped bodies.

"Deep-sea squid," said Jim Bob. "They use chromatophores to generate complex light patterns, which in turn seem to cause other squid to modify their behavior in complex ways."

"You mean they're talking?" said Baker incredulously.

"We can't go that far. We just don't know. But in terms of complexity, these signals come surprisingly close to human writing. And this is a *small* species. There may be good reasons why we've never caught a live giant squid."

Baker let out a low whistle. Dupres, the psycholinguist, looked skeptical.

"From the data I've seen, the Object's camouflage system is to an octopus's as a human brain is to a marmoset's," concluded Jim Bob.

"But that doesn't mean it's sentient!" erupted Dupres, who could stand it no longer. "Computers can match the complexity of human brains, but they're not self-aware."

"I didn't say the Object was sentient," said Jim Bob. "We don't even know if it's alive. But the data you've given me don't preclude either life or intelligent life."

"Why do these conversations always end with some variant of 'I don't know'?" sighed Baker. "Okay. One hypothetical at a time. Assume for a moment that this thing isn't sentient, but a very smart critter. What could we predict about its behavior?"

"Well, I'm sure Jerry will point out that we can't necessarily predict alien behavior from earthly models." (Karpov smiled and nodded slightly.) "But the traits you've observed look like precautionary, non-aggressive defenses. It's extremely slippery; when you approach it, its portal disappears, like a snail's siphon retracting. It camouflages itself when moving or disturbed. If you don't get past those defenses, you're not a serious threat. But if you penetrate them, you can expect a more active response: flight or fight."

Baker whistled. "Jesus. If this thing's weapons are as sophisticated as its passive defenses . . ."

"We're in deep do-do," said Dupres.

"But none of this proves it's an animal," noted Karpov. "A machine programmed to defend itself might act exactly the same."

Baker thrummed his fingers. "We need to bring the whole group in on this. Computer, call a meeting, Committee Piney A-1, ASAP, Priority One." Thrum. "Meanwhile, we might as well hear from Dr. Wozniofsky. Could this thing be a plant?"

"Yes," said Wozniofsky. "But probably not a growing plant."

"Not a growing plant?"

"No chlorophyll. No evidence of multiplying cells. No roots, although some plants do absorb nutrients from the air."

"Well, how can it be a plant if it doesn't grow?"

The botanist smiled. "Consider the resemblance between the object's shape and that of a peach pit."

Baker's fingers froze in mid-thrum. "This thing is a seed?"

"Makes sense," said Karpov. "Instead of sending a mature creature across space, why not send the data to create one, inside a relatively small packet of starter materials?"

Thrum. Silence. Thrum. Images of Audrey II danced in their heads.

"This isn't my specialty," added Wozniofsky,"but it could also be a fungoid growth—a spore case. A single puffball can emit thousands of spores. An object this size . . ."

"If that's true, we should destroy this thing immediately," said Grubb, so upset he actually frowned.

"How?" said Jim Bob. "Plant or not, it still has animal-like defenses. Who knows what it's got up its shell?"

"And we may not know until it's too late!" said Grubb. "It could shoot millions, maybe billions of spores into the atmosphere at once."

"Wonderful," said Dupres. "If we don't understand it, kill it. I hope you aren't following that philosophy with those poor people you're holding at Fort Leonard Wood."

"I'm an M.D.!" fired Grubb. "I don't kill my patients. If one died, the interest of public health would demand an autopsy. But I don't kill people!" He sat back, his face again a benign mask, but pulled taut as a drumhead. "Those people's symptoms haven't run their full course. They may be a danger to themselves or others. Until I—until we've completed our study of this syndrome, we have to keep them under observation."

"Gad. People with fair skin have an increased risk of skin cancer. So you'd define 'fair' as a disease, and lock up all blondes?" Dupres asked, and shook his head.

"Don't be silly," retorted Grubb. "At any rate, my Hippocratic Oath does *not* apply to alien spore cases."

"Great. Just wonderful," said Baker. "So if this thing's a plant or fungus, we need to destroy it before it starts growing. If it's an animal, we mustn't do anything to provoke it."

A moment of silence followed, as everyone regrouped.

"You forget the other possibility we mentioned," pointed out Karpov. "What if it's *intelligent* life?"

Long pause.

"We try to talk to it," said Dupres. "Not just test it or try to kill it. We talk."

XXV

The Rat-Father

Sander had expected a black jet or a James Bond submarine or something. Reality was an aged C-140B transport plane.

Not that he ever actually saw the plane. He just heard the roar of its big turbojets through the walls of his crate.

Granted, the Q-14E Mobile Quarantine Module was a pretty sophisticated crate. There was a mattress on a little riser, both bolted down, and a chemical toilet with clamp-down lid for minimal spillage, and an overstuffed seat that might have come from old Ford pickup. (In fact, it had cost the US Government $53,295.85). The air-conditioning unit supplied filtered air so cold it made the bed's lack of blankets rather distressing.

A box bolted beside the chair contained dehydrated food-stuffs and a square plastic bag of drinking water. Sander wasn't quite ready to tackle the foil packets labeled "20C112 ENER-GY BAR" or "34D1582 MEAT PRODUCT STICKS." But he tucked one marked "20F152 CHOCOLATE" into his pocket for further consideration.

There was even a rack with an odd assortment of maga-zines: *Time, Newsweek, Soldier of Fortune,* a foreign policy quarterly, a dog-eared *Penthouse* and four journals in assorted non-English languages. One, apparently in Japanese, Sander had put on the floor for Ratty-san. But even aside from the challenges of reading with rat eyes, Ratty-san couldn't make much of it. Despite his accent, his Japanese vocabulary seemed to be limited to a few common words.

In *Time*, Sander found an article entitled "Is the Saucer a Hoax?" A *Newsweek* article compared the UFO's shape to that of a rather unsuccessful model of septic tank, which had a tendency to "float" out of the ground during freeze-and-thaw weather. The "saucer," theorized the story, was literally a crock of . . .

"They're giving people an excuse to forget," Sander told Ratty-San, grimly. "Maybe deliberately—leak misinformation, cover up, keep the goods. My dad had a friend who worked in northern Thailand in the late 70s, at refugee camps for that mountain tribe—what were they called, the Mong?—the ones the CIA armed in Laos during the Vietnam War, then abandoned. My dad's friend saw women and children coughing up bits of their lungs from mustard gas the Communists dropped on them. But a US spokesperson announced that the yellow stuff falling on the villages was *pollen*. And everyone believed it! Everyone except the refugees and camp workers. . . ."

"I think maybe people want to believe comfortable things, Papa-san," suggested the rat.

"I think you're right, Ratty-san. I mean, look how I had to be dragged kicking and screaming into believing Dick existed. If something tears a hole in the walls of our rational world, we reach for the bricks and trowels."

"What about me, Papa-san?" asked Ratty-San. "Are you walling me in, too?"

Sander laughed. "It looks like the CIA did that for us." Then his face went sober again. "I think you kind of came with your own built-in wall, Ratty-san. What did you say in the dream? 'The first key opens the door between dreams and reality'? I had a moment of pretty bad stress and fatigue, and somehow you popped through. That makes sense, sort of. But I don't remember dreaming Dick." He shook his head.

"Always this Dick. What about me, Papa-San? Why did you make me?"

Sander looked tenderly down at his little companion. "I don't know why, Ratty-san. I didn't even know I was making you. You just happened. I'm sorry."

The rat dropped on all fours and turned away. "Do you know how that makes me feel, Papa-san?"

"I think I do, Ratty-san," said Sander. "God, doesn't every child want to know why his parents made him or her parents made her? But we don't want to hear the answer that's most often true. Parents don't know why, not really. It just happened."

"That's sad, Papa-san. That's very sad."

Sander smiled, though his eyes remained sad. "You're right, Ratty-san. And you know what's even sadder? We ask God the same question. We think He must be all-knowing, all-powerful. But what if He's just a father? Look at you—you're supposed to be a Japanese rat, but you know exactly as much Japanese as I do. Maybe we don't know everything because God himself doesn't. Maybe from His viewpoint, He's no more immortal than we are."

Ratty-san stared at him. "You aren't immortal?"

Sander stared back. "You thought I was?"

The little rat turned away, scurried a couple of feet, then turned and scurried another way.

"That means I'm mortal, too," he squeaked.

"I'm sorry, Ratty-San. But I'm mortal, so far as I know."

"You are not a very good father, Papa-San. Why would you create me, knowing I'm going to die?"

"I don't know why, Ratty-san! Every father does that! *Every* father. . . ." He felt like sobbing. "I guess that's part of parenthood. Creating children when you know they'll die—not really knowing why you do it, not having an answer for them. Just hoping some insane hope that something will change."

The rat scurried to Sander's foot and leapt to his knee. It stared at him for a long moment, then shivered. "I'm cold, Papa-san. Hold me, or wring my neck, or something."

Sander cupped his hands around the little creature. "I'm sorry, Ratty-san. I really am," he repeated. "I can keep you warm, at least." He unzipped his prison jumpsuit a little. Ratty-san crawled into the gap and curled up against his side.

"Thank you, Papa-san."

"Now, if I can just keep warm, myself," muttered Sander, folding his arms and tucking his legs.

Afraid to dream, he fought sleep by reading most of the *Time* and *Newsweek* articles. He eyed the *Penthouse*, thought of Jenny, and picked up the Japanese magazine instead. He couldn't read it, of course, but some of the pictures were almost as bad as *Penthouse*. One ad featured what appeared to be "before" and "after" photos of a woman's naked torso. The advertised product apparently lightened the color of women's aureoles. Sander stared, then turned the page.

"It's sure taking a long time for them to fly back to Missouri," he muttered sleepily. . . .

The plane landing jolted him awake. He looked around in panic. Nothing new seemed to have escaped his dreams. The plane halted; the crate shuddered as the C-130's unloading system dragged it to the door. Something ground against the floor. They jolted upward, lurched around, dropped and stopped.

"Well, we're here," said Sander. "But where are we?"

They were, in fact, stacked with two other modules at an undisclosed military airport. One crate was from a university lab with a government contract to create a genetically modified mold that produced ten as-yet-unpatented antibiotics. The mold had escaped, resulting in hundreds of fuzz-coated petri dishes, lab coats, computers, etc., in storage pending the current administration's decision on the previous administration's reversal of the administration before that's edict converting a remote Pacific atoll from a chemical/biological/nuclear disposal facility into a wildlife refuge.

The other crate housed two experimental chimpanzees with an immunodeficiency disease that a rogue germ warfare unit of the Chinese People's Liberation Army had developed as a solution to the population crisis and the deteriorating morality of Chinese youth; unlike HIV, the new virus really could be transmitted by kissing or fondling. The CIA had outbid two pharmaceutical firms for the chimps on the Hong Kong black market, and had hoped to ship them to the personal petting zoo of a certain Mid-East dictator, as soon as the attorney general finished writing a legal opinion on why this would not violate the anti-biological weapons treaties. But that attorney general had resigned, and his successor had dithered until her boss left office. So the plan, and chimps, remained in limbo.

Sander and Rat-San, of course, didn't know all this, just as they were unaware that a SNAFU had occurred, switching their module's lading number with that of one of the other two crates.

That may have been accidental. Or, just possibly, NASA had struck.

XXVI
Things That Go Bump

"Yes, but what happened to Dick?" you may be fairly screaming by now. Or maybe not. You may prefer cute little white rats, and hope that big, ugly armadillo never reappears. You may be worried about Jenny, alone in Hawai'i with a killer on his way. Or maybe you're the type who goes to see *Friday the 13th, Part 22: Jason Fillets Lady Gaga,* and you're rooting for the maniac. So go check out Chapter XXVII already. But be warned, Harlan's just riding in an airplane at the moment, and Jenny's just reading a magazine at Hilo International Airport.

Which makes it a good time to go back a few days and check on Dick.

Dick rather enjoyed being a poltergeist, now he understood the rules—at least some of them. In a sense, he truly was imaginary: he occupied a path of possibility slightly out of phase with most people's conscious "reality." He and humanity shared the same planet, but their paths and his intersected the world at slightly different points, so he and they (most of them, anyway) never quite touched. If he deliberately tried to, say, pee on their shoes, the little golden stream would never get there in time—though they'd notice a puddle afterward. If he charged straight at them, he'd never reach their location until after they'd moved out of it. Similarly, they could never step on him, because their feet landed somewhere else or took more time to land than they'd planned. The results could sometimes be quite hilarious.

His most immediate problem, after tumbling out of the Object, was hunger. The Facility wasn't impervious to insects, but the population when he arrived consisted mainly of two species of cockroaches. Adult roaches were usually too fast even for his nimble tongue, though the nymphs were sometimes available.

Then he discovered the elevator to the surface. He sneaked aboard, accidentally sending one human occupant sprawling as they disembarked. Clutching his injured ankle, the man spewed a string of very graphic curses. Even to armadillo vision, the man's dark clothing looked military; he probably was trained to commit very graphic violence as well.

Dick scuttled guiltily around the two guards who'd come to the man's aid. *They're treating this like a war,* he thought. *I guess casualties are to be expected.*

He was in a wooden cabin. The door was closed. He waited ravenously for half an hour. Finally two people stepped out to smoke. He hurried out with them, and emerged into pastoral night.

A cold, wet breeze bore aromas of strange vegetation. Cattle grazed on gentle slopes between huge, twisted dead trees that towered blurrily in the moonlight. Fallen trunks and limbs lay scattered, overgrown by a layer of tough grass.

There wasn't the scent of an ant anywhere. But the termites—oh, the termites! Fat, juicy, complacent termites, which until that moment had gone uncounted generations without knowing, in their collective termite gestalt, that such a thing as an armadillo existed.

Well, one did now. Tearing into one corner of a rotten log, Dick wondered, briefly, why he couldn't touch humans but could lap up bugs. Apparently termites lacked humans' stratified levels of reality—no imagination to relegate him to.

Three hours later, stuffed so thoroughly that his armor felt tight, Dick returned to the shack. He'd briefly considered sleeping outside, but he wasn't sure if bulls dreamed, so he decided he'd take his chances with humans. He slipped in with another pair of smokers and rode the lift down with them.

"Any luck with the infrared test, Jim?" one smoker asked the other.

"Not much," said Jim. "The whole thing seems to be a heat sink. No matter how much infrared we threw at it, it stayed constant. Not that they let us throw that much."

"No difference between the external and internal?"

"Hell, Joan, the aperture doesn't even show on the heat signature. I'm beginning to think it *is* just an illusion."

"Matt's laser reflection tests indicated it had real depth," said Joan.

Ah, the things I could tell you, thought Dick. *Only I can't.*

The woman's dark clothes looked like a uniform, but her odors were distinctly un-military. The mingled reeks of hair spray, deodorant, perfume, fabric softener and cigarettes played havoc with Dick's finely tuned nose. He wanted to bolt at the first chance, but the humans stood between him and the elevator door. He let them exit, then tried to dodge out after them.

For some reason, Joan paused a moment just beyond the door, throwing off Dick's timing. The door closed on his head. Door and armadillo retreated, then charged again at the same time.

"What's wrong with the elevator?" asked Joan.

"I dunno. I heard one of the MPs broke his ankle in it earlier this evening," said Jim.

"Ouch," said Joan, as they headed down the hall. Dick was saying considerably more pungent things at that moment.

He spent the day curled up under a tableful of electronics. The next evening, after dining topside, he still had a couple of hours before daylight and naptime again. What to do next?

Contact Sander, was the obvious answer. The scientists here didn't seem in immediate danger of prying secrets out of the saucer. But Sander, who'd gotten those secrets without even realizing it, was carrying a planetary time bomb with a random fuse. He had to be warned, before he triggered it by accident.

The problem was, Dick had no idea how an invisible armadillo could contact someone a very long plane flight away. He didn't even know where he was, himself.

He slipped back inside and spent the early morning eavesdropping on conversations. References to "Hilo," "Mauna Kea," and "lousy surf" suggested the Facility's location, though he'd have expected Hawai'i to be warmer.

Dick pondered. There had to be a way to send a message.

Except for Sander and Jenny, humans apparently couldn't hear him. He could, however, interact with objects . . . an e-mail? But even if he found a computer at armadillo level, his eyes couldn't read the monitor.

He was still pondering when he chanced onto the main security station.

He froze. The bank of monitors was blurry but unmistakable. A chill went down his spine. Cameras didn't dream.

But the soldier watching the monitors showed no awareness that an armadillo was in the vicinity. That seemed a good sign.

Dick decided to press his luck. He trotted into the hall, did a little tap dance with his digging claws, then returned. "Hi. See any interesting wildlife?" he asked.

No reaction.

Okay, I don't show up on TV—at least, not to them. The screens are tuned to sync with their eyes. Maybe I'm onscreen, but they can't see the image. Or I'm registering only at some subconscious level. Hoo, boy.

It probably worked the same with sound. Or did it?

He sat for a long time beside the bored private, and pondered the relationship of an invisible armadillo to the universe.

And came up with a plan.

Two nights later, an emergency staff meeting convened to discuss a rash of "unexplained phenomena." The primary phenomenon also attended, unnoticed.

The base security chief, a captain named Arthurs, was quick to pooh-pooh theories of ghosts or invisible aliens. "Either someone's pulling pranks in very bad taste," he said, "or we have an inside agent or saboteur."

One scientist, whom everyone but Arthurs called "Will," was skeptical. "What sort of sabotage is it to push boxes together, or pull all the books off a bottom shelf?" he asked.

"The agent was probably looking for information in the books," said Arthurs. "He read them at the desk, and dropped them in a pile as he discarded them."

"In the dark?" snorted Will. "You said six witnesses walked past my office during that period. But nobody saw any lights."

"We all work overtime, Will," scoffed Captain Joan Postlewaite, one of the smokers Dick had "met" on the elevator. "Why would anyone notice if the lights were on?"

"Dr. Weismuller, did you tell anyone about anything you'd found in a book in your library?" Arthurs asked Will.

"I haven't looked at any of those books since I unpacked!" said Will disgustedly. "But I might need one of them ten minutes from now, so I do hope you'll return them ASAP."

"We need to process them as evidence," said Arthurs. "You should have them back within a week or so."

"A *week or so*? But . . . but . . ." Will sputtered into incoherence.

"Were any of the boxes opened?" Joan asked.

"No," said Arthurs. "We think the perpetrator may have moved them over by Dr. Dupres' desk to get at something behind them."

"But the boxes were set against the wall!" protested Dupres. "There was nothing behind them. They were just personal effects I hadn't unpacked yet."

"The intruder didn't know that," said Arthurs. "Maybe he pulled them over to your desk to examine, but was interrupted."

"Yeah, right. Who interrupted him?"

"We don't know. We'll return your effects as soon as they've been processed. Probably within two weeks."

"But you said you'd have Will's books back in a week!"

"The books get priority. The perpetrator handled them individually, so they're more likely to yield clues. Also, Dr. Weismuller says he needs his books for his research. Did we take anything you require for your own work, Dr. Dupres?"

"My coffee mug would be useful," muttered Dupres.

"I'm sure we can find you a mug," said the man whom Arthurs addressed as "General." "Meanwhile, Captain Arthurs has my full confidence. Everyone please cooperate with his investigation. He's just seeking the truth, like the rest of you."

A phone rang. The general picked it up. "Williams. Yeah. Do that."

Crouched under the conference table, Dick saw the phone cord jiggle as Williams put down the receiver. "I've been going at this from the wrong end," the armadillo muttered wonderingly.

But this room was too public. He inched carefully around table, chair and human legs to reach the general's, then sniffed to be sure of the scent. *If anybody has a private office, he does,* thought the armadillo. He waited while the scientists chewed up theory after unsatisfactory theory. For some reason, no one suggested that an invisible armadillo might be trying to reach a telephone.

The meeting finally broke up without conclusions. Dick managed to follow General Williams out without tripping anyone.

"I don't care how! Just do it!" Buffalo Bill Williams barked, and slammed the telephone. "Damned dry cleaners," he muttered, glancing at his watch.

"Wha . . . ?" said Dick, awakening in his corner by the file cabinet. He saw Williams arise and cross the room. The lights went out, the door slammed, the general's footsteps receded down the hallway. Dick stood and stretched, listening for any more footsteps, then swung into action.

"If you can't bring the armadillo to the phone, bring the phone to the armadillo," he chuckled, hooking the phone cord with one digging claw.

He pulled. The phone slid off the desk with what, to an armadillo's ears, was an awful crash. The dial tone hummed in the upturned handset. Dick listened again for footsteps, then nudged the phone's base upright.

His blurry eyes couldn't read the keypad numbers, but the top three rows were obviously one through nine. That left the bottom two rows to figure out.

Dick's digging claws weren't designed for punching keys, but he did possess one superb precision instrument. His ant-catching tongue probed the bottom left-hand button. The receiver blurted a series of tones. He hurriedly cut off the call. Bottom left: "redial" button.

He tried the center button, next-to-bottom row. A single tone: '0'? He got the dial tone again, pushed '9', then re-hit the center button.

"Thank you for calling Hawaiian TelCom," said the telephone. "This is Louise. How may I help you?"

Now the moment of truth. He hummed a note, and focused his finely tuned ears on the responding vibration. He was *almost* in sync with human reality anyway. He just had to make the receiver vibrate a tiny bit differently. . . .

"Hello?" said Louise. "Hello?"

"Uh, hello. What's the area code for Brazito, Missouri?"

"One moment please. That area code is 573."

"Thank you." She'd heard him on the first try! He got the dial tone back, then dialed 1-573-555-1212.

"What city, please?"

"Uh, Brazito, Missouri."

"What listing?"

"Uh, Appollonasia Duenckel. D-u-e-n-c-k-e-l, I think."

"One moment, please. We have an 'A. Duenckel', sir. Here's that number. . . ."

He listened, then punched the "hang up" button and dialed again. The phone rang four times before a rather sleepy voice answered.

"Hello? And you'd better not be a reporter."

"Hello, Appy? Hi. It's Dick."

"Dick who? Wait a minute. If this is a crank call, there are curses that'll reach a man, even if I don't know his name."

"Uh, what if I'm not a man? Thanks for the sandbox, by the way."

Pause. "Sander's not here. Where are you, Dick?"

"Uh, on vacation. Can you take a message for him?

"Certainly. I don't know when he'll get it, but go ahead."

"Tell Sander, 'Greetings from the Big Island of Hawai'i.' Tell him this: 'You hold the keys to unlock the soul and end the world . . . Weather's fine. Wish you were here.' "

"I'll tell him. Take care of yourself, Dick."

"You too, Appy."

"Oh, and Dick?"

"Yes?"

"Next time, call a little earlier? It's two o'clock in the blessed morning here."

"Oh. Sorry."

"All right. 'Bye."

"'Bye."

He eyed the phone's handset, considered his next move, and decided his next move was simply to wait.

"Beepbeepbeepbeepbeepbeepbeep," screamed the phone.

Someone in the hallway finally heard the noise. A few minutes later, three MPs darted through the door, combat style, one covering the other, fanning out left and right. Dick scrambled out the open door between them, and was gone.

XXVII

And Thirty-Eight
Deer Died for His Sins

Harlan Chillingworth had flown before, twice: once to get to boot camp, and once when he'd washed out. But a C-130's Spartan benches were nothing like the first-class section of a 767.

That was the problem with the military, he thought, reclining in the luxurious red-and-blue airline seat. The military had no style anymore. A while back, he'd rented "Elizabeth: The Golden Age" because it was rated R and Cate Blanchett was hot. The sex had proven rather disappointing, but the film had still made a deep impression. He'd started renting other medieval films. Gleaming suits of armor. Sailing ships gilded and carved from figurehead to the sterncastle. Cannons spewing death from the mouths of bronze lions' heads.

"Shoulda been born a century ago," he muttered. "Two centuries. Whenever. Knights in armor. That's what it's all about."

No more. Tanks were terrifyingly ugly. Humvees were the ugliest truck ever built. Apache helicopters—the Apaches should sue—all lumps and spindles and harsh angles. B-2s like giant bats. F-15s with lumpy, two-barreled bodies, squatting like toads. And A-10 Warthogs—*warthogs*, for Chrissake! Not a lion's head anywhere. Where was the romance of war?

But the rifle had been beautiful. For Harlan Chillingworth, abandoning the rifle had been like Moses giving up the Tablets. A prophecy had come true: *his* prophecy. He'd known the gun was going to kill someone, and it had—even though it had just been a sort of soggy crunch under the gunstock, not the muzzle flash and a CRAHCK! of large-caliber ammunition that he'd pictured. He'd halfway expected the rifle to go off and kill him as he drove the butt down on that damned reporter's neck.

But maybe it would still kill someone the proper way. The prophecy could come truer, even if he wasn't there to see it.

If I hadn't drunk so much, he thought, *maybe I could've figured out how to get it through the airport. Okay, Harlan, no more vodka.*

But he'd been clever enough, so far. They weren't going to find that little asshole reporter's body, not in that old farm well. He'd left McDermont's car in Springfield Regional Airport's general parking lot, so they'd figure the little shit had gone off somewhere without bothering to turn the car in. Then Harlan had hitchhiked back for the Karmann Ghia, and left it in a shopping center parking lot. He'd never registered the Karmann's title, so he didn't figure the police would trace it.

And it had been real hard, but he'd wiped his fingerprints off that lovely rifle and locked it in the Karmann's weird front-end trunk, then taken a cab back to Springfield Airport.

A stewardess approached: silver-haired, craggy-tanned, lean almost to the edge of bony.

"Can I refill that for you, sir?" she asked, flashing an overly-white smile.

Probably false teeth, Harlan thought. *I might've flown her, 30 years ago. Damn women's lib and unions, anyhow.*

He handed her his glass. It was just champagne. You couldn't get drunk on champagne. "Ma'am, could I ask you a question?" he drawled.

"Yes, sir?"

"Ma'am, if you're still up here, who's raising the next generation of little airline pilots?"

She flashed that pearly smile again, a little tensely. "My daughter is, sir." She walked away with his glass.

"Probably while she's working as a waitress, 'cause they got no stewardess jobs open," muttered Harlan. "Granny stewardesses. What a concept."

Stoppit, Harlan! Don't even think about other women! Knights in armor! You're on a crusade, goddammit. She's gonna see your fine new clothes and your new attitude, and know that you're a changed man, that it's all gonna be different. . . .

That, or he'd threaten to kill himself. That had worked before. He'd have to buy another gun when he got to Honolulu.

Then he'd drive to Kapoha or whatever it was and find her. *Hawai'i might be a big island, but it's just an island,* he thought. *It can't be that hard.*

Meanwhile, a tow truck was hitching up to the Karmann Ghia. As the truck's hydraulics raised the car's front end, the rifle slid backwards over an improperly stowed tire iron, accidentally dislodging the gun's safety catch. The gun slid to the rear wall of the trunk, where the trigger guard came to rest against the mouth of an empty vodka bottle. Then the tire iron slid into the rifle, with just enough force to push the trigger guard over bottle's mouth, gently but firmly pressing the trigger.

CRAHCK! went the rifle. The high-caliber bullet easily tore through the Karmann Ghia's thin sheet metal, which deflected the projectile just enough that it passed through the skull, brain, and left eye of a 50-year-old mother of four on vacation from Enid, Oklahoma, where she had worked, rather bad-temperedly, as a receptionist at her ex-husband's chiropractic office.

And so Harlan's second prophecy—that he'd be gone when his first prophecy came truer—was fulfilled, albeit in what appeared at first glance to be a purposeless fashion. But in fact, the receptionist's death actually had many purposes, though none likely to console the bereaved. One purpose was to start an inheritance battle, in which two of her offspring discovered their true feelings about their family, and one, the 23-year-old, was involuntarily "outed"—a change that, she decided, had its drawbacks, but at least it stopped some of the pressure to find a husband.

Another purpose was to provide a job opening for a 25-year-old unwed mother of two, who improved the quality of life for nearly all who came to the chiropractor's office and gave the chiropractor better head.

A third purpose was to provide a high school senior with some truly "killer" wheels. He bought the Karmann Ghia for $950 at a police auction, repainted it metal flake black at the school auto shop, airbrushed ruby-red lips around the bullet hole and droplets of ruby metal flake blood trickling from the corner of the mouth and down the fender, and named the car "Christine."

Another purpose was to place the rifle, eventually, in the hands of a police sergeant, an avid hunter, who lovingly cleaned traces of blood from the grooves in the gunstock, figuring they'd gotten there when a previous owner posed with a big buck. The rifle has since reduced Missouri's deer overpopulation by 26 bucks and 12 does (7 wounded and unaccounted for), including a state champion 13-point buck, whose mounted head may someday be donated to Bass Pro Outdoor World, its successor or spiritual inheritor, by the sergeant's vegetarian grandchildren.

Yet another purpose was to provide a liver transplant that lengthened a 66-year-old man's life by four days, in which he repented and backslid at least six times—no one was sure how he ended up, as he was in a coma by then. At his funeral, a relative joked that his body rejected the liver because its donor was a teetotaler. She wasn't. But no body really likes liver.

And another purpose was to generate an arrest warrant on Terrence Harlan Chillingworth for involuntary manslaughter and illegal possession of a firearm, after the police got his name from the Kharmann Ghia's previous owner. A small news item about this appeared on a local TV station's website, where it came to the attention of Appy Duenckel.

Also the attention of the FBI.

Also the DIA.

Also the president of an Islamic nonprofit that had once received a check for $257.98 from a Cayman Islands account linked indirectly to a known associate of Osama Bin Laden.

Also the Israeli Mossad (despite its student agent in Springfield being distracted by a heavy date with a co-ed "sleeper" agent of Persian extraction).

(The Russians missed it.)

Also an obscure office in the French aerospace industry.

Also the Northern Alien Spaceship Advocacy.

One of them acted.

XXVIII
That Gnawing Sensation

Sander was awakened by small claws scratching his belly. He nearly fell out of the chair before he remembered Ratty-san.

The little rat scrambled from Sander's shirt and hopped to the floor. "It's hot," Ratty-san squeaked, wrinkling his nose. "And it smells. Papa-san?"

"What, Ratty-san?"

"How long do rats live?"

"You don't want to know."

"Papa-san, is it that bad?"

Sander considered, then opted for honesty. "I think they normally live a year or two. But I may be wrong."

There was a moment of silence.

"Fuck you, Papa-san. Why didn't you dream an elephant?"

"Inside an airliner?" Sander shuddered, remembering the imaginary rhinoceros. He took a deep breath, then wished he hadn't. The air conditioning had been off since their second flight ended. It was like trying to breathe cheese.

He decided to try the intercom again. He walked over to the door and pushed the "talk" button. "Hello?" he said.

Not even static.

"I'm hungry," squeaked his companion.

"Me, too, I think," said Sander, though the air was a distinct appetite suppressant. "There are those rations—but they look like they were packed a long time ago."

"Especially in rat years," said the rat, reproachfully. "Could I eat this magazine?"

Sander eyed the publication dubiously. "I wouldn't eat the cover. I'm not sure that slick paper would be good for you."

"I'm a rat," said Ratty-san. "I can eat anything."

"Thus spake the rat, as he gobbled up a tasty tray of Warfarin," said Sander. "Okay, it's your stomach. Just don't eat the nipple-bleach pictures when I'm watching, okay?"

He leaned back on the sticky seat, and noticed a strand of sweet odor weaving through the general cheesiness. He drew a warm, limp, sticky mass from his pocket. The chocolate bar had finally succumbed to the laws of thermodynamics.

"A year to live," mumbled the rat, gnawing a magazine corner. "It's just not fair. Hey, what's that?"

"I'm sorry, Ratty-san," said Sander, peeling the flaccid chocolate bar's paper jacket. "You're right. It's not fair. No matter how long you live, it's never fair."

"It might be more fair, Papa-san, if I could try some of *that*," said the rat, working his nose energetically.

Sander stared at the brown mass in his hand. He'd had a wide range of chocolate experiences, from stale Oreos to a dark chunk of heaven from The Fudge Factory in St. Louis, where crews danced and chanted over the hot fudge as they mixed it. This current goo promised a new low. Still, chocolate was chocolate.

"Sure," he said. He ripped off a third, unwrapped it as best he could—the gooey chocolate unfolded with the foil—and set it down on the floor. "Don't eat the foil. Maybe I'm wrong, Ratty-san. Maybe rats live longer than that in captivity."

"You're going to put me in a cage, Papa-san?"

"Ratty-san, we *are* in a cage." Sander shook his head, then straightened. "And we need to get out—especially since they seem to have forgotten us. If you've got so little time, you shouldn't have to spend it in here." He looked around. "I wonder how thick these walls are?"

"I started a hole earlier," said the rat. "The wood is not very thick. But then I hit steel."

"Really? Where?"

Sander examined Ratty San's test hole, thought hard, went to the inside-outside intercom and punched the button one last time. No response. He began wiggling and prying at the button, finally pulled it loose, then attacked the metal socket that had held it. After a few more minutes, it also came off as well.

The wire behind it disappeared into a tiny hole in the wood.

Sander looked at the bit of metal in his hand, and sighed. "Destruction of government property. Now they've got another charge to hang on me. But this wire's gotta go through."

Using the metal piece, he began prying splinters from the edge of the hole.

Heavy machinery rumbled outside. There was a crunch and a jolt, then the noise of something large sliding under the floor.

"God, here comes the forklift again!" said Sander.

He braced himself as best he could. The module jerked into motion, careened like an elevator on a pendulum, then jolted to a halt. The forklift scraped out from under them. Then a new vibration rumbled up through the floor. The crate lurched again. Sander lost his footing and fell backward into the seat.

"I bet this is a truck," he shouted to Ratty-san. "I wish I had a seatbelt."

For the next hour, as they jerked and rumbled along, Sander tried to brace himself and chip at the hole around the intercom wire. The crater slowly grew to nickel size before he reached bare metal. But instead of piercing the crate's steel skin, the wire disappeared upward between the wood and metal layers.

Meanwhile, Ratty-san had enlarged his earlier hole to two inches in diameter. Sander dropped down to help him. "Stand back," he said, and kicked hard at the hole, then went to work prying off the loosened splinters.

30 minutes later, the hole had grown another two inches. And it was getting harder to breathe.

"If we keep it up, maybe we can get a hole big enough for me to kick at the steel itself. But I gotta rest a minute," Sander panted. Effort, tension, bad air and truck motion had combined into nausea. "Stand clear!" he gasped, and gave the wall another desperate kick. Pain shot through his bruised foot. But at least it distracted him from his stomach—and the fact that CO_2 must be building up in the air, slowly killing them.

Then the motion stopped. Moments later, pounding and grating noises began coming from the far side of the crate's door.

"Ratty-san," whispered Sander. The rat ran up his body to sit on his shoulder, as the door slowly, jerkily opened. A blast of welcome cool air cut like a cheese knife through the atmosphere. Man and rat blinked against the bright light.

On the truck bed outside, surrounded by fresh air and pines, stood four men in cowboy hats and boots, Western-style shirts and faded jeans. The man in the lead held a crowbar he'd used on the door. With a full, salt-and-pepper beard and mild pot belly, he resembled Santa Claus at a younger, boozier stage of life.

"Pee-*you*!" said the jolly middle-aged elf. "I bet you're right glad to be out of *here*. Welcome to Arizona, Mr. Keynes."

"Thank you. Uh, who are you?" Sander asked, numbly.

"Martin Origen," said the elf, extending his hand. "NASA."

"NASA?"

"Not *that* NASA."

XXIX

The Real Purpose
of the Soviet Union

As it so happened, Martin Origen owned an aged Dodge Power Ram 50. Sitting in the passenger seat, Sander felt a wave of nostalgia for the little old truck that he'd driven so briefly. Martin's truck had almost no rust, but years of wind-blown sand had scoured the gray paint down to bare metal in places.

"Damn good thing we stopped when we did," Origen remarked, as they drove through the pines of Longhouse Plateau. "Sorry about the bad air. Shoulda realized the crate wasn't running right. That grocery bag at your feet's got some of your personal effects, by the way. We intercepted 'em a couple days ago. You might want to change. That jumpsuit kinda sticks out."

In the bag were the clothes he'd been wearing when he was arrested. His wallet was there, but the money and fake ID were gone. There were even the folded hard copies of Hawai'i maps that he'd been carrying. They'd found the cash under the Odor Eater pads in his shoes—but had missed the three $100 bills in the little pocket that Appy had created in the double-fold of cloth over his pants zipper, and another tucked behind the jeans' leather label. Sander was a little surprised at that. But then, those people missed whole drug shipments.

The plaid shirt that Appy had bought him wasn't exactly his style, but it beat Prison Orange. He unzipped the jumpsuit to change. Ratty-san tumbled out into his lap.

"Hey," the rat said sleepily.

"Sorry, Sander mumbled. "I forgot you were there."

"Huh?" said Martin.

"Uh, nothing," said Sander.

"I'm going under the seat, where it's safe," grumbled the rat. "I *have* to get some sleep."

"Uh, Martin, how'd I end up in Arizona?" Sander asked. "And who exactly are you guys?"

"First questions first," replied his host. "You're here 'cause you were mistakenly scheduled to get incinerated as hazardous waste, but the disposal facility where they were shipping you was still on hold, so they diverted your crate to Luke Air Force Base for shipment to a secure warehouse in Nevada. Only we picked you up instead."

"And you're NASA. But not *that* NASA."

Origen nodded. "Darn tootin'. We used to be the Northern Arizona Saucer Advocacy. But then we recruited some NORAD guys up in Alaska and a branch opened up in Idaho. So we changed the name to Northern Alien Spaceship Advocacy and kept the acronym. It's helped sometimes—just take advantage of the confusion, not actually break the law. But I suspect liberating an Air Force truck, an Army quarantine module and a government 'guest' just might get us into some hot water."

"You stole that flatbed?"

"Nah, not really—'just got it assigned to us. Easy computer job, once you crack the codes. We've got some pretty good hackers in NASA. We know more about the CIA's secret UFO files, for instance, than Keyhoe and Davidson ever found out."

"Keyhoe and Davidson?"

"'Couple of first class UFOlogists. One was a retired Marine Corps major, the other a Ph.D. in chemical engineering. They nearly blew the lid off the CIA files, with Mike Wallace's help."

"Oh."

"No need to feel embarrassed, Mr. Keynes—no reason you should've known about 'em. The government's been awful good at keeping the shades pulled on the UFO War."

"War?"

"Sure. They've been at it since the '50s. The aliens must've had a listening post on the moon. They didn't get too upset until we started broadcasting images of atom bombs, but since then they've been down here pretty regular. The local governments keep chasing 'em off. That's what NORAD was really for.

"NORAD?"

"Matter of fact, that's what the whole Cold War was about. The U.N. knew about the saucers, and figured they had to develop the technology to stop 'em if they needed to, but they knew if the public got in on it, the aliens would find out the minute it hit the airwaves. So we had the Rosenbergs slip the Russians enough secrets to get the arms race going. Then we started the space race, so we could send Apollo to the moon to find their transmitter. The minute the US managed to achieve lunar orbit, the Russkies dropped out."

"Uh—that makes sense, uh, I guess, but . . ."

"We went up and made a landing or two, just for form, then left, as if we hadn't found anything. Then we started Star Wars to develop anti-spacecraft technology, and the minute we got those programs established, the whole freakin' Soviet

216

Union had no use anymore. So the CIA, World Bank and UNICEF pulled their subsidies, and the USSR collapsed. So how come you tried to hijack that plane, Mr. Keynes? If you don't mind my asking."

"I didn't try to hijack a plane. I found a fingernail clipper in the restroom at the Los Angeles airport."

"Huh. Seems reasonable. Hell of a lot you can do with a nail clipper. Especially if it's got one of those manicure files. Even more if it's got alien chip technology. So why'd you risk flying? That's kinda like screaming, 'Catch me!' "

"We—I was going to Hawai'i."

"Hawai'i, eh? That makes sense, too. Hey, I remember somethin' . . ." He grabbed a cell phone from its perch on the bench seat between them, and punched in a number while steering the pickup down Longhouse Pass with his knees. "Don't worry," he said. "This phone's got a double scrambler. Hello, Ho? 'Got the package. Say, where's Harlan Chillingworth right now? Yeah, I'll wait. Do tell. Okay, get us a couple. Nah, coach. See you in two-three hours. 'Bye." He set the phone down. "That was Ho Chi Minh Begay. Good guy. Full-blooded Navajo. His daddy was in 'Nam, and decided he was fightin' for the wrong side. Ho's gonna meet us in Kayenta, with tickets and your new ID. You're now Andrew King of Tucson, Arizona, by-the-by."

"What was that about Harlan Chillingworth?"

"He just bought a first class ticket to Honolulu."

"Oh God. Oh, hell!"

"Yeah, if your girlfriend's there, she could be in big trouble. She was on the same plane with you, wasn't she?"

"Look, Mr. Origen . . ."

"Call me Marty."

"Marty, I'm grateful to you for getting me out of that crate, but I really do have to get to Hawai'i now, as fast I can."

"That's why I had Ho order the tickets. I bet he'll have us a flight booked before we get to Cow Springs."

"Uh-thanks, Marty. I'm *really* grateful, now."

"Think nothing of it, Sander. 'Least we could do for one of the Chosen."

"Uh—the chosen?'

"Sure. One of the Exalted, whom Those on High have touched."

XXX
Calling on the Sisterhood

For two days, Jenny had called the airline to ask if a Mr. Sandy Kinny was aboard each incoming flight. The airline had finally offered to help her file a missing person report. Jenny had hastily declined.

But if Sander had evaded custody, he might try to fly in under a different name. It seemed she had no alternative but to haunt the airport.

Her vigil was now in its third evening, and only one flight remained. The security guards knew her by sight now, if not by her real name. They cast sympathetic eyes in her direction as she sat on a concrete bench, watching the top of the escalator for the first trickle of debarking passengers.

More sunburned American tourists in screaming-bright aloha wear. More Japanese tour groups, pale-skinned and clustered as tightly as if they were still in a Tokyo subway, despite their outfits from Hilo Hattie's. More tired local businessmen in aloha shirts several shades less gaudy than the visitors'. More tearful, lei-festooned reunions.

And then, at the top of the escalator, there appeared . . .

Apollonasia Duenckel?

"Mom!" Jenny cried and ran toward the escalator.

Appy looked up in surprise, then trotted down the moving steps until a pair of Japanese honeymooners in matching orange-and-blue floral outfits blocked her progress.

"Jenny!" she called, anxiety etched across her face. "We have to get you out of this place, right now!"

"What? Mom, Sander never arrived! He's not on the flight with you, is he?"

Appy shook her head. "I'm sorry, hon! Uncle Gilroy told me he hadn't arrived!" She reached the escalator's base and side-stepped around the newlyweds, just in time to collide with her daughter's hug. "Listen, Jenny," she gasped, "we have to leave this airport, *now*. Harlan may be in Hawai'i."

"Harlan?"

"He's wanted for negligent homicide. A gun went off in the trunk of a Karmann Ghia he owned."

"Huh? Harlan would never drive a foreign car," said Jenny. "He always bought American—wait, McDermont had . . ."

Appy nodded. "When I couldn't reach you, I called *MorningStar* to confirm your phone number. They said McDermont was missing, that he went off to look at a car and never came back. Harlan may have lured him in with the Karmann Ghia, then—I don't want to think about it. . . ."

"Oh my God. I've been meeting every flight. . . ."

"Jenny, we have to get you out of this airport, *now*."

Jenny had three options at that moment. She could have fainted. She could have panicked. But instead, the third option kicked in: the personality she called the Numb One, the survivor who took over after Harlan had beaten her or trashed the place; the one who spoke softly and without emotion, said the right things, called her mother or the ER when she got the chance, made the right decisions, because her life depended on it. The one who'd finally called the Family Crisis Shelter, packed her bags and gotten herself out.

"Mom, if Harlan wasn't on your flight, this may be the safest place we could be," she said. "That was the last flight this evening. Let's get your baggage, then go to the coffee shop."

Her mother nodded. Jenny felt strange, telling Appy what to do.

Over coffee, they talked strategy. If Harlan had gotten McDermont to talk, then returning to the beach house was out (Jenny thought wistfully of the reef fish). So were the Banyan Drive resort hotels in Hilo, because Harlan was likely to book a room there. But as usual, Appy had a plan.

"Before I left, I got on the Net and got the names of some local SOBA members," she said.

"'SOBA'?"

"You remember. The Sisterhood of Old Bellydance Artists. One of them runs a B&B in Pāhoa. She's got an opening."

"Pāhoa? Mom, I've heard that place is pretty wild."

"Good," Appy said. "Maybe we can hire some protection there. And maybe get some clues about where Dick is."

"Why would they know about that in Pāhoa?"

"Honey, trust me. If you want to find a secret UFO research facility, you don't go to the local police."

An hour later, after getting dinner and buying a few essentials, they arrived in downtown Pāhoa: a 7-11, an ancient movie theater, a natural food grocery, and a block of rickety but brightly painted wooden buildings with covered boardwalks right out of a Wild West movie. A few bearded men in colorful and/or ragged T-shirts stood chatting over beers in the Akebono Theater parking lot, but no one acted especially threatening.

Following a map Appy had printed from the Web, Jenny turned onto a side street and pulled in the third driveway on the left. The Aveo's headlights revealed a rambling, faded blue structure with a wraparound second-story lanai.

"Doesn't look particularly luxurious," remarked Jenny.

"It's in better shape than *my* house," said Appy.

The main residence was on the second story. Nancy Wolf, a.k.a. Nancy Applebaum, a.k.a. Sarai, proprietor of the Pāhoa Pride Bed and Breakfast, met them at the head of the lanai stair. "Sister Asfura, I presume! So glad to meet you! And this must be Jenny. Do you do Balledi, too?"

"Mom taught me some when I was young," admitted Jenny. "But I haven't done it in years."

"Jenny's just coming off a bad marriage," explained Appy. "Her ex didn't approve."

"It's funny. That's how he met me," said Jenny. "A group of us danced at a friend's party. Some fraternity drunks crashed it and started trouble. Harlan came to our rescue...." She dropped her eyes. Harlan had stood those college bullies off like a gallant little knight. No wonder she'd fallen for him. No wonder he'd decided she needed "protecting." She sighed and added, "Doomed from the start."

"You poor thing," said their host, a tall, hollow-eyed, fifty-ish woman with waist-length black hair shot with a little gray. Her large, somewhat saggy breasts bounced unsupported under a tie-dyed T-shirt. "I don't put my own belly on display much anymore," she admitted. "But I have a few students. Come on in. I'll show you your rooms, then maybe we can talk dancer talk for awhile."

Soon they were spraddled on Nancy's eclectic collection of papasans, beanbags and Indonesian carved teak furniture, and sipping Malaysian Boh tea with turbinado sugar, cream and cloves. In the background, the TV muttered CNN.

"I hope you don't mind if I leave it on," said their host. "I want to get the latest on that Navajo hostage standoff. I'm one-eighth Cherokee, you know. So you danced professionally, Asfura?"

Appy nodded. "For over thirty years. The fair circuit, Greek restaurants in Kansas City and St. Louis, Seattle, a year in Alaska. Even San Fran, for a few months."

"Nobody's got that kind of experience, here," said their host enviously. "There are some decent dancers, but we just don't have the polish, the isolation. Wanna earn a little cash as a guest instructor while you're here?"

Appy shook her head. "We want to keep a low profile. Jenny's ex may be tracking her."

Sarai nodded. "I know how *that* goes. Hey, here's the story." She hit the remote. The sound of the newscast suddenly filled the room.

". . . Standoff in Northern Arizona took a strange turn to-day. Authorities now say some of the holdouts are not Navajos, but members of an obscure flying saucer cult. One hostage is believed to be Sander Keynes, the so-called "Saucer Man," who disappeared with his female companion after discovering an alleged UFO in Missouri. Federal officers have surrounded the compound on an isolated mesa. . . ."

XXXI

Not another Ruby Ridge

"Fuck," said Ho Chi Minh Begay.

"Fuck," said his father, Homer Begay. He put down the cell phone and rattled off something in Navajo. His wife listened sorrowfully, nodded, then spoke in Navajo to the children.

"I'm too old for this shit," said the elder Begay.

"You always wanted a revolution," pointed out his son.

"A revolution, yes," said Homer. "Not a fucking Ruby Ridge."

"Well, they keep saying they want a peaceful conclusion," pointed out Sander, hopefully.

"Yeah, they just told me that again," said Homer. "The question is, do I dare believe them? They've offered Martha and the kids safe passage down the canyon. All of them but Ho." He shook his head. "Now I've gotta think about what happened to that guy's wife when she stuck her head out the door at Ruby Ridge."

"They *don't* want another Ruby Ridge," said Martin. "Too much publicity. But if something happened up here, who'd know it?"

"Look, it's me they want," said Sander. "Why don't you just tell them I'll come out, if they leave the rest of you alone?"

"Look, Sander," said Homer. "I know you white men are supposed to know more than us poor *Dineh*, but let me point out a few things. First, by your own account, you're wanted for attempted skyjacking. I know, you say the charges are crap. And Marty and Ho didn't kidnap you. But those men out there disagree. They've got us either for kidnapping or for harboring a fugitive. No cop in Arizona'd pass up the chance to bag a Joe on charges like that."

"A Joe?" asked Sander.

"A Navajo," explained Martin. "Not a respectful name. Don't use it."

"Second point. Again, by your own account, they're locking up everybody who's had anything to do with that UFO. So what happens if my family goes out the door?" He answered his own question. "Those bastards will stick them in some damn crate like Martin busted you out of, and haul them off to that fucking fort in Missouri. We *Dineh* have this thing about being hauled off our land. We're never sure we'll get to come back."

"Pop, look," said Ho. "I don't know how much choice we've got. This isn't a *hooghan*, with nice, thick earth-and-log walls. It's a wooden house, and they've got assault rifles. The bullets will go right through these planks."

"I know, son. I know," said Homer grimly, peering through a crack in the door. "That's why Mr. Keynes has to stay inside and play hostage. If he goes, we're all done."

Sander sighed. "I'm beginning to think you should have left me with the CIA."

"That wasn't the CIA," said Martin.

"Excuse me?"

"That was the MIB."

"The MI—nahhh. . . ."

"Mutual Investigations Bureau. 'Clandestine branch of the NIA. They put together info from all the other agencies, then check it out. Bush the First started it, Bush the Second made it bloom. They always say they're CIA or FBI so folks won't know there's an MIB."

"Uh, okay," Sander said.

"Too bad we can't call your alien buddies for a lift," joked Ho grimly.

"I never saw any aliens," said Sander. "I just saw the saucer." He glanced around the tiny, unpainted cabin. He couldn't believe that a whole family lived in this place. If the FBI didn't flush him out, claustrophobia would.

Mrs. Begay and her three daughters huddled against the far wall. Ho kept watch with a well-worn deer rifle at one window, and Martin, with a .22, at the other—both men trying not to become targets in the process. Beside the door sat Homer, an aged M-16 cradled lovingly in his arms. The cabin had a fine view of the canyon and the trail up to the mesa. But one whole wall was windowless, a blind side. If the Feds decided to, they could rush this place easily.

"Any chance some of your relatives will come to the rescue?" asked Martin. "I mean, there's Begays all over this country."

"What, an *Indian uprising?*" said Ho. "We've tried that. It doesn't work."

"There was a place called Bosque Redondo," explained Homer. "Back in the Civil War, a batch of Union troops from California arrived in Santa Fe too late to help run the Rebs out of New Mexico, so they decided to round up the *Dineh* instead. We had peach orchards then, and fields of corn. They burned us out, starved us out, hauled us all down to Bosque Redondo on the Pecos, stuck us in pueblos like fucking Hopi, and said they were going to *teach us how to farm.* But the soil was bad, the water was alkali, the weather was wrong. There was a *reason* why nobody was farming there. They hauled ten thousand of us to that reservation. When they finally let us go home, there were seven thousand left." He glared at the two whites. "So now we don't plant peach orchards. We graze sheep, keep moving, keep our baggage light. We let you say stupid things and we grin, because we know you'll be gone in a few decades. . . ."

"Cultures like yours burn out quick," added Ho. "It's the damn Hopi we really have to worry about."

". . . And we don't pick fights with the US Government," concluded Homer, "unless they try to take our children."

"Besides, it's bad for tourism," added Ho.

"A lot of people are going to be real pissed off that I let this get out of hand," said Homer. "But then, they're generally pissed off at me anyway."

"Well, aren't they *trying* to take your kids?" asked Sander. "Why not call your relatives and tell them the Feds want to haul your children off to a fort in Missouri?"

"I tried," said Homer tiredly. "They're jamming the damn cell phone. The only number I can get is the FBI man."

"Let me try something," said Martin. "Sander, watch the window, please."

"Uh, all right." Sander crawled across to where Martin crouched, but refused the proffered gun. He took a quick glance out the window, ducked back, waited, and glanced again.

Meanwhile, Martin opened the briefcase he'd brought in from the car, and pulled out a notebook computer. He opened it, extended a little telescoping antenna, began typing, then shook his head. "They're jamming my modem, too."

"So what's left?" said Sander. "Smoke signals?"

"*Smoke signals?*" Homer exclaimed in disbelief. "That's *plains* Indians, you fuckhead! Do we look like fucking Sioux?"

"Easy, Pop," said Ho. "He's just an ignorant white guy from Missouri. How would he know?"

"Smoke signals," muttered Homer disgustedly. "Okay, I got an idea." He picked up the cell phone and punched in the one working number. "Yeah, Special Agent Shipley, I know it's you. Or I know it's *allegedly* you. I still can't rule out that you're a batch of drug runners posing as Feds. By the way, are you any relation to that asshole Agent Shipley that we cornered at Round Rock in 1892, after he tried kidnapping our kids for that religious school? Nah—Indian Agent, not FBI. Oh—from Boston, eh? Welcome to the Southwest, Agent Shipley. Say, I noticed Sampson Begay's squad car down in the canyon. I don't suppose you could patch me through to him? Yeah, I know you'd rather I talked to you. Yeah, you're a trained hostage negotiator—or so you say. But you haven't even established that anyone here's a hostage, have you? Why don't you put me through to a real expert on Navajos, like Sam? Besides, Sam's a duly constituted authority here in Dinetah, whereas you're just a foreign emissary, even if you aren't a drug runner. Yeah, I'm sure this is just a big misunderstanding that'll all be worked out. Meanwhile, we all want to avoid another Ruby Ridge, don't we? Or a Waco or a Wounded Knee? So why don't you just put me through to Sam, so it won't all be on your head anymore."

Long pause. Homer grinned and winked. "Hi, Uncle Sam," he said, and switched to Navajo.

"Step one completed," he finally said, hanging up, then mused, "How come everyone in the FBI is a 'Special Agent'? Why don't they have any *regular* agents?"

The phone rang. Homer answered. "Hello? Hello, Agent Shipley. I see. Good. Now, if you'll just patch me through to Sam. . . . No, it's not that I don't trust you—well, actually, yes, I don't trust you—but even if I did, your *bosses* just don't have a lot of credibility here. We all want to avoid another Ruby Ridge, don't we?"

He waited, then spoke to someone else—presumably Sampson Begay—in Navajo, then addressed his wife in the same tongue. "Okay, we're getting Martha and the kids out," he announced. "The Feds agreed to let Sam take them to the Tuba City hospital for a few days, instead of sending them to Missouri. Meanwhile, Sam'll be talking on his squad car radio, all the way to Tuba. By tomorrow evening, every tribe in the country'll know about this. That's a lot of gambling dollars for media coverage." He sat in silence a moment, then added, "Sam says they're locking people up in Missouri because they're afraid of some alien disease. That true, Sander?"

"Do I look sick to you?" Sander asked, a trifle nervously. "Aside from the old bruises, that is?"

"Well, you do look a little pale. But then, what can I say? You're White."

Soon they heard a four-wheel-drive grinding slowly up the switchbacks toward the canyon rim. "That's Sam's Explorer," said Homer, listening. "All right. Here goes."

The SUV pulled up outside the cabin. "Hey, Homer!" called a voice from the vehicle.

"Come on in, Uncle," said Homer.

"I'd rather not, Homer! Those Feds really are all hinky about some kinda alien disease. They want me to wear a mask and gloves while I drive your kin down to Tuba."

"Is that true, Sander?" Homer asked loudly. "You got some disease that my kids might catch?"

"I don't think so," said Sander.

"What're the symptoms, Sam?" Homer yelled out the door.

"They say people who got exposed to that saucer are seeing things."

Homer turned to his guest. "Anything like that happen to you, Sander?"

Sander hesitated, then thought, *These people are risking their lives. At least be honest with them.*

"I've talked to an armadillo," he said. A tiny paw prodded his ribs. "And a rat."

Pause.

"So what's wrong with that?" asked Homer.

"Jeez, one of their own has a spirit vision, and they try to lock him up," said Ho disgustedly.

"An armadillo?" said Martin.

"He's fine," Homer yelled to Sam, added something in Navajo, got a response, and then shouted, "Okay, they're coming out. Remember our agreement."

"Will do," acknowledged Sam.

"*Ahe'hee.* And Sam?"

"Yeah?"

"See if you can get someone to check on Che and Fidel?"

"Sure."

"My brothers. They're out with the sheep," explained Ho to Sander.

The woman and children filed out. Soon Sam's 4WD was grinding its way back down to the canyon floor.

"Okay, time to hunker down," said Homer. "Now the psy-war starts."

The first move wasn't long in coming. The noise of the departing SUV was drowned out by the thrumming roar of helicopter blades. The chopper cruised directly over the cabin, so close that the floor shook. The noise receded, then increased as the copter came around for another pass.

Homer risked a quick glance out the window. "Now, that's adding goddamn insult to injury!" he exclaimed. "Buzzing us with an *Apache!*"

XXXII

Undercover, Underestimated, Under Desk

Being a poltergeist was especially fun the day after Dick's phone call to Appy. People were scrambling like ants on uppers, trying to avoid General Williams, or to look *very* busy if he caught them. Dick had to shift his sleeping spot three times, as teams of MPs moved equipment and furniture and muttering scientists moved them back. Two staffers suffered mysterious falls by dodging into the path of an also-furiously-dodging invisible armadillo.

The day culminated in another senior staff meeting, which the poltergeist of course attended.

"People, come to order!" roared Buffalo Bill, glaring at the unruly scientists in his charge. When they had settled down somewhat, he continued: "We're here to discuss an extremely grave security breach. At 22 hundred hours, oh-seven minutes last night, someone placed a call from my office phone. I, myself, had locked the office at approximately 21:55. The perpetrator accessed the room, made the call, locked the door again, and escaped down a brightly lit corridor. If he or she hadn't knocked the phone off the desk and left it, we might not have known anything was amiss.

"We hit the redial button, and learned that the call went to the personal phone of one Apollonasia Duenckel in Brazito, Missouri."

"Oooh . . ." moaned the armadillo under the conference table. If he could have slapped himself, he would have.

"Apolla-who?" asked Mike Dupres.

"Apollonasia Duenckel. The mother of Jennifer Duenckel-Chillingworth, Sander Keyne's canoe partner."

"My God. Could that poor woman have been inside the Object all of this time?" asked Joan Postlewaite, whom Dick now knew was an aerodynamics expert who ran the wind tunnel experiments.

"Get a grip, Captain," said Buffalo Bill. "Some fast food waitress solves the portal mystery in a few minutes, when we've been working on it for weeks? Then pops out one night, makes a phone call from a locked room, and disappears again?"

"Maybe she didn't have to solve it," volunteered Dupres. "Maybe the saucer let her in."

"And gave her a course in picking locks?" the general's voice dripped sarcasm. "I sincerely doubt it."

"The builders of that ship are probably as superior at locks as they are at stealth technology," pointed out Dupres. "Look how much luck we've had getting *in*." Then he suddenly stopped, dumbfounded at the connection he'd just made. "My god. Stealth technology. Could whoever built the Object have applied the same technology to some sort of personal device?"

"A stealth suit?" said Will Weismuller, and whistled. "Whoa. This is getting heavy."

At that moment, Captain Arthurs entered.

"You got it?" Buffalo Bill asked the captain, who nodded grimly.

The general accepted a flash drive from Arthurs and plugged it into his notebook computer. "People, the conversation I'm about to play was obtained by agents monitoring a foreign aerospace company that we shall leave unnamed. Said company had an illegal wiretap on Apollonasia Duenckel's phone. One of our agencies has a tap on that company's lines, per a Patriot Act investigation. The recording was delivered to us with remarkable alacrity—an indication of the urgency being given this project at the highest levels of our government."

(Actually, that speed was due mainly to a recent breakthrough in the computerized sorting of CIA message intercepts—but only one person in the room was privy to that fact. He smiled slightly, but said nothing.)

The computer's speakers came to life. Everyone listened, slack-jawed, to Dick's conversation with Appy.

"'The keys to unlock the soul and end the world,'" Weismuller repeated, after the tape ended. "What the hell does that mean?"

"What a weird voice," breathed Joan. "It really doesn't sound human."

"But with perfect Midwestern pronunciation," said Arthurs. "High pitched, yes, and distorted. But we believe it belongs to a human agent speaking through some sort of distortion device. And it is *not* Jennifer Duenckel. We digitally filtered for the distortion factors, then compared voiceprints with her home answering machine message. The two weren't even close."

Buffalo Bill leaned on the table with both hands. "People, we have an agent inside this facility. A very clever agent, with very sophisticated equipment."

"Who has to borrow your telephone to call a fast food waitress's mother?" asked Dupres. "And then leaves the phone off the hook?"

"We believe he was interrupted," said Arthurs.

"Aw, come on," said Dupres. "This person knocks over the telephone, then takes time to lock the door after himself? Moves books and boxes and leaves them where they'll obviously be noticed? That sounds to me like an amateur, or a small-time professional who's lucky but out of his depth. My guess is that if our visitor's human, then this Midwestern granny found out about the Facility and hired a local detective to look for clues of her daughter."

Amateur, eh? Out of his depth? thought Dick. *Well, maybe we'll do you a little special haunting, Dr. Dupres.*

Arthurs flashed a brittle smile. "Dr. Dupres, your area of expertise is alien intelligence. But mine is human intelligence."

"A statement rife with unconscious irony if ever I heard one," said Dupres dryly.

Arthur's smile hardened. "And how would a retired belly dancer in Missouri find out about a top-secret facility in Hawai'i?" he asked. "A gumshoe with a voice-disguising device that even we can't duplicate? That's more plausible than a clever agent who just doesn't have time to cover his tracks?"

"Your theories are both goddamn equally alarming," said Buffalo Bill. "Either there's been such a huge breach of security elsewhere that a granny in Missouri can discover us, or there's such a huge breach here that an agent can get into my locked office at will. Either way, we have to act. Captain, are the filtered versions here?"

"Yes. Saboteur M and Saboteur F," said Arthurs. "These are approximations, of course. There actually appear to be several different distortion effects, and we don't know exactly how much the original pitch was modulated. So we had the sound lab prepare two different versions, one male and one female."

The speakers came on again. A woman-like voice said, "Weather's fine. Wish you were here." Then a male voice repeated the phrase.

"People, one of those voices is the voice of our saboteur," said Buffalo Bill, melodramatically.

"We've been infiltrated by a cartoon character?" said Dupres.

"Do any of you recognize this voice?" asked Buffalo Bill. "No? Well, we're going to find him or her. The FBI will place an *authorized* wiretap on Ms. Duenckel. And as of now, *all* incoming and outgoing calls will be recorded. Everyone on this base will submit a voice sample. That will be all, people."

They stood to leave, still arguing. Dick wondered which pompous ass most deserved to be tripped up. He settled on Buffalo Bill, who fell into Dupres, who, flailing for support on his way down, accidentally grabbed the left breast of Captain Postlewaite, which would complicate their professional relationship for the rest of their period of association.

Later, under a table in the coffee room, where a steady rain of crumbs and spills supported a burgeoning cockroach nymph population, Dick had a leisurely snack and considered his options. So far, he decided, he'd not done well. He'd gotten Appy's phone bugged, given Sander's message to the US Government, and possibly lured Sander out here.

There was nobody sitting at that conference table, Dick thought, whom he would trust with the secrets the saucer was keeping. Scientists or not, their judgments were all clouded by ambition, with the possible exception of Karpov—and Karpov didn't care how knowledge was used, so long as he knew it. It was ironic, thought the armadillo: either the saucer had shown preternatural good judgment, or the world had really lucked out, because the only person Dick had met whom he would have entrusted with the saucer's secrets was an unassuming fish keeper who had already shown the good sense not to try to claim credit for the one of the biggest discoveries in human history.

And thanks to Dick, Sander might even now be headed for Hawai'i, into the clutches of all these ambitious men.

If the former fish feeder did come, Dick suspected, the TSA was a bigger danger than Captain Arthurs. But there wasn't much Dick could do about that. He didn't even know where the local airport was. Still, he shuddered to think what would happen if Sander found this place and tried to get in—especially now that, thanks to Dick, the base was on an even higher alert.

"Well, I've stirred up a hornet's nest anyway," Dick told himself. "I might as well keep stirring. Maybe I can slow them down. Maybe Sander can slip in during the confusion."

He went upstairs for a real meal, while plans began forming in his head. It was time for some *serious* haunting.

The next night, he got busy. First he tried striking at the heart of the matter. He entered the big garage-like room where the Object was kept. Two men—one to push, one to guide—were trundling the thing into the adjacent wind tunnel by themselves.

"If it's that light," Dick told himself, "maybe an armadillo can move it." (He'd taken to talking to himself out loud quite regularly now, since he was fairly sure no one else could hear him without a phone. If they did, so much the more confusion.)

He waited until the saucer stopped, then tried his hand—or forehead, rather. But for *him*, the saucer wouldn't budge.

"I guess that's the trade-off for me being able to use the portal," he speculated. "It must be almost as unreal to them as I am, and they feel the fraction of it that's real to them, or something like that. I don't know. Probably the 'something like that.' " He suspected that he might be able to tune his body a little differently and get the job done, the way he'd tuned his voice to the phone. But what if he became visible?

"On to Plan B," he said. The technicians were still doing things in the wind tunnel. The control room door was ajar. Inside, he smelled Captain Postlewaite.

She was sitting at the control panel and relaying instructions via intercom to the team in the wind tunnel. Dick eyed the situation. He couldn't interact with *humans*, but . . .

"Privates, we're now 30 minutes behind. Get a move on in there!" the woman barked, leaning with both hands on the console, as Dick backed up, gave a bull-like snort just for the heck of it, and charged full speed at her rolling office chair. At the last moment he put on the brakes, skidding on the tile floor, and slammed sideways into the chair, taking the blow on his armor. The chair spun into the console, smashing Joan's well-padded chest into its hard edge. She squealed, then clutched wildly as the chair tipped out from under her. Her hand swept across the console, hitting, among other things, the switch that activated the wind tunnel's huge fans. She landed hard on her buttocks and sat there, stunned, until she heard the frantic yells of the men in the tunnel. . . .

That had worked even better than expected. Dick trotted out of the room and headed for his next destination.

In the coffee room, Mike Dupres and Rupert Samuelson were rehashing the old "anthropomorphic alien" debate.

"But what we call consciousness is evolutionarily defined by our biology," maintained Samuelson. "Have you read that Frank Herbert novel, *Destination: Void*? Not a great novel, but it *is* a great Socratic dialogue on the nature of consciousness. It argues that consciousness derives from the interaction of basic biological drives—including the urge for sex."

"Oh, bull roar," said Dupres. "By that argument, if we cloned people, they wouldn't be conscious."

"No, they'd still be conscious, because they'd have all the hardware and software of a sexually reproductive creature," snorted Samuelson. He'd had the misfortune of being stuck with a first name that had no nickname that wasn't even sillier than his name was, dooming him to grow up formal and coldly defensive. Intent on his point, he barely looked at the Mr. Coffee as he reached for the pot. At that same moment, Dick got one claw firmly hooked around Mr. Coffee's electric cord.

"Hey!" Samuelson squawked as the machine suddenly slid past his hand. Dupres shrieked something much less polite, as the falling pot sluiced scalding coffee down his pant leg.

As Dick trotted from the room, the tone of the two scholars' argument changed drastically. It had been decades since anyone had called Samuelson a "god-damned moron."

Three doors down, Jim Dubinsky was showing Matt Meyers a digitized graphic model of infrared data he'd been collecting on the Object. "I've been working on this for a week," Dubinsky said proudly. "Every pixel equals a value on a ten-square-centimeter section of hull surface. We can also show an entire side of the hull, but screen resolution only allows one value per 400 square centimeters at that scale, so I had to devise subroutines to average the data."

"Cool," said Meyers. "How much trouble do you think it would be to adapt the program for other ranges of the spectrum?"

The screen flashed, then went black.

"What the . . . ?" breathed Dubinsky. "Damn—the power's off! I told them I needed a UPS on this machine. . . ."

"Jim, the ceiling lights are still on," observed his companion. "There's no blackout."

"Oh. Damn. What's wrong, then?" Dubinsky flicked the computer's on-off switch, then dropped from his chair and crawled under the desk to peer behind the CPU tower. He backed out again, then froze.

"Matt, you stepped on the surge protector."

"What?"

"The power strip. Six inches from your foot. It's off."

"Uh, I don't think I did, Jim."

"Matt. . . ."

"Okay. Sorry." Meyers reached down and flicked the switch. The screen lit up and hard drives whirred to life. " 'Oughta put that strip behind the desk, Jim," Meyers admonished.

"I didn't want to crawl back there every time I hooked something else into the system," Dubinsky said defensively.

"This is a Windows machine," observed Meyers. "Oughta switch to a Mac, if you're going to leave the power strip out like that. Four out of five times, though, it'll reboot okay."

The Object's glowing false-color image swam back into existence—then novaed and faded again.

"Dammit, Matt, you did it again! God, I need a smoke. . . ."

"Four out of five times, eh?" mused the armadillo, unheard. "Then three more times oughta do it. . . ."

Twenty minutes later, Buffalo Bill was getting an informal briefing from Arthurs, with the aid of a bottle of single malt Scotch.

"Hysterical blame-shifting, is my best guess," said the captain. "She dumped herself out of her own chair, and couldn't accept that she'd done anything so stupid. So she started raving about poltergeists." Arthurs took a respectful sip, and smacked his lips appreciatively. "Smooth, sir. Anyway, I recommend that Captain Postlewaite be relieved."

"Can't do it, Jeb," said Buffalo Bill. "Political ramifications. The damn broad's the only woman in our command structure. Besides," he lowered his voice, "between you and me, you just don't find boobs like that in the military too often. I'll give her a few days of R&R. I'll tell her the wind tunnel needs repairs, whether it does or not."

"Uh, respectfully, sir—she'll want to supervise the repairs."

Williams winced. "You're right. Okay, she's temporarily relieved, pending an enquiry. I'll see if Personnel can round us up another captain with boobs, just in case. So you've got all the voiceprints?"

"Yes, sir. Dupres was the last. He was threatening a civil rights complaint. I told him it was strictly voluntary, just like his participation in the project. I'd just consider that if he didn't cooperate, he no longer wished to participate."

"Good work!" The general knocked back his glass and poured another. (In fact, he knew, Dupres' participation was not entirely voluntary, but he saw no point in troubling Arthurs with that.) "Anything else?"

"Uh, there's those two chimpanzees. They're a mistake, sir. None of the scientists ordered animal subjects."

"Wonderful. Can we send'em back?"

"We haven't traced the source yet. It was extra-military—probably CIA. Conrad says we could keep them in one of the ETQ chambers until we know where they belong."

"ETQ chambers? Refresh my memory."

"Rooms designed for quarantining live ET's, if we happened to acquire such. Sir, if I may suggest—Joan's psych profile says she's fond of animals. They could be a good distraction."

"Splendid idea. You're doing a hell of a job, Jeb. Hell of a job. It's sure not the hell easy, keeping goddamn scientists in line." He took another sip. "Damn smooth. Hell, Jeb, back at Huntsville, we knew what to do with goddamn chimps. We shot 'em into space."

"You'd think that with all the brains here, sir, someone could find a good use for animal subjects," mused Arthurs.

"Hell, I can think of one myself," said Williams. "Have the monkeys look into the damn saucer. That's how you use monkeys. You use damn monkeys where you don't want to waste people."

"Excellent idea, sir," agreed Arthurs. "That new biologist—whatshisname? Jim Bob something—I'm sure he could design something like that."

"Hell, *I'll* do it. Oughta have a little fun, now and then."

"Good idea, sir," said Arthurs. "You could assign Captain Postlewaite to assist." A fine alcoholic warmth had spread from his tongue to his toes, making saboteurs, scientists and generals all seem faintly ridiculous.

"That's a damn fine suggestion, Captain Arthurs. Damn fine," said his ridiculous commanding officer, taking a noisy sip.

The general's phone rang. He picked up the handset. "Williams."

"Howdy, Buffalo Bill," piped a maddeningly familiar reedy voice. "Did you know your Head of Security was a total boob?"

The general clapped his hand over the receiver. "It's him!"

"What?"

"The infiltrator! Get to another phone and order this call traced!"

Arthurs bolted out, ran to his own office, fumbled the key into the lock, threw open the door and rushed in. But somehow his left foot didn't go where it should have. He arrived at his desk head first.

He awoke to the sight of one metal desk leg a few inches from his face. On the carpet nearby lay his telephone handset.

"Beepbeepbeepbeepbeepbeepbeep," it said.

XXXIII

The Night of the Living Bee Gees

As night fell on the mesa, the Great Rock Assault commenced.

To pass the time, Ho had been explaining the Navajo creation myth to Sander.

"Let's see," the former mused, "we've covered First Man, First Woman, First Boy, First Girl, Talking God, Calling God, Coyote, White Light of Dawn in the East, Blue Light of Noon in the South, Yellow Light of Twilight in the West, Blackness in the North. . . . Who'm I leaving out?"

"What about Changing Woman?" asked Martin.

"Uh, I don't think Changing Woman is one of the original *diyin Dineh,*" replied Ho. "Right, Pop?"

Homer responded with something very pointed in Navajo.

"Oh, come off it, Pop. They could get all this off the tribal website. Besides, you're a fine one to talk."

Homer responded angrily in Navajo. Ho replied with equal heat. Sander nervously eyed the weapons in both their hands.

Suddenly Homer shrugged and nodded. He smiled with his mouth, but his eyes were still angry. "My son says I'm rude, talking in front of guests in a language they don't know, when we may die here together," he said. "He may be right. He also says I'm not a very good Navajo myself. He may be right about that, too . . . no, he *is* right. I haven't heard the *nil chi'i* speak in my ears for years, and I never took their advice when they did. I haven't had a Blessingway ceremony since 'Nam. But I know this, Ho. It wasn't being a good Navajo, or a good son, to bring strangers to your mother's house to die."

"Wait a minute," Sander said. "Who said anything about dying here? I'll give myself up before I let anyone die."

"I'm sorry, Pop," said Ho, ignoring him. "That was stupid. I was taking Sander and Martin to the airport, and that cop came up behind us with his gumball machine lit up. He had a sedan, so I figured we could lose him in the desert. And we did, I thought. I didn't think about . . ."

"You didn't think about choppers. This isn't the damned 19th Century, Ho. You *always* gotta think about choppers."

"Look, why don't I just give myself up?" said Sander.

"There's one Navajo tradition I do believe in," said Homer. "When someone dies before his time, you break a hole in the north side of the home so the spirit can leave, and you abandon the house. I believe that. A mother shouldn't have to live in the same house with a son's death, or a husband's. Even if you give up, Sander, there's a good chance they'll come in shooting. I'm not taking that chance, even if it's certain I'll die elsewhere. When it's dark, I'm going to slip away from this house." He shook his head. "It used to be we owned the night. That was before damned night vision goggles."

"Too bad you didn't talk to Coyote instead of an armadillo, Sander," remarked Ho. "We could use a good trick right now."

Homer nodded. "Armadillos just dig in, curl up and wait."

"What about the rat, Pop?" said Ho. "Sander, what did the rat tell you?"

Sander cocked an ear. "The rat is scared silly. He asks if we'd mind if he went and hid under the house."

"The rat's with you, now?" Ho said.

What the hell, Sander thought, and nodded. "He rides in my shirt."

"Can you show him to us?" asked Martin, dubiously.

Sander shook his head. "'Sorry. I think I'm the only one who can see him."

Homer smiled. "Must've been some pretty good peyote."

"That tears it," said Ratty-san. "Nobody calls Papa-san a druggie." He popped out of Sander's shirt, scuttled over to an M-16 ammunition clip, and began tugging it across the floor.

"Hey, Ratty-san!" exclaimed Sander. "Where are you going with that?"

Ratty-san spat out the end of the clip for a moment. "Just over to the stove."

"Wait a minute! No you don't!" Sander reached for the clip, but Ratty-san had jerked it just out of range. Sander lurched forward and just managed to grab it. "Okay, you've made your point. Let go!"

Ratty-san hung from the clip by his teeth. He let go, dropping into Sander's lap. Sander looked up. All three of his companions were staring.

"*Really* good peyote," breathed Homer.

"I saw it move across the floor. Did anybody else see it move?" asked Martin, wide-eyed.

"We all saw it move," said Ho.

"So, Sander, what *did* the armadillo say?" said Homer. "Now I'm curious."

"He said lots of things," said Sander, then thought again, *what the hell*. "The last message I got from him said, 'You hold the keys to unlock the soul and end the world.'"

"Huh. Interesting," said Homer. "Did he . . ."

IN-A-GADDA-DA-VIDA HONEY, DON'TCHA KNOW THAT I LOVE YOU?

Twelve giant directional speakers shattered the desert's silence. The cabin floor shook with the bass line.

"They think we're fucking Noriega!" yelled Homer. But his voice almost disappeared in the din.

Hour after hour, the assault pounded on. Two hours of Iron Butterfly. Then Alice Cooper, then Eminem, then Snoop Dog, then Christmas Carols with Alvin and the Chipmunks. The cabin's occupants stuffed their ears with toilet paper, wrapped their heads in wool blankets, wadded another blanket for Ratty-san to hide in—but the noise still crawled into their eardrums through their own bones.

Sander thought he could hold out. But just before dawn, loudspeakers started playing "Staying Alive" over and over and over. Sander screamed, but couldn't hear his own scream. He cast about mentally for anything that he could think, and somehow keep thinking, that wasn't that awful music. But a howling hurricane of Bee Gees finally stripped away every rational thought—stripped away most of consciousness itself.

And drowning in the void between consciousness and dreams, Sander Keynes instinctively grasped the Second Key . . .

. . . And found another song playing, tiny but brave, in the far reaches of his skull. He began singing along, keeping it going like a tiny boat cutting a wake against giant waves of disco:

> Well, the surge rolls in and the surge rolls out
> And the breakers keep on breaking and
> And the searchers, they would all long since have gone

But her eyes keep them out on the waves
And the surf ski riders brave the spray
Trying to find a body for her to take home . . .

He didn't try to think of the rest of the song—just kept weaving the same verse stronger and stronger, an incantation against Bee Gee overload. Slowly, the beach swam into focus. Huge breakers rolled in, dashing against white sand and an old wooden pier. Dozens of surfers were out on that roaring seascape, but they weren't surfing. They were paddling in the same area, watching the water.

Then he saw her. She was watching seaward, with her back to him, but he knew what color her eyes would be.

"Where the hell are we?" breathed Ho, beside him.

"What's happening?" asked Martin, pulling nervously on his Santa Claus beard.

"Quiet. Let him sing," said Homer.

A beachcomber walked away, carrying a radio blaring the Bee Gees. The disco music grew fainter and fainter.

I can't stay here. This is the early '80s, thought Sander. He moved on to the next verse . . .

Well, she's had two kids with another man,
and she doesn't think he'd understand
So she's never told him why they're always here,
So she walks along the sand alone
And her kids ride skim boards in the sun
And he sits under an umbrella and has another beer.

. . . and the beach faded imperceptibly . . . into the same beach. Now the pier was even more decrepit. Children glided on plastic foam disks along the ocean's margin. *So that's what skim boards are,* Sander thought. There was the umbrella, and there was the woman: a little bit of a pot now, but still attractive. Still watching. . . .

> And her body's not so perfect now,
> It was never perfect anyhow,
> But a few of us who see her cry inside,
> For the moment that defined her
> In the eyes of forty searchers
> Is still frozen in the stare of her green eyes . . .

Stop now, before the song repeats! Sander clamped his jaw shut, but the song kept playing in his head. He desperately cast about for another song, and set *Californication* spinning in his mental CD player, and hoped it wouldn't waft him off into a video game. Then he ran down the beach to where the woman was striding, and stood in her path, staring at her, until she nearly walked into him. She turned from the ocean, and their eyes met. Those green eyes, so intense. . . .

"He's not coming out. I'm sorry," he told her.

She stared a moment longer, then nodded. "I know," she said. "But the waves come in every day. I still like watching them."

He watched her pass, then slowly walked back to Homer and Ho, who still sat bewilderedly on the sand. Ratty-san peeked timidly from the wadded blanket beside them.

"Hey, Sander, where the hell are we?" asked Homer.

"California," Sander replied.

"You took us off our land?" said Homer angrily.

"Yeah, but all you've gotta do is hitchhike back."

"*How* did we get here?" asked Ho. "Or can you explain that?"

Sander shook his head. "You know the story you told about Changing Woman's twin kids, who chanted up a rainbow and walked over an ocean on it to see their dad? Something like that."

"Heavy, man," said Ho, bemused.

"Saucer powers, eh?" said Martin. "Not surprised"—though he clearly was. "Reckon we can still catch our plane?"

Sander glanced at his calendar watch. "We should. We've got almost three days." He stared at the woman walking down the shore. "The Second Key unlocks the doors between *here and now* and *then and there*," he murmured, and started toward the parking lot.

XXXIV

The Heaven of Rats

"So, is this real?" asked Martin Origen, sitting on a bay-front park bench in San Francisco.

"I think so," said Sander, sitting beside him. "Whatever 'real' means."

"I mean, we're not going to wake up, and find ourselves back in that cabin with a batch of assault rifles pointed down our throats?"

"I hope not," said Ratty-san.

Sander shook his head. "You might want to keep your voice down. No, I'm pretty sure we can't 'wake up.' I might be able to dream-weave us back into Homer's cabin—but I'm sure you'd rather I didn't." He stared out on the bay, and muttered, "I wonder how big a hole I've torn in the universe."

Before the Begays had left, he'd warned them not to try returning to the cabin to warn themselves, because he didn't know what sort of a feedback loop such a paradox would create.

"I hope things work out for Homer and Ho," he said aloud, though softly. "We sure messed up their lives for them."

"Don't worry," said Martin. "They've got two very experienced covert societies taking care of them: us, and the Navajo

Nation. Besides, you know what Homer told me at the bus station, while you were in the john?"

"Obviously not," said Sander.

"Hey, after that beach trip, I'm not sure what you might know. Anyhow, Homer told me, 'Martin, I'm glad you guys pushed me off my butt. I was just sitting up in my cabin, stewing and having kids. Now I've *got* to start the revolution.'"

"Wonderful," said Sander. "Does that make me an accessory to a conspiracy to overthrow the United States?"

"Not so loud," shushed Martin. "Nah, you were kidnapped, remember?"

"Yeah, Papa-san, it's not your fault. It just happened," chimed in Ratty-san, ironically, from Sander's jacket pocket.

Sander had wanted to leave the rat at the motel, but Ratty-san would have none of it. "I've only got a year to live, and you want me to spend a whole afternoon in a motel room?" he'd huffed. "Sorry, Papa-san. You have a disobedient son."

"I sure hope the self-destruct fail-safes worked on my computer," remarked Martin. "Otherwise, the whole organization's got some fast covering up to do."

"We've got a lot worse than that to worry about," said Sander. "Look what I've done. Talking animals. Teleportation. I barely understand how I did it—I didn't really do any of it consciously. What's gonna happen next? Am I going to accidentally make a dragon out of the Golden Gate Bridge? Or maybe make Oakland disappear?"

"Hey, it just occurred to me," said Martin, "why didn't you just dream-weave us over to Hawai'i? We could've saved the ticket money."

"God, Martin, this isn't a toy. Besides, we're only losing the cost of the feeder flight from Albuquerque to here." Sander stared out into the bay. "I'm glad it routed through San Francisco. I've got bad memories of L.A. International."

"You should be glad I had the tickets in my pocket when you started singing," Martin harrumphed. "Hey, maybe we could transport back four days, and have Ho buy just the San Fran to Hawai'i tickets. . . ."

"Dammit, Martin! Remember the last half of Dick's message: 'The keys to unlock the soul and *end the world*.' We can't play around with this!" He stared moodily out over the water again. "The Golden Gate really does look a little like a big dragon, you know. . . ."

"That's the Bay Bridge, not the Golden Gate," pronounced Martin nervously. Sander had finally gotten through to him, and he was anxious to change the subject. "See that dark spot in the middle of the bridge? That's an island. Ever see an island in the middle of a picture of the Golden Gate Bridge?"

Sander couldn't recall that he had, and he didn't want to think about bridge-sized dragons, either. "So why would they haul a UFO to Hawai'i?" he asked.

"That's easy," said his companion. "It's been reported that Maui is the 'Flying Saucer Capitol of the World.' That's actually a little inaccurate. The Flying Saucer Capitol *was* a few miles south of Maui."

" 'Was?' " repeated Sander.

Martin nodded. "They call Kaho'olawe the 'Target Island,' because the Navy and Air Force shelled, bombed and strafed the place for fifty years. They claim it was for gunnery practice. But the real reason was to drive out the aliens."

"Hmm," said Sander. "Sorry, Martin, but even I find that one a little far-fetched."

"Is it any more far-fetched to believe our military would spend 50 years bombing the hell out of an island that we claim as US territory, when they could have practiced on some Central American country whenever they wanted? But that's why they pushed for Hawaiian statehood, even though they knew we annexed it illegally back in the 1890s. They wanted to keep bombing Kahoʻolawe without anybody asking questions.[1]

"Anyway, the military probably established a secret facility on the Big Island so they'd have a place to examine a UFO if they ever captured one. My guess is that it's somewhere in the Pōhakuloa Army Training Area. Meanwhile, we think the aliens finally left Kahoʻolawe in the mid-90s. The Native Hawaiians had been lobbying to get the island back for decades, and then suddenly the Feds let them have the place. They're still clearing unexploded ordnance, though."

"Hmm," said Sander noncommittally. Something besides the possible End of the World was nagging him. The weight of his clothes didn't feel right—maybe just because they were new. They'd used much of his zipper-money to replace things they'd left in the cabin. He'd even found a jacket with big pockets for Ratty-san ... *wait* ... "Ratty-san? Ratty-san's not in my pocket. Oh, no—Ratty-San!" he called, staring about wildly.

He heard an answering squeak. Something white skittered across the grass, dragging something shiny. Ratty-San stopped at their feet and began stripping the foil off a brand new chocolate bar.

"Ratty-san! You stole that!" Sander scolded.

"Of course, Papa-san. I'm a rat."

---

[1] Martin was wrong about this. Some local sources in Hawaiʻi maintain that the saucer base is actually located on the ocean bottom 12 miles south of Kailua-Kona on the Big Island. But this doesn't mean that the military didn't *think* the base was on Kahoʻolawe. And once the military decides something, it's awfully hard to get them to admit their mistake. Ask any Iraqi.

Sander could think of no immediate answer to that.

Martin stared. "A chocolate bar's unwrapping itself and disappearing before my eyes," he said wonderingly. "Or more like *before* and *after* my eyes. . . . Y'know, I've spent most of my life investigating stuff that other people find unbelievable, but I gotta admit, this is freaking even me out just a little."

"Think what it's doing to *me*," Sander replied, with a brief, humorless laugh. He stared at the dragon-bridge, then looked away. "I've gotta figure out exactly what it is I'm doing, before I accidentally bring reality crashing down entirely. But what if it's something you can't figure out? What if the keys are down in the part of the brain that evolved before reason did?" He shook his head as if to clear it. "I think I liked it better when I was just worrying that I'd gone nuts."

A third of the chocolate bar was already gone. Ratty-san eyed the rest dubiously. "I don't feel so good."

"Ah, you've just learned the lesson of gluttony, my son," said Sander. "For every action there is an equal and opposite stomachache."

"Bleah," said Ratty-san. "Can we wrap the rest of this up and take it with us?"

Then Sander's eye caught a glimpse of something else. "Leave it, Ratty-san," he said quietly. "Get up here now."

"Oh, come on, Papa-san. Nobody else will want it."

"Do it now, Ratty-san," said Sander.

"Why?"

"Because there's a cat stalking you."

Ratty-san froze. "Where?"

"*Now*, Ratty-san. Run up my leg *now*," said Sander, drawing curious stares from a couple of passing women, but no other repercussions, since this was San Francisco.

Ratty-san sprang, grabbed onto Sander's pant leg and scurried up into his pocket. Then he peeked out. "Where's the cat?"

"Over there." Sander nodded toward a black-and-white alley cat that was still watching them intently.

"Is Ratty-san out of the way?" said Martin.

"Yes," said Sander.

Martin jumped up, advanced on the cat and waved his arms. "Shoo!"

The cat bolted.

"I still don't see it," said the rat. "Are you two playing a joke on me?"

"No joke," said Sander. "Humans have better distance vision than almost any other mammal. I think it's one of our most overlooked evolutionary assets. You've gotta be more alert, Ratty-san, or your life-span's going to be even shorter."

But the rat's attention had slipped back to his overloaded stomach. He hung his head out of the pocket, his black eyes looking slightly glazed. "Can a rat throw up?" he asked.

"Uh, I saw a Discovery Channel program once that said they couldn't," said Sander. "That's why rat poisons work so well."

"Rat poisons?"

"Uh, not everyone likes rats, Ratty-san. You have to be careful what you eat."

"Cats. Rat poison. What kind of world did you bring me into, Papa-san?"

"Not an ideal one, Ratty-san."

"I'm going to learn how to throw up," vowed the rat.

"Well, if you're going to try, get out of my pocket."

"Your pocket? I thought you bought it for me."

"I bought the jacket for both of us, Ratty-san. We have to share."

The rat scrambled out. "Uh, Papa-san, do you mind rat pellets in our new jacket?"

"Yes!"

"Uh, I'm afraid it has some already."

"What?"

"Sorry."

Ratty-san scuttled to the bench's edge and engaged in a couple of experimental dry heaves, while Sander turned the jacket pocket inside out. "Damn," he said softly, as a couple of very real rat droppings tumbled out.

Martin shifted uncomfortably. "We'd best be heading back to the motel, before the bar crowds start getting too happy," he said.

They'd discovered that their motel was reasonably priced because it was in the Tenderloin District. This being San Francisco, even the Tenderloin was a somewhat upscale slum, but it still had its share of rowdy bars and urine-soaked walls. Martin wanted to take a cab for safety's sake. But Sander was adamant.

"The money's going fast, and I don't know how or when I'll get any more," he said. "Let's at least take the cable car to the other end of the line, so cab fare isn't so high."

They found the cable car turnaround with some difficulty, and caught a chilly, hilly scenic ride. Ratty-San rode on Sander's shoulder for much of the trip, sticking his nose into the cold, odor-laden breeze and squeaking with delight.

At the other end of the line, though, they found themselves in the midst of downtown and not a cab in sight. San Fran had a perfectly good bus system, plus the cable cars and BART trains. If you knew their routes.

And this being San Fran, that most egalitarian (and highest-rent) of American cities, the homeless weren't confined to the Tenderloin. Every fourth or fifth doorway held a figure huddled in layers of old army jackets or Salvation Army castoffs to stave off the cold, foggy San Francisco spring night.

Sander's small-town Midwestern upbringing had not prepared him for beggars. Despite his meager cash reserve, he found himself searching his pockets for change. But the change gave out long before the homeless did. His last quarter was already gone when they passed a young Black couple and two children, huddled in the doorway of a closed luggage shop.

"Please, mister," the young man said. "They had no supper."

Sander felt his hand moving toward his back pocket, then felt Martin tug his arm, propelling him on. "Don't reach for your wallet out here," Martin hissed. "You want to get us mugged?"

"But . . . but . . ."

"How can humans be so powerless?" mused Ratty-san. "Those wonderful eyes, those hands, that huge body. That man could go down to the wharf and club a sea lion, and feed his kids for a week."

"It doesn't work that way, Ratty-san," said Sander. "It just doesn't work that way."

"You can't save them all in one night," Martin said. "Gotta be a reason why two strong young people don't have a place to stay or a bite to eat. Gotta be a big reason. You can't fix that with a quarter, or a dollar, or a hundred dollars."

"Maybe I *could* fix it, somehow, with what I can do," pondered Sander.

"What? Transport'em to a beach? They still won't be able to feed themselves." Martin shook his head. "Or maybe you *could* end the world. Maybe that's why the saucers are here: to put an end to the misery."

"I don't know," said Sander. "If you put an end to time and space, does that mean for sure that you put an end to misery?"

They were passing a fast food place, bright and warm and stainless-steel-sterile. Sander suddenly swerved in. "Four double-cheeseburgers to go," he told the counter girl. He paid her, then handed Martin his wallet.

"Put this in a safe place," he said, and headed out the door.

"What . . . ," began Martin.

"There's gotta be a reason why two healthy young people aren't out mugging us," was all Sander offered in explanation, as they strode back toward the luggage store.

The young family was still there. Wordlessly, Sander held out the bag.

"Why, thank you, thank you," said the man. The woman simply snatched the bag, and began grabbing out burgers and handing them to the children.

"You're welcome," said Sander. They turned to go.

When they started to walk away, the young man called, "Sir, I don't suppose you could spare a couple dolla for coffee?"

Sander paused. "Sorry," he said, and strode on.

A few minutes later, a cab stopped for them.

This last event may have been coincidence. But in a world of infinite purposes, there really are no coincidences. In such a world, the path from *here and now* to *there and then* usually leads through other *here and nows*. But other purposes are always at work, closing doors to some perfectly good *here and nows* and opening doors to others. And sometimes doors open into elsewhere else; sometimes they lead through a song or a dream. Sometimes, as any ancient Aztec or Hebrew could have told you, the only route to a taxi goes through a sacrificial offering.

Sander was beginning to understand this, as they rode through the Tenderloin to their motel. But he was only just beginning.

Riding Sander's shoulder, meanwhile, Ratty-san was on sensual overload. The rich, cold air from a stuck-open cab window buffeted his fur. His beady eyes took in a whirl of towering lights and shadows; his ears caught the rumble of the cab's engine and hiss of its tires echoing off millions of wonderful crannies. His nose worked furiously, processing an incredible kaleidoscope of rich smells—pizza and stir-fry, curry and garbage, auto exhaust and spilled wine and ice cream, chocolate and vomit, urine and frying French fries. And he knew in his deepest being that the purpose of humankind was to build the Heaven of Rats, and he was gazing upon a work in progress. Not perfect yet, but getting there. He just had to learn how to puke.

He sighed deliriously, dropping a couple of processed chocolate rat pellets down the back of Sander's jacket.

They reached the motor inn and got out. Still on his shoulder perch, Ratty-san wriggled his whiskers more furiously than ever.

"I smell a rat," he said lasciviously.

XXXV
The Lost Carrion Club

Sander awakened to the sound of a tiny moan beside his ear. He rolled over to hit the light, heard something skitter out of the way, and found three small spots of blood on his pillow.

"Ratty-san?" he asked, peering about. Then he saw the rat sitting on the bedspread. Ratty-san was attempting to put his fur in order. A piece of his left ear was missing.

"Ratty-san, are you all right?"

"Do I look all right, Papa-san?" The rat lowered himself stiffly to all fours. In addition to the ear wound, a bloody scratch scored his left shoulder.

"My god, Ratty-san! What happened?"

"Papa-san, a small favor? Could you just lay off the 'Ratty' business? I'd rather be just 'Rat-san.'"

"All right, but what happened?"

"I nearly got laid, Papa-san. But the local rats didn't like it. *Big* local rats."

"God, what am I going to do, Ratty—I mean *Rat*-san? I can't take you to a vet. The vet couldn't see you, literally."

"I'll be all right, I think. Just let me clean myself up." He went back to grooming his fur, very carefully.

"I've gotta rent a Teenage Mutant Ninja Turtles movie," said Sander. "You need a positive role model."

"Huh? Wha . . . ?" said Martin, awakening in the other bed.

"Ratty-san got beat up. He's hurt."

"That's *Rat*-san," the rat corrected.

Martin sat up and rubbed his eyes. "How bad?"

"It looks like he met the rat equivalent of Mike Tyson. What time is it?"

They ended up renting a car to drive to Napa, where a feed store sold a line of antibiotics for "Guinea Pigs, Chinchillas, Hamsters and Rats." Their journey was slowed considerably by the fact that the Oakland Bay Bridge was closed for repairs, forcing a detour through horrendous traffic jams. While they were stuck in traffic, Sander spent the time studying the five Hawai'i maps he'd copied, with their exotic-sounding place names and odd diacritical markings: Hāmākua, Kailua-Kona, Hilo, Ka'ū, Puna. The district of Puna, he'd figured out, held Kapoho, where Jenny presumably was. But which of those maps held a flying saucer and a talking armadillo?

On Yerba Buena Island, near the midway point on the Bay Bridge, engineers Wiley McGinnis and Russell Yee stared dubiously at the network of cracks that had appeared overnight in the base of one of the bridge's massive peers.

"This doesn't make sense," repeated McGuinness, for the seventh time that morning.

Yee's cell phone rang. He answered it. "Yee. Hi, Tom. Yeah? Really. Hmm. That doesn't make sense. Okay, thanks." He put the phone back on his belt. "That was Tom Loggerfeld. They've got the revised figures on that quake swarm last night. The largest temblor at most a 2.9."

McGuinness frowned. "A 2.9 shouldn't do damage like this."

"Triangulation puts the epicenter directly under the bridge, and very shallow."

"If there was a known fault under here, they wouldn't have built this bridge."

"Hey, they built three dams right on top of the San Andreas Rift Zone. That's why I don't live in San Mateo."

"And look at these cracks. Tensile and compressive stress fractures—like something pulled straight up on the pier, then dropped it again."

"Or the ground dropped from under it."

"The ground would have to have subsided several decimeters, but it's only changed a few millimeters. And a drop like that would have triggered a measurable tsunami. It doesn't make sense."

The two men debated a while longer about what *might* make sense. Then, being engineers, they moved on to the more fascinating topic of how to fix the damage.

Neither man advanced the theory that at precisely 9:47 on the previous evening, the San Francisco-Oakland Bay Bridge had briefly considered becoming a dragon.

It had even checked to see if it could lift its feet. It decided that it could, but that it would require a horrible effort—and then, to fuel its enormous body, it would have to eat the city of Oakland, which was no great loss, but then it would have to eat San Francisco.

The hell with it, it had thought, and settled back down to be a bridge again.

"This stuff tastes awful," commented Rat-san, finishing off a cupful of Rat Chow and antibiotic. But that was only his opinion, of course.

"I thought rats could eat anything," Sander remarked.

"We can. But we'd rather have chocolate." He chewed the last bit, then scampered into Sander's jacket pocket again.

The traffic was crawling toward the airport. They were in grave danger of missing their flight. Martin drove, cursing and lane-jumping, while Sander navigated.

"I've had bad experiences at airports," worried Sander. "What if they're still looking for me?"

"They shouldn't be," said Martin. "You're in a cabin on the Navajo reservation, surrounded by FBI agents."

"Uh, yeah, I guess," he said. "Rat-san, remember, once we get to the airport, no running around, and I can't talk to you again until we reach Hawai'i. If Papa-san starts talking to invisible rats on the jet, he's liable to end up locked in a little room again."

"Um-hoommf," replied the rat, sleepily. It was past noon, and rats, of course, were nocturnal.

They finally reached the airport. Sander's new fake ID was much better than the one Appy had bought for him in Missouri. The new one even had a film of holographic security plastic, peeled off a real driver's license and transplanted to the fake. Still, he was relieved when the TSA officer gave it only a quick glance.

They made their plane just in time. Their seating assignments on the 767 were crammed into the middle of a bank of seats that marched, four abreast, down the plane's center. A bearded, 40-ish traveler in a sport coat got up with a small smile to let Sander and Martin in, then resettled in the seat beside Sander's and resumed writing on a palmtop computer. Sander thanked his lucky stars he wasn't sitting between the two huge women, both reeking of perfume and body odor, who had taken seats just in front of theirs.

"I do hope we're headed for the right place this time," worried Sander. "I still think my original flight was to Hilo."

264

"There weren't any direct flights to Hilo available," sighed Martin. "Only to Kailua-Kona. To go to Hilo, we'd have had to change planes again in Honolulu."

The attendants started their safety mime show. The bearded man pocketed his Ipad and pulled out a paper notebook.

After 45 minutes on the tarmac, the big plane finally lumbered into the sky. Drink service began. To avoid UFO discussions, Sander started telling Martin about his Carrion Club Theory of Human Evolution.

"The basic thing is that we weren't killer apes or mighty hunters," he explained. "The facts don't fit. Hunters usually have a keen sense of smell—or if they hunt by sight, they're really fast, like the cheetah. But we've got the worst noses of any mammal, we can't outrun anything, and our wedge-shaped feet are prone to trip us up in a cross-country sprint.

"Some people've theorized that we had great endurance, and just ran things to death. But in the sort of broken veldt-and-grove country that Africa was back then, your prey could've just left you in the dust, popped behind some trees and hid out. If we hunted like that, we'd have evolved noses like a bloodhound's. Besides, endurance runners need carbs. I don't think marathons were possible before the invention of pancakes."

"So what does make sense?" Martin asked politely.

"We were pack scavengers. Picture *Homo erectus:* nearly as tall as we are, whole body probably naked as a vulture's head. Those incredible eyes. Not as keen as a vulture's—but keen enough to *watch* vultures. Legs strong enough to get you there before the other scavengers carry off the bones, and tools to break the bones open for marrow. None of this is new, by the way. Johanson even talked about marrow-scavenging on a TV documentary." He sighed.

"Yeah, but how did they fight off the other scavengers?" asked Martin. "I mean, no claws, little bitty teeth—those hyenas are mean customers."

Sander nodded. "That's where my theory comes in. Individual male chimpanzees swing tree branches in threat displays. Think of the damage a baseball bat can do. Now imagine a whole phalanx of *Homo erecti* swinging six-foot cudgels. Hyenas get their teeth bashed in before they're in range to bite. No predator on the veldt, short of a pride of lions, could stand up to a coordinated cudgel attack. And the lions would be awfully sore afterwards. And then pretty soon somebody breaks his cudgel, and accidentally shoves the broken, pointy end of the stick through a hyena's hide. . . ."

The bearded man next to him had become interested. "For such an attack, referential utterances would be useful," he said.

"What?"

"Referential utterances. Vocal signals referring to specific things or actions. One of the building blocks of human language. Vervet monkeys, for instance, have alarm calls to denote different predators, such as leopards or eagles. But they're still just general warnings, like a human screaming "Eek! A rat!""

"Huh?" said Rat-san, sleepily, from Sander's pocket.

"The main response is still reactive and emotional, like a scream. A vervet can't say, 'A rat? Where?' or 'Kill the damn rat with that cudgel.'"

"Hey!" protested Rat-san. He stuck his nose out of the pocket, and glared sleepily about for the speaker.

"I don't suppose vervets have anything in particular against rats, anyway," Sander pointed out timidly.

"But your scenario would be ideal for evolving combinant referential utterances. Imagine the advantage to a band of *Homo erecti* standing siege around a carcass, if they could call out, 'Hyena on your right, Og!' or 'Two hyenas at 10 o'clock!'"

"Right!" said Sander. "Hunting scenario advocates always point to the cooperation of a communal hunt as a perfect breeding ground for language—but the carrion club scenario works just as well, and fits human anatomy better."

"Keen sight, dull nose, nakedness," said the bearded man. "Upright stance to enhance vision, *and* allow one hand to carry the carcass while the other swings the club. Carrion luggage, so to speak. Good fit. Good fit."

"Yeah, but what's he got against rats?" said Rat-san.

The drink cart arrived. Sander had orange juice; Martin, a beer; the bearded man, a white wine. Rat-san wriggled his whiskers at the interesting odors.

"Only one problem," said the bearded man.

"Nobody's found a club or a spear that old," said Sander.

"Right. Without evidence, it's not science, just speculation."

"So people have to keep building scenarios around stone tools, even if they're the wrong scenarios."

"It's too bad wood rots," observed the stranger.

"Not always," said Sander. "Look at the Petrified Forest, or the coal swamps."

"But humankind isn't designed for swamps," said the stranger. "With all his weight on two feet, he sinks in. We still drain swamps whenever we get the chance. By the way, my name's Jerry Karpov." He extended his hand.

"Uh, King. Sandy King," said Sander, extending his own hand. Karpov's eyebrows arched slightly when he heard Sander's assumed name, but the handshake had a friendly enough grip.

"I can't believe you're shaking hands with that rat hater," said Rat-san. "I'm thirsty."

"You know, there's another way wood can be preserved— or at least, its image," Karpov said. "This island where we're headed has lots of 'lava trees.' They're hollow casts, made when the lava flows around a tree and cools as the tree burns."

Sander nodded. "They found casts of wooden furniture in the ash at Pompeii. 'Plenty of volcanic activity in Africa's East Rift Zone. I really want to go there someday. Johanson and the Leakeys and Tim White may have found the bones. But I want to find the first club."

"So you're a paleoanthropologist, Mr. . . ."

"Uh, King," Sander repeated.

"Yes, *King.*"

"And I'm afraid I'm just a paleoanthropology wannabe," said Sander, sadly. "Uh, are you, Mr. Karpov?"

Karpov shook his head. "Let's just say I'm a professional thinker. I look at incomplete puzzles and ask what could be missing. I've got a few advanced degrees, but I spend most of my time these days on theoretical physics and the nature of human thought. So are you coming to the Big Island to study evolution, Mr. King? It's a fascinating place for that. Especially the extinction aspect." Karpov's eyes were focused on Sander's face with a steady attention that was both flattering and slightly unnerving.

"Uh, I'm just sort of here on vacation," said Sander. "Maybe to find a job. I do have a degree in biology."

"Why don't you ask him how a rat could talk?" asked Rat-san.

Why not? thought Sander. "So, do you think there's any way animals could use language?"

"Hmm. Human language, or their own?"

"Uh, either one."

"Well, start with human language. Most critters don't have the right vocal apparatus for speech. Truly human-type sign language—chimps and gorillas, probably not. They can express desires, yes. Understand syntax—no, at least not so far. Bonobos, however—yes, at least occasionally. There's one named Kanzi who's pretty much doing it."

"What about, uh, other species?"

"Well, the most popular candidate is dolphins. They've got big brains and use a wide range of native vocalizations. One big problem, though, is that they grow up too fast. The female's sexually mature at 5 years. Its brain's probably hard-wired much sooner than a human brain is. And a huge part of the dolphin brain is devoted to physical coordination and echolocation. You never see an adult dolphin do something clumsy—but you also never see one that seems lost in thought."

"So could creatures with *smaller* brains learn to speak?"

"Good question. Physically, yes, in a very limited fashion. There's a harbor seal that can pronounce several English words. And parrots."

"Yeah, but they just imitate, don't they?"

"We thought so until recently. But there have been some remarkable breakthroughs in the past few years. Some birds in studies are talking back, following detailed directions, showing a crude grasp of reference and syntax. And nobody can figure out how they do it."

"What do you mean?" Suddenly, Sander realized that Rat-san was no longer perched on his knee.

"Consider a bird's beak," said Karpov. "Can you imagine anything less like a human mouth? No lips, no teeth, the larynx in a different position, the throat a tiny fraction of the size. And parrots have big brains for a bird, but they're still bird brains. If parrot brain size is a measure of verbal potential, then howler monkeys should be reciting Shakespeare."

Out of the corner of his eye, Sander caught a glimpse of white. He glanced at Martin's lowered food tray, then tried not to stare in horror. Rat-san was lapping up Martin's unfinished beer.

Relieved, by Karpov's intervention, of listening to non-saucer-related conversation, Martin had put on his headphones and closed his eyes. Sander surreptitiously elbowed the sleeping man. Martin stirred and looked around groggily.

"Sorry," said Sander.

"No problem," said the UFOlogist. He reached for his beer.

"Hey!" yelled Rat-san, scuttling frantically aside. Then, before Sander could think what to do, Martin put the cup to his lips and drained it.

"Anyway, nobody knows how parrots manage to do it," continued Karpov. "It's like they're channeling some reincarnated soul."

"You did that on purpose," Rat-san accused Sander. "Hey! Watch it!"

The cup slammed back down. Rat-san dodged, fell off the tray's edge and disappeared under the seats.

"Uh, you said you were also studying physics," Sander said, somewhat desperately.

Karpov nodded, smiling. "The other great mystery."

"Is it possible for something to, uh, exist, without, uh, well—being detectable?"

Karpov looked at him, startled. "You mean, like a stealth aircraft?"

Sander shook his head. "No—well, yes, maybe. I mean, a stealth aircraft makes itself invisible to radar by absorbing or scattering radio waves, right?"

"Yes." The scientist was watching him like a chocoholic eyeing a slab of Fudge Factory fudge.

"So the plane exists, but it doesn't exist within the radar's range of senses, right?"

"Uh, almost. It exists a *little*, from the radar's perspective."

"So could something exist, while being out of tune with the light and sound frequencies we humans usually detect? Or maybe detectable to only one or two people with unusual, er, tunings?"

"Hmm." Karpov looked thoughtful. "Interesting idea. You know, they've been trying to detect dark matter particles unsuccessfully for years, though we know they exist because of their gravity. But we've been looking for particles. Maybe we should be focusing on waves. . . ."

In the row ahead of them, one of the fat women shrieked, then moaned, "God, wine all over my pants!" A flight attendant left the dinner cart and rushed to the woman's aid.

"Some theoretical physicists postulate alternate universes," Karpov added. "Things could well exist that are perfectly visible relative to each other, but barely detectable to us."

A tiny voice piped up from somewhere in the seats ahead of them. "Roll me over, in the clover . . . ," it sang giddily.

"Jeez," said Sander.

The singing was getting closer. Suddenly Rat-san scrambled up Sander's leg. Sander tried not to flinch.

"So based on our conversation, it's possible an invisible talking rat could be sitting on my knee right now," said Sander.

Karpov chuckled. "Could be," he said, as Rat-san hopped from Sander's lap to Karpov's serving tray.

"Or even drinking your wine as we speak," said Sander.

"Maybe," Karpov laughed. He reached for his cup, just as Rat-san began lapping wine. Somehow Karpov's hand went astray, knocking the cup over. Rat-san slipped on a small river of spilled wine and fell off the edge of the tray again.

"Damn." Karpov fished his notebook out of the wine and began mopping up with his napkin. "That'd never happen to a dolphin," he grinned ruefully. "You know, Sandy, you're a pretty bright, creative man. You say you may be looking for work?"

"Uh, maybe," said Sander, distracted by the weight of a small, soggy body clambering up his pant leg again.

The scientist pulled out his wallet. "I've heard there's not much work over here right now, just like everywhere else. But I'm working on a project you might find interesting, and there just might be a place for you. Let me give you my card."

"You did that on purpose, Papa-san," said the rat, slurrily. "I oughta bite you in the crotch."

"Ah, here's lunch," said Karpov, as the cart arrived.

"All right!" said the rat. "Food!"

And passed out.

When Mike Dupres found Karpov at Kona Airport, the theorist was staring bemusedly at the baggage carousel. He acknowledged Dupres' greeting with a small wave. Dupres smelled wine.

"Sander Keynes is here," Karpov said.

"Here on the island?"

"Here in this airport. At least, he was until a minute ago. His baggage came off the carousel before mine did."

"You're sure it was him?"

Karpov nodded. "He's using an alias, but it's him. He sat next to me on the plane. We had some interesting conversations. He's not unintelligent."

"Well, that's—hey!" A thin, leather-faced man who'd been standing at the adjacent carousel suddenly bolted past them, nearly knocking Dupres over with a suitcase. "What's with him?"

"Hasn't caught the spirit of aloha yet, I guess."

"At any rate, I started to say, that's very interesting," said Dupres, "because the CIA told us two days ago that they'd found Keynes in LA, where he'd tried to hijack a plane with nail clippers. And Fox News just announced that he's being held hostage on the Navajo Reservation by a flying saucer cult."

"Really? Then someone's obviously mistaken. This man matched the physical description and interest profile perfectly, and he was asking about stealth technology. And the possibility of intelligent beings that no one else can see."

"Jesus. So did you call airport security?"

Karpov smiled. "Why, Michael, I'm not a policeman. And there's no evidence that the condition of any of the so-called 'victims' is contagious—or that confinement is helping any of them—or even that they're diseased."

"Wait a minute—you're saying all the weird stuff they're seeing is *healthy?*"

"We all see visions. Dreams, daydreams, mirages, theories. They're what our brains do when we confront things that don't make sense yet. It's how we *react* to visions that matters."

"It doesn't make sense that Keynes would just happen to sit down beside you," muttered Dupres. "What are the odds?"

"Actually, the odds are pretty good," replied Karpov. "The same events drew both of us here. There aren't that many direct flights, and this is the closest airport."

"But there must have been 400 seats on that plane!"

"I'd have noticed him if he'd been seated adjacent to me in any direction, including diagonal. That's eight seats—one in 50 odds. And this flight had at least three other people from the Project that *I* know about, each covering another eight-seat grid. That makes the odds about one in, um, 12.1875. Add press people, military personnel, spies, UFO buffs. . . . Once he boarded the plane, it was almost certain that he'd meet *somebody* who could recognize him. Ah, my bag." He grabbed a battered overnighter off the carousel.

"So you met Sander Keynes. And you just let him go."

"I didn't say that."

"What?"

"I gave him my card."

Harlan Chillingworth paused, out of breath, at the parking lot's edge. Kona International Airport was not large, but with a 767 and two local flights unloading at once, the grass-hut-shaped terminal buildings were boiling with people. He had no idea where Keynes had gone. "Well, at least I got my bag this time," he muttered. "Get the car, Harlan. You'll find him."

He found the rental car agency without much problem. The clerk smiled her best Smile of Aloha at him. She had almond eyes, but much more cleavage than he was used to seeing on the Southeast Asian refugees' daughters back in Springfield.

"Worley McDermont," he told her. "I got a car reserved." *I've never made it with an Oriental woman,* he thought. Somehow, doing it with an Oriental seemed more okay than doing it with a Black woman. . . . *Stop it, dammit! Knights in Armor!*

He waived the insurance (whatever that meant) and got his keys. *I'm getting the hang of this traveling business,* he thought. He found the car: a Mazda. He'd reserved a Caddy. Damn. Well, when he'd found Jenny, he'd come back and rent a Lincoln.

As he was emerging from the parking lot, a dark blue Chevy SUV drove by. A face peered out the rear seat window. It was one of the men who'd been discussing Sander Keynes.

Harlan hit the accelerator and pulled in behind the vehicle. It had US Government plates.

If I can't find Keynes and Jenny, he thought, *maybe they can. The damn government can find anything except a tax refund.*

XXXVI

The Official First Mauna Kea Car Chase Scene

&

What the Cows Saw

Car #3:

"I'm not at all sure this is a good idea," said Sander, as their rented Toyota minivan pulled in behind the blue Chevy Blazer. "I think the first priority ought to be to find Jenny."

"She's in that much danger?" asked Martin.

If Harlan's on the island, she could be. He was supposed to arrive when?"

"I'm not sure any more. Let's see. Today we're under siege in Homer's cabin. I think—or was that yesterday? Jeez, time travel's enough of a bitch for keeping track of dates, without adding time zones."

"And it's not just her ex. The government could find her. Or somebody's secret agent. Look out!"

A white Mazda subcompact suddenly pulled out in front of them. Martin slammed on the brakes. A tiny moan came from the minivan's back seat.

"Damn. He cut us off," muttered the UFOlogist. "But I can still see the Blazer's taillights. So you'd risk mad husbands and murderous spooks for this woman? She's that important?"

"Jenny? Of course she is. She's a nice girl. You know how rare nice girls are?"

"Not as rare as you think. Just look for the nearest mean, stupid asshole, and you'll find a nice girl propping him up. Same thing with the nice guys. The bitches grab them first. Survival of the fittest. Jeez, that guy's really tailgating."

"Hmm—for once, Marty, you've spun a theory I can believe. Think about it. The bitchy gene gets passed along by grabbing the nice person, because without nice mates to restrain them or pick up the pieces, the nasty people would kill each other off. The nice gene gets passed on because the bitchy person needs the nice gene's owner, even if that person leads a miserable life. It's like a male praying mantis, mating at the cost of getting its head bitten off."

"Could you two talk a little softer, up there? I don't feel so good," came Rat-san's voice from the back seat, where Sander had carefully deposited his jacket.

"Let me guess," said Papa-san. "Headache? Nausea? A mouth that tastes like it's full of cotton?"

"Cotton tastes a lot better. But yes to the other two."

"Congratulations, Rat-san. You've got your first hangover."

"Oh, great. Is it fatal?"

"Sorry, you'll just have to live with it."

"Very clever, Papa-san," moaned the rat.

The Mazda stuck to the Blazer's tail all the way out to Queen Kaʻahumanu Highway. Then both vehicles turned left. The minivan and its occupants followed.

Martin scratched his beard. "I'll just sit back here until he passes. With him tailgating like that, our scientist ain't gonna notice anybody else following. So, navigator, where does this road go?"

Sander squinted at the rental-car map by the light of the passing argon street lamps. "Someplace called 'Kawaihae,' I think. However it's pronounced. . . ."

"We're headed north, right?"

"I think so. What makes you think this guy's going to lead us to Saucerland?"

"Hey, while you two were talking on the plane, I was only pretending to be asleep, most of the time. That guy was way too interested in you. He had to have an ulterior motive."

"Hey, he's a scientist. He's supposed to be curious."

"Hey right back again. Scientists aren't usually that far-rangingly curious. They're fascinated about their own field, but they tune you out the minute you try to talk to them about something else, like the fall of the Soviet Union."

"I see," Sander said, privately rolling his eyes.

"Besides, what's a scientist with that man's range of interests going to do on a little island in the middle of the Pacific, besides work on a flying saucer?"

"Maybe he's going to one of the observatories on Mauna Kea."

Martin snorted derisively. "Hunh. Let me tell you about those observatories. Have you noticed how they're building all those big new telescopes in pairs now? Like the Keck telescopes, and Gemini? That's 'cause one of each pair isn't a telescope. It's a camouflaged, advanced Star Wars laser. Keck I's a real telescope. Keck II was designed to burn out the alien relay station on the Moon."

"But what about those wonderful composite images they get, using both scopes? I've seen them on the Web."

"Hell, Sander. You're smart enough to figure that out. They take two pictures with one telescope, use computers to adjust for the difference between the positions for the first and second pictures, and combine the images. They could make a hundred-fold more powerful image that way, by combining a hundred images. They don't *need* a second telescope."

To Martin's surprise, the Mazda didn't try to pass the Blazer on the long straightaways just beyond Kona International Airport. The three cars fled together across the black, inhospitable lava landscape of South Kohala. Messages from lovers, gangs and tourists, spelled out in lumps of white coral on blackness of the old lava flows, flashed by in the headlights. Finally the Blazer turned inland. The other two cars followed, winding uphill toward the dark, ancient mass of Mauna Kea, the highest of the Big Island's five volcanoes.

The road climbed steadily through lava flows and desert uplands, which had expanded into a gray-and-black immensity in the light of the rising moon. Sander craned around to take in the spectacular sight of fifty miles of coastline necklaced with the amber lights of resorts and villages and subdivisions, sprawled out between two mountains with all the moonlit South Pacific beside them. Nothing in Missouri could have come close to preparing him for this beautiful vastness.

His reverie was interrupted when the little convoy hit a T-intersection and turned left. "That looks like a cloud bank up ahead," Martin noted, his Santa Claus profile looking even more gnomish in the glow of the dashboard instruments. "Hey, navigator, where does this road go?"

"I can't see the map," said Sander. "Martin, maybe you should drop back a little. That guy up ahead is weaving."

"This looks like a pretty deluxe model. I bet there's a map light. Maybe even GPS."

Sander wasn't even sure what a GPS looked like. But there was a map light, anyway. After a little groping, Sander found it and flicked it on.

"I'm glad they ran out of compacts and gave us this free upgrade," said Martin.

"We're headed for a town called Waimea," said Sander. "From there, the road cuts across a corner of the island, then winds along the coast to . . ." He flicked the page ". . . to Hilo."

But they never got to Waimea. Just past a highway sign that read "SADDLE ROAD," the government vehicle turned right, headed uphill again. The little Mazda swerved after them. The minivan and its passengers followed.

"Uh, Martin," said Sander, "isn't this the road that the rental car company said we weren't allowed to drive on?"

"Doesn't look that bad," Martin said. "Sander, check the map. I bet Pōhakuloa Military Reservation's up ahead."

"Uh—yeah, there it is. "

"I knew it! I knew it!"

"Please! A little softer!" whimpered Rat-san

The road was good, but was obviously designed for 45 m.p.h. The blue Blazer was averaging at least 60, which made the quiet curves a bit hair-raising as they tried to keep up. Even more hair-raising were the antics of the Mazda driver, who wasn't particularly staying in his lane.

As they ascended the flank of Mauna Kea, the road grew steeper and windier, sweeping past giant ancient cinder cones.

"Uh, Papa-san?" said Rat-san.

"Yes?"

"I did it. I puked. Sorry about your jacket."

"You're the one who has to live in it."

Banks of fog began to appear, causing the vehicles ahead to fade in and out of existence. A jacked-up black pickup suddenly loomed out of the fog, forcing all three ascending vehicles to take to the narrow shoulder. Gravel crunched under tires, rattling as ominously as the snare drums before an execution.

They topped one last rise, crossing the mountain's shoulder and leveled out. Fence posts and bridge rails whipped by. Before them loomed an enormous wasteland of black lava: the Mauna Kea-Mauna Loa Saddle. To the right, silhouetted against brilliant stars, Mauna Loa's 75-mile-long bulk loomed like the Black Goddess of Slugs fallen to earth, confined and humiliated by all that saltwater. To the left towered Mauna Kea, the tallest mountain between California and Asia. Clustered against the mountain's base were lights of what looked like a village.

"That must be Pohakuloa Training Area," said Martin.

A roadside sign flashed by, announcing DANGER LIVE AMMUNITION AREA, as the road skirted the border between Mauna Kea's aged ash-lands and Mauna Loa's raw lava. Aside from the lights of the base, the whole area seemed eerily empty.

Just then, they hit a particularly nasty bump. "Gad! Do you guys have *any* idea how this feels to a little bitty rat with a great big headache?" wailed a plaintive voice in the back seat.

The Blazer ignored both the army civilization on the left and plunged onward into the night. They passed a desolate collection of huts and trees with a brown-and-white sign proclaiming MAUNA KEA STATE PARK, then hit a section of highway flanked by giant, ancient cinder cones and chain-link fences. The LIVE AMMUNITION signs had reappeared. Then the road plunged out onto a black field of pāhoehoe lava, rumpled and mounded and rippled like the petrified black wax drippings from a giant candle, where nothing grew but a little grass and a few grotesque mullein stalks that clung to the road's edge.

"Gad," breathed Sander, his brain's language-processing facilities overwhelmed by the immense alien landscape. "Gad."

"Yep," Martin said. "Reminds me of home. Grants, New Mexico. Uranium Capital of the US. Lava fields like this there, too. There ain't nothing, not even an atom bomb, that obliterates everything quite so thoroughly as a good layer of hot, molten rock." He shook his head. "That's what puts the lie to this place as a training area. How many times do you end up fighting a war in a lava desert?"

"Maybe they think if you can fight a war here, you can fight a war anywhere."

"Maybe. Like on Venus, or Olympus Mons. Or maybe Io."

"So where is this Blazer going to turn off?"

Martin shook his head again. "Don't know. Never been here."

They plunged into another fog bank—only this time, there was no apparent end to it. There are no good words in English for such a fog. But native Hawaiians call it *kauanoe*. It is essentially a pregnant rain cloud come to earth, birthing its rain against rocks and trees and windshields before all that water has a chance to become proper raindrops. The minivan's windshield wipers couldn't keep up with the drenching.

"Jeez, I don't know how that drunk up ahead can stay on the road in this," commented Sander.

"I don't know how *I'm* keeping it on the road," Martin shouted back. "Let's hope the Blazer's still ahead of him, because I can't see a sign of it in this crud! I wonder how high we are?" He turned on the van's heater, then flicked it back to "Air" again when the windshield instantly fogged up. Sander thought longingly of his San Francisco sweatshirt, buried in his new suitcase. But he resisted reaching for his jacket.

The fog suddenly lifted—but only a few feet. Their head-lights seemed to illuminate an eerie, low, infinitely broad chamber, with about ten feet of clear air between wet lava floor and cloud ceiling. Both cars were still ahead of them. An old cinder cone loomed on the right, poking its tree-covered sides out of the bare lava and into the cloud.

Then, abruptly, the Blazer turned left, Mauna Kea-ward, on a two-lane black top. So did the Mazda, barely braking in time. The minivan followed.

"Where does this road go?" asked Martin.

Sander flicked on the map light and flipped pages. "This must be the Mauna Kea Observatory Road," he said, and suddenly grinned. "I told ya!"

Car #1:

"Hmph," said the driver, Specialist 4th Class Danny Hollings-worth, glancing back in his mirror.

"What?" said Dupres. Then the track of headlights pivoted across the interior of the car. "Oh, no! Don't tell me that idiot turned in behind us *again.*"

Hollingsworth nodded. "Must be an astronomer," he said. "Hey, here comes the other one, too."

"You've got to be kidding," said Karpov. "Who ever heard of a drunken astronomer?"

"Oh, I've known a . . . ." began Dupres, then realized that Karpov *was* kidding. Another sign flashed by:

CAUTION
OPEN RANGE

"Is this a firing range, too?" asked Karpov.

"No, sir. Cows," said the driver. "No fences up here."

"Ah, 'range' as in 'Home on the Range,'" said Karpov.

"Better cows than unexploded ordnance," muttered Dupres.

"Cows *are* unexploded ordnance," said Karpov.

"What?"

"Cows generate huge amounts of methane gas from the deteriorating plant matter in their stomachs. Never hold a match up to a cow's behind."

"Oh. I didn't know," was all Dupres could think to say.

"That true, sir?" said Hollingsworth. "I oughta try that sometime. Say, *both* those cars are still sticking with us."

"So what's the chances of three cars coming all the way up here from Kona airport together at night?" asked Dupres.

"If they're telescope staff, they're getting here kind of late, I'd think," Karpov remarked. "I doubt if the astronomers themselves go up the mountain very often any more. They can stay in Hilo or Waimea and get images and data cabled down to them—or get them via the Net. I've pulled data from the observatories myself, but this is the first time I've physically been here."

Dupres nodded. "All the thrill of discovery, none of the altitude sickness. I've never had occasion to use any of the Mauna Kea eyes, myself. We use mostly large radio arrays. And I'm not even the radiotelescopist. I'm the psycholinguist."

"Hey, I saw that movie," said Hollingsworth. "That was pretty good."

"Uh, what movie was that?" asked Dupres.

"*Psycho.* Man, that shower scene was awesome. But I think they should have shown a little more. . . ."

"Uh huh," said Dupres, politely.

"They might be some of our own people, just off the plane like me," said Karpov.

"Maybe," said Hollingsworth, doubtfully.

"Hey, wait a minute," said Dupres. "Haven't we passed our turnoff?"

"Yes, sir," said Hollingsworth. "We're taking a little detour. SOP, if we think someone may be following us."

"I see, said Dupres.

The Blazer surged onward, growling up a giant road fill. Even the SUV's big engine had to drop back a gear or two on the steep slope. Dupres twisted around to look behind them. "They're still coming, but they've slipped back a little."

"That subcompact's engine is probably laboring," observed Karpov. They were now rising rapidly above the silver expanse of moonlit cloud that stretched off toward Hilo. "My guess is they're sightseers, out to get a view to remember."

"They might be coming up for those public stargazing sessions at the half-way house," said Dupres. "There's a dormitory at about 9,000 feet, so telescope staffers can avoid the worst effects of long-term oxygen deprivation. They have a visitor's center there, too, with a couple of small telescopes that they trundle out for public viewing."

"Could be," said Karpov, "but those jokers have been on our tail ever since the airport. They'd have had to know about the viewing sessions before they arrived, and prioritized stargazing over finding their hotels. What are the chances of two different visitors doing that, if they aren't professional astronomers?"

"Or Psycho Linguists?" Dupres said, grinning maniacally in the dark. "So what's left? You really think we're being followed?"

"If we are, they're being pretty blatant about it," said Karpov. "Oh, how I love a good mystery."

"Well, we'll know in a couple of minutes," said Hollingsworth. "Brace yourselves, sirs. It'll get a little bumpy."

The Cows:

Three of the roaring things with bright lights went by. Most of the herd kept grazing, but the nearest cow looked up.

Run?

She trotted back a little as the first thing rushed past. The blinding lights stupefied her; one side of her head was seeing day while the other saw night. She stood splay-legged, trying to decide what to do, as the other two things roared past.

Vaguely, she tried to plug this experience into others in her memory. The roaring things sometimes stopped, and two-leggers got out. Sometimes they brought good things: feed or salt. Sometimes they separated the calves and yearlings and put them into bigger roaring things that took them off and . . .

Don't think about it.

She lowered her head to graze again

Car #2:

Harlan had no idea where the hell he was, except that he was on Hawai'i, The Big Island. The cable TV travelogue at the Waikiki Hilton had showed pictures of a huge mountain or two, and a batch of stark white observatories on one of them. He bet the hotel here would have more about this island, just like the O'ahu hotel had mostly O'ahu stuff. And more blue movies, too. . . .

Dammit, Harlan, stop that! Knights in Armor!

The travel channel (and the blue movies) had been almost the only saving grace of a nightmare stay in O'ahu. He'd wandered the airport for two hours before finding where the baggage came off the planes, and then discovered one of the biggest rooms he'd ever seen: miles of moving conveyer belts that somehow went around corners—and he'd had no idea which belt to look on for his suitcase. He'd finally decided just to buy new clothes. Finding out how to get a rental car had been even worse. And then he'd gotten on the highway, and discovered Honolulu.

He'd expected grass shacks. He'd found a goddam skyscraper city, its crosswalks filled with more people than Springfield had *anywhere*, even at Walmart. Men with hairy legs sticking out of white shorts and hairy arms hanging from gaudy gay floral shirts. And women! Women in bikini tops and shorts, little patches of vivid color far more disturbing than the men's expanses of flowery cotton. Blondes, brunettes, redheads, Orientals, Oriental fake-redheads, and incredibly striking women who seemed to blend every combination of Oriental and Caucasian features: Chinese eyes gazing out of freckled faces, petite golden-skinned women with flashing green eyes, big Western-style boobs arching golden-brown from straining floral bikini tops. But also gaunt, bikini-clad blondes with prematurely leathery skin, and pruny white-haired bikini-clad matrons, and white women and golden women with luxurious folds of belly fat bouncing over the waistlines of near-bursting shorts, their jelly-thighs bulging through the leg-holes. And little golden twelve-year-olds barely blooming into their strapless elastic tube tops. Every shape of beautiful and ugly womanhood, all dressed for sin. He'd steeled himself for a few bare-breasted wahines dancing under coconut trees. But this was too goddamn much.

It wouldn't be adultery, exactly. She divorced you. It was her hardness of heart, not yours—you gotta satisfy your needs somehow. . . . Stoppitstoppitstoppit! Knights in shining armor!

Then there had been that awful moment when he'd finally struggled free of the city, driving past Diamond Head and another little mountain to the island's eastern tip. And there, like a ghost floating on the waves, had been another island. . . .

He was jolted back to the present by the crunch of tires on gravel, and swerved back onto the narrow asphalt strip just in time to avoid crashing into a jagged mass of black rock.

The weather was getting worse. He'd never seen fog like this, or rocks like this. It was creepy.

He followed the blazer as it turned left and kept climbing. They quickly left the fog behind. Through the windshield, he caught occasional glimpses of the most brilliant stars he'd ever seen. Then he risked a look out the right window. He was looking *down* at *clouds*. . . .

He swerved away from the guard rail. *I can't be drunk. All I had was a couple of tequilas at the Honolulu airport, and a little tiny bottle of wine on the plane. But this damn road's tricky. 'Gotta stay on my toes.*

They started up a long, curving grade, so steep that the car's little engine was dragged down to a crawl. The damned government truck was pulling ahead. He floored the gas pedal, and managed to accelerate a little in overdrive. He wondered, briefly, where the car behind him was headed. Probably to whatever city this road led to . . . which maybe was coming up. He spotted lights. No, too few. Two or three buildings, and a solid black mountain behind them.

He was catching up again. The Blazer seemed to be slowing.

Then, a hundred yards before the first building, the Blazer turned off. Harlan slammed on the brakes, skidded, and turned after them.

Shit! This isn't a road. It's a damned cow path. There was no paving, just ruts and a cloud of dust hanging in the moonlight. He got about two hundred yards, all the while dodging rocks and hummocks. Then a rock loomed that he couldn't avoid. It disappeared under the front bumper and scraped along the bottom of the car. Suddenly liberated from its muffler, the little Mazda's engine bawled a race car challenge.

"Shit!" yelled Harlan, skidding to a halt. He remembered that the car was an automatic, stopped feeling frantically for the clutch pedal and shifted to park. The Blazer's tail lights disappeared beyond a hummock.

"Goddammit," he muttered. "I gotta come back with a Jeep or something." He put the car into L2, lurched forward into a little dip where there didn't seem to be any major rocks, and managed to turn the car around. Watching for the muffler among the ruts and hummocks, he crept slowly back to the highway.

He didn't learn the muffler's whereabouts until he reached the pavement again. The jolt as the car climbed back onto the road shook another hanger loose, and the muffler, separated but still clinging to its perch under the car, dropped into contact with the asphalt. Harlan drove a few feet, stopped, then breathed, "Ah hell," and hit the accelerator, putting up with the awful racket. After a while, the part touching the pavement wore off, so it didn't sound so bad on straightaways. On every dip and curve, though it renewed its clattering protest.

It was hard not to do 70 or 80 going down. He rode the brake until the odor of hot metal seeped into his consciousness. But by then, the crossroads had to be only a few more miles ahead.

The fog had crept higher while he was up the mountain. The little Mazda plunged into it. Something else suddenly gave, and the muffler dropped to the pavement again.

Which distracted him at just the wrong moment. By the time he saw the cow *jacklit* in his high beams, it was too late.

Car #3:

"Whoa, Nelly," said Martin. He brought the car to a halt at the point where the other two had turned.

"Martin, don't do it," said Sander. "That's no road for a passenger car."

"It's no road, period," said Martin. "But the guy in the subcompact went on. Maybe he knows something we don't."

"I bet he doesn't," Sander said. "He's probably from some intelligence agency, or the media. The people in the SUV probably figured out they were being tailed, and went that way to throw us off. Jenny and I once got rid of a reporter that way."

"I wonder what these buildings up ahead are?" said Martin. He started the minivan on up the blacktop toward a large steel-and-glass structure. A sign announced ELLISON ONIZUKA VISITOR CENTER. In the parking lot beside it, a small crowd of people clustered around two portable telescopes. "Hmm . . ." Martin said, cruising slowly past. Beyond lay another building that resembled a college dormitory.

"Definitely a facility of some kind," said UFOlogist. "Maybe they're hiding it in plain sight." He pulled into a parking lot by the second building and killed the engine. "We better investigate."

Suddenly, Sander was surprised to discover that he was out of patience.

"Martin, even if I were going to hide something in plain sight, I still wouldn't put it right next to something marked 'Visitor Center.' It's probably 10 p.m., I think I'm discovering the meaning of 'jet lag,' and I don't feel like barging into somewhere and getting arrested again—at least not until I've found Jenny and had some sleep."

"Oh, all right. We'll consider this a scouting trip and come back later." Martin started the car and headed back downhill.

"What's wrong with that car ahead of us?" asked Sander. The vehicle in question was trailing a shower of sparks.

"Looks like he's dragging something," remarked Martin. "Hey, is that that little Mazda?"

"Whether it is or not, he's going way too fast . . . Uh-uh. Don't even think it, Martin."

"Don't wanna trail him?"

"Please, enough adventures for tonight!"

"All right, all right."

Sander flicked on the map light. "If we turn left down at the intersection, it'll take us into Hilo. They ought to have a hotel there."

The minivan handled the downhill curves surprisingly well, but Martin had to ride the brake. Finally he shifted to L2 to control their descent somewhat. The Mazda, still trailing occasional sparks, had disappeared into the cloudbank below. Soon they had re-entered the cloud themselves.

And almost missed noticing the Mazda, lying upside down in the cow pasture beside the road.

"Reckon we should stop?" Martin asked.

"Of course we should stop!" said Sander.

Martin hit the brakes, backed up, and pulled off. "Rat-san! *Please* stay in the car, unless you want to spend the rest of your life in a very cold cow pasture!" Sander ordered.

"Don't worry, Papa-san," moaned the rat. "I'm never moving again."

"Well, here *I* go again," Sander muttered. He got out and trotted back to the disabled vehicle. "Martin!" he yelled. "Can you turn our car around so the headlights are on this?" He knelt beside the cracked driver-side window. The minivan's headlights swept into the upside-down car's interior, where a man hung upside down, staring at an airbag's collapsed remains. The air reeked of gasoline. Sander yanked on the door handle, with no luck. "Martin?" he yelled again.

"Yeah?"

"Can you bring the tire iron?"

"Coming right up!"

Sander tapped on the window. "Are you all right in there?"

The man slowly turned his head and nodded, which looked very strange upside-down. He began struggling with the shoulder harness, then suddenly dropped. Stunned silence. Then a muffled blasphemy penetrated the glass barrier. The man began pounding on the door. "Get me out of here!" he yelled.

Martin arrived with the tire iron. "Get away from the window!" Sander shouted, grasping the iron. After a couple of quick swings, the safety glass collapsed into glittering crystals.

"Shit!" the man yelled. "What the hell'd you do that for? Goddammit, I gotta pay for all this!"

"It was cracked anyway!" Sander said. "Get out of there, mister! There's gas leaking!"

A hand emerged, then another, then a head. A lean, leathery face. "Did I miss the cow?" it asked.

"I guess," said Sander. "I don't see a cow, anyway."

"Shit. I wanted it to suffer." A lean, almost emaciated body crawled out. The Mazda's occupant stood up, shaking bits of glass from his clothes. He looked vaguely familiar. "Damn, It's cold," he said wonderingly.

"Let's get you to the car," said Sander. "You've got some cuts." It *was* cold, and this liquid fog was rapidly drenching them all to the skin.

The rescued driver stared down at his former vehicle. "Hell," he said, numbly. "Gonna be hell to pay." He calmly, if slightly unsteadily, walked over to the minivan and got in.

Martin looked at Sander. "I don't even know this guy," he said. "But I get the feeling we're gonna regret this."

Sander stared after the accident victim, and didn't argue.

XXXVII

The Traffic Jam of the Self

The rest of the trip down the mountain would prove to be nearly as hair-raising as the observatory road side trip—partly because of the road, and partly because of their new passenger.

By the time Sander and Martin had gotten back to the car, the accident victim had already deposited himself in the front passenger seat and reclined as far back as it would go.

"We'd better check to see how badly he's bleeding," said Sander.

Martin nodded, and opened the passenger side door. The dome light came on, revealing a livid bruise on the stranger's left cheek. He held up a hand displaying several small cuts, probably from the bits of "safety glass" he'd crawled out over. "Hey! It's raining, dammit!" he said.

"How do you feel, Mister?" asked Martin.

"Like shit," said the stranger. "Shut the damn door!"

Martin complied with the stranger's request. "How far do you think it is to Hilo?" he asked Sander.

"I don't know," said Sander. "He's sitting on the map."

"I didn't see any massive bleeding," said the UFOlogist. "And if he's got a spinal injury, it's too late. He's already moved himself. But he could be in shock."

"He didn't sound like it," said Sander, "but if he is, we don't even have a blanket to throw around him."

"Let's just get him into Hilo," said Martin.

Sander nodded agreement. They got into the car, with Sander piling into the back. Rat-san was sitting on his jacket on the seat beside him. "Who's *that?*" the rat asked grumpily.

Sander held his finger to his lips in the classic "Shh!" gesture, then gently shoved the jacket and its passenger a little farther away.

"Hey!" protested the rat.

"Shit. It smells like puke in here," said the stranger.

"You don't smell so good, yourself," remarked Rat-san.

"Hey, you guys haven't been drinking, have you?" said the stranger.

"Nah," said Martin. "Just got off the plane. Somebody got airsick on my friend's jacket." He put the car into drive. "Why don't you just lie back and rest, mister? You've had a big shock."

"Hell, I can't believe I did that," said the man. "I just can't fucking believe it. Shit, I'm bleeding."

"Polite, isn't he?" said Rat-san.

"Are you bleeding anywhere beside your hands?" asked Martin.

The man looked down at his body. "Hell, I can't tell," he said, more loudly than he needed to. "I'm so fucking wet, I don't know what's water and what's blood."

"If you press your palms together, that'll help stop the bleeding," suggested Sander.

The man gingerly pressed his hands together, then stared at them as if he'd never seen them before. Suddenly he grinned and guffawed. "Pray for forgiveness, sinner!" he intoned, and snorted with laughter. "Why'd you suggest this?" he said, when he'd recovered. "You a doctor or a preacher?"

"I'm a—a biologist," Sander said. "Direct pressure usually helps stop bleeding."

"Well, that's fucking close enough to a doctor," the stranger said. "Just so's I know you're not just pushing the power of prayer, which I already know about. I'm going to heaven, but God's sure treating me rough on the way there." He dropped his hands. "Shit, I can't believe I rolled that car."

"I can't believe you got out in as good a shape as you did," said Martin. "Somebody was sure looking out for you."

"He was looking out better for the goddamned cow," said the stranger. "Fucking beef cow, headed for the slaughterhouse anyway. Should've just hit the goddamned thing."

"It's a good thing you didn't," said Sander. "If that cow had gone through the windshield, you'd be a dead man."

That stopped the man for a moment. "Jesus Christ, you're right. I could be dead. I nearly fucking *died* back there." That shut him up for a while.

They reached the Saddle Road again and turned left, toward (they hoped) Hilo. For a while, the pavement ran fairly straight. Jagged lava still loomed frighteningly close on either side, but occasional small trees also flashed by in the headlight's glare.

The stranger held his silence for a while, except to repeat "I nearly fucking died . . ." every few minutes. Finally Martin broke in to distract him. "So, was that Mazda a rental car?"

The stranger nodded. "Shit, I can't believe I did that. At least I signed that waiver to get insurance."

Sander mulled that one over. "Uh, I believe when you sign a waiver, it means you *didn't* accept the insurance."

"Shit. Hell, I don't know what I did." Then an evil grin spread across their passenger's face, as if he'd just remembered something embarrassing to tell about an enemy. "Don't matter anyway. My company'll pay for it. They're rich. They pay people thousands of dollars just to tell cock and bull stories."

"Really? What business would you be in?" asked Martin.

"The writing business. I write for a magazine."

I told you so, thought Sander.

"Huh," said Martin. "Which magazine is that?"

"The *MorningStar,*" the man said proudly. "Best pile of bullshit in any supermarket. You know, we sell mostly to women. Women'll believe anything."

"This man's disgusting," noted Rat-san. "Can I bite him?"

Lord. This one's even worse than McDermont, thought Sander. *But maybe this is a piece of luck. If he's from* MorningStar, *maybe he knows where Jenny is.*

But first he had to get a word in past Martin.

"I read your mag sometimes," said Martin. "In my line of work, I can't rely on the mainstream press to keep me informed. You guys are sometimes more right than you think."

"So what's your line of work?" said the stranger.

"I'm a UFOlogist."

"Sir, do . . . ," began Sander.

"A *What*-ogist?"

"I study UFO's. Unidentified flying objects. I run a little UFO museum in New Mexico. So, were you following that guy up the mountain for a story, Mr. . . . ."

"Uh, McDermont. Worley McDermont."

Sander sat bolt upright. *Oh my God,* his lips said voicelessly.

"Pleased to meet you, Mr. McDermont. My name's Martin Origen. And my friend back there is Sa—"

"Samuel. Samuel Johnson," Sander interjected hastily.

Martin shot him an odd look. "So you were tailing that Blazer for a story, Mr. McDermont?" he asked again.

"Uh, yeah. Yeah, I sure was. And I bet you were following it for the same reasons, given your line of work," said the man posing as McDermont.

Who is this guy? wondered Sander.

"A UFO story?" asked Martin.

"Bingo," said the imposter. "The guy in the truck maybe knows where the Saucer Man is—you know, that Sander Keynes guy."

"Really?" said Martin "What a coincidence. I—"

"I heard he was over on Maui," Sander interrupted again.

"He was?" said Rat-san.

"Really? Shit," said their passenger. Then he seemed to recover. "Well, the guy in the Blazer said he saw Keynes *here,* this very night, at the friggin' airport. Maybe the sumbitch just flew back. How far off is Maui, anyway?"

"Uh . . . ," said Sander. *Yipes,* he thought. *I was recognized?*

"It's the next island west of here—not counting Kaho'olawe," said Martin. "You know about Kaho'olawe, right?"

"What about it?" the drunk said, somewhat suspiciously.

While Martin explained the NASA viewpoint on the bombing of Kaho'olawe, Sander tried desperately to figure out how to simultaneously warn the UFOlogist and find out their passenger's real identity, without giving away his own—a mental task made all the harder by the fact that they were now careening down a terrifying serpentine, shrouded in rainy fog and flanked by groves of stunted trees or fields of jagged lava, while the odors of tequila breath and beery rat vomit drifted through the air. The road here had been repaved, but was crossed again and again by rippled sheets of flowing water, threatening to send the car hydroplaning at any minute. Martin had to ride the brake to stay under 45, as they swooped past curve sign after curve sign marked "35" or "25." Stuck in the back seat for the first time since childhood, Sander was on the edge of carsickness.

So Sander sat, as paralyzed as a cow in headlights, thinking *Don't think about vomit* and listening helplessly to the conversation unfolding in the front seat:

"So the goddamned aliens invaded the US fifty years ago?"

"Well, I wouldn't exactly use the word *invade.*"

"Why the hell not?"

"Well, first, the native Hawaiians sort of dispute that it's US territory. . . ."

"Fuck'em. We stole it fair and square. 'Sides, they voted for statehood, so they musta liked us once they got used to us."

This logic would have gotten the drunk a severe beating in many bars on the Big Island, but Martin talked right past it. "Second, the aliens may have been here 'way longer than that. In fact, they may well have been here before the overthrow of the Hawaiian kingdom. We suspect they even had secret permission from Queen Lilli'uokalani to establish their base."

"Queen who?"

"The last queen of Hawai'i. She openly defied a powerful clique of American businessmen. Then, when the businessmen staged a coup, she told all her supporters not to fight. I think she was counting on the aliens to throw the bastards out for her, but the aliens chose not to intervene."

"Do tell," said the fake reporter.

"Which brings us to my third point. I wouldn't call it an invasion, because there's no evidence the aliens ever shot back."

"You mean they just sat there and *took* it for fifty goddamn years?"

"Sure."

"Then why the hell'd we wait so long, before trying to invade *them?*"

"Hey, if you left hooked a six-foot-five boxer, and he just stood there and grinned at you, would *you* bore in close? Besides, they didn't want the aliens to find out the US was deliberately trying to drive them out."

"Huh? Say again?"

"That's what that whole elaborate concoction about the 'Target Isle' was about. They wanted to make it so hot that the aliens would leave, but they didn't want to appear to be deliberately attacking aliens. You know, 'plausible deniability.' So they created this whole ruse about using the island for 'target practice.'"

"Huh. Well, I'll be. So just what exactly *were* the aliens here for?'

"Why, to save us, of course."

"Shit, I'd rather have 'em trying to kill me. Ain't no fucking alien can save the human race. The only one who can save the human race is Jesus."

"Ah, I see. Sorry—I hadn't picked you as a believer type."

"Oh, I'm a sinner. No doubt about that. But I know I'll be saved in the end, because I've said those blessed words. I've said, 'Jesus I believe in you, come into my life.' And I know that I fall away from Him pretty often, but I still know I'm saved, 'cause I know the one deepest thread in my life is a pure, true love, and Jesus is never going to throw such a love away. And there ain't no space alien's ever gonna understand that."

Ohmygod, thought Sander. He remembered Jenny talking about this speech.

"Has it occurred to you that Jesus might *be* an alien?" riposted Martin.

Sander almost intervened, but Rat-san chose that moment to upchuck again. "I don't know which is worse, the driving or the conversation," the rat commented, when he was able.

Sander wanted to lift the suffering rodent to the back of the seat and tell him, "Watch the road, it might help." But with the car swerving around curve after curve, he wasn't sure he could pick Rat-san up without crushing him. And he couldn't talk to the rat, not when a stranger sat in the front seat. Especially not *this* stranger. Two more dilemmas crashed into his mental traffic pileup.

"Jesus is an alien," repeated the stranger, amusedly. "You know, that's fucking blasphemy. You're a fucking kook."

"Well I may be a 'fucking kook,' quote-unquote, but Sander and I . . ." He nearly swerved off the road, as Sander's knee jabbed against his back through the seat.

Too late. "SANDER AND YOU?" erupted the stranger.

"They met on Maui," said Sander, desperately, his mental block overcome by the sheer adrenaline of fear.

"YOU KNOW THAT SUMBITCH?"

"Yeah, we talked extensively. I might even be able to get you an interview," said Martin, quickly.

"WELL, I'VE GOT NEWS FOR YOU, MAN! WE'VE ALREADY INTERVIEWED THAT SUMBITCH ONCE. HE'S A FUCKING LIAR."

"Really?" said Martin. "What did he lie about?"

The stranger subsided a little. "The man's a fucking lying adulterer! He claimed he and Jenny Chillingworth were *just friends*, an' told all sorts of lies about the lady's husband, just to . . . to turn our magazine and the whole public against the man. If that sumbitch were president, he'd be impeached! I'm here to EX-POSE that fucker!"

Tell him to calm down, that he's had a bad accident, that we need to get him to the hospital, part of Sander's brain told himself. But simultaneously, he thought, *Don't call attention to yourself. This is Harlan Chillingworth, it's got to be. If it occurs to him that you're Sander . . .*

Then he realized that two thoughts were going on in his head at the same time, and his tongue was paralyzed because it didn't know which one to obey. And he suddenly knew that his mind wasn't just a single line of thought. It was a huge amorphous mass of thoughts, all going on at once. A tiny bit of that chaos called itself *I*, picked out a single tiny thread of firing neurons, and decided that was what he was consciously thinking. When *I* couldn't decide, his tongue and a lot of the rest of his body didn't work.

Then Sander knew what the Third Key was. And was truly, truly terrified.

At the moment, Martin appeared to be tongue-tied, too. Which left the initiative to Harlan. "I tell you what. Why don't we just go see this Sander Keynes tonight?"

You've gotta risk it, said Sander's *I*, coming unstuck. "L-look, you've been in a bad accident, Mister," he said aloud. "We've got to get you down to an emergency room. Meanwhile, you shouldn't be getting upset like this."

"I'M NOT FUCKING UPSET. LOOK, I'VE GOT A GUN IN MY POCKET. WE'RE GOING TO GO SEE SANDER KEYNES RIGHT NOW!"

Suddenly, Sander's *I* was dead calm. "Mister, I watched you crawl out of that car," it said. "You're wearing a wet Aloha shirt and skintight Levis. There wasn't anywhere you could have hidden a gun."

"I TELL YOU, I . . . I . . . I. . . ."

Ego jam. Go for it! "Look, we'll just forget you said that. You've been in an accident, you've had a little to drink, you're upset. The important thing now is to get you down the hill and get you checked out. We can try to contact Sander Keynes later."

"I am not drunk! I am not a drunk! I . . . Look, just let me out of the goddamn car. . . ."

"Keep driving, Martin," Sander said. "Look, mister, if we let you out up here, you could die of exposure before morning. You've been in an accident, your hands are cut up, you could be injured internally. I don't want the responsibility for reading tomorrow morning that they found your body."

"I don't wanta go to the hospital! I don't . . . I can't. . . ."

Suddenly, Sander realized that Rat-san was perched beside the headrest of Harlan's seat. "Shall I bite his ear?" the rat said. "If he's bleeding more, maybe he'll go to the hospital."

Sander shook his head violently. "Let's make a compromise," he told their passenger. "We'll drop you at the nearest emergency room. You can choose to go in or not. If you're feeling okay, you can walk away and call a cab."

"But what about Sander Keynes?"

"We can call you in a couple of days and try to set up an interview, okay?" said Sander. "What hotel are you staying at?"

"It's, uh . . . wait a minute." He pulled a soggy sheet of paper from his shirt pocket. "I can't read in this light. Shit."

Martin silently reached over and switched on the map light.

"It's the Hilton," said their passenger. "The Hilton Wai— The Hilton Wai-ko-lo . . . Wai-ko-loa?"

We passed the exit to Waikoloa on the other side, before the Saddle Road, thought Sander. *You're in for a long night, Mr. Chillingworth.* "The Hilton Waikōloa," Sander said. "Okay. We can remember that."

"Drat," said Rat-san. "I wanted to bite him." Just then the car went around another sharp curve. The rat lost his balance and tumbled forward, out of sight.

"Okay, I guess," mumbled Chillingworth, as Rat-san crawled back from under the front passenger seat and paused to put his bedraggled fur in order.

Scattered clusters of houses began to appear. They reached a long straightaway and flew down it, despite the 35 MPH signs, then hit another series of steep curves. Over the next 20 minutes, Sander watched not only mileage markers, but altitude markers slip past: 3,000 feet, 2,000 feet. . . . Their passenger broke into quiet sobs, which both Sander and Martin carefully ignored. By the time they'd passed the 1,000 foot marker and re-entered civilization, Chillingworth was snoring.

Martin managed to pull the damp map from beneath the accident victim's buttocks, and turned the dome light on so that Sander could navigate them to the hospital. They missed the turnoff where Kaūmana Drive diverged from new Pūainakō Extension of the Saddle Road, but found Komohana Road and took it back to Waianuenue, spotted a hospital sign and followed it up a steep mile's climb to the medical center, pulled in to the Emergency Room and roused their passenger.

He got out reluctantly. "You're gonna call me, right? To set up that talk with Keynes?"

"We're gonna call you," Sander assured him.

"You know, you guys are being pretty damned nice, for a couple of flying saucer loonies," the man said.

"It takes all kinds, Harlan," said Sander, tiredly. "It takes all kinds."

"Yep." Then Harlan did a double take. "Wait a minute. What did you call me?"

"Martin, drive," said Sander. "Drive!"

"Wha . . . ," Martin said, then peeled out.

They whipped around the circle drive and turned downhill, and saw their erstwhile passenger running a mad intercept course down the concrete handicapped ramp to street level. There was death in his eyes—his death, or theirs, or somebody's.

"Go, go, go!" yelled Sander. The minivan roared, ignoring a stop light and the QUIET HOSPITAL ZONE sign. They whipped past Harlan Chillingworth just in time to avoid his second accident of the night.

"So, Samuel Johnson," said Martin. "I guess we're not calling on the Hilton in a couple of days?"

Meanwhile, halfway up on Mauna Kea, a herd of cows trooped slowly through the *kauanoe* fog, and stopped to stare at the metal hulk that lay like a giant white beetle on its back.

Don't think about it, they thought, and dropped their heads to graze.

XXXVIII
Meanwhile, Back at
the Reservation

"Any answer, Shipley?" asked Senior Agent Daniel Whittaker, watching the cabin with his field binoculars. The place looked deceptively peaceful, perched against the mighty backdrop of sky on the canyon rim.

Shipley, the hostage negotiator, shook his head. "They're letting the phone ring. Not a good sign."

Whittaker shook his own head grimly. "This had better not turn into another Ruby Ridge, or all our asses'll be nailed to the wall." The helicopter took off behind them. Disgustedly, Whittaker let the dust settle a little, then wiped the new layer off his binoculars, hoping he hadn't damaged the special polarized coating that kept the lenses from winking in the sun and drawing hostile fire. After shivering all night, he was already starting to sweat.

"Sir?" called Special Agent Benchley. "What's that?" He pointed across the mesa behind him, at a small cloud of dust.

Whittaker brought his glasses to bear on the phenomenon. "It's an SUV. How'd a damn SUV get up here?"

"Those things can go just about anywhere these days," observed Special Agent Waldrop.

"Goughsky, call base. See if you can find out who that Jeep belongs to. Halsey, can you detail a sharpshooter to track it?"

Halsey shook his head. "The SWAT team's all deployed forward, per your instructions."

"Damn," Whittaker focused his binocs on the approaching vehicle again. "Huh. It's a Navajo squad car. Waldrop, you're checked out for an AAR, aren't you?"

"Yes, sir."

"Get one of Halsey's spares, deploy someplace inconspicuous, and keep a bead on that vehicle, just in case."

"Sir?"

"We don't want to get surprised by some Indian uprising, do we?"

"No, sir."

"But do be careful. We don't want any friendly fire incidents, either."

"Of course not, sir."

Whittaker turned back to the negotiator. "Anything, Shipley?"

"No, sir."

"What's your expert opinion? What's happening in there?"

"I don't know. There's any number of scenarios. Worst case, they've committed suicide. Or they don't want to talk anymore, which is almost as bad. Or maybe they just fell asleep. They had a hard night of rock 'n' roll."

"Then we'll just have to wake 'em up. Goughsky, cue up the Zappa set. Ear plugs, people! In five, four, three, two, one . . ."

Eight giant, highly directional speakers bombarded the cabin with the dissonant strains of the Mothers of Invention's "It Can't Happen Here." Unfortunately, with all of canyon country's echoes, the sound didn't stay highly directional. His own people's nerves were nearly as frayed as the alleged terrorists' must be. But the damned Joes had to be near the breaking point.

He had Goughsky cut the music as the squad car pulled up.

"Special Agent Whittaker? I'm Sampson Begay," said the Navajo cop. "We've talked on the radio. I ferried the women down to Tuba City yesterday."

"Begay, how'd you get up here?"

"I took the back way." Begay scratched his grizzled head. "I've got some interesting news for you folks. That's not Homer and Ho Begay in there."

"What?"

"I talked to Homer on the phone half an hour ago. He's been in a jail cell in Alameda, California, for the past 48 hours. So's Ho. They allegedly got into a bar fight with each other. He heard about all this on TV at the jail, and got real upset."

"But—didn't you talk to him when you hauled his wife and kids from that cabin?"

"I thought so. I guess I was wrong." Begay grinned that infuriating Navajo grin. "I didn't actually see Homer then."

"You didn't recognize your own nephew's voice?"

"Hey, I got a lot of nephews. You know we all sound alike."

"Well, didn't you ask his wife?"

"Now, why would I do that? We thought we knew who was in there already. She was upset enough, without being *Mirandized*."

Whittaker stifled a sigh. *Damn Navajos. Everything's a joke to them.* "So how'd you know it was Homer calling from jail?"

"I called the jail afterward. They faxed me his prints. I'd say he's got a pretty airtight alibi, wouldn't you?"

"Goughsky!" Whittaker barked in frustration. "Goughsky, call Alameda PD and check this story out. Shipley, get through to that cabin, and find out who the hell's in there!"

308

"I'm trying," said Shipley. "Still no answer." He shook his head. "I'm now extremely concerned. There's an excellent chance something's gone very wrong in there."

"Oh, just wonderful. Halsey, are your men ready to move?"

"We've been in position since 8 p.m. last night."

Suddenly, Whittaker felt icy calm. "Well, lay in some tear gas, and let's get on with it."

"Uh, sir, shouldn't we check with Washington?" asked Shipley. "They're kind of sensitive, you know, after . . ."

"This is an emergency situation," said Whittaker. "I'm authorized to act if lives are in immediate jeopardy."

"Mr. Whittaker, I also have a message from the Tribal Council," said Sam Begay. "They asked me to relay their extreme concern. They say you've entered our land with a massive armed presence and encroached on local authority, without establishing that a Federal crime has been committed. They're lodging protests in Washington, and urge you to act with due respect for the people whose lives are in your hands."

"Those *people* may be dying over there right now, whoever they are," said Whittaker grimly. "Do it, Halsey."

Four tear gas canisters arced toward the cabin. The first two bounced off the walls. The next went in the cabin window, sending shards of glass flying. The fourth flew through the window as well. The cabin's stovepipe suddenly tilted.

"Shit," said Sampson Begay. "I think you just knocked over the stove."

"Move it, McCloskey!" barked Halsey into his headset. "Be there when they emerge!"

No one emerged. Smoke began billowing from the windows.

"Goddamn," breathed Whittaker. "Send'em in, Halsey, quick."

"Go in! Go in!" Halsey shouted into his headset.

Two agents in bulletproof vests sprinted onto the cabin porch. One covered as the other kicked the door in. Flames roared out the doorway. Both agents beat a hasty retreat.

"Damn. God *damn* it," breathed Whittaker, verbalizing the curse that had just been laid on his career.

"Well, it's not another Ruby Ridge," said Sampson Begay. "Looks more like Waco, to me."

XXXIX
Paths of Convergence

A teacher at the local high school once called Pāhoa "an entire dysfunctional community." Hilo residents often refer to the citizens of Pāhoa and the surrounding Puna district as "Punatics." Some Puna residents have adopted that name as a badge of honor.

This is partly a fault of geography. Literally. The East Rift Zone of Kilauea (the World's Most Active Volcano), runs just east of town. Four Puna communities have disappeared under a layer of lava in the past three decades. Pāhoa could go tomorrow. The fact that it hasn't in over 150 years—though there was a close call in 2014—gives some residents confidence that it probably won't go for a while yet. For others, this same fact suggests that Pāhoa is overdue to undergo a going-under.

This, of course, puts a damper on real estate prices. So during Hawaiʻi's real estate boom 70's and 80's, and again in the boom between 9/11 and the Crash of '08, when island homes often sold at thousands of dollars per square foot, Lower Puna became the haven of the tired, the poor, the huddled masses yearning to breathe free, or breathe cannabis fumes, or "whatevahs." Prospective homeowners flooded into swatches of jungle and fields of old lava with names like "Hawaiian Paradise Park," "Orchidland Estates" and "Hawaiian Beaches," that had been partitioned off by Honolulu investors with visions of stupid Mainland vacation lot buyers dancing in their heads.

No one had actually expected anyone to live on those little squares of jungle, so there were no provisions for things like water or sewer lines. Undaunted, thousands of hardy souls erected above-ground swimming pool kits or galvanized live-stock tanks and hooked them up to gutter systems, trapping East Hawai'i's abundant rain for their bathrooms and laundries. Middle class families built dream homes they couldn't have afforded elsewhere, while their poorer neighbors assembled "Puna skyscrapers": two-, or three-, or even four-story plywood shacks, whose top floors peered over the jungle to catch the trade winds and an "ocean view." Some of the pioneers paid for plywood by starting little patches of *pakalolo* (marijuana) in the jungle, and those patches often ended up paying for very nice houses and "*pakalolo* Cadillacs"—four-wheel-drive pickups with *everything*—until the local police realized how lucrative helicopter-borne marijuana raids could be. Undaunted, one local entrepreneur started selling "Birds of Puna" T-shirts, identifying the various types of helicopters used by military and law en-forcement agencies.

And the dowdy queen of it all was Pāhoa, the Town Where the Sixties Never Died, the capitol of the Wild West of East Hawai'i, where hard-working hippies opened little crystal bou-tiques and health food stores, New Age smoothie shops and tasty ethnic restaurants, right next door to the bar and the pawn and thrift shops; where earnest-faced environmentalists ped-dled organic limes before the Akebono Theater by day and dealers pushed ice and crack by night; where the *Puna Press*, for years, ran issues containing two stories about police conspira-cies and four pages of "The Bionic Toad" comics; where teach-ers worried daily about the possibility of assault, but the little public library was crowded with children the minute school let out, and the Christmas Parade one year featured one Santa who passed out candy canes, and another who tossed handfuls of (sterilized, legal) hemp seed into the crowd.[1]

And where, early one evening, Nancy Wolf took Appy and Jenny to meet Gregor Norman Dennison, local NASA chapter president, at a local Thai restaurant.

Dennison was a big, bony man with a jowly face, piratical mustaches, and a body vaguely reminiscent of a grizzly bear after a hard winter. That was partly because, these days, he got all his sustenance from plant-based foods, including a daily dose of potato-derived vodka. But he was sipping a large Thai iced tea as he greeted Nancy and the two Duenckels.

"I've got news about your boyfriend," he said, grinning.

He wasn't my boyfriend. We were just dating. We . . . , Jenny started to object, then decided it just wasn't worth the effort. Especially not after watching the evening news tonight. . . .

"We heard about the fire," said Appy. "If that's your news, we'd rather not talk about it just now."

"Oh, no, no, no," Dennison drawled. "It's like, wow, it's much, much, *mucho* better. Like, what *didn't* burn. Like, *who.*"

"Sander didn't . . . ?" Jenny asked, not quite daring to hope.

"Nope. Now, I gotta be a little freakin' cautious here. Sander Keynes and his friends gave those Feds in Navajoland the total, awesome slip, though how they freakin' did it has got us just soulfully baffled, too. *Jesu-Christo,* man, it was just totally wild. I

---

[1] This figment neither endorses nor condemns the use of hemp products or their wilder cousins. In fact, this figment was composed entirely without the aid of mood-altering substances of any sort, excepting caffeine and sugar. Otherwise, the above passage might have read: "Hey, like, uh, Pāhoa was really, uh, really wild, with, uh, like those weird colors and shit."

got word from a *compadre*—I'm not saying who nor where—that Sander and a soulmate of mine are headed this way."

"Thank God," said Jenny, and realized she meant it. *God, what have you done to me?* she thought. *He's wanted for hijacking, he's been in a standoff with the FBI, he talks to invisible armadillos, and when people call him my boyfriend, I let it stand . . . and I'm thanking You for it? Heavenly Father, You've got some heavy explaining to do, when You've got a moment. Amen.*

"So when he shows up, you'll let us know?" Appy asked.

Dennison shook his head. "Sorry, pretty lady. That, no can do. I mean, I'll let you know if he shows up to *me*. *No problemo.* But unfortunately, I happen to know that my soulmate doesn't have my phone number. His notebook computer burned up when the Feds set the place on freakin' fire."

"But the news said the flying saucer cultists—I mean, the people inside—set fire to the cabin," protested Jenny.

Nancy Wolf tossed her graying black mane contemptuously. "So who do you think the newscasts got their information from? The *FBI?* You expect them to say *they* started the fire? That's why I brought you to see the man with the real news."

"So where do we go from here?" Jenny asked.

"I'd say we order lunch," said Appy.

"Try the pineapple curry," said Nancy. "It's just outa orbit."

"How can you all just talk about eating?" exploded Jenny. "Sander's alive, he's coming, but he doesn't know Harlan's out there. For all we know, they could be on the same plane!"

"Has Harlan ever seen Sander?" Appy asked.

"Uh, not that I know of. But his picture's been in the papers."

"Hon, nobody recognizes *anyone* from one or two pictures in the paper. An untrained person's got to see a picture at least six times before her memory starts tracking it—and even then, most people can't make the jump from a still photo to a living person. And Sander's changed his hair since then. Nah, unless those two happen to sit down beside each other and start chatting, Sander's not in much danger from Harlan, so long as he's not traveling with *you*."

"So who's this Harlan dude?" asked Gregor.

"My ex," answered Jenny, flatly. "He's violent."

Gregor sighed. "I know that old song. It's real common here. The most chilling phrase in Pidgin is 'local love.'"

"What?" asked Jenny.

"It's what local people say when they hear a woman screaming in her own home," said Nancy.

There was a brief silence around the table. Then Jenny called to the waitress. "Ma'am? We're ready to order."

At Nancy's suggestion, they ordered Thai-style fried rice, basil chicken, *gang sapparot*, and two plates of *satay*. Soon the rich aromas of curry and peanut sauce wafted from the kitchen, as they sipped glasses of the sweet, milky, orange-colored iced tea.

"This is almost like drinking a milk shake," remarked Jenny, trying hard to get her mind off what they'd just been discussing. It didn't work. She noted that the restaurant's broad doorway and open windows offered a clear view of the street—glanced to check where the kitchen entrance was, in case she needed an escape route. She wondered when she'd gotten into the habit of always sitting where she could watch a restaurant's door—and if she'd ever have a chance to get out of that habit.

"So, if I were going to haul a captured UFO to the Big Island, where would I put it?" Appy asked Gregor.

The gaunt man tipped back his chair and grinned. "Hey, ask me a hard one. *Everybody* knows where that freakin' place is."

Harlan Chillingworth emerged from Sears with two shopping bags full of clothing. It had taken time to find five aloha shirts that didn't have flowers on them. He was wearing one: a purple shirt printed with yellow marlins that looked like Jenny's refrigerator magnet. His face, bruised from the rental car's airbag, was even gaudier than the shirt.

The next step was a vehicle. He was sick of taxis already. *Fuck rental cars,* he thought. He'd just check the want ads and buy something, an old 4WD that could go up the trail where that Blazer had disappeared.

"Excuse me," he asked a passerby. "Where can I buy a paper?"

"Uh, try Long's Drugs," the woman said. "It's out behind the mall. Take that exit over there. . . ."

Following her pointed finger, he exited Prince Kuhio Plaza and started across the lot asphalt in the deepening tropical dusk.

Then stopped cold.

Parked between two SUVs was an old-fashioned enduro-style motorcycle, a big air-cooled Yamaha. The gas tank had been repainted stark, gleaming white, mellowed by the argon parking lot lights to the color of bone. The frame, oil tank and up-raked tailpipe were the matte black of an unlit cave. Street legal headlights, high clearance frame; big nasty two-stroke engine, probably a 450. Not sprangly and rangy like the newer enduros. It was a bear, a bull-gorilla of a motorcycle. Where could it go? Anywhere it wanted to.

And taped on the gas tank was a sign proclaiming, FOR SALE.

Jeb Stuart Arthurs finally had his man. He was sure of it. The problem was, his man didn't admit it.

"Come off it, Private Collins!" Arthurs barked, leaning in. "We've been over the rosters. You were the only man on duty during all these incidents!"

"But I was at my post, sir!" drawled the distraught young MP. "Ask my partners!"

"Private Collins, haven't you and the other sentries gotten into the habit of 'spelling' each other for bathroom breaks on long watches?"

"Uh, well, yes sir, but I never take more'n a minute or two!"

"That haste just explains some of the sloppiness—books left on the floor, phones knocked over."

"But where's your evidence, sir? Sir, I'm a good soldier. I got a clean record. Where's your evidence, that you'd go besmirching my record? I know I'm not on any of those security cameras, 'cause I wasn't there."

"Are you *sure* I haven't got any evidence? Think hard, soldier. If you confess now, we might be able to work out a deal where you don't do so much time. Maybe you can convince me you just thought they were harmless pranks, not betraying your country." Arthurs unconsciously fingered the stitches on his forehead from the collision with his desk. "But if this comes to a court-martial . . ."

Just then, the phone rang. Arthurs looked at it with dread, but resolved to answer it anyway.

It was the general, not the reedy-voiced saboteur. "Jeb, Poundstone thinks he's got something," said Buffalo Bill. "Get your ass up here to his lab."

"You sit here and think about it, Collins," Arthurs snapped at the unfortunate private. "He stays right here," he told the M.P.s outside the door, then hurried up to the Visual Electromagnetic Spectrum Laboratory.

"Ah, Captain Arthurs," said Dr. Hanson Poundstone, as the security chief entered. "I was just telling the general. I was working on some theories about how the saucer cloaking device works, and I remembered somebody's remark—I think it was Dupres'—about a "stealth suit." So I borrowed some security tapes, with the general's permission." He clicked his mouse, and the computer screen revealed an empty hallway. "Here's the hallway outside your office, the moment you hit your head."

He should have asked me for those tapes! thought Arthurs. But he held his tongue, for now. "So?"

"Did you notice that slight flicker to the image?"

"No."

"Let me replay," said the scientist. Arthurs' own figure charged through the scene, on his way to the rendezvous between his head and the desk. Arthurs winced.

"There!" said Poundstone. "That slight flicker, right after Captain Arthurs ran through. Gentlemen, unlike our phones, these are state-of-the-art digital cameras. That flicker shouldn't be there. But it's predicted under one of our models. Ah, hi, Jim. Hi, Matt."

Dubinsky and Meyers had entered, and pointedly moved to positions as far as possible from each other while still in sight of the computer monitor.

"I was just explaining to our military friends," he continued. "One of our physicists has a theory that the Object disappears when it moves because it defracts and scatters its image across time—maybe the Object itself even moves that way. Instead of going elsewhere, it travels else*when*—or else*maybe.*"

"Huh?" said Buffalo Bill.

"Think of it this way. You're going from Point A to Point B. The most efficient path would be a straight line—but straight lines are a physically impossible ideal. Instead, we have to take one of a virtually infinite number of actual paths through space-time."

"So?" said the general.

"Hi, Will. Hi, Rupert," acknowledged Poundstone, as Weismuller and Samuelson entered the room. Then he continued, "We usually think of time as a single line of events. We can deal mentally with other time lines, but we shunt them off into categories of possibility. If Dupres were here, he'd start talking about "if" and "could" and "should" and "might.""

"Where is Dupres, by the way?" said Weismuller.

"He's off with that fellow from MIT, setting up that idiotic communication experiment," said Samuelson, his voice dripping condescension.

"Well, at least we've *got* an experiment," remarked Dupres, entering with Karpov behind him. "We're not just sitting around reading bad science fiction novels for their Socratic wisdom."

"Hi, guys," said Joan Postlewaite, as she entered with a young chimpanzee riding on each hip.

"What are *those?*" Samuelson asked distastefully.

"This is Pandora, and this is Pandemonium," said Joan, giving each of the little creatures an affectionate kiss on the forehead. "Aren't they just adorable?"

"Uh, yes, they certainly are," said Poundstone. "At any rate, as I was explaining, some theoretical physics models extrapolate multiple paths through space-time. Most of these paths don't affect us; we can speculate about them by using our marvelous human linguistic and mathematic tools, but unless events are in sync with our own universe, they just don't register. The Object, and perhaps our poltergeist friend, could be moving on a closely related but slightly different path through time/possibility, like two people walking down the same hallway."

"Hmph?" said the poltergeist. He'd been sleeping under Karpov's work table when Buffalo Bill's summons had arrived.

It had taken the armadillo a little time to yawn and stretch and decide to check out whatever was happening.

"So the poltergeist is in a parallel universe?" said Dupres.

"Not at all," said Poundstone. "If it were a parallel universe, the Poltergeist's path and ours would never cross. Besides, like I said, the real universe holds no straight lines, so how can there be parallels? Paths of probability meet and diverge with reality all the time. In this case, our poltergeist's path may be so close that it intersects our own reality at myriads of points just before or after *we* intersect it. He's just never quite there when we are."

"So how do we detect him, Poundstone?" asked Buffalo Bill. "That is, assuming that any of this crap is true."

Poundstone ignored the "crap" and concentrated on the question. "Our digital cameras synchronize with human reality— otherwise the picture would be snowy or out of focus. But they're still not as finely tuned as our own eyes. So they're catching this flicker, which *may* be our poltergeist."

"I take it this, uh, cloaking device doesn't affect sound?"

"The telephone receiver is a much grosser instrument," said Poundstone. "Especially *these* telephones. Aside from the computer trunk lines, the phone system here is a dinosaur, and sound is a much grosser signal anyway. It's *always* got a good deal of the past mixed up with it, in the form of echoes and bounce back. Our brains normally help us filter them out. But telephone receivers don't, which is one reason why we get so much static and distortion. I bet if you took those phone recordings and 'cleaned them up' with digital filters, the intruder's voice would almost disappear from the recording."

"Splendid," said Arthurs. "So what do we do to catch him?"

"We're already doing it," said Poundstone. He touched a computer key. The screen slowed, then froze.

"Huh," grunted Weismuller, staring at the screen.

"So?" said Samuelson.

"What? What?" said Dick.

"See that little curve?" said Poundstone. "That's our intruder."

"Our intruder's a little curve?" said Dubinsky.

"Not *all* of our intruder. The bit that happened to intersect our own space-time at that moment."

"That's not much of an ID," pointed out Arthurs.

"No, it's not," admitted Poundstone. "But it's a piece of the puzzle. With a little help from Matt, I designed a data compilation program based on a filter routine we borrowed from a program that Jim designed."

"Stole, you mean," growled Dubinsky.

"We're supposed to *share* information, remember?" said Meyer.

"Information. Not patentable software under development," snarled Dubinsky. "Who knows what sort of bugs crept in, once these two cretins got hold of it?"

"Well, it checked out well enough, *despite its source*," said Meyer, icily.

"Enough!" said Buffalo Bill.

"At any rate, it was a huge, complicated undertaking," continued Poundstone. "I had to design enhanced filter/compilers to sort through millions of still frames and spot anomalies of a certain type, then assemble them into a three-dimensional composite, compensating for different angles, distances and rates of movement. It was so complicated that I had to arrange for time on the Cray supercomputer on Maui. Then I input the entire image stock from our security cameras. . . ."

"You did *what?*" exploded Arthurs. "You transmitted all our security tapes to a computer in *Maui*? And didn't even *ask* me?"

"I authorized it," growled Buffalo Bill.

"At any rate, the Cray's crunched the data and used them to construct an image of the intruder. It's like a forensic sculptor re-creating a victim's face from bits of an old skull, only exponentially more complicated. The results are downloading now."

"Oh, shit," breathed Dick.

"Sir, I have to protest this!" exploded Arthurs. "You don't solve one security breach by creating another one!"

"I don't know that you've solved *any* breach, Arthurs," said Weismuller. "And I *still* haven't gotten my books back!"

"And you don't steal patentable subroutines and send them off to other computers, goddammit!" shouted Dubinsky.

"What about the ones *I* helped *you* write?" demanded Meyers.

"Please! Please! You're upsetting Dora and Mony," said Postlewaite, rocking the chimps. "They're not feeling good, anyway, poor things."

"QUIET, PEOPLE!" roared Buffalo Bill. "Something's coming through!"

A hush settled, except for Pandemonium, who was screeching plaintively. Joan hurried out, singing a lullaby. The rest stared at the screen—except for Dick, who sincerely wished he could. "Ohmygod," he muttered. "If this works, I'm gonna need a new home, fast." He started edging through the forest of legs, toward the door.

Suddenly Dubinsky burst out laughing.

"*That's* your intruder?" said Weismuller, then broke into guffaws himself. Laughter quickly spread to the others, except Poundstone and Arthurs.

"I don't know how this could have happened!" exclaimed Poundstone.

"Face it, Poundstone," chortled Meyer. "We've been hoaxed."

"But a program this complicated . . . the man would need access to a Cray, himself!"

"Or a much simpler program that dispersed digital images in a manner similar to sound waves," said Dubinsky.

"This still has to be a very clever opponent, with some big technical resources, to pull this one off," said Arthurs.

"That could describe any of us," noted Weismuller.

"And a sense of humor, to boot," said Buffalo Bill. "Shit, an *aardvark!*"

"I believe that's an armadillo," said Meyer, and broke into chortles once more.

They all offered their condolences to Poundstone, then dispersed, still laughing.

Wait till the wife hears about this one, thought one of them.

They're going to love this one in Tel Aviv, thought another.

They're gonna have a hoot at the Company, when they hear about this, thought a third.

Then they were gone, except Poundstone and his nemesis.

"You bastard," said Poundstone staring at the computer. "How did you do it? *Why?"* Then he broke into sobs.

"Well, score another one for the evil armadillo," said Dick, settling warily under the table. "You just probably ruined a scientist's career. You know, Poundstone, I really wish I could talk to you. You're generally a decent guy. And it gets lonely. . . ." He sighed. "But I can't trust you guys. You're just interested in finding out how and why, without considering the consequences. I don't know how much longer I can keep you guys safe from yourselves. This can't go on. . . ."

And he was right. Several paths were now converging like satellites in dying orbits, for the primary shape of motion in the real universe is not a straight line, nor even a curve, but a spiral. Converging purposes were drawing the people they controlled into a tighter and tighter tangle.

New Agers often speak of fostering "harmonic convergence." But dissonant convergences are just as likely. In fact, the difference between harmony and dissonance may simply be which side of the spiral you happen to be on.

That's were peace comes from. And explosions.

XL

The Man Who Didn't Know

Sitting in a small Internet café in downtown Hilo, Sander pulled up the familiar web page with its cupids and scroll. In the message window, he typed,

> Dear Madame Asfura,
>   My girlfriend's on vacation, but I just learned her ex knows where she's gone and is stalking her. How can

He frowned, then deleted what he'd written. The time for hints and subterfuge was past. Instead, he wrote,

>   Jenny and I became separated, and I don't know where she is. Contact her if you can. Tell her Harlan's nearby. She has to get out of here. Tell her I've found the Keys. I love her, but I'm too dangerous to be with. I'll find Dick myself.
>   Armadillo Man

He watched the scroll burn up and disappear, then decided to check if Appy had left any messages for Lost My Heart in

Armadillo, TX. He found one new scroll in the chest, and stared at the message.

"Okay, I'm done," said Martin, sitting the computer beside Sander. "I'm back in contact with my compadres."

"I'm done, too," said Sander. He looked up, and pain showed in his eyes. "I found a two-day-old message for Jenny and me from Appy. Harlan killed somebody in Missouri. I want you to phone Crimestoppers with an anonymous tip that he's here." He wrote down Madame Asfura's URL and his password to the treasure chest, and handed them to Martin. "Here. Keep checking for messages."

"You sure you want to go through with this?" Martin asked. "Don't you want to keep looking for this lady?"

Sander shook his head sadly. "Harlan could pick up my trail as easily as hers. If we're both together, it doubles his chances. She's better off without me. And if the saucer gives those people what it gave me, then I have to be there to control the damage, if I can. If I choose . . . "

Martin nodded gravely. "Anything else I can do?"

Sander shook his head. "Just ask your friends to find Jenny and keep her safe. Now I have to go see a man about a job."

They exited the café, shook hands and parted. Sander walked past a black-and-white motorcycle parked outside an Army surplus store, on his way to the vaguely New-Agish little cafe where he'd arranged to meet Karpov. He bypassed the wrought-iron sidewalk tables and settled at a table inside, carefully shifting the camera pouch on his belt so he wouldn't sit on it. Keeping a nervous eye on the street, he ordered a slice of blueberry cheese cake and an iced Red Zinger from the gingham-smocked waitress.

Karpov appeared on the sidewalk. He shaded his eyes, trying to peer from the tropical sunlight into the cafe's depths.

Sander waved.

The scientist entered. "Hello, Mr., uh, King," he said, advancing with a smile and an extended hand. Sander stood and met it.

"I see you've already ordered," Karpov continued.

"Feel free," said Sander.

Karpov snagged a cream Danish and an all-natural cherry cola from the counter girl, then sat down. "So, you're interested in employment at my little, uh, enterprise."

"Maybe," said Sander.

"You know, as a biologist, you should find this island fascinating," remarked the scientist. "If Darwin had seen what's happening up on Mauna Kea right now, he might have written a very different Theory of Evolution."

"Really? How's that?'

"There are whole new ecosystems evolving, based on introduced species—but it's not species against species. It's *team* competition. Some old, established teams, like grass and cows. Some brand new coalitions, like the pigs and the poka."

"Pigs in the poke?"

Karpov chuckled. "Uh-uh. Not 'poke.' 'Poka.' Banana poka. It's a vine related to passion fruit. Feral pigs gobble the fruit, then root up the native forest understory, and poop poka seeds on the freshly-uprooted earth. The poka vines smother whole forests—creating a tangle that pig hunters can't get through." He took a sip of his cola. "'Survival of the fittest' is survival of those that fit together."

"So I'd be studying alien species?" asked Sander.

Karpov fell silent a moment, then smiled. "Yes, you might say that."

"Hmm. Just how alien?"

Karpov chuckled. "Some of them are really weird. Especially the humans. But my interest is broader than that. You might say I'm seeking the keys to unlock the soul."

Sander's heart sank. But he'd more than half-expected this. "Are you sure you want to know the answer?" he asked.

Had there been more light in the cafe, Karpov's eyes would have glittered. "If I did, would you help me?"

His voice was nearly drowned out by an engine reverberating on the street. A man on a black-and-white motorcycle cruised past the café's open front. A huge machete in a green canvas sheath was strapped to the handlebars. Hawai'i had no helmet law; there was no mistaking the rider's gaunt, bruised face.

Then it was gone. Sander heard the bike's engine growling at the next stoplight. It roared off uphill, toward the Saddle.

"You look like you've just seen a ghost," remarked Karpov.

"Worse than that," said Sander. "So you know who I am?"

"I think so. Speaking of ghosts, you're looking awfully good, for a man who supposedly burned to death yesterday."

"No one came with you?"

Karpov shook his head. "Naw. I'm on my own. Nobody really believed that I saw you."

"I know the feeling," said Sander, fingering his camera pouch. "This place is a little public. Do you have a car?"

"Sure. But we might as well eat our sweets before we go."

A few minutes later, they were cruising up Kaūmana Drive toward the Saddle, with fresh sugar coursing through their veins like a New Age mantra. They rode the first three miles in silence, negotiating the stop lights and traffic of Hilo. When they were above the last 7-11, Karpov could restrain himself no longer.

"So," he said, "have you really found the keys to unlock the soul and end the world?"

"Yes," said Sander.

"Do they work?"

"I think so. Do you really want me to find out?"

"I don't know."

"I could try them, I suppose," mused Sander. "I don't know if using the keys would end the world. I'm pretty sure that they could end *me,* as I know me. But at this point, it doesn't matter much one way or the other."

"That sounds a little glum."

Sander shrugged. "Since finding that thing on the sand bar, I've lost my job and had to flee my home. I've been spied on, arrested for hijacking, and I just lost my woman. And it wasn't much of a job or a home to start with, and I'm not sure I ever really had a claim to Jenny."

Karpov nodded. "My condolences."

"But that's not the worst of it. I've seen the press peddle lies for profit and public servants hound people out of their homes for the public good. I've encountered a police system that hunts down innocent people and lets maniacs walk free, and a medical system that puts people in boxes without even a trial. And I've seen love used as a sick excuse for all sorts of nastiness." He gave a short, bitter chuckle. "I guess they picked a pretty chancy guardian for the world's future, didn't they? By the way, you might want to go slow. There's a motorcyclist up ahead whom we *don't* want to catch up with."

"Okay," said Karpov. "This isn't a fast road, anyway. Some poor slob flipped his car up here, the night we arrived."

"I know," said Sander.

"Let me guess. You were in the second car following us."

"The third, actually."

"And the man in the other car?"

"He wants to kill me."

"But he was following us, not you. You were following him."

"I didn't know who he was, then. But he knew you'd seen me. He was following you to get to me."

"Hmm. Our security chief said he was a tabloid reporter. Why would he want to kill you?"

"He's not a reporter. I knew that reporter."

Karpov nodded. "So you did. Now I remember. I read that interview. Very interesting."

"I lied a lot."

"I know. Why?"

"Because even *MorningStar* wouldn't have run it, if I'd told the truth. But there's one thing I didn't lie about. That motorcyclist—he's the man who was following you. He's Jenny Duenckel's ex. He's dangerously nuts. "

"I see."

The Blazer wound around the first serious set of curves. Ahead, clouds were already building on the Saddle.

"Some other people who had contact with the saucer have reported seeing some odd things," said Karpov. "Some of their descriptions sound like paranoid delusions."

"Do *you* think they're seeing delusions?"

"I don't know," said Karpov. He gave a little chuckle. "That's my secret, by the way. Some people think I'm a genius. Actually, I'm not that far above average. But I'm willing to say when I don't know. That gives me a huge edge."

Sander nodded. "I see things, too. But some of my delusions leave real poop behind, and eat real ants."

For once, Karpov lost his cool. When he'd gotten the Blazer back on the road, he said, "Eat ants? Like an armadillo?"

Sander stared at him. "You've seen Dick?"

Karpov's hands were actually trembling on the steering wheel. "I've seen a composite computer image of an armadillo. Everyone dismissed it as a hoax."

"Thank God!"

Karpov shot him a curious glance. "That little outburst seemed genuine."

"Yeah, I guess it was," said Sander. "Look, I don't know if I'll use the soul keys or not. But if you want my help with the saucer, I need *your* help with two things. One, help me lock up that maniac before he finds Jenny. And two, help me find Dick."

"Hmm," said Karpov. "If the base security officer hears that the missing reporter is really Jennifer Duenckel's homicidal ex, I'm sure he'll pass the word on to the local authorities. Would they have reason to arrest him?"

"Yes. There's a manslaughter warrant in Missouri."

"Good. As for Dick, we're already hunting frantically for him. He's made a damned nuisance of himself."

They climbed a long straightaway and swung around the curves past an isolated subdivision, crouched in the rainforest where it shouldn't have been. An ominous sign ordered, TURN LIGHTS ON. Ahead loomed the waiting maw of the *kauanoe* fog.

"Do you want to go up to the facility with me?" asked Karpov.

"They'd just let me in?"

"Of course not." said Karpov. "But we can try a couple of things. I could try issuing you a clearance as my assistant and colleague. After all, you *are* the world's foremost expert on the Object. And if that doesn't work . . . ?"

"If it doesn't?"

"Well, I'm sure they'll be happy to arrest you."

XLI
Love in the Gorse

"What, Mom? *What?*" Jenny stared at her mother's face, which itself was staring into space over the screen of her notebook computer, her morning coffee cup suspended in her hand perilously close to the keyboard. A whole series of emotions played across the older woman's face.

"It's a message from Sander," she said. "It says . . ."

But Jenny had already jerked the little computer around to stare at the screen. She read the message on the scroll from Madame Asfura's treasure chest, then walked away and sat down heavily into one of Nancy's batik-covered bean bag chairs. ". . . I love her, but I'm too dangerous . . ." she repeated softly, then fell silent. Her face went through its own workout.

"Honey, he . . . ," her mother began.

"He's still trying to *rescue* me!" Jenny erupted. "That bastard! Shit. . . . Sorry, Mom."

"Honey, *I've* never tried to curb your language, remember? You did that to yourself, to spite me. Well, we'd better . . ." She stopped herself. "No. If you don't want a man to rescue you, you don't want me to, either."

One expression finally had won out over the others on Jenny's face: a rigid mask of determination. "You're right, Mom. I don't. But I could use your help."

"What are you going to do?"

"I'm going to rescue *him*, the bastard."

A couple of hours later, Gregor Dennison pulled up in his battered Chevy pickup. "So, ladies, like—oh, man, wazzit?—like, are you ready to hunt *flying saucers?*" he chortled as Jenny and Appy trotted out of the Pāhoa Pride B&B.

Jenny immediately had a bad feeling about this—partly because of the odor of alcohol in Gregor's vicinity (contrary to popular alcoholic belief, you *can* smell vodka on the breath). But alcohol was not the predominant drug in Gregor's bloodstream this morning. A distinctive smoky aroma also hung about him. It wasn't tobacco smoke.

Appy grasped the situation instantly. "You know, there doesn't look like a lot of room in your cab. Why don't Jenny and I take our car and follow you?

"What? Oh, man, you can't take a rental car . . . uh, you can't take a rental car where . . . where *we're* going."

"Why not?"

"Well, uhm, like, they don't let you and shit. It's bad up there. Gotta have a four-doubleyou-dee to get there, anyway."

"Uh, why don't we compromise?" said Jenny diplomatically. "We'll follow you up to the point where we have to go off-road, then we can get in the truck to go the rest of the way."

"Uh, well, all right, man, if that's how, uh, like, you want to do it. Like, how you want to *do* it, right?" He sniggered at whatever it was he had just said that he thought was clever.

"I'll go start our car. We'll be right behind you," said Jenny.

"What are we going to do when we get up to where he wants to turn off-road?" she asked Appy, as they pulled out.

"He may be a little less high by then," said the elder Duenckel. "Providing, of course, that he's not carrying three or four joints with him."

They followed the pickup back out onto the highway and on into Hilo, then started up the Saddle Road, with which the reader is now familiar: curves, *kauanoe*, etc.—which didn't make it any less frightening for Jenny, encountering it for the first time. Fortunately, the pickup they were following seemed to handle the curves fairly well. The nimble but underpowered subcompact was straining to keep up.

"Maybe marijuana *doesn't* affect your driving as much," said a somewhat astonished Jenny.

"Don't you believe it, Hon," said her mother. "It might not affect his reaction time as much, but he's even more likely to forget something important, like the fact that he's driving."

They followed the pickup to the little tree-covered cinder cone at the base of Mauna Kea Observatory Road. Gregor pulled off into a cinder parking lot beside an empty Hunter's Checking Station. The women followed, and stepped out into a biting wind.

"Gad, why didn't you tell us to bring jackets?" shouted Jenny, hugging herself as she ran toward the pickup.

"Oh. Wow. I'm sorry. I didn't think about that," said their guide. But he didn't look quite so unfocused as he had before. He had stepped out of the car to shrug on a battered sheepskin coat, and had squashed an equally beat up cowboy hat down over his mane. Suddenly he looked like an extra from Clint Eastwood spaghetti western. Jenny almost expected his next words to be, "Hey, Blondy!"

Instead, he said, "They call this 'Pu 'u Huluhulu.' That's Hawaiian for 'pubic hair hill.' Isn't that just wild, man?"

Appy eyed the little cinder cone critically. "I can see a vague resemblance," she said. She rummaged in her purse and pulled out a plastic emergency raincoat.

"Uh, this isn't the place, is it?" asked Jenny.

"The place . . . ," repeated Gregor. "Uh, what place?"

"You know, the place where, uh, the saucer . . ."

"Oh!" Gregor laughed. "Nah. But you'd better leave your car here. We got some monster trails to cover from here on. . . ."

"Jeez, it's freezing," said Jenny, shivering.

"Yeah, 'n my heater don't work, either," Gregor said. "Hold on, I got something." He rummaged in the cab, and drew out first a mildewed Mexican blanket, then a huge beach towel emblazoned with the nude figures of John Lennon and Yoko Ono—fronts on one side, backsides on the other. "All right. One for each of you," he beamed. "Well, crowd in, and let's get this show out of the hoosegow. Or you could ride in back. The view's gonna be awesome."

"That sounds like a good idea," said Appy. She accepted the blanket and clambered over the tailgate. Shaking her head and shivering, Jenny took the beach towel and followed.

"What on earth were you thinking, Mom?" she whispered harshly, as she climbed into the truck bed. "Even if he doesn't roll the truck—we're going to freeze to death back here!"

"Yes, but we don't have to worry about getting groped," said Appy. "And he *has* come down some. Take it from an old hitchhiker, girl. A pickup bed's the best seat in the house!"

They huddled behind the cab to avoid the occasional banks of *kauanoe* as much as possible. But the pickup soon left the clouds behind as it complained its way slowly up the mountain. After that, the high-altitude sunlight did fair combat with the chill air. The view truly was spectacular, as they gazed out over cloud belts and upland pasture and rainforest—and beyond, the incomprehensible immensity of blue water. . . .

The truck turned off the asphalt. The ride became rougher, though the views remained breathtaking. But close at hand, the sights were less pleasing. The pasture here had once been an upland tropical forest. A few twisted, scrubby trees remained, their lower branches denuded and broken off by cattle. The huge old cinder cones that they passed had an oddly terraced effect from scores of cow paths winding around them. (Cattle, unlike people, have the good sense to never wear a path straight up and down a hill).

But in some places the trees seemed to have discovered an unexpected ally. Thistle-like shrubs with yellow flowers crowded over the ground, and the few remaining trees among them seemed to be recovering their greenery.

Jenny found out why, half an hour later, when the truck finally bounced to a halt.

"Pit stop!" called out their driver, emerging from the cab. "Uh, you ladies may want to get out on the other side of the truck, so everybody's got a little privacy?"

Jenny got up stiffly, wishing she hadn't abandoned her neck brace a few days before. She winced as the feeling returned to her butt, activating nerve endings in the fresh bruises there. Then she walked to the back, swung herself carefully over the tailgate, lowered herself into the bushes—and shrieked.

"What's wrong?" cried Appy, forcing her older muscles to hobble to her daughter's aid. But Jenny had already helped herself, scrambling back up on the bumper. "Those bushes!" she gasped.

The yellow-flowering shrubs bloomed in profusion just below the tailgate. They were extremely, wickedly thorny. Even the leaves were edged with spines, which had sunk into her calves as easily as a hot wire slips into butter.

Gregor had hastened around the truck to see what the fuss was about. "Oh," he said, and laughed as he finished zipping his fly. "That's gorse. They brought it from Scotland a make cattle hedges, only it decided it didn't like growing just in straight lines." He gazed sadly about. "Yeah, take a look. We're sitting in the middle of a genuine, freakin' post-human ecology. This stuff is making its own rules now, and we've got no part in it. Now, if you'll excuse me. . . ."

This particular patch of gorse had spread over hundreds of acres. There were no cows in sight.

A few minutes later, they were on the trail again, bouncing over ancient Hawaiian cobbles that alternated with stretches of pure dirt ruts. Gradually, the gorse dwindled into outlying patches, then disappeared. The pickup turned off on a branch trail that was even rougher than the first, and began climbing steadily.

Downslope, a new vista was slowly opening up. They had traveled two thirds of the way around the mountain, and were now looking down toward the pasturelands of Waimea and the green ruins of a far more ancient volcano, which looked as if half of it had already eroded into the sea. Beyond, they could even see the misty summit of another mountain on another island.

Finally the truck pulled to a halt again.

"Awri-i-i-ght!" bawled Gregor, emerging from the cab again.

"So we're really here?" Jenny asked. "Where's the entrance?"

"Entrance? Oh, we're not *that* close. I thought you'd want to see where it was, before you freakin' drove up to the front door," said their guide. He swung easily up into the truck bed, and pulled a small, cylindrical leatherette case from his pocket.

It held an old-fashioned brass spyglass. He unlimbered it and scanned the landscape below. "Right . . . *there.*" He lowered the glass and pointed. "See where that blue SUV's approaching those three ranch buildings?"

Jenny squinted. "I guess so. That's it? That's all of it?"

"What you can see of it. Here, take the scope. Watch what freakin' happens when the truck reaches that cabin."

Following Gregor's instructions, she adjusted the spyglass's focus by pushing the smallest telescoping segment in and out. The image jumped around with every breeze, but finally she located the ranch's cabin-sized bunkhouse. The little scope was surprisingly powerful; she could make out individual clapboards in the cabin walls.

The blue truck pulled up beside the cabin. Then the truck began sinking. A face in the passenger window peered anxiously out. Jenny adjusted the focus, lost the truck, found it again.

"Ohmygod. Ohmygod," she gasped.

"What's wrong, Jenny?" asked her mother.

"It's Sander! I just saw Sander disappear into a hole in the ground!" She lowered the glasses in disbelief.

"At that distance? Are you sure it was Sander?" said Jenny.

"I'm pretty sure. . . ." But in that last moment, that tiny white face, so clearly full of surprise in spite of distance and inexpensive optics, had reminded her of someone else. A frantic white rabbit, calling out, "I'm late!"

"Well, we expected him to go there," Jenny said resolutely. "That doesn't change the plan. It just makes it stronger."

"What's that flash down there?" Appy asked, pointing.

Gregor squinted. "It's some dude on a motorcycle. Dirt bikers come up here all the time. You probably saw the sun on his mirrors. I don't grok why he's stopped out there in nowhere land, though. Maybe he's got problems. Let me borrow my scope back." He focused the spyglass on the biker. "Hey, he's checkin' us out, too. Watching us with a big pair of binoculars. Man, how bi-polar reciprocal! Light reflected from him, watching light reflecting from us, watching his light. Awesome!"

"What? Let me see!" Jenny snatched the spyglass back, and struggled to bring the finicky instrument to bear on the motorcyclist. "Oh, God. Oh, SHIT! Mom, it's Harlan!"

The motorcyclist dropped his binoculars and revved his bike up the mountain slope toward them.

"Gregor, get us out of here!" barked Appy.

"Hey, what's the . . ."

"That's Jenny's crazy ex on that bike!"

"I grok, I grok. Roger, Wilco and we're outa here!" Gregor vaulted over the side of the truck bed and scrambled into the cab. The truck roared to life.

It had been over two decades since Harlan had owned a motorcycle. That one had been a Honda 350 "Thumper" enduro, the world's largest one-cylinder four-stroke. He'd bought it because he couldn't afford a car at the time. The previous owner had ridden the hell out of it. Harlan had even had to have the frame welded after the cracked tail fell off. But he'd loved the vibration of it in his bones. He'd sold it only after he'd proposed to Jenny, because a husband needed more serious transportation, especially with the kids Harlan was sure were coming. But somehow the kids had never come, and he'd gotten fired from one job, then another, and drifted from one junker car to the next. . . .

It felt wonderful to have a bike between his legs again: a good, powerful old bike, from the days before emissions standards and stupid little radiators. The big two-stroke roared like a horny caged demon. Riding jockey-crouched like a wild kid, he

flew across pastureland and stony scrub, dodging rocks and ancient logs, whumping perilously across deep-cut cow paths. "Wooooeeee!" he yelled, on his joyful-desperate way to a reunion with his true love. . . .

"He's trying to cut us off!" yelled Jenny.

"If I go any faster, I'll flip this thing!" Gregor shouted back. Jenny and Appy were already taking a beating, clinging desperately to the pickup's sides to keep from being flung across the bed. They lost sight of the motorcyclist as they passed a big cinder cone. Then Jenny spotted him again. He had come up to a paddock fence and was running parallel, looking for a route up to them.

The pickup was narrowing the gap itself, though. They were descending more rapidly, heading for the cloudbank that was piling up on the eastern side of the island. *If we just make it to the fog, we can lose ourselves,* Jenny thought. *If I can just hang on.* The altitude or the jolting or both were getting to her stomach. She felt nauseous; her head throbbed. She glanced at her mother, clinging white-faced beside her, and felt even sicker. An angry bruise was swelling on Appy's forehead, where she'd banged it against some part of the truck. "I'm sorry, Mom!" Jenny shouted, suddenly realizing that her mother was really a rather frail-looking, sixty-four-year-old woman who should never have had to accompany her grown daughter on such a venture. . . .

They wouldn't have made it, if the motorcycle hadn't come to a corner in the fence that turned the wrong way. Harlan pounded the handlebars in frustration, then turned and sped away, looking for a gate.

The truck hit a stretch of ancient basalt cobbles, rattling every joint in the vehicle and their bodies. Then they plunged into the first tentative finger of fog. Jenny welcomed its chilly touch, almost as much as she'd welcomed the sun when they'd emerged from the clouds earlier.

Then something, some other noise, impinged on the flood of relief surging through her. An angry buzzing swelled in the mist behind them—a giant Weed Whacker, a demon-prince of chainsaws, coming up fast behind the pickup. A headlight appeared, then the outline of a huge machete strapped to the handlebars, then a mud-streaked, purple-wealed face.

"Shit! Here he comes, Mom!" Jenny shrieked, looking wildly around for her purse, which held the can of Mace she'd kept in case this moment ever happened. But her purse had slid back to the tailgate of the wildly bucking pickup. And what could a little can of Mace do against that monstrous blade, anyway? She risked letting go of the bed wall with one hand, and groped for anything that could be used as a weapon.

The black and white bike roared onto a cow path beside the main road, and swept up alongside the truck.

"I love you, Jenny!" yelled Harlan Chillingworth, just as John Lennon and Yoko Ono's nude terrycloth backsides sailed from the truck and wrapped themselves around his face.

The bike and its rider went down, bounced into a stand of gorse, and then disappeared into the fog in the pickup's wake.

Jenny let out a shriek of triumph. But the emotion was short-lived, as Harlan's words—perhaps his last words—sank in. She stared back into the mist.

"Mom, what if he's hurt?" she shouted to her mother.

"Good!" Appy shouted back.

"But. . . ." She couldn't finish the thought.

"Men can go back and save their enemies," shouted Appy. "Women can't afford to."

"He loved me, Mom," her daughter said.

"They always do!" shouted her mother. "And yet they can do that to someone they love. That's why they deserve to die!"

Jenny shook her aching, tormented head. Then the Numb One took over again. *You may have just killed your former husband,* she thought. *Okay, you can't change that. Move on. Your current male friend just sank down a rabbit hole.*

"If the police ever trace that towel to us, we say it blew out of the back of the pickup," she told Appie. "I tried to grab it, but lost my grip."

Appy nodded. "Okay. Let's make sure Gregor hears that version, too. All he probably saw was the towel flying out in the rearview mirror. But no prosecutor's going to try a case of murder by beach towel, anyway."

"All right," said Jenny.

"So what's next?" her mother asked.

Jenny thought for a moment. "Mom, when we get back, I want to go on the Net. I want the e-mail addresses for Reuters, CNN, Fox, the Huffington Post, all the networks. I want you to help me set up a Twitter account. I'm sick of running. Everybody else has used the media. Now it's my turn."

A patch of gorse saved Harlan's life. But being gorse, it exacted immediate payment. His new leather jacket protected him somewhat, but hundreds of spines, each a fraction of the diameter of an average sewing needle and twice as pointed, still lanced through Harlan's clothes and flesh, all the way down to the big nerves that lurk in the lowest layer of skin, waiting to scream havoc. He shrieked and rolled frantically out of the patch, taking more lances in his hands, wrists, shins and right cheeks (both fore and aft), then scrambled to his feet in a frantic war dance of pain. He saw the motorcycle, its motor still purring as if it weren't lying on its side, ten feet into the gorse patch. John and Yoko lay nearby, smirking their peaceful Om-ishness, despite the myriad of spines protruding through their private areas.

"Jenny," Harlan moaned. "Jenny, I loved you. All I ever wanted was to love you. How could you do this to me, when I loved you?"

He didn't even notice that he was using the past tense.

The spells of love and hate are mixed from many of the same potions: obsession, denial, powerful emotion, fierce devotion to the cause. Like many opposites, they are actually more alike than different. In some relationships, it's already difficult to tell them apart. It's not as hard as one might think to transform one into another.

By the time Harlan got back down the mountain, the metamorphosis was nearly complete.

XLII
The End of the World's Fair

The camera crews arrived first, drawn by footage on YouTube of a Humvee slowly sinking into a hole in the ground. Then the faithful started to assemble. The saucer cults arrived within hours of the first podcast, and were quickly followed by other cults that had suddenly decided to incorporate saucers into their theologies. The VonDanikenians for Jesus and the Neo-Cargoites were especially troublesome, marching repeatedly straight toward the military cordons in hope of setting off the Apocalypse, but triggering pepper spray instead.

Little did they know how near the Apocalypse might be.

And at first the cordons had started at the boundaries of Pohakuloa Training Area. After all, the Facility was located within the larger Army base. (The cattle were there by lease to a local rancher who happened to be a retired Army colonel.) But the rangeland was just too open; there were too many hunters' trails and ranch roads. Anyone who wanted to knock down a couple of fences or hacksaw the chains on a gate or two could drive or hike or ride right across the rangelands.

The cults were soon joined by anti-nuke protesters, drawn by reports that the saucer might be radioactive. Then Native Hawaiian activists showed up, demanding to know why a secret military facility had been bored into the bowels of their sacred mountain, whose lava tubes often housed ancient burials. Then more Native Hawaiians arrived to protest the first group of Native Hawaiians. Meanwhile, the Training Area's attempt to close the Saddle Road met with howls from local politicians, prompting senators and representatives to intervene. (In an effort to maximize profits for certain real estate interests, the Big Island was zoned with most of its job-producing resort hotels on one side of the island, and most of the so-called "affordable" housing at the other end, leading to a mad 5 a.m. derby of maids, janitors, groundskeepers and bellhops commuting over the Saddle Road. The developers paid for political campaigns, but the janitors voted.)

Pohakuloa, it seemed, was one fort that couldn't be held.

The administration in Washington considered action. At a cabinet meeting, someone pointed out that the protestor's chaotic encampment presented a perfect opportunity for Islamist bombers. Someone else pointed out that if the terrorists struck there, it wouldn't kill anyone important, so long as they could be kept out of the Facility itself, and it might divert attention from the current economic unrest. The President, who until now had been Kept Out of the Loop to Maintain Plausible Deniability, listened with a fair amount of interest to all this.

"We really have a flying saucer?" he asked, finally.

"Yes, Mr. President," said Walter Baker. "We believe it's the genuine article."

"Hmm," said the Commander in Chief. "Walter, why don't you go over and check this situation out personally?"

Meanwhile, all those saucer-loonies were spending badly needed money at every level of the island's economy. A flood of better-heeled New Agers were filling Kohala resorts and Hāmākua

B&Bs. The Puna T-shirt entrepreneurs began joining the morning commute, their old pickups and minivans crammed with T's bearing imaginative renderings of UFOs and aliens on the front and ALOHA ALIENS or FREE SANDER KEYNES on the back. Shave ice trucks and lunch wagons picked their way up the mountainside to the tent city that had sprung up on the range; homeless families brought their tents and camp stoves up from the beaches, and pedaled *manapua* and *pasteles* and *malasadas* and spring rolls, steamed or deep-fried on the spot. By the fifth day, local restaurants were setting up their own catering booths. Local teenagers showed up in droves to check out the excitement. So did the local pot, ice and crack dealers.

By then, the topside defense perimeter had shrunk to about a 500-yard radius in the immediate vicinity of the Facility's now very public "secret entrance." Guards patrolled one side of the perimeter's hastily-erected chain-link fence. Aging hippies and saucer cultists hung banners on the other side.

And among all this wonderful chaos on the mountainside, Jenny Duenckel strode like a slightly out-of-shape goddess in a FREE SANDER T-shirt, the red-gold starting to gleam again at the roots of her dyed auburn hair. She gave endless interviews and recruited her protesters, led her sign-wavings and shouted in her bull-horn, protected by a small bodyguard of NASA members and by the tide of her own publicity.

And high up on the mountainside, crouched in the gorse, Harlan Chillingworth watched through army surplus binoculars. He'd hunted for a long-range rifle, but Hawaii had the strictest gun control laws in the nation, and Harlan just didn't know the right people. So he kept the machete strapped to the bike's handlebars, and waited, and bit his cheeks in rage and despair.

Meanwhile, the koa log lay under its layer of Kikuyu grass, a dozen yards from Jenny's and Appy's tent. It wasn't lying in wait. It was a log, after all. Simply lying there was sufficient.

XLIII
A Better Rat Trap

Mike Dupres was pouring a cup of coffee when he noticed a faint but unpleasant odor. Then he remembered the traps.

Like everything else in the beleaguered base, the vermin problem had gotten out of hand. As the once-minimally-staffed Facility had sprung to bustling life, smaller life forms had crept in and multiplied, dining on a growing abundance of coffee spills and food crumbs.

So on his last trip to town, Dupres had bought some glue traps out of his own pocket. He'd set them inside the coffee room cabinets, then forgotten them. Until now.

Gingerly, he opened the sink cabinet door. A less than appetizing odor rolled out. Holding his breath, the scientist peered inside.

"What the . . . ?" he breathed.

He'd laid three trays inside. The victim in one had expired. In another, a rat still twitched, its breath raspy with ingested glue, its tail and legs and head all stuck down. Not a pleasant death.

But rats and glue were all coated with bits of white tissue. Not a millimeter of stickiness remained exposed. A roll of paper towels in the cabinet had been knocked over and gnawed for the raw material.

By the time Dupres had hauled out the third tray also covered with gnawed paper towel, the first two had drawn a small crowd. For once, even Dupres was at a loss for words.

"Damn. Smart rats," was all he could manage.

XLIV
Family Reunion

Mauna Kea isn't as solid as it seems. It is, after all, a dormant volcano (a fact that many astronomers, ranchers and towns-people—not to mention the cows—would rather forget).

Big "shield"-type volcanoes such as Mauna Kea are naturally as hole-y as sponge cake and gaseous as a cow's gut. A shield volcano is built from rock so hot that it isn't just melted, it's *boiling*—full of sulfur dioxide and other extremely unpleasant gases that should have been minerals. (An active volcano smells of planetary farts.) When this lava hits open air, it freezes in mid-boil. The resulting spongy rock makes a great insulator, eventually forming a continuous roof over lava flowing to the ocean. When something finally plugs the plumbing, the lava already in the system flows onward, leaving a cave.

As volcanoes go, Mauna Kea is not quite an old fart. But it has reached sedate middle age, only venting its guts once every few millennia. And it remains riddled with millions of cold, damp and extremely black lava tubes.

By excavating rooms off of these natural caves, the builders of the Facility had saved untold man-hours of clandestine tunneling. But the resulting hallways were a sloping compromise between the needs of military engineers and of molten rock, who usually thought in very different ways.

Lava logic also tended to grate on the nerves of the military and scientific types currently in residence. They had spent their whole lives imposing Order on Chaos, but now found themselves laboring every day up and down tunnels that Chaos had taken a large hand in shaping. The Chaos factor, along with old-fashioned claustrophobia and the Poltergeist's continued depredations, had played a major hand in the "Morale Crisis" that now loomed nearly as large as the "Security Crisis" in the minds of both Buffalo Bill and Jeb Stuart Arthurs.

Both crises came to a natural head in the matter of the Jerry Karpov's guest.

It was the champions of order who were reduced to screaming near-incoherence. Karpov, who had written papers on Chaos Theory, was doing a much better job of keeping his head.

"What do you mean, 'not a security risk'?" shouted Arthurs. "The man's a subversive!"

"Oh, come off it, Jeb," said Karpov. "You know that as Head of Research, I have authority to screen and recruit experts. I ordered a background check on Keynes the minute his name became known—after all, he's the *only* authority on the Object's interior. You know what the FBI found: not even a traffic ticket. He was a rather boring model citizen, right up to the moment his canoe beached on that sand bar."

"The man tried to hijack a 767!"

"He was *accused* of attempted hijacking," said Karpov. "TSA found a nail clipper on him and freaked. The FBI found no substantial evidence."

"The same FBI who had a shoot-out with this man over in Arizona?"

"Oh, come off it, Arthurs. I was sitting beside him on the plane, the day he was supposed to be in that cabin! In fact,

351

everyone they thought was in that cabin was out of the state that day. Didn't *you* read the FBI file?"

"I-I haven't had time to complete it, it's so damn thick!" sputtered Arthurs.

"This is the information age, Arthurs. The FBI could generate 300 pages on a ten-year-old."

"Well, you know what?" growled Buffalo Bill, "I don't goddamn care what Airport Security thought he did. And I certainly don't care about the damn FBI, who don't know their goddamn ass from a goddamn Navajo in the ground. I just know someone used my own goddamned telephone to leave a message for this man."

"Someone else breached security," pointed out Karpov. "We don't know that this 'Dick' did so at Keynes's instigation, or even with his knowledge. And we don't know that what was transmitted actually constitutes a security breach."

"Hell, we don't know what it means at all," said the general. "But it could've been 'The Itsy Bitsy Spider,' for all I care. It was transmitted without authorization, and Keynes was the goddamn intended recipient, which makes him a security risk. This base is on goddamn maximum security, goddamn it, for so long as that goddamn Object is here. I can detain *anyone* who risks its security-including you, Jerry, goddamn it."

"I see," said Karpov, slowly. "So, should I cancel the test and tell everybody they can reach me in the brig?"

"No, you're not going to goddamn cancel the test. And Keynes is goddamn staying in his cell, at least until Grubbs's psycho-med squad gets here to check him out. Then I want him off this base, unless he helps us apprehend his saboteur friend-maybe even after that, if I'm not satisfied he's clean. Arthurs, I want all the FBI material on him on my desk by eleven hundred hours."

Karpov smiled. "I thought you didn't goddamned care what the FBI thought, Bill."

Just then, the "urgent" pager tone beeped on the general's computer. Buffalo Bill picked up the phone. "Williams. Yeah, he's here. One moment. It's for you, Arthurs. Sergeant Glauber."

Arthurs took the phone. "Arthurs," he said. "You're kidding. Damn. We'll be right down." He handed the handset back. "We've got another security breach—a major one. Glauber just recorded a network news feed. He's down in the media room."

"Goddamn it. Okay, let's goddamn go," said Buffalo Bill. "We'll talk more about this later, Karpov."

The media room was just a few steps downhill. As they arrived, a monitor was blaring,

". . . newest weapon of terror, as the wave of cow bombings continued in northern India today, with three animals exploding in New Delhi and four more in the Gujarat province. . . ."

"Sorry, sirs. Over-rewound," said Sergeant Glauber. "Here it is."

"White house sources today confirmed that the saucer-like object discovered in Missouri three weeks ago apparently was not lost in a flood, as previously reported, but was moved to the same secret research facility in Hawai'i where eyewitnesses say Sander Keynes, the so-called 'Saucer Man' who discovered the UFO, is also being held . . ."

"White House sources!" fumed Buffalo Bill. "How the hell are we going to maintain security when the damned White House itself leaks stuff? Arthurs, I want the perimeter guard doubled."

Arthurs shifted uncomfortably. "Uh, we can't, sir."

"Why the hell not?"

"We don't have enough guards. You've already ordered double shifts."

"Well, draft some cooks or something! When are the goddamned Strykers arriving?"

Arthurs shifted to the other foot. "They can deploy in about two weeks, sir."

"*Two weeks?* Goddammit, a Stryker brigade is supposed to be a *rapid deployment force!*"

"Yes, sir. But the President ordered it flown in."

"So?"

"Uh, there was a glitch with the specs when they ordered the Stryker vehicles, General. A C-130 can't safely fly a Stryker vehicle with full combat equipment up to Bradley Field at Pohakuloa, and most of our C-17s are deployed forward in the War on Terror."

"Well, what about those criminal trespassers terrorizing this base? What about the terror from the skies, when these goddamn saucers start coming down in real numbers?"

"I'm on your side, sir," Arthurs reminded him. "Anyway, they're stripping the vehicles down, flying them in one by one, then re-equipping them. Colonel Sakamoto has sent a request to the President to countermand and send the vehicles in by barge from Honolulu. If they did that, we could have a significant force here in four days. But the request is going through channels."

"Well, get me a conference with somebody at CINCPAC about expediting that request. We don't need a whole Brigade Combat Team. Four or five Strykers with supporting infantry oughta be enough to put the fear of God into these goddamn hippies."

Arthurs shifted feet again. "I suggested that to Colonel Sakamoto. But the Army's a little sensitive about under-deployment after—you know—Iraq. Uh, permission to be frank, sir?"

"Granted."

"Sir, I suspect somebody's dragging their feet upstairs. The President probably doesn't want to be seen cracking down on unarmed demonstrators. It's not like the old days."

"Damn! Dismissed, all of you!"

The general strode angrily back to his office. On top of everything else, he was late for his private appointment with Captain Postlewaite, who wanted to return to her wind tunnel duties. The general allowed himself a grim smile. That woman at least knew how the game was played, in the *real* military.

That evening, Dick prowled the winding corridors uneasily, noting the new phone jacks that had appeared during the day. Why were they putting phone jacks in hallways?

He decided to stop by the canteen for a late-night roach snack. The counter boy, a young private, was asleep at one of the tables; otherwise, the place was deserted except for various small skitterings. The base's bug population had swollen so much that he didn't have to go outside to forage anymore.

The armadillo's ears swiveled like sonar, tracking targets. Giant flying cockroach on the floor at two o'clock. *Too big.* Cave centipede at five o'clock. *Don't mess with that buggah.* A mouse or rat behind the counter, or maybe under it. *Not on the menu.* Five adult German cockroaches. *Too fast.*

Ah, roach nymphs.

Dick ambled happily around the counter, sending the rat scuttling for cover. Several nymphs were working a piece of bacon that had fallen between the stove and the counter. The rat had probably wanted the bacon, too, but the space was too cramped for even a rat to get at. An armadillo's tongue, however, fit quite nicely.

He lapped up a couple of bugs and munched contentedly. The rest of the nymphs scurried off. No matter. They'd return shortly. He settled back, tracking.

The rat ventured out of hiding. Dick ignored it, focusing on roach noises, until his fellow mammal ventured into range of his starboard eye. Not just any rat. A white lab rat.

"Hey, where'd you escape from, little guy?" he said.

"A dream," said the rat. "Also a prison in Los Angeles, and a quarantine crate, and a camera case."

That got Dick's full attention. "You can talk."

"Likewise," said the rat. "You must be Dick. I hate you."

"What? Who are you, anyway? Did you get into the flying saucer or something?"

"I have never seen the flying saucer. I'm Rat-san. Sander dreamed me up, but all he talks about is you!"

"Sander's here? Where is he?"

"I'm pleased to meet you, too," said the rat, sarcastically.

"I'm sorry. Where are my manners? Rat-san, you said?"

"Rat-san. Until I think of something better. He gave *you* a *real* name."

"Yeah. What a great name it is, too," Dick said, not yet truly aggravated, but getting there. "Is Sander here?"

"He was somewhere in these tunnels. I don't know if he still is. They took all his things, including the camera case I was in. This is all your fault. He came here looking for you."

"Are you sure he didn't come here looking for answers?" said Dick. "The meaning of life, or how do talking armadillos spontaneously appear in bathtubs, or some such nonsense?"

"He came looking for you," the rat said. "I'm the one who wants answers like that. He never gives them to me. All I know is that he dreamed me, and now I'm stuck here, and I'm going to die too soon. But at least now I've gotten laid." He gave a little snort. "Big deal."

"That *is* a big deal," said the armadillo, remembering a female armadillo's untimely demise. "You could be a father."

"That's no big deal to a rat."

"It might be to your kids," said Dick, picturing little piebald rats—half-gray and half-invisible?

He decided not to pursue the thought, for now. "Where did you last see Sander?"

"In a town called, uh, Hilo," said the rat. "I rode up here in a camera pouch with him. . . ."

"Must've been crowded," Dick observed.

"You know what I mean. Anyway, I was asleep when the trip started, then I got so carsick I didn't want to even stick my head up. The next thing I know, someone opens the lid, says 'There's nothing in here but a goddam bad smell,' and tosses my case on a shelf." Rat-San shuddered. "Since then, I've been living like a *real* rat. Scuttling around in the walls. Eating garbage. Fighting for food, for sex. I'm not big, but I figured out how to sidestep a charging rat, grab him by the ear or the neck, and steer his nose into the wall until he squeals to get away. I've tasted rat blood. I've seen sick rats, dead rats. I've seen glue traps. Have you ever seen a glue trap?"

"Well . . . uh . . ."

"I can't imagine the mind that thought up a death like that. Conscious, terrified, becoming more trapped the more you struggle, your mouth bloody from trying to chew the plastic to free yourself, the glue getting down your throat. . . . I wonder if they have the brains to wonder how the end will come? Exhaustion? Thirst? Choking? Beating by some blunt instrument, while you can only look up, unable to dodge?"

Dick didn't know what to say.

"Rats are condemned to death just for living," said the rat.

"So are all living things," said Dick, but that didn't make it seem more fair.

"Okay, so we've met," said Rat-san, after a pause. "Now what?"

"I bet Sander's down in the brig," said the armadillo. "No—quarantine, come to think of it. Okay, let's go."

"Where?"

"To rescue Daddy." Dick set off at his best armadillo scuttle.

They had nearly reached the quarantine area, and had just rounded a bend in a corridor near Arthurs' office, when Dick suddenly stopped.

"What . . ." began his companion.

"Shh!" Something wasn't right. Dick swiveled his supersensitive ears, sorting the myriad noises that crowded the hallway. Air rustled and fans hummed in the ventilation ducts, as usual. A rat was gnawing on electrical insulation in the wall on the right. Conversations rose and fell in distant rooms. A computer keyboard rattled in Matt Meyers' office, a hundred feet or so up on the right. From the darkened office on the left came noises of clothes rustling against carpet and lips smacking on flesh. But he'd heard those sounds before. They weren't what had put him on alert.

The ears kept swiveling, then locked on.

Ahead, one of the newly installed phone hookups had been covered with a slightly bulging plastic plate. From behind that plate came a faint hum, pitched above the threshold of human hearing.

Dick turned carefully and retreated, with no more noise than the faint click of an armadillo's digging claws on floor tiles.

A couple of hundred feet back down the corridor, he breathed a small sigh of relief.

"What was that all about?" asked Rat-san.

"Shh. They're installing microphones in the hallways. There's one under that plate in the wall up ahead."

"They can hear you with a mic?"

"A telephone receiver can pick up my voice sometimes. I thought I had to work at it to make it happen, but at least one of the scientists thinks the phone would pick me up anyway. You, too, probably. Oh, by the way, I'm not exactly popular around here, though they haven't figured out exactly what I am."

"Wonderful. Have *you* figured out exactly what you are?"

"I'm a misincarnation—an armadillo with a human soul, a dream that accidentally got an identity stuck inside it. There are all kinds of names for it. But mainly, I *am.*" He let out another sigh. "Gee, that felt good. Do you know how long I've been waiting to give someone that speech?" He paused thoughtfully. "I don't think I'm going to alarm anyone too much if I walk quietly past one speaker. But if they wire the whole place...we've got to act fast. But how are we going to get Sander out? Wait a minute, I've got an idea. . . ."

Mike Dupres and Technical Specialist First Class (Signals) Wiley Standish were tuning the new listening array in the sound lab when the alarm happened. Dupres was setting up modified versions of software he'd designed for SETI's radio telescopes: filters set to sift through the random noise of the universe and winnow out certain sound patterns that might indicate speech, even alien speech. They'd already installed subroutines to recognize the vocal harmonics that had characterized Dick's telephone messages. (Dupres personally thought that was silly.

"Dick" wasn't going to speak through an electronic tempero-randomizer unless he was disguising his voice on a telephone—was he?)

"One through five are checking out normal," said Standish. "We've still got static on Six. Some clicking noises on Three—maybe rodents."

"Well, get 'em working," growled Dupres. "The speakers, that is, not the rodents. We need an operational array extended to the UFO chamber by oh eight hundred tomorrow."

Gad, listen to me, Dupres thought. *I'm starting to sound like Arthurs. This place is getting to me, too.*

Then the scream hit.

"FIIIIIIIIIIIIIIIRRRRRRE!"

"Where's that coming from?" Dupres yelled.

"Number three!" Standish pointed at the readouts for the third of the four test speakers they'd installed. The numbers were going crazy. Whoever was screaming was doing so at a pitch an octave or so above that of the normal human voice.

Dupres looked up at the TV monitor. The section of corridor around Microphone 3 was totally empty.

"Switch to headset!" Dupres yelled.

"Do I have to put it on?" Standish yelled back at him.

"No! But we've gotta report this! If I pick up a phone now, the feedback will blow the skull off the guy at the other end!"

"How about if I just turn the volume down?" yelled the phone specialist, and he did so. Then he rang up Emergency Control. "Norm? Hi, it's Wiley. I'm in the Sound Lab. Some-body's screaming 'Fire!' over one of our new mics. Yeah, Cor-ridor 3C, Section 15, but there's nobody there. Crossed wire or something. Yeah, I got it on screen right in front of me."

Captain Archer was having a private interview with Captain Postlewaite. *This woman knows how things work in the real Air Force,* he thought appreciatively.

"You know, I didn't . . . really . . . think you'd . . . do it," he murmured.

"I'm really very good at my job," Captain Postlewaite replied, between pants. "Do you realize that? *Oh!* But if there's one thing—*uh!*—that I learned in the Air Force Academy, it's that . . . to get ahead—Oh, *God!*—a woman has to be more than that. She has to be a bitch—*uh!*—and a whore. God, I'm gonna . . . have rug burns."

"You *are* . . . very good . . . at your job," Captain Archer agreed.

Then the fire alarm went off.

"Okay, stay calm," Archer said, scrambling to his feet. "Oh, for Christ's sake, stay away from the door until you've got your bra . . . I mean, there might be a fire on the other side."

"Shit! Just help me with my goddamn bra, goddamn it!" said Captain Postlewaite.

If bras sometimes seem difficult to take off when one is in a hurry, they can be hell to get back on in a panic. Somehow, with some cursing, the job was done. While Joan struggled with her blouse buttons, Jeb pulled up his pants, straightened his tie, and cautiously touched the doorknob. It was cool.

"Ready?" he asked. "I'll go first." He opened the door and peered out. People were boiling out of their offices, headed uphill. A phalanx of military firemen, advancing nervously up the corridor, were already almost up to his office door.

"Just stay calm, people!" Archer shouted in his best command voice. "All civilians proceed in an orderly fashion to the nearest exit! Military, stay at your posts unless otherwise ordered!" He stepped out in the corridor—and suddenly his feet went out from under him. He fell sideways, flailed his arms frantically to avoid the nearest firefighter's ax, smacked his forehead into the next fireman's metal extinguisher—which left nearly as bad a gash—then hit the floor hard as Captain Postlewaite tripped over his legs. The third firefighter stared in horror, then opened a frequency on his two-way. "Corridor 3C-15. We have a man down. Repeat, we have a man down. Make that two men down—er—a man and a woman. Two casualties. Wait, the woman's getting up. No, she's down again. . . ."

"Hey," said the second fireman. "Aren't a lot of women trained to call out 'fire!' when they're being raped?"

"Yeah. It's supposed to get more attention than yelling 'Rape!' Why? Oh, I see. . . ."

Sander and Karpov were playing chess in the quarantine unit when the alarm went off. Sander was losing, of course, but not as badly as either man had expected.

Karpov looked up when the alarm erupted. "I do hope they remember to let us out of here, if that's genuine."

Sander smiled. "Self-contained air supply, stainless steel walls inside solid rock—could you think of anyplace safer, if they don't?"

Nothing else happened for several minutes. The alarm shut off. Then it resumed again.

"This makes it really hard to concentrate," said Sander. Then another buzzer went off: the chamber's air seal was being broken. An M.P.'s surgical-masked face appeared in the door. "I'm sorry, sirs," he said, "but we need to evacuate you."

"So the fire's real, Harry?" Karpov asked the M.P.

"We think so," Harry answered. "Mr. Keynes, would you please present your hands for cuffing?"

Sander sighed, and held out his hands.

They stepped through the air-seal door into the corridor, then past the guard at the doors to the quarantine zone. But a few yards down the hallway, Harry's feet suddenly went out from under him.

"Dick!" said Sander. "Hi! Ah! Rat-san! *Konishiwa!* I was worried sick about you two! Are you all right, Harry?"

Sander started to kneel beside the guard, but was interrupted by an invisible questioner.

"What? But I don't want to leave," the prisoner replied, apparently addressing the floor. "Not yet, anyway. Dick, Rat-san, this is Jerry Karpov. Oh." He turned to the scientist. "They both say you've met, sort of. They've met you, anyway."

"Invisibility does limit one's social life," observed Karpov. "Er, what about the fire?"

"They say it's a false alarm. Dick yelled, 'Fire,' then they slipped into the light lab in the confusion, and knocked off a laser, then—what?—then they used it to fry a smoke detector."

"We definitely have the wrong person locked up," remarked Karpov. "Or the wrong mammal, or mammals, or whatever."

"I wonder if it was the laser you were going to use in the experiment?" said Sander.

"No, that one couldn't fry anything. We were very careful to specify *that*," said Karpov. He knelt beside the fallen guard. "Out cold—probably a concussion. Let's see, assault and battery, destruction of government property, espionage, trespass . . ."

"Dick says, 'Just try and prosecute,'" said Sander. "Let's get some help for Harry, then we can talk in my room. No, Dick, I *don't* want to leave."

He went back to the quarantine block and buzzed the intercom on the outer door. "Hi, Corporal Hardy. This is Sander.

Harry tripped and hurt his head. Can I come back in where it's safe?"

"I don't believe this," muttered Dick, as they followed Sander back into his stainless steel womb.

"At least the ETQC's not quite as Spartan as that crate was, eh, Rat-san?" Sander remarked. "Look, a real bed, a real easy chair, a real bathroom with a shower. We've even got cable."

"That's the toilet?" asked Dick.

The object in question was lower and flatter than the average American john, and had a seat with adjustable "swing wings."

Sander chuckled. "Dick's asking about the toilet," he told Jerry Karpov.

"That's the MT83-H, the most humanoid of several different models designed to snap into the plumbing," explained Karpov. "This chamber was designed to quarantine aliens, after all. The human furniture came from the Officer's Club."

"I am *so* glad you're okay, Rat-san," said Sander. "I wish you'd have let me leave you with Martin, like I wanted."

"Papa-san, Martin is *weird*," protested the rat.

Sander sighed. "Teenagers," he said apologetically.

"Oh, that reminds me. I got laid," Rat-san added.

"Congratulations. I'm not going to even ask you if you practiced safe sex."

"There *is* no safe sex for a rat. Papa-san, there's no safe anything for a rat." The little rat shuddered. "Have you ever seen a glue trap in action?"

Sander shuddered. "Yes. Those things should be banned."

"Excuse me, but I have a question," said Dick. "What are we doing here?"

"Dick, you've always had that question," observed Sander.

"I mean, *here* here. Locked in a stainless steel tank," the armadillo elaborated.

"Dick, I've been running ever since I found you in my bathtub. Every time I ran, things got worse. I finally realized that I really didn't have anything to run from."

"But isn't this place going to get boring rather fast?" asked the armadillo.

"Let me guess," said Karpov. "Dick's mad because he went to all that trouble to spring you, and you didn't leave with him."

"He's actually being pretty restrained about it," said Sander.

"I don't think he'll be here long, Dick," said Karpov. "His girlfriend's been busy. Which reminds me. . . ." He pulled several envelopes from his pocket. "Letters of introduction, recommending you highly for a paleoanthropology field internship, as an intelligent, original thinker, proven steady and adaptable in exotic and high-stress situations. Most are for Board Members at Nairobi Museum. I met Meave and Richard Leakey years ago at a conference in London. Charming people. And there's a letter to Tim White—I once spent an afternoon with him, debating the shape of pithecanthropine voice boxes over a few beers. I'd stay away from Johanson, though. He's a bit of a stinker. That's just my opinion, of course."

"Thanks, Jerry." Sander stared at the letters, and remarked wonderingly, "It all seems sort of childish, now. But on the other hand, why not play?"

"I wanted to make sure you got them, in case something unexpected happens," said Karpov.

Sander nodded grimly. "If something unexpected happens, there may not be an Africa to go to. Jerry, I sincerely hope the saucer doesn't tell you guys what you want to know. You, maybe, could handle it. But those other folks. . . ."

Karpov nodded. "If you give humanity a gift, the saints and villains both get it. Well, I've got to go. We can finish the game later, if you'd like."

"Sure. Dick, you want to stay and chat? Otherwise, this may be your last opportunity to leave for a while."

"Do me a favor?" said Karpov. "If Dick's leaving again, don't tell me about it."

Dick swallowed. 'I, uh, guess I'll stay. But this place gives me the creeps."

"He's gonna stay," said Sander.

"All right, I'll be going, then. And Sander? Remember that Grubb and his psych/med team are coming in tomorrow. Don't do anything too weird, okay?"

"Sure, Jerry. See ya."

"What did he mean by that last remark?" asked Dick suspiciously, after the theorist had left.

"He was reminding me about the camera and microphone in the ceiling, and the team on the way here to decide if I'm loony."

"Oh, so you shouldn't be talking to us figments of your imagination?"

Sander smiled. "I didn't say the camera and microphone worked."

"You sabotaged a camera, and they didn't fix it?"

Sander smiled. "I've been practicing a few things. Small things—safe things, I hope. The camera's still running. It just doesn't show the quite same reality. I'm afraid it hasn't occurred to the repair people that the screen could be black because they're looking at the inside of a rock."

"Dick and I made a great team, Papa-san!" Rat-san burst out, tired of being ignored. "He knows where everything is, and I can get up everywhere he can't! We ran this whole place silly!"

"Yep, and then walked into the brig," sighed Dick. "Why are you so interested in staying, Sander? What the hell's going on?"

"The end of the world, maybe," said Sander quietly.

There was a moment of silence.

"I'm glad I had sex, then," said Rat-san.

XLV

What Belly Dancers Don't Show

The end of the world didn't come the next day. This was, after all, a government-sponsored project.

Nor the day after that. After all, the military was a part of it.

Nor the third day, since this effort involved inter-service and interagency cooperation.

But by the fourth day, some progress was being made, even though the media had gotten involved.

On the fifth, Mike Dupres was ready to sacrifice chickens or stick pins in voodoo dolls or pledge his unborn son to the Great God Poobobo. Whatever it took to exorcise poltergeists.

". . . chewed through, too. Probably a rat," Wiley Standish said. "It would have electrocuted the rat, except somebody had already pulled the plug."

"I can't believe this!" said Dupres. Then he remembered the glue traps. *Uh-uh. Nah.* . . .

"I think the rodent damage is incidental, even though it's gonna be expensive to fix," said Standish. "It's weird that a rat would gnaw the same part in four different modules. Maybe there was some trace element it craved. Jeez, with all the mildew in here, it's a wonder these things run at all."

Dupres nodded grimly. "The rats and the mildew are both way out of hand. Damn. So how soon can we be back online?"

"I'll have to order the parts. We might have one or two replacements in stock, but not four."

"Damn. We'll have to postpone the experiment again, or risk having the Poltergeist present. Well, do what you have to do."

He strode angrily back to his office and poured a cup of strong coffee from his own drip machine. (He avoided the coffee room these days, since it might lead to chance encounters with Rupert Samuelson, Joan Postlewaite, or a very smart rat with a grudge.) What was really annoying was that while the poltergeist still seemed to have it in for his particular project, it had been showing a softer side lately. There was that bouquet of orange tritonia and white native poppies that was left outside Poundstone's door the morning after his armadillo fiasco. And Spfc. Canton, who'd lost her engagement ring between the stove and the counter in the mess hall during her KP shift, and hadn't dared ask anybody to move the stove because she wasn't supposed to wear jewelry while on duty. The stove never had gotten moved, but the ring had somehow magically appeared on her bunk the next day. Maybe those incidents were just anonymous humans being nice, though. He didn't really want to think about it.

Ignoring his government-issue PC, Dupres opened his own notebook computer to log a personal diary entry. But the minute he switched the machine on, a small Liberty Bell icon began flashing in the upper right-hand corner.

"Damn. *That's* all I need," muttered Dupres. He pulled up his e-mail program and unscrambled the message. "We have traced the crate . . . ," it began.

Dupres read the rest in horror. He had to let people know about this. But how, without breaking his deep cover?

Then he grinned savagely. "Okay, Poltergeist," he said. "Let's have you do something *really* useful." He started a cloaking program to disguise his computer's identity, routed through two Internet "safe house" sites, pulled up Yahoo, opened a new, pseudonymous e-mail account, typed a message and posted it to Grubb's CDC mail cache. The message read:

> I suggest that you not touch the chimps in Hawai'i.
> I suggest you not touch anyone who has touched
> the chimps.
> —DICK

Sander was playing triple deck solitaire when the door seal hissed (the alarm buzzer had "broken" two days ago, when he'd gotten tired of the noise). He swallowed to quiet the faint rumble in his ears as the air pressure equalized.

"After you, Dick, if you're there," came Jerry Karpov's voice. Dick ambled into the room, followed by the theorist.

"Hi, you two," Sander said. "How's chaos?"

"Chaos is doing quite well, thank you," said Karpov. "The rest of us are a bit frayed. Have you worked out the odds yet?"

Sander shook his head. "With three decks, I'm winning more than three times as often. But if I keep point totals, I'm falling hopelessly behind even faster. I'm still not ready to make my fortune in Vegas."

"What's with the rat?" asked Dick.

Rat-san was sitting on his haunches on a back corner of Sander's bed. "Ommanipadmehumommanipadmehumomma-nipadmehum," he chanted, at a pace Alvin and the Chipmunks would have envied.

"Rat-san's trying to achieve Enlightenment," said Sander. "I don't think he's going to make it in time—but then, rats work fast. So what's new, Jerry?"

"Well, the entire base is under medical quarantine," said Karpov. "Some disease the chimps brought in. Life-threatening, and moderately interesting. We're not supposed to hug anyone."

"Too bad," remarked Sander. "I haven't gotten to hug anybody in a long time." He thought wistfully of Jenny.

Karpov nodded. "Come to think of it, neither have I. Oh, well." He took a deep breath. "Williams has ordered the experiment to proceed at 2100 hours tonight. He's not waiting any longer for the listening array to be fixed."

Just then, the little speaker in the room's ceiling crackled. "I thought you'd fixed that," said Dick.

"I did," said Sander. "It can talk. It just can't listen."

"Attention, Dick, wherever you are," rumbled the speaker. "This is General Williams speaking. Would you please contact me? I'd like to arrange a truce."

Outside, as dusk grew into night, the carnival atmosphere in the tent city increased. There were no power outlets (at least, not of the electrical variety), but the campers had brought along so many sources of light that the astronomers on the mountaintop were complaining. There were Coleman lanterns by the thousand, and portable generators, and scented candles blending with the smoke of incense punks in every sweet odor imaginable. (It was generally agreed, however, that sandalwood was in poor taste, given that tree's sad history on these islands.) There were pottery lamps and stone lanterns, luau torches and bonfires and little torches made from strings of oily *kukui* nuts. There was the occasional burning tent.

Jenny had gone off to an emergency meeting of the tent city's ad hoc town council, where the main agenda item was toilets. Meanwhile, Martin and Gregor were keeping a discrete eye on Appy, who had agreed to conduct a belly dance workshop at the New Age Church of Jesus Dharma revival tent.

"Kids, I've done Balledi, and I've done so-called 'exotic dancing,'" Appy told the heavily female audience. "If they look a little alike, it's just because they're exact opposites. 'Exotic' dancers move from the crotch, the ugliest, most utilitarian part of the whole body. Balledi centers on the navel, the body's purist ornament, which has no purpose but to remind us where we came from. A Balledi artist may display her navel. She *never* displays her crotch.

"The purpose of 'exotic dancing' is to make a beautiful woman look cheap. The purpose of Balledi is to take a woman who isn't valued enough, and show everyone—including herself—how beautiful she is. Watch this old belly."

She'd donned a halter top and shorts for the demonstration. Her abdomen was nothing to be ashamed of, for all its six decades; it lacked the baby fat of youth, but also lacked the blubber of prolonged neglect. She took a deep breath, then released it. Suddenly that slim old abdomen was still, almost unnaturally still, without sagging. A relaxed, balanced still, like a deer listening, alert but not yet alarmed.

Then it flexed: first the right side, then the left. A ripple rose from her thighs all the way to the base of her ribcage, and hung there, graceful as a hawk about to bank into a dive. It rolled right, then left, then full circle; swept clockwise and rolled smoothly into counterclockwise. An exquisite shiver passed up and down her white skin. Then the shiver moved in circles.

By then every eye in the audience, whether male or female, was transfixed on a single spot: the spot from which life had entered her before she left the womb, the last spot where she had been part of someone else, the starting point of her journey into Apollonasiahood. Her navel described its own small circle, like the center of a whirlpool. That tiny movement controlled a spiritual maelstrom, sweeping them all to its center. She glided forward, stepping so evenly that her body appeared to lift and sway only as much as her navel dropped or swung in its orbit: the navel became the still point around which her whole body moved, gliding slowly, electrifyingly, toward them. . . .

She stopped, then took another deep breath. The watchers drifted, released, helpless and grateful as shipwrecked sailors. A sigh filled the tent as her audience breathed again.

" 'She moved in circles, and those circles moved,' " murmured Gregor.

"What's that?" whispered Martin, still staring like a man in the grip of a very powerful daydream.

"From a poem, man," Gregor said softly. "Dylan Thomas. 'I knew a woman, lovely in her bones . . .' "

"That she is," agreed Martin. "That's sure right."

"That's called 'isolation and control,' ladies," Appy said. "You don't just move your belly. You learn every muscle in your belly, so you can move each one individually. Then you bring all those isolated movements together. You become their friend and mentor; you lead them like a symphony. If you can do that, you don't need breast implants or even tummy tucks. Any man looks at that movement, and he *knows* this body is something special. Gad, if her belly can do that, just think what her vulva can do!

"But he knows the woman inside that body is special, too. There's a soul-creating beauty, a mind dancing with its own spirit inside that belly. He looks, and he *knows*. And what's more important, *she* knows.

"Okay, let's try a couple of things. . . ."

An hour later, Martin and Gregor accompanied a flushed and glowing Appy back toward the cabin tent Nancy Wolf had loaned them. Nancy herself joined them for the walk; she'd come up for the class, though she had to go back to greet her B&B guests in the morning.

"Wasn't that just incredible?" she asked the men, beaming.

"That it was, ma'am," said Martin, glancing at Appy with a new respect.

"It has its cost, like any power," Appy said softly. "I nearly sucked my own daughter back down that whirlpool in my belly."

"Well, Appy, I think she's escaped now," said Gregor. "This whole awesome carnival's revolving around her."

Appy stopped to survey the scene. A squad of shrieking children ran past, flying saucers painted on their cheeks and an invasion fleet of Frisbees clutched in their young hands. Rich odors of hot oil and frying batter wafted from a malasada stand. On a propane-lantern-lit plot of grass, seven young women danced *hula kahiko* to the throb of ancient percussion and the hypnotic tenor of a Hawaiian chanter. A few tents away, a boom box reveled in the Grateful Dead. Everywhere, people quarreled and laughed, performed and fondled, ate and drank and bought and sold and moved from music to music. In short, life went on, if a bit more intensely than usual.

"My daughter helped to start this," Appy said, finally. "And now she's riding the crest, and it's a big one. But no, she's not the center. This is a carny, and a carny's got its center deeper than any one human can hope to be. Carny rides always end where you got on, and the shows go on over and over, and when you've circled the fairground, you leave again, or you're lost. But when you're in it, you just see happy chaos. The carny goes in circles to help people *forget* where they're going for a while. If this one sucks Sander and his familiars out of that hole over there, then that's just incidental."

"I think you're wrong, Appy," said Martin, after a moment. "I think the center *is* down that hole over there. It's the saucer that brought us all here, and it did it for some purpose that we don't know yet, but we're gonna find out."

"Aw, bullshit," said Gregor. "These paranoia games are fun. That's why I do 'em. But the world doesn't have to be some huge conspiracy to be just freakin' awesome, and a flying saucer doesn't have to be God to be just awesomely holy. Let it be a saucer, man, just let it be what it is, and worship that."

And Gregor would get the last word. Because the End of the World was about to arrive.

XLVI

The Pandora Code,

or

Be Careful What You Ask For

Mike Dupres used machines without liking them, and liked people without liking to use them. But his love always had been language. Not necessarily language as literature, though he found difficult poems intriguing as puzzles. But he loved language as a great, abstract puzzle in itself, whose pieces could fit together an infinite number of ways—but there were some ways the pieces didn't fit, and others where they fit exceedingly well, and still others where they fit, but formed astonishingly strange pictures: where anyones lived in pretty how towns and colorless green ideas slept furiously. And, most intriguing of all, there were pictures you just couldn't quite make with words, though you knew the pictures were there. . . .

As an undergraduate, he'd discovered Noam Chomsky's transformational grammar, and fallen in love with the idea of "deep structures": core meanings that lay hidden beneath the surfaces of sentences. Then, while working on his doctorate, he'd read about the gold-plated audio records and etched diagrams winging beyond the solar system on the Voyager spacecraft. He'd marveled at the crudeness of those messages: music, voices, a cartoon of a male and female. It was like sending hieroglyphics to the universe without a Rosetta stone.

The Rosetta Stone provided the key to ancient Egyptian Hieroglyphics by containing the same passage in both Hieroglyphics and Greek. But how could one supply a Rosetta Stone for aliens who didn't know *any* human language?

Most people working on the problem had proposed messages based on scientific constants, such as prime number sequences or the periodic table. But Dupres had a different idea. Any sentient living creature, he reasoned, would have certain concepts embedded in its language by the nature of being alive: *consume, reproduce,* and *die,* for instance. Could one start with simple pictographic representations of those deep concepts, and build a symbolic language based on them?

He'd worked up a proposal and sent it, through several carefully researched channels, to NASA. No reply. He'd learned the ugly truth about the American Graduate School Pyramid Scheme, which created new PhDs far faster than it retired old ones. He'd substitute-taught, hated it, spent two years teaching in Saudi Arabia, hated it, gone on welfare, hated it, all the while working on his theoretical human-to-alien language.

Then one day, out of the blue, a grant offer arrived. One of his NASA proposals had found its way to another government agency, which was willing to underwrite his work on the deep structure code. But the agency wanted something in return. If deep structure could be used to create a language aliens could understand, could it be useful in deciphering codes sent by humans? Could he look into this for them?

And thus Mike Dupres had gotten ample funding to work on his beloved artificial language, and later, to claim listening time on some of the biggest radio telescope arrays on the planet, including some the public didn't know about. All for the small cost of selling his soul to the CIA.

Usually, the Company's burden was light. They shared in the results of his research. And since his work wasn't political, they accepted it when his answers weren't always the ones they'd wanted to hear. Deep structure analysis hadn't proven that useful in cracking modern encryption matrices, for instance. But it *had* yielded a screening program for rapidly sorting the millions of unscrambled messages that the Company intercepted monthly.

Other requests made him less comfortable. Sometimes he was asked to attend specific seminars or conferences and report anything of possible interest, or even to make the acquaintanceship of certain people. And of course, he could never reveal his CIA connection.

That was the worst of it. Every time he talked to someone, that small lie tainted the conversation. He caught himself wondering, *what would this person think of me, if he knew I was a spook?* Or worse, *if* she *knew I was a spook?* Or even scarier, *what if she's a spook, herself?* Those nagging little fears had had a great deal to do with one failed marriage and a string of superficial relationships.

Which was why Mike Dupres was walking down the hallway to the fulfillment of his dream (and the end of the world) with no photos in his wallet.

A few minutes behind him strode Dr. Harrison Grubb, his usual expressionless face masking a state of high-endorphin battle euphoria. First there had been the identification and writing up of Grubb's Syndrome, the brand new combination of mental symptoms suffered by the UFO witnesses. Then news that the most advanced case of all, Keynes, had shown up—and had matched Grubb's predictions perfectly! And now he, Dr. Harrison Grubb, was leading the struggle to contain a new and deadly virus! And in ideal conditions! A small, contained population, the nation's best facilities at his disposal (if he was allowed to ship samples to them), the nation's security dependent on his success . . . and the lives of some of the country's top scientists at stake. Men with Nobel pull! He'd be in the history books, right up there with Pasteur and Fleming and those Brits with their cloned sheep! Just so long as he didn't hug anyone. . . .

Buffalo Bill Williams had more than hugged someone. As he walked down the hall to the Observation Room, he was wondering how to break the news to his wife. Jessie had always put up with his little escapades before, more or less. She'd entertained a captain or two, herself. And these days, he not so much loved her, as honored her as the long-suffering mother of his children. But they did take advantage of each other's company when he was home. Or had, until now.

Grubb had sent a requisition list across his desk this morning. All those drugs, for one little virus. . . .

"What the hell's a 'protease inhibitor'?" he muttered. "Sounds like something to keep you from going into goddam strip joints."

He hadn't reported for tests yet, himself. He'd wait for Grubb's official recommendation, then order *everyone* on base to take an exam. Grubb had said this bug appeared to be a melding of DNA from normal HIV and some hepatitis-like virus. Unlike HIV, which had never documentably been transmitted by even the Frenchest of kisses, the new virus could be passed on in saliva, even in sweat. All it needed was warmth and bodily moisture.

The general tried to remember if he'd ever given Joan Postlewaite a friendly hug in public. Unfortunately, he wasn't the type who hugged in public. He wondered if he could claim the new virus had been passed on by a sweaty handshake.

And so he walked down the corridor, still mentally ducking and dodging and trying out counterpunches, resolutely not accepting the fact that his career, his marriage, and his life were all riding a cataract down the inside slopes of a toilet bowl. Maybe the goddamn aliens would have a cure.

Walter Baker walked down the corridor with Karpov, getting briefed as they went. Baker had arrived just in time to get caught by the blasted quarantine. He was appalled at what he'd found. Laboratories sabotaged and in shambles. The Chief of Security in quarantine under guard. An epidemic threatening to break out. Vermin infesting the corridors and mold covering everything. Half the staff not speaking to each other. If he ever got back to Washington, Williams's head was going to roll! No—*when* he got back to Washington.

"Is this deep structure business really necessary?" he asked. "I mean, sure, for a deep space message to a civilization that's never encountered us. But if an alien comes here, surely it's watched some TV first. What better Rosetta Stone could you get than millions of TV images with voiceovers?"

Karpov nodded. "The Sagan scenario. I wonder, too. But Dupres argues that if an alien learned human language from broadcasts, it's probably developed at least as many misconceptions as correct interpretations. Dupres thinks it's better to start afresh—there's less likely to be misunderstandings with the Deep Structure Code."

"And what exactly is this 'deep structure,' again?"

"A linguist named Chomsky thought it up, a few decades ago. I haven't read Chomsky directly in years, so this summary may be mixed up with a few of my own ideas. But here's the basic concept: Language is built up in layers by the brain. Traditional grammar is only the surface layer. Under that layer are older, deeper layers of meaning—deep structures. Both 'The dog ate the cat' and 'The cat was eaten by the dog' share the same deep structure, the way *Homo sapiens* and *Homo neandertalensis* share a common ancestor."

"Like men and gorillas."

"Right, only the difference between men and gorillas is more like 'The pitbull chowed down on the pussy' versus 'My poor Siamese disappeared down the gullet of that vicious canine.' " But the common ancestor's still there: 'Dog ate cat.' "

"So what's that got to do with talking to aliens?"

"Bear with me a moment longer. We haven't finished our deep structure analysis yet. Words like 'dog' and 'cat' contain even deeper structures. In fact, they have a common ancestor—something like 'carnivore.' 'Carnivore' itself bundles together 'animal' and 'meat-eating.' And 'animal' contains concepts such as 'alive' and 'thing' and 'eats organic matter.' "

"So?"

"So Mike's idea is that if we dig deep enough, we find basic concepts that all language-using creatures would have to share. Concepts like 'eat' and 'reproduce.' He calls those concepts 'deep structure elementals.' If we can assign those concepts to pictographic symbols that aliens would understand, we can build a common language from the ground up."

"I see," said Baker, shaking his head. He changed the subject. "Do we know who this Dick is, and who he's working for?"

"Not really," said Karpov. "I have a strong theory, but I can't prove it yet—and it's the sort that's going to require strong proof. I *can* say that he claims to have been inside the saucer, and his demonstrated abilities seem to justify that claim.

There's no evidence that he's working for any government or company."

"He can really make himself invisible?"

"We have no evidence that he's been visible since he entered the base," said Karpov, "though Keynes claims to be able to see him." He neglected to add that Dick was probably walking beside them right now. There was no point in upsetting Baker over an unprovable hypothesis.

"A personal stealth cloak," breathed Baker. "Can you picture the strategic value of such a thing?"

"Hmm. 'Picture' may be an ironic word choice," remarked the theorist. "But yes, I can imagine. Look at the havoc that a single, uh, sentient being has wreaked here, with some of the best brains in the country trying to track him down."

"There's going to be a hell of a fight over who controls this technology," said Baker, "even within the branches of government. Just imagine totally undetectable planes that reach hypersonic speeds on a few hundred pounds of thrust. Invisible armies. Intelligence agents who can walk into any closed meeting in the world. And the commercial applications. . . . This saucer could pull us out of the recession."

"Imagine policemen who can walk into any bedroom," added Karpov. "Politicians and mobsters who can walk into any bedroom or private caucus or campaign headquarters or cabinet meeting. Businessmen who can walk into a competitor's office or an employee's home. Invisible terrorists. . . ."

Baker nodded, boggled. "If this works, I've got to call Washington immediately. This really is Pandora's box, isn't it?"

"Yes," said Karpov.

"But we're going to open it anyway, if we can, aren't we?"

Karpov shrugged. "We were headed there already. For a couple of hundred dollars, I can go on the Net and buy a camera embedded on a single silicone chip, with a lens that can peek through a nail hole. It's impossible to obtain cash without getting your picture taken. Department stores watch people in dressing rooms, and Amazon monitors every book we buy. There are thousands of websites devoted to peeping tom cams. And, shades of Orwell, there's software available now that can turn any video screen into a camera. And hundreds of websites where every fetish and perversity imaginable—cannibalism, urine-drinking, scatophagia, necrophilia, erotic hanging, child rape—is on display for all to see. For the first time in history, we may have to live with the entire truth about ourselves."

"Yechh," said Baker. "Pretty good rationalization, though."

"Thank you. Pandora couldn't help herself, either."

(And beside them, a figmental armadillo marched, lost in his own contemplations.

If I hadn't charged Joan Postlewaite's chair, he thought, *she wouldn't have ended up with chimp duty. She wouldn't have slept with Archer, and probably not with the general. . . . Can people survive without hugging? Whatever happens today—have I already started the extinction of humankind?*

"It's been fun," he muttered. "But Dick, my boy, you've also been acting like a real shit. . . . Wait a minute—I was doing Sander a favor by disrupting everything. Can I be an angel and a dung ball with the same act?"

He was still pondering this, when he saw his two unknowing companions stop at the Observation Room door, and Karpov said:

"Well, here we are. The prime seats for the grand opening."

The viewing room, separated from the UFO chamber by a wall of bulletproof glass, already held most of the senior staff except for Dupres, who was still in the main chamber with the technicians.

Buffalo Bill glared at the two newcomers. "Gentlemen. So good of you to join us. The show's about to start."

Baker glanced around guiltily. "You know, we should have had at least *one* woman present on an occasion like this."

"I'm afraid Captain Postlewaite is still indisposed," said Karpov. "There's been a shortage of women in SETI research, ever since they saw how Jody Foster got treated. Hi, Bill. Hello, Dr. Grubb. Will, Rupert, Jim, Matt. I wonder why Lacey Hatfield didn't come for the show?"

"Maybe he knew about the damn chimps ahead of time," growled Williams. "That was a goddamn CIA crate they arrived in."

"Deliberate sabotage?" asked Baker, alarmed.

"With the goddamned spooks, who knows?" said the general. "Mike, are you about ready in there?"

"One more calibration check, General," came Dupres' voice over the intercom.

The saucer stood at the chamber's center, on the same hydraulic lift that had carried it down from the surface. The lift was raised 150 centimeters from floor level, creating optimum angles between the laser projectors and the tantalizingly open-appearing portal. Dupres spent a few more minutes checking the equipment, then waved the technicians out of the room. "Ready!" he said.

"Dupres, you aren't staying in there, are you?" said Williams. "I thought this was rigged to run from in here."

"It can be worked from either place, General," said the linguist. "I thought I'd better stay in here to mind the equipment. Besides—uh, if this works, the thing may want to talk to someone in person."

"What the—now just a goddamn minute, Dupres. You hold everything until I get in there! I'm not letting *you* talk for the whole goddamn human race!"

"But that's what I'm *trained* to do!" protested Dupres.

But the general had already charged into the main chamber. "Look, Dupres," he said, low and fast. "I know who you really work for. I'm damned if I'm going to let the goddamned Company get a monopoly on whatever this thing says!"

The chamber door opened again. The two turned to find Harrison Grubb entering. "Hello," he said. "If there's going to be a delegation, wouldn't it be good if the aliens saw a healer as well as a military man?"

Then Baker burst in. "Hold it, folks!" he said. "You're forgetting who's at the top of the pyramid here. If I'm going to report to the President, I'd better be as close to first hand as possible."

Then Jerry Karpov sauntered in.

"So what's your excuse for horning in on history?" said Dupres, exasperated.

Karpov shrugged. "The same as always. Just curious."

Fortunately, the rest of those present in the Control Room decided that they were quite close enough to history already.

"Well, gentleman, shall we start?" asked Dupres.

The single laser flicked on. A bright ruby band shot into the saucer's portal. Inside the far wall of the saucer, the pulsing laser traced a circle. Not a zero nor a letter o. A circle, a self-contained entity: existence, the starting point.

The circle grew a line down its center, then split into two circles. Lasers #2 and #3 switched on, helping with the complex image sequence. The circles divided again and again. Then all but the primary laser switched off. The image froze at the moment two circles were about to split apart: Life.

The laser switched off, came on again, traced the original circle and then began pulsing. The circle broke into four uneven fragments. The fragments disintegrated. The laser repeated the sequence, then froze as the circle broke into pieces: Destruction, Death.

To circles rolled toward each other, then disappeared when they met. The sequence repeated, then a diagonal line sliced through them at the moment of their meeting destruction, and the image froze: Negation. A circle engulfed a smaller circle, amoeba-like: Consumption. A circle bulged out into a square: Transformation.

Sequence after sequence appeared, defining symbol after symbol. Equal: two identical circles rolled across each other within two parallel lines, then froze. Unequal: a "not" symbol before an equal symbol. Larger: three progressively larger circles, from left to right. Smaller: the opposite. A dozen such symbols displayed themselves, then the lasers shut down.

"End of Lesson One, folks," said Dupres. "Let's wait to see if our friendly giant peach pit has anything to say about all this."

It did.

Suddenly the room filled with flashing lights of every color from infrared to ultraviolet. More and more rapidly they reeled about the five men, tracing rhythms and patterns almost faster than the eye could follow. Then, abruptly, the sequence ended.

For a long moment, there was only silence.

Then Buffalo Bill Williams began screaming, and didn't stop, even as he began swallowing himself. Dr. Grubb began dividing endlessly into smaller Dr. Grubbs. Walter Baker thrummed his fingers on his knee, yelped in pain, and stared in shock at the hammers his fingers had become. Mike Dupres simply disappeared.

"Hmm," said Jerry Karpov. He walked bemusedly to the door. "Hi, Dick," he said, on his way out. "Nice to see you."

In some strands of possibility that may have survived afterward, a man matching Jerry Karpov's description may have appeared at an isolated Tibetan Buddhist sanctuary on the slopes of Mauna Loa. There he may have been recognized instantly as the 347th reincarnation of the abbot of a Tibetan monastery destroyed by the Chinese in 1964. He may have spent the rest of his life at the sanctuary, in revered and serene seclusion, although his picture may have appeared on millions of fundraising letters.

But it would have been nicer if Karpov had stayed around the Facility that evening to help. Because that Tibetan stuff was all just possibility.

In reality, meanwhile, all hell broke loose.

XLVII

Mass Consumption

Sander first learned that something had gone seriously wrong when a tiny *doppelganger* of Dr. Harrison Grubb ran through the closed door.

"Help! Help!" it cried. "Eating us! Help!" Then it ran through the stainless steel wall into the rock beyond, and was gone.

"Uh-oh," said Sander. "Well, maybe it's time to go investigate. 'Want to come along, Rat-san?"

"*Ommanipadme*No*humommani*Thanks*hum*," said Rat-san.

"All right. Suit yourself," said Sander.

He didn't undertake this journey blithely. He had spent days attempting to map out the route, in case something like this occurred—only to realize that the route couldn't be mapped, because it continually changed. That's why people can't get from Point A to Point B in a dream. There are no still points.

Of course, there are no still points in "reality" either. The earth spins around the sun spins around the galactic core spins around the Big Bang, with a closed infinity of other spinnings thrown in just to make things even more confusing. But most of us still generally manage to get around passably well, thanks to an illusion that we call *I*. If you believe in yourself, you basically create a single point in relationship to everything else in the universe, and then go from there. *I* is, first and foremost, a navigational tool.

But believing in *I* also essentially walls humans off from all the rest of the multiverse, which the human brain's *I* mechanism only allows it to see as "will" and "was," "could" and "would," "can" and "might" and so forth. But you can escape into them if you loosen the fetters of *I*, which is very close to the same thing as the soul. It's like crossing a river by hitching rides on flotsam. You have to abandon your maps, leave your smart phone and its GPS behind—they'll just short out anyway—and go with the flow.

Sander's route out of the isolation cell started with one of Rat-san's "oms." He caught a quick ride on it to the image of Buddha with one hand upraised, playing patty-cake—no, giving a high-five to Sally Jessica Morgan, age 8, of Cowgill, Missouri, who was trailing a fuzzy purple dinosaur in the playground dirt—wait, back up, Barney the Dinosaur riding his patrol car through Mayberry to Aunt Bea's house to pounce savagely on a blueberry pie as blue as a 1991 Honda CRX's custom paint job, riding a highway to heaven where angels sang, "That Old Devil Moon," which shown down on two armadillos having sex on a highway in Texas just before they were squashed by the armored SUV of Rep. Ted Cruz, cruising down the highway as he pondered his next move in the Chess Game of Politics. . . .

"Checkmate," said Jerry Karpov. "Good game, though." He got up and stretched. "Well, I better get back to see what Mike is doing."

"Thanks for stopping by," said Sander-of-the-Past. This game had happened maybe half an hour ago.

"My pleasure, as always," said Karpov, as Sander, moving just a little outside of "real" time to remain invisible, stepped around his earlier self and followed the theorist out the door. Sander strode down the winding hallways, got lost a couple of times, then found the elevator and went topside. He was astonished at the size of the apocalyptic protest revival carnival that had sprung up across the upland pastures of Mauna Kea. A chain-link perimeter fence, capped with eight strands of barbed wire, now surrounded the little fake ranch cabin that stood directly over the Object's hanger. The wire mesh of the fence was festooned with banners, readable by the yellow glare of the freshly erected security lights:

FREE SANDER KEYNES!

ALIENS FOR THE NATION

HELL, NO, WE WON'T GO!
SCREW YOUR WAR WITH UFOS!

IT'S OUR SAUCER, TOO

JENNY LOVES SANDER

"Jeez," murmured Sander. "She *has* been busy."

He slipped past the checkpoint and wandered into the tent city, read the time off a drowsing fortune teller's watch, then spent the next 20 minutes, Sander-time, hunting fruitlessly among the tents and campers, jugglers and hula dancers, cultists and entrepreneurs, searching for the one face he needed to find now. Finally he synched with normal time and stopped a long-haired gentleman in a FREE SANDER T-shirt.

"Excuse me. Do you know where I can find Jennifer Duenckel?"

"Uh, haven't seen her, man," the Punatic replied. "But I think her old lady's giving a belly-dancing demo in that tent over there. I hear she's a really hot old lady."

"Thanks," said Sander. "Uh, what time is it?"

At the man's answer, he set out for the revival tent at a trot. But the balledi class was already over. One of the participants pointed him in the direction that Appy and her escorts had taken. He caught up with them a few moments later.

"Let it be a saucer, man, just let it be what it is, and worship that," one of her companions was saying.

"Appy!"

"Sander!" said the elder Duenckel. "Jenny's been worried sick about you."

"I have to find her, fast," Sander said. "The world's about to end. I have to ask her a question."

"Uh, she's probably still at the Council Arena," said Appy. "Just duck between those two malasada stands over there. You can't miss it."

"Thanks!" Sander said, and disappeared again.

"Who was that dude?" asked Gregor.

"That, you moron, was Sander Keynes," said Martin. "And if he says the world's about to end, we'd better believe it."

"Wow, man, that's really heavy. Like, what should we be doing at the End of the World? I'd like to be screwing, I mean, that's sort of traditional, but then, I mean, what's the point, 'cause it's all designed to create children, and—what the hell is tha

The Council meeting was about five minutes' walk from where he'd found Appy. Fortunately, Sander found an imaginary short cut that saved seven minutes.

"I agree totally," Jenny was saying. "We can't just go poop-ing everywhere on the landscape. The cow pies are bad enough. So how are we going to come up with 25 more porta-potties?"

Just then, Sander appeared out of thin air.

There were several shrieks of startlement. Jenny's was among them.

"Sander?" she asked, when she'd recovered.

"Hi, Jenny. Jenny, listen. The world's about to end. Do you want me to stop it from happening?"

"Uh, uh, yes," she said.

He hesitated a split-moment. "Okay," he answered, gave her a quick, wet kiss, and disappeared again.

Jenny stood in shock, then called out angrily. "Hey, wait a minute! You're trying to save me again! And you kissed me without asking my permi

Back in the Object's chamber, five minutes earlier, things had already gotten pretty bad. After the non-thing that had been Buffalo Bill had finished swallowing himself, it began consum-ing everything else. For a while, it was kept busy consuming Dr. Grubblets, as the good doctor, having discovered the ultimate instant cloning method, proceeded to create Grubbkind in his own image, which he loved most in all the world, and bade them be fruitful and divide and replenish the earth. Perhaps he thought an army of Grubbs might cure the world's diseases— or if that didn't work, perhaps one Grubb per microbe would do the job.

The problem was, he got the initial set wrong. Instead of shaping a Grubb in his own image, he made two of himself out of himself. But that meant that each was only half of him. Neither of the second generation had enough brains to correct the mistake. (Fortunately Grubb had a massive IQ to start with; and incredibly fortunately, it was a second-generation Grubblet that had run through Sander's cell; it still had the mental capacity of an australopithecine, and was the last generation with any ability to talk.) Soon the once-General was scooping up Grubblets by the non-handful, then non-licking the film of Grubblets off the floor.

The Baker-thing, meanwhile, had also transformed itself beyond recognition. It had become ice to soothe the bruises from the hammer-blows, then fire to warm the frostbite, then water to put out the fire, evaporating most of itself away. Everything it became only generated more pain. Finally it metamorphosed into an utterly innocuous, quivering mass of strawberry-flavored gelatin. And of course, there's always room. . . . The not-thing that had been Buffalo Bill consumed it with a single un-slurp, did a Tasmanian Devil routine with Dupres' language equipment, then not-looked around for more substantial fare.

By then, most of the remaining staff, already naturally selected for prudence, had fled. But Rupert Samuelson had never seen a *Halloween* movie, nor a *Friday the 13th* sequel, nor a *Nightmare on Elm Street* clone. He even disdained to watch newscasts. So he was utterly unprepared for the horror in the next chamber. He was still standing, as frozen as a jack-lighted cow, when the disembodied hunger next door noticed him. It unreached through the transparent barricade and pulled him through without even bothering to break the glass, which pretty much strained poor Rupert into particles fine enough for even a Grubblet to suck up, if Grubblets at that point had had mouths.

Sander was trotting down one of the winding hallways, knowing he was headed toward the Object chamber because everyone else was headed in the opposite direction, when he met Dick. "How bad is it?" he asked the armadillo.

"Bad," replied Dick. "Buffalo Bill just consumed himself with rage, then ate a lot of Grubb. Then Baker made dessert." He described in a little more detail what had happened. Not much detail, because there wasn't much time.

"So what are we going to do?" he concluded plaintively.

"You know what?" said Sander. "I don't have the faintest idea. I know how to end the world myself. But that doesn't mean I know how to save it."

"Too bad Dr. Karpov didn't stay around," said Dick.

Sander snorted. "He wouldn't have done any good. He already knows the ultimate secret, and that's all he wanted; he doesn't really care, now, whether the world ends or not. What did you say happened to Dupres?"

"He's disappeared, completely gone," said Dick. "Even I couldn't see him."

Sander thought a moment, but only a moment. "That doesn't necessarily mean that he's gone entirely," he said. He took a step off in one temporal/possible direction, then stepped back into Common Reality. "Did you see me just then?"

"Yeah, but you were a little blurry."

"I thought so. General Williams had a hookup to the PA system in his office, didn't he?"

"So I'd think, from all the announcements he made."

"Where's his office?"

As they ran and scuttled toward the general's office, Sander explained his idea. "You can see me and Rat-san, even when we're not in Common Reality, because we're all three basically the same soul—but even I can pursue some paths that aren't easily seen by you. Someone else could be walking an even more remote path."

"So how are you going to track him down? Hold a seance?"

"No. The same way you contacted me," said Sander. "By phone." They reached the general's office, which was locked, of course. Sander peered at the obstruction. "It would take a few moments for me to find my way in," he pondered. "Then I'd have to wait for you and me to arrive. Sometimes the old ways work best." He stepped back, kicked the door in, and rushed to the desk. The computer was locked and under password, of course. But fortunately the PA/intercom system, like the phones, had not been upgraded since the early 70's. Sander fumbled with the buttons, then found the right one.

"Attention Dr. Dupres," he said. "Paging Dr. Dupres. This is Sander Keynes. I'm calling from General Williams's Office. Extension numbers 12 or 13. If you're within the facility, please call me."

"So what if the MPs hear that, and call on us first?"

"I suspect the MPs are pretty busy right now," said Sander. Then the phone rang.

Sander picked it up. "Hello?"

"Mike Dupres, here," came the slightly tinny voice. "Except I'm not Dupres anymore. And 'here' is kind of iffy, too."

"Uh, hi. We seem to have a little problem."

"A rather large one, actually," non-Dupres said dryly.

"Any idea what to do about it?"

"Not really. But I think I know what's happened. The thing sent back its version of our own message. But the message acted like some sort of subconscious command, or restructured us in the image of the signal, or something. We turned into deep structure elementals. Grubb became Division—Baker, I think, Transformation. Williams turned into pure Consumption."

"So what are you?"

"I'm not sure. It's tough to see me as others see me."

"I understand that it's tough to see you, period."

"It could be that I'm Not, or Death, or maybe just Hidden. It's kind of neat, though, being a *real* spook. I'm sort of enjoying it."

"It gets lonely," said Dick, listening in with his supersensitive armadillo ears.

"So do you have any idea how to stop Consumption?" Sander asked.

"None at all," said the ghost of Dupres. "Hey, I grew up in America. We were always taught that Consumption was a *good* thing."

"Great," said Sander. "If we do figure out a way to stop this thing, somebody'll probably try to arrest me as a Communist."

"Nobody's going to be left to arrest you. This thing is growing fast. In fact, there goes the wall of this office now. It's getting the other end of the desk, it's

"He's gone?" said Dick. "I can't believe it. I mean, he was a jerk, but not as big a jerk as most of the other jerks. . . ."

"I'm not sure he's gone," said Sander. "Remember, he's outside of the normal time line, the same way you are."

"You mean if this thing comes up to me, I might survive?" said Dick. "That's encouraging."

"You might. But remember, it ate the Grubblets," Sander said.

"Then maybe we should get out of here?" suggested Dick.

Sander shook his head. "We can't outrun it in normal space-time. But the Grubblets were too stupid to dodge."

"Some of them had more of a brain than I do," noted the armadillo.

"Oh, come off it, Dick. Most of your mind is already outside normal space-time. You're just *channeling* through the armadillo."

"But it's the only body I've got!"

"No, it isn't. I think you may be a part of me that's channeling, like a split personality. If worst comes to worst, you've always got my body. Only if we reunite, you wouldn't remember being an armadillo, just like right now you don't remember being me. But we can't argue about that now. Consumption could be here any second. Have you tried traveling through time/possibility, yet?"

"I've been sort of avoiding that."

"I can understand why. Well, try following me. Look out! Here it comes!"

Just then the wall dissolved into

. . . slow dissolve into a closet full of stuffed animals, and a little brown creature with huge eyes. Fast forward to an outlandish contraption assembled from various household items. "ET phone home," the creature said. Fast forward and suddenly they were flying, flying through the air on a bicycle and cows passed and houses and a cackling witch on a broomstick. And then the house was falling, falling, and it landed in Munchkin land, and the delegation solemnly presented a giant lollipop goes the weasel, and they sprang out of the box into a darkened child's room, and a closet full of animals where . . .

"Uh-oh. We've been here already. Dick, are you still with me?"

"Scuttling as fast as I can," panted Dick.

"Quick, out the door!"

They charged past the startled mother, and since that wasn't in the movie, they were suddenly behind the screen. They ran around it just as the lights were coming up in the Akebono Theater. "Damn projector broke again," mumbled a bearded white man in a Rastafarian tri-colored cap and dreadlocks, sitting in one of the ancient sofas that lined the back of the little theater, in place of regular seats. Moving just out of sync with normal time/space, Sander trotted up the aisle past the sparse collection of aging hippies, braless mothers and restless children, and stepped back into reality in the lobby, where a man sat behind a table full of M&M's and Skittles.

"Uh, 'scuse me," said Sander. "What time is it?"

"About 10 o'clock, man," said the candy-vendor. "Listen, I'm sure they'll get the projector fixed soon, if you wanna just hang for a little."

"Naw, that's all right. Uh, which town is this?"

The vendor laughed. "Had some of the good stuff, eh, my man? This is Pāhoa. Step outside and assure yourself. Just walk it off for a while, and don't try driving, okay?"

"Uh, uh, yeah, man," said Sander, and sauntered out after Dick. They got out on the Akebono's front verandah just in time to see the wall of Consumption eat the Young Buddhists Association building.

"Shit! We've lost ground!" breathed Sander, as Consumption swallowed the Bank of Hawai'i and the First Hawaiian Bank and

They jumped for their lives into a big puddle in the Akebono Parking lot, and sank into the Russ Mire. A roomful of surreally large breasted women beckoned, mostly naked or dressed so that they might as well have been. One went into wild orgasm, then opened her eyes wide, realizing that there was a pistol barrel in her mouth. The gun went off. Red-colored corn syrup solution geysered from between the woman's lips.

"Jeez, what sort of sick movie is this?" exclaimed Dick, lapping a roach from among the spilled popcorn in the balcony.

"Crap," exclaimed Sander. "It's *Beyond the Valley of the Dolls*. The worst movie I ever rented."

"Gad, I wish I hadn't written that," said Roger.

"Trash, pure trash," said Gene, shaking his head sadly. "Well, that's my Last Judgment. The balcony is

They fell out behind the screen of the Akebono Theater, and lay there, trembling and exhausted, as the lights came up. "Damn projector's broken again," they heard the bearded man say, on the other side of the screen.

"It's like we're caught in a loop," gasped Dick, "and the loop keeps getting shorter. . . ."

"A bubble," panted Sander. "Consumption's got us surrounded. We're trapped in a bubble of reality, and it's shrinking. And the imagery's getting older. I think maybe we shifted in time, but consumption's consuming *all* times."

As they emerged into the lobby, Sander asked the Snack bar attendant, "Excuse me, but what year is this?"

"Had some of the good stuff, eh?" said the attendant. "It's 2001."

Then Consumption ate the theater's front porch.

They fled back into the theater. "So what do we do?" asked Dick.

"We dive back into non-realities and other realities, and stay there until we can find another bubble. If there is one," said Sander, trotting back toward the screen. "Hell, we just went through the worst movie I've ever seen. Let's try for one of the best."

"Hell, we all know how this ends," said a voice on the other side of the screen. "What's the

". . . the most resilient parasite? Bacteria? A virus? An intestinal worm?" said Leonardo di Caprio. "An idea. Resilient . . . highly contagious. Once an idea has taken hold of the brain it's almost impossible to eradi—" *Fast forward.* "You're infecting my mind!" Mal cried—*Fast forward.* "Here comes the kick!"

They spilled out of a wide screen TV into a living room, ran out past the startled couple who'd been necking on the couch, and emerged onto a street high up on a slope above a town sparkling with sickly yellow argon lights around a dark bay. Off to the right stretched the blue lights of a pair of airplane runways.

"Okay, we're out of the bubble," said Sander. He stared down at the lights of an airplane making its final approach. "I've seen this before. We must be above Hilo, in one of those subdivisions just off the Saddle Road. That means we've not just time-shifted, but possibility-shifted. Consumption would have gotten here before it reached Pāhoa."

But Dick was staring uphill. "Crap!" he exclaimed. "Here it comes again!"

"Hell," said Sander, as the house and the lovers inside disappeared. "Let's just

"Let's just get this over with," said the cowboy with the noose
    no the man wearing the blindfold

no the teenage prostitute to herself, staring up at the sixty-
five-year-old Senator

no the baby at his B'rith

no the racehorse with the broken leg to the startled vet

no the dangling preposition

no the young man whose fraternity brothers had just won a
bet and the loser had to screw a trombone

no the suicidal poet whose magnum opus, *Water Needle
Rags,* had just fucked his girlfriend and run off with Har-
per and Row

no the jazz pianist fielding the fourth request of the night for
"Feelings" from the only couple that was actually listening

no California waiting for the Big One

no the battered wife as her husband approached with the ax

    no approached with the two-by-four

    no with the Maori war club

    no with the pit bull

    no her daughter's new home address

    no the frozen haunch of caribou

    no the cutting torch

    no the search warrant for the heroin he'd planted

    no the machete

but she decided to get in one last, desperate kick, just for
the hell of it. As he raised the machete, her heel somehow hit
home in his crotch. The blade thunked into the grass between
her arm and her chest.

"Shit!" Harlan shrieked, buckling over. Jenny got up dazedly,
seized the machete, and felt its power as the man staggered
away in pain and fear. She wondered if she should just use it,
just get it over—

"Jenny!" yelled Sander.

She hesitated, and Harlan staggered away to an idling black and white motorcycle that lay on its side in a mud slick. He dragged the bike upright and took off, roaring away toward the oncoming wall of Consumption.

"Damn. He got away," said Jenny, lowering the machete. "Sander?"

"This has gotta be the future," Sander gasped. "Did you see me before, at a meeting about toilets?"

"Uh, yes," said Jenny. "I think so. It's all been so confusing . . ."

"Then we stopped it somehow! Or at least delayed it. Jenny, I don't have time to explain," said Sander. "You must have seen part of the saucer's signal. That's why you could at least hear Dick. You've gotta have some ability. Please, just take my hand, and watch me closely, and step the way I step, okay?"

The motorcycle, meanwhile, had spun to an abrupt halt beside a malasada vendor's stall. The rider grasped one of the stall's aluminum tent poles and yanked it free, just as

"Is that you, Dick?" Jenny asked, wonderingly.

"In the flesh, I think," said Dick.

"I can *see* you . . . ."

"We've gotta keep moving," Sander reminded them. He picked his path carefully now, rejecting myriads of possibilities, until he found one that led to a rather large fragment of the Facility's reality. They stepped into a familiar hallway. The door to the isolation area stood open in front of them, the checkpoint unmanned. Consumption stood, impossible to visualize but undeniably there, a few yards down the hallway in the other direction, but it didn't seem to be advancing.

Echoing down the hall was the faint sound of a tiny voice, chanting rapidly.

Sander stared at the open doorway. "Rat-San!" he suddenly exclaimed, and trotted into the Isolation Zone.

"*What*-san?" said Jenny.

"Oh. That's right. You haven't met," said Dick. "Sander's got another familiar. Come on!"

The guards' monitor station stood empty, but the monitors revealed that the cell's occupants had been left behind when the guards fled. Jeb Archer paced disconsolately in one cell, the lines of stitches on each side of his forehead making it look as if he'd just been dehorned. Joan Postlewaite lay curled up with Pandora and Pandemonium in another cell.

Sander's cell lay at the very end of the hall. But it was rather difficult to reach because of the rats. They clustered around the door by the hundreds: tawny Polynesian rats not much bigger than mice, and huge gray Norway rats, and even a few rangy roof rats, who normally preferred Hawai'i's remaining forests, where they were rapidly filling a niche occupied elsewhere by squirrels. The rats all sat on their haunches, reverently staring at the cell door. A tiny, steady chant poured out of the speaker beside the door: "*Ommanipadmihumommanipadmihum. . . .*" But it had changed since Sander last heard it—had taken on a bell-like purity.

"Funny," said Dick. "I thought you 'fixed' that mic."

"I unfixed it," said a voice in another speaker.

"Hi, Dr. Dupres," said Sander.

"Please, I'm not Dr. Dupres anymore," said the ghost. "But you can call me Mike, for convenience, I guess. No point in standing on formality, when we may be the only surviving members of the human race. Except I'm not human anymore."

"So what's keeping this place intact? You?" asked Sander.

"Nah, the little guy," said the ghost reverently. "I think he reached Nirvana, just before Consumption hit. Consumption won't come near him."

"My son," breathed Sander. "I'm so proud."

"Your *what?*" exclaimed Jenny.

"Don't worry," said Dick. "He's imaginary. No child support involved."

"It makes sense," said Sander. "Consumption is afraid of nothing. If I understand what I've read of Buddhism, Nirvana is the purist nothingness that there is, or rather isn't."

"*Ommanipadmehum*," the voice continued, like Alvin the Buddha Chipmunk.

"But you're also pretty close to nothing, Mike," Sander pointed out. "Couldn't you keep Consumption at bay yourself?"

The ghost snorted. "I'm Negation, I think," it said. "Negation is *part* of Consumption. You don't eat, without destroying something. I can pass through unscathed, but I can't stop it."

"Hmm. Why aren't you trying to negate us?" asked Dick.

"I *am*. Haven't you noticed? I've contradicted everything you've said. But negation's subjective. Undoing something is always doing something else. I'd rather undo Consumption, at the moment."

Jenny was still staring at the mass of reverential rodents. "Gee, what'll the world be like if it does survive?" she wondered. "Rats were bad enough before. What happens now that they've got religion?"

"Are you sure they didn't have it already?" asked Dupres' disembodied voice.

"Well, right now, folks, we don't really have to worry about that," Dick pointed out, "because outside this little island of peace, the world *isn't* surviving."

"Listen, Sander," said Mike. "Consumption hasn't eaten the saucer, either. It's still out there."

"Hmm," said Sander, considering all this, then made up his mind. "Okay. I think I know how to stop Consumption. But I probably won't be around afterward."

"Sander, what are you planning?" asked Jenny.

"I'm sorry, Jenny. I'm going to use the Third Key. I don't see any other way. You'd better stay here."

"Listen, Sander, I'm *sick* of you rescuing me. And I'm *not* staying here while you sacrifice yourself. I'm going with you, even if I fall behind and get swallowed in the chaos out there."

Sander looked at her helplessly, then steeled himself. "All right. If I don't succeed, it won't much matter. And if I do, maybe you *can* rescue *me*. Maybe my only hope is for you to pull me back. If there's anything to pull back."

"I'm coming, too," said Dick.

"I don't know if you'll do any good," said Sander. "This place will be safe for as long as Rat-san's body keeps chanting . . ."

"Hey, I certainly don't want to spend eternity with a batch of holier-than-thou rats."

"Gee, thanks," said Mike. "I'm not a lot of things, including a rat. But I'm not staying, either. It's not like I've got something to lose."

By now, Sander had become more adept at navigating this chartless realm. "Isolation cell, cell of life, Life Stinks, Mel Brooks, Brooks Brothers, suits me, me and you, UFO," he chanted aloud, as they ducked and dodged past traps and dead ends of non-space. Consumption kept mindlessly extending un-pseudopods to engulf them. Just as it seemed there was nothing but Consumption left, the Object loomed in before them.

"Okay, everybody, listen carefully," Sander said. "If this works, I hope you'll end up back at the moment of the experiment. If that happens, then you've got to keep the saucer from sending its signal. I suggest you use the elevator."

"The elevator?" said Dupre's ghost. "Oh, wait, I see, but. . . ."

Sander made his last wish. Then he used the Third Key.

XLVIII
The Third Key

There is a basic problem in thinking about the soul. We can say what it is not: it is not the body, it is not a thing. The problem is, we don't usually understand what it *is*. So we keep expecting it to act like a thing, even though it's not.

What the soul is, is a container—or perhaps three containers, or one container with three aspects—who knows or cares which? The important thing is that when the soul is unlocked, it doesn't escape. The soul is the jail.

The Third Key unlocks the innermost portal between self and not-self. Opened, the soul ceases to have any function, like an empty box. Since it is defined by containing, it essentially ceases to be a soul.

When Sander used the Third Key, he ceased to be Sander.

What was inside the box was nameless and needed no name. It didn't even need to exist. Buddha called it Nirvana; the Brahmins called it Atman; Mushashi called it the Void. But they were all wrong by necessity, because what was inside the soul wasn't an *it*. It wasn't even nothing, and therefore it couldn't truly be named. There were no words, are no words, and never can be words for What was Inside.

Faster than a fly's wing/eye coordination, Consumption rushed to devour the husk of what had been Sander Keynes. But before it could, it met What was Inside.

Consumption tried to devour What was Inside. There was nothing to devour. It tried to surround What was Inside. There was nothing to surround. It tried to ignore What was Inside. There was nothing to ignore.

But What was Inside could surround and consume Consumption, even as What was Inside less-than-ignored it, just as nothing always surrounds and consumes and less-than-ignores anything (only more and less so).

Consumption started being sucked into What was Inside, faster and faster. Consumption could not get away, because it did not know how to get away. It only knew how to consume.

(Actually, whether Consumption was sucked into What was Inside, or What was Inside expanded to engulf and disperse Consumption, was just a matter of perspective, and both perspectives were ultimately both true and false. But the relationship between the two changed as they came together, anyway, and the change was not in Consumption's favor.)

Suffice it to say that Consumption was put in its place. And as this happened, *place* began to emerge again. Consumption shrank and shrank, until it was a squalling baby of itself, then an embryo . . . back to the moment of its conception.

Something very peculiar happened at that moment. Falling down a tunnel toward light, Consumption suddenly knew that like all things, it would have to cease to be, even though it desperately wanted to go on being. And then it knew that it was loved, and that it was forgiven. Maybe these last two thoughts were merely the final desperate delusions that it granted itself as a consolation for ceasing to exist. But maybe they were part of the true nature of the Multiverse. It would never know for sure until

And time began again.

"Everyone, stop what you're doing and DUCK!" screamed Mike Dupres' voice from every loudspeaker in the Facility.

The startled scientists, including Dupres-still-incarnate, obeyed.

"Jenny, if you don't want the world to end, hit that switch on the wall beside you!" commanded Dupres-disincarnate.

"Uh—okay."

Jenny did so. Beneath the floor, behemoth engines sprang to life. Giant hydraulic pistons, designed to lift thousands of tons of starship if necessary, began rising ponderously beneath their relatively miniscule load. Rising, in motion, the saucer began to disappear. So did its counter-message, just as it began to transmit.

"Sander?" Jenny asked, then saw the husk of Sander Keynes collapsed on the floor. "Sander!" She knelt beside him, frantic. "Sander! Come back!"

And the last dormant shred of Sander's identity awoke within the husk of his soul, responding to the command it had been told to wait for. The soul swung shut. And of course, What was Inside being what it was (and wasn't), there was still as much of it (and wasn't) inside the soul as there had been before.

"Gad, I'm hungry," mumbled Sander.

"God, Sander," said Jenny. "Are you all right?"

"I have no idea," said her future lover, getting up groggily. "What's it feel like to be all right?" He shook his head as if to clear it.

"Uh, folks," asked Dick. "What happens when the Object gets to the surface and stops moving?"

"Oh my God," Jenny breathed. "All those people up there will get the message. . . ."

"Where'd those people come from?" roared General Williams. He wasn't referring to "those people on the surface." He pointed at Sander and Jenny. "Stop those people!"

"Sander," said Dick urgently, "Sander, put me in the saucer."

"What?" said Sander. "But . . ."

"Just do it! Trust me! Then get ready to follow!'

The Object had disappeared for most of those in the room, but Sander had only to twist a little *should*-ways and slightly to the *might* to bring it into focus again. The light-show message was still broadcasting, dancing on the walls a few inches above normal human eye level. The portal was already six feet above the floor, and rising. Sander grabbed the armadillo and thrust him through the opening.

"Shut up!" came Dick's voice from inside the saucer.

The portal closed. When it opened again, six inches higher and still rising, the light show was gone.

"Get in!" shouted the armadillo. "Hurry!"

Sander boosted Jenny up and watched her tumble headfirst into the portal. By then, MPs were rushing into the room. Sander backed up, looked for an opening, then took a flying leap into approximately thirty seconds ago, and landed inside the vehicle moments before he had boosted Jenny up, and cushioned her fall when she slid in on top of him.

"Oomf," he said.

The saucer rose up through the roof, before anyone else in the panic-stricken room could remember where the switch was.

"Uh, Dick," said Sander, as the object came to a halt topside. "Just out of curiosity—exactly how did you stop this thing from transmitting?"

"I told it to stop," Dick replied. "The last time I was in this thing, I said something like "What am I doing here?" And then the lights came on, and it told me, sort of. Dr. Karpov guessed it might understand English. He was right. Nobody in the Facility ever just asked it something."

"But why didn't it change you into something, just now?" Jenny asked.

"It wasn't talking to me," the armadillo replied.

"Hmf. 'Makes sense—I think," said Sander. "All right, everybody out."

He scrambled out, and stared up in bemusement at the little ranch house, suspended on a giant swing-arm ten feet up and to one side of the saucer. "Gad, Jenny, look at this."

As Jenny joined him, a spotlight struck the ranch house, then swept down to focus on the saucer.

"Jenny, help me push this thing!" Sander shouted.

"You're going to try to take it with us?" Jenny asked incredulously.

"I've heard it's really light," said Sander, already pushing.

The thing wouldn't budge.

"Wait," said Sander. "We're still in sync with the saucer. We're going to have to go back to reality for a moment. Watch where I step, and follow me. . . ."

When they shoved again, the thing started moving with less effort than it took to roll a small motorcycle.

"ALL RIGHT, YOU AROUND THE SAUCER . . . ," began a loud speaker.

"Hey, you guys forgot somebody!" called Dick's voice from inside.

"That's okay, Dick. Jenny, hop back in!" Sander shouted. He gave her a boost—she may or may not have needed it, but what the hell. . . .

". . . PUT YOUR HANDS IN THE AIR!"

Sander took a quick look at the landscape downhill and gave the saucer a final shove, just as the elevator started to sink again. The saucer started accelerating on its own. He leapt through the portal, just as a warning shot plunked into the ground beside where his feet had been.

The saucer disappeared—except to the people inside, to whom it went only mostly transparent, with a thin band around the perimeter remaining opaque for some reason. As smoothly as a bobsled on Teflon, it slid down the slope toward the perimeter fence, gaining momentum as it went. Then it shot up the side of the hummock where Sander had aimed it with his last shove, and sailed into the air, like a stone skipping across a pond under lunar gravity. It sailed toward the perimeter fence—then hit the top of the fence, tried to squeeze between the strands of barbed wire, and squirted backward into the perimeter again.

At the end of the ride, the saucer's occupants all found themselves tangled in a pile at one side of the chamber. Obviously, if there was gravity control or inertial damping, it either wasn't turned on or wasn't designed for this kind of ride.

"Well, at least we landed right side up," said Sander.

The portal reappeared. The rest of the interior went opaque.

"Uh-oh. I bet we're visible, now," said Jenny.

"YOU IN THE SAUCER," repeated loudspeakers outside. "COME OUT WITH YOUR HANDS UP."

"So what now, Sander?" Jenny asked.

"We're safe in here for now," said Dick. "It's not like they can come in and get us. On the other hand, I'm hungry, and I don't see any ant dispensers."

Sander disentangled himself from the others and shook his head. Then a look of inspiration shot across his face.

"Saucer, fly!" he said.

Lights flashed around the saucer's inner equator.

"WE REPEAT, COME OUT WITH YOUR HANDS UP," rumbled the loudspeaker outside.

"I don't care," Sander replied to the saucer. "How about straight up?"

And they flew.

The lights of the End of the World's Fair shrank beneath them. The lights of Hilo appeared, no longer blocked out by the top of Mauna Kea. A moment later, every argon light on the Big Island stretched out beneath them. Then the lights of Maui and Molokai and Lanai, and even a few on Kaho'olawe. Then Honolulu. Then the fiery crescent of sunrise on the earth's edge. . . ."

Saucer, stop! Hover!" Sander shouted hastily. "Now go down twenty feet!"

And it did. Apparently when it was under its own power, there *was* inertial damping, or they'd have been squashed against the ceiling, then the floor.

"Well, it doesn't surprise me that it understands English," said Dick. "But I hadn't realized it was obedience trained."

"This was all so obvious that nobody dared to think of it," mused Sander. "Nobody even considered just asking it to fly for them."

"It's like Aladdin's lamp," breathed Jenny. " 'Your wish is my command' "

"Only we're the ones inside the lamp," said Sander. "Anyone want to play djinni?"

Jenny shook her head. "Who do we know who deserves to have their wish granted?"

"Well," said Sander quietly, "I think that if we leave the solar system, your mom will wish she had her daughter back."

"You're right. She will," said Jenny.

The sun was starting to peep over the horizon again.

"Saucer, drop down to 30,000 feet above sea level, then hover," Sander said.

The blurry patches of light on the island chain below them grew larger, then resolved themselves into city lights again. The lights of a commercial jet from Honolulu climbed to their altitude, then winged past.

"There goes the redeye to San Fran, I bet," giggled Jenny.

Meanwhile, something more ominous was scrambling out of Hickam Air Force base in Honolulu, and Kāne'ohe Marine Corps Base, and Wheeler Air Force Base in Wahiawā. But the crew of the saucer didn't notice that, just yet.

"So, want to go pick up your mom?" asked Sander.

"That makes sense," said Jenny. "But then what? Go explore the universe?"

"What's the point?" said Dick. "We already know the ultimate secret."

"I don't think there is any ultimate secret," said Sander. "We know a big one, that's for sure. But it just opens up more questions, like 'Why are there souls to start with?' And 'What is a soul made of, that it can contain what's inside?' Not to mention the big one: 'What happens if we tell the world?'"

Dick shuddered. "Buffalo Bill Williams would start a weapons design team for targeting souls."

"All the intelligence agencies in the world would be peeping into our souls," said Jenny, also shuddering.

"All of our *mothers* would be peeping into our souls," said Sander. "And our nosy little sisters and our spouses. . . ."

"Oh, God, think what Harlan would do with this," gasped Jenny.

The discussion was interrupted by a fireball that whipped perilously close, then exploded with a roar that reverberated even inside the saucer. The spaceship winked completely out of reality for a moment, until the flying debris had passed.

"Jeez, what was that?" asked Jenny. "A meteor?"

"Sander, we're hovering," noted Dick. "Is that the same as 'not moving'?"

"They can see us!" exclaimed Sander. "That was a missile!"

Two more fireballs whipped past.

"I don't think they can actually hit us," said Sander, "though it's getting hard to hear ourselves think."

'Well, we're about to test that theory," said Jenny, as a phalanx of two dozen little fireballs approached.

"Saucer, go down two thousand feet!" said Sander, quickly. "How about it, Jenny? Shall we go see your mom?"

Jenny shrugged. "Why not? But I don't guarantee that I'm going to follow her advice from now on."

"Okay," Sander said, then considered how to tell the saucer where to go. After all, neither the Facility nor the protesters' camp had official names. "Saucer, go to a point 1,000 feet above the spot where you, uh, first left the earth with us."

Lights flashed.

"Right, right, we haven't left the Earth. Go to a point 1,000 feet above the spot where we left the *ground.*"

The saucer obediently descended.

"I've got a stupid question," said Dick.

"What's that?" said Sander.

"Why do we need this thing now, anyway?"

"Uhh . . ."

"You know, he's right," said Jenny. "I mean, if I understand what's happening, we can take ourselves anywhere and anywhen and any possibility on our own power. The saucer can probably tell us some more things. But we've got enough to keep us busy the rest of our lives, already."

"Hmm. Well, why not ask it? Saucer, why do we need you?"

The lights flashed. When Sander had fed it flying instructions, he alone had seemed to understand the Object's responses. But this time, perhaps since Sander had said "we," everyone got the message.

It was a little embarrassing.

"Compound question," groaned Sander. "Jeez, I learned about that in sophomore English. Like, 'Have you stopped beating your wife?' Oops—sorry, Jenny, bad example. . . . Okay, Saucer, *do* we need you?"

The lights flashed.

"Oh," they all said, together.

But being humans, they still had to debate the issue for a while, to look at all the ramifications, to ask more questions, to discuss the answers and the questions that arose out of the answers. Sander told the saucer to rotate while they were doing that, so they stayed in motion and invisible and kept their privacy while all this was happening. They'd been in the saucer for nearly three hours, and their butts had fallen asleep, before they decided it was time to go down and find Appy.

They descended slowly toward the Facility, which looked like a disrupted anthill. The ranch house still hung on its swivel arm, and people were still at work, photographing, measuring

416

and taking notes, along the saucer's path from the elevator to the fence.

"Saucer, go west a thousand feet," said Sander hastily, before anyone below noticed.

They did so, though Sander was a little surprised at the direction that "west" turned out to be.

"Uh, saucer, go, uh, north, slowly."

Lights flashed.

"Uh, about 3 miles per hour."

They cruised slowly over the protesters' encampment. "Do you think you can spot her tent, Jenny?" Sander asked.

"Maybe. Wait—there's the Council Arena. We can put down there."

"Saucer, go, uh, east, uh, 100 yards. God, I'm glad this thing isn't geared only for metric. Okay, saucer, go north, uh, about 30 yards. Now go east another, uh, 20 yards. Okay, saucer, land."

The thing seemed to drift down to the ground. But the moment of landing was still a bit abrupt. Sander stood. "Okay, Jenny, how's about I go first, then you can hand Dick down to me?"

"'Sounds good to me."

"Are you sure you're not worried about leprosy?" Dick asked, but the edge had gone out of his sarcasm.

They disembarked, and stood looking at the saucer for a long moment. Then Jenny took a deep breath.

"Go away," she told the saucer.

She'd expected it to fly. But it didn't have to. It just gave itself a slight boost, which started it sliding downhill. It caromed gently off a couple of tents and slid out into the makeshift main street that the tent city had spontaneously developed.

It was all downhill from there, literally. Invisible, it shifted slightly to avoid a few tents and a sleeping dog, then scooted out of the encampment and tobogganed down the long, long slope of Mauna Kea. It swooshed off the sides of a couple of cinder cones, bounced along the grove of trees that lined the last leg of the old Saddle Road, crossed the upper Belt Road, then slalomed over the lava fields and fountain grass of the South Kohala desert, clipping a few prickly pear cacti along the way.

By now it had considerable momentum, even for an object only a few percentage points into reality. It skipped over Queen Ka'ahumanu Highway, made some interesting new dimples in the Hapuna Prince Golf Course, sailed over the palm trees inches from the Hapuna Prince Hotel, and landed in the water off Hapuna Beach with such a splash that the resulting tsunami climbed all the way up the beach and the little bluff behind it to spray the hotel's ground floor. The saucer skipped a dozen more times, then settled into the water over a mile out to sea. It decided that this was probably an adequate definition of "away," and settled down to drift endlessly on the ocean's currents, continually rocked invisible by the waves—perhaps joining a great invisible fleet of ghostly Objects that had come before. Or perhaps not. Who could tell?

Sander, Jenny and Dick saw the Object disappear on the first leg of this journey, then started toward Appy's tent. The protest fair had mostly closed down for the night, though somewhere in the dark, a few voices were singing "Take Me Home, Country Roads" to the accompaniment of a single badly-tuned ukulele. The three newly retired astronauts wandered between two darkened vendor's booths to the trampled and tire-tracked open space of the ad hoc main street.

"There's our tent, over there," Jenny said, pointing.

A gasoline engine suddenly roared to life behind them. They turned just in time to see a black-and-white motorcycle accelerate from between two booths, its rider waving a huge machete.

"Duck!" screamed Jenny.

Sander dove to the ground. Unfortunately, hidden under the matted Kikuyu grass where his head landed was the koa log. Three hundred thousand termites suddenly found themselves at new angles to the world, as Sander lost consciousness.

Jenny had rolled the other way. She had thought Sander would be the object of Harlan's charge, and was still recovering from the shock of seeing the machete whistle so close to her head that she'd felt the breeze. She rolled over and screamed. But it was not a scream of fear for herself.

"Sander!"

Scrambling on all fours, she reached him, and felt wet stickiness on his scalp. Then she screamed again, in rage. "Harlan! I'm gonna kill you!"

All around, in their tents and booths, sleepy protesters and entrepreneurs awakened to the racket of the big Yamaha engine and Jenny's screams. "Local love," said some, and rolled over and went to sleep again. "Local love," thought others, and cowered deeper into their sleeping bags. But others thought, "That sounds like Jenny," and scrambled into consciousness.

It takes time to come awake, though, even with the sound of primal rage ringing in ones ears. As Harlan wheeled around for another pass, only one creature was in a position to intervene. And that creature was in a hell of a position.

When the motorcycle first swept by, Dick had scuttled out of the way, then popped into a near-ball out of pure instinct. When he uncurled again, he could make out the blurry shapes of Jenny and Sander, downhill from him, and the motorcycle headlight pivoting back toward them, even further downhill. There was no way to intervene in time—at least, not in real time.

Dick was not as good as Sander, yet, at the business of traveling outside real time-space. He scanned frantically for possibilities. Only one path seemed to put him in position to intervene—and a very unfortunate position, at that.

"Well, Dick, you were going to start doing more favors," he muttered. "Did you want to be an armadillo forever?"

The black-and-white Yamaha launched itself uphill. Jenny scrambled to her feet, looking wildly about for something to use as a weapon, anything that would let her take a stand and protect herself and Sander.

"Bansai!" screamed Dick. He galloped downhill, then popped into a near-ball again and rolled, caroming off five different improbabilities like a scaly pinball.

Harlan saw Jenny looming like a deer in his headlight's beam. Then something blurred into existence from out of nowhere, directly in front of the Yamaha's front wheel. The bike hit it, went airborne, landed sideways and went down, still sliding uphill. Jenny had to leap out of the way to avoid being bowled over like a ninepin. She hit the ground hard, knocking the wind out of her lungs.

While she lay gasping, Harlan struggled out from under the bike. His left leg had lost a lot of skin, but he'd managed to keep his head from hitting anything important. The leather jacket he'd gotten at the surplus store had taken most of the rest of the damage. The bike's rear wheel was still spinning madly. He slapped the kill switch, then crawled out of the remains of the pastele stand that had stopped his slide. The machete lay on the ground nearby. He grabbed it and started toward the prone woman, just as heads were starting to pop out of various tents.

"Time to die, bitch," he said, matter-of-factly.

Still gasping, Jenny rolled over and stared up at her tormentor. "'Might as well get it over with," she said. But she decided to get in one last, desperate kick, just for the hell of it. As Harlan raised the machete, her heel somehow hit home in his crotch. The blade thunked down in the grass between her arm and her chest. "Shit!" Harlan cried, buckling over. Jenny scrambled dazedly to her feet, then seized the machete. She felt its power as the man staggered away in pain and fear, and she wondered if she should just use it, just get it over. . . .

"Jenny!" cried Sander.

And Jenny hesitated, as her tormentor staggered over to where the black and white motorcycle lay on its side in the middle of a collapsed manapua stand. He dragged the bike upright and started it and roared away from them.

"Damn. He got away," said Jenny, lowering the machete. "Sander? Are you all right?"

"This has gotta be a different future," Sander gasped. "I should have reappeared. There's no wall of Consumption. . . ."

"Uh, yes," said Jenny. "I think so. It's all been very confusing."

Just then the motorcycle spun to an abrupt halt beside a malasada vendor's stall. The rider grasped one of the stall's aluminum tent poles and yanked it free, collapsing the front awning of the little business. Then he popped a wheelie and started downhill with his makeshift lance, toward where Jenny stood, machete in hand, grimly awaiting his charge.

Before he got there, he ran face first into the two-by-four in Appy Duenckel's hands.

The shock of the meeting spun Appy off her feet. It also sent the bike into an uncontrolled wheelie that turned into a twisting end-over end-flip, while Harlan flew twisting off in a different direction.

"Mom!" screamed Jenny.

The little woman struggled to her feet and dusted herself off, looking slightly dazed. "Okay," Appy said shakily, "I promise: That's the last time I'll come to your rescue."

She walked over to where the erstwhile motorcyclist lay, unmoving.

"This is Harlan Chillingworth," she told the gathering, predominantly female crowd. "He was trying to kill Jenny. I didn't hit him. He hit the two-by-four."

Silently, the women surged forward. One of them had an ax. Another had a Maori war club. Another had brought her pit bull. One ran to get the cutting torch from her truck. Yet another attacked with a needleful of heroin that she'd found planted in her tent. There was no haunch of frozen caribou available, but one woman made effective use of a five pound box of partially frozen chicken thighs.

There would be no charges filed afterward, because the coroner couldn't prove that Harlan Chillingworth hadn't been dead already when he hit the ground, and nobody wanted to put Appy in front of a jury for defending her daughter. Besides, the investigating officer's wife was the one with the cutting torch. For the rest of his life, he had nightmares of getting drunk some night, and waking up to find himself Bobbitized in a most searing fashion. . . .

Harlan slid screaming down the long, long tunnel to the argon light at the end.

He landed in an enormous, featureless room. As far as the eye could see, there were only naked men.

"Hi, there," said one of them. "You must be new. My name's Gacy."

"Where am I?" Harlan mumbled.

"Why, you're in the largest single room in all of Hell. It operates a little differently from most other rooms, I'm afraid. In most rooms, people do what they loved above all else in life for all eternity, until they're infinitely sick of it. But that's not possible here, because what we loved most was abusing people who weren't that fond of being abused. So in this room, we all have to take turns."

Harlan suddenly felt a strange wave of heat pass through his eternal body. He looked down, and stared in horror at the breasts swelling out from his naked chest.

"I guess it's your turn," said Gacy.

The women finished their work on the remains of Harlan Chillingworth, then turned to where Sander and Jenny knelt over a quivering, half-visible, armored mammalian body.

"He's . . . he's . . . *real,*" Jenny whispered, although the little creature slipped into and out of reality with each shudder. "Oh-oh, Dick . . ."

"Face your fears," the armadillo gasped. And gave up his soul.

Then the crowd gasped as his body fully materialized. It lay, plated and bristly and squashed, as solid and improbable a creature as any of the alien species that had invaded Hawai'i's shores.

"Can we bring him back?" said Jenny. "Should we?"

Sander stared a moment longer at the smudge of tire rubber on those damaged armor rings, then shook his head.

"There are other probabilities where he's still alive," he said. "There are *shoulds* where he exists, and *coulds,* and *mays,* and a few *might have beens*. But I suspect that in most of them, you and I are dead."

"But maybe there are a few where we're all still alive."

"Maybe. Probably. But if we go there, we'll just be trading places. This will just become another probability where he's dead."

Jenny nodded slowly. "So what do we do, now, here?"

"We preserve his memory," said Sander, grimly. "We might never use what we know about the soul again, might never share it. But everyone should know that Dick did exist, and could exist again." He stood up, cradling the still-warm body. "There's a shop I saw in Hilo, not too far from that Internet place. . . ."

Half an hour later, as the first rays of dawn crept down the slopes of Mauna Kea, the long funeral cortege started out: pickups and dirt bikes and SUVs, old army Jeeps and water trucks and lunch wagons and even a few Volkswagon microbuses, winding around the Māna Road to the Mauna Kea Observatory Road, then down to the Saddle Road, and onward through the *kauanoe* mist, toward the taxidermy shop in Hilo.

A butterfly, disturbed by the passing vehicles, erupted into the air, its barely-warmed-up wings glinting in the low, rosy light. Its shadow slipped briefly across a caterpillar, which froze in fear, then recognized the bright colors flitting past.

"Flower fuckers," the larva thought disgustedly, and resumed munching with a renewed fury.

Dick watched his funeral procession go by, deeply impressed. No tunnel had opened to carry his disembodied soul away to Heaven or Hell. But as the last of the convoy passed, the final vehicle, a battered Winnebago motor home, pulled to a stop beside him. The passenger door swung open, and a heavyset man with dark, friendly eyebrows grinned down at him.

"Care for a ride?" the man said.

"Sure," said Dick, and scrambled in. The driver lifted him up to the passenger seat so he could see better.

They drove in silence for a while. Then Dick spoke. "Sander never had a dream about armadillos, did he?"

The driver shook his head. "Nope."

"So what am I?"

"Well, for now, you're the ghost of an armadillo—which isn't that much different, practically speaking, from what you were just prior to this."

Dick nodded. "So what else am I?"

The heavyset man shrugged. "Well, think about it. Your entire life was spent working miracles—heck, you couldn't help working miracles; you were invisible. You gave your life so that men—and women—might live. And you couldn't have had a much more virgin birth."

"Really? Me?"

The new Patron Saint of Byroads and Stragglers shrugged again. "Well, that's one possible purpose for it all."

"Hmm. So if that's so, how'd I do this time, do you think?"

"Well, as a religion, I think it's got an excellent chance of taking off. There are already more little flying saucer cults around than there were little Jewish cults last time. Sander's no John the Baptist, but he's at least as charismatic as Moses was. . . ."

"Well, at least he doesn't stutter . . ."

". . . And Jenny will make sure that they treat the women better this time."

"Yeah. And last time I ascended, but I didn't leave any evidence. This time, they've got a *corpus delecti*."

The driver grinned. "And Mike Dupres will make a hell of a Holy Ghost, if he takes the job."

"He's still around—I mean, *not* around?"

The driver nodded his head. "Exactly. Dupres in the flesh is around, too, but the disembodied one still exists in other possibilities, and he still knows how to cross over. Imagine the Voice of Conscience with unlimited telephone access and a predilection for Thou Shalt Not."

Despite his lack of expressive facial muscles, Dick still managed to look doubtful. "Yeah. But really, an armadillo? They're going to buy that?"

The driver chuckled. "Why not? Most religions teach about the same moral realities—be generous, don't kill your friends, don't screw your neighbor's wife. It's the absurdities, the divine jokes, which set them apart. The stuff in the goblet may smell like wine, but it's Christ's blood. Your salvation depends on turning to face a certain stone in a desert thousands of miles away when you kneel to pray. If you do bad things, you'll come back to life as a dog. Or my personal favorite: if you cut a piece of your winkie off, it shows you're the Chosen of God."

"Hmm. Okay. Maybe we've got a new religion. I wish I'd known. I mean, I didn't even get to preach a sermon."

"Oh, well. They never get them copied down right anyway. But I'm sure they'll come up with some collected sayings. . . ."

"Wonderful. 'And thus spake Dick, his first words: *Damned if I know.*'"

"And those who think they know are the truly damned," added the driver. "'And his last words were thus: *Face your fears. Not bad.*'" He shrugged. "But really, do you think they need any more sermons? Like I said, a good Buddhist and a good Christian act just about the same way. It's the miracles that people need—the knowledge that the rules could change, the world could end. . . ."

Dick nodded. "But they're not going to end the world, any more than they did last time."

The driver shook his head. "No. Every couple of thousand years, though, you do have to offer one or two of them the chance."

"Yeah, you're right," said Dick. "And sometimes when the End of the World comes, you just have to tell it to go away again." He flicked the electronic window button with his tongue. The bracing air of upland Mauna Kea whirled in, along with a few light flecks of mist, as the sun rose in a thousand pastels over the cottony layer of clouds that blanketed Hilo.

"Well, what the hey, we're in Hawai'i," said Dick. "I could use a good vacation."

Epilogue

"You know about road reflectors, don't you?" Martin Origen asked Gregor Dennison, as Gregor's pickup truck wound down the Saddle Road toward Hilo.

"Naw, man, what about 'em?" said Gregor.

"You notice how they've sprung up everywhere?" said Martin. "Those little yellow reflector bumps going down the center of the road, and the ones along the edge, that are white facing one direction and red facing the other way?"

"Aw, man, they've had those in Hawai'i for, like, forever. They're great, man. Little lights, twinkling like stars in the night, leading you home."

"They've had them here forever, because Hawai'i was the pilot project. You know what their real purpose is?"

"Yeah, man, like, if you're drunk or stoned or just tired, and you start to drift, and you hear that little *whumpwhumpwhumpwhump*, and you know you're either running off the road or you've got a tire that's about to blow, and the old adrenaline rush is like ten cups of coffee straight up your nose, and you don't head-on somebody. It's an awesome concept, man."

"Well, that's the surface reason, maybe. But the real reason is cameras. Every tenth reflector's got a tiny camera in it."

"No shit, man? What for?"

"Originally it was a project of the Big Three auto makers. It was gonna be the prototype guidance system for a new generation of automatically-steered automobiles. Every fifth bump was gonna have a radio transmitter in it, too, to tell the car what to do, based on what the cameras see. Not only can it keep the car on the road; it automatically tells if there's another car in the way, or if there's some obstruction like a tree or a telephone pole, or even if there's a roadkill to dodge."

"Yecch, man."

"Yeah. But then GM figured out it would be cheaper to use GPS—spinoff technology from the Saucer War. But then the government took over GM in the Great Recession and got the whole system, and it's spreading them on every highway in the country, so they can track everybody going everywhere. The MIB's paying for it."

"Wow. Cool, man."

"Cool?"

"Yeah, man. Then nobody'll ever be alone again."

The truth about roadside reflector bumps is even stranger than Martin's theory, however. Reflector bumps are symbio-technoviruses.

All life is characterized by the urge to reproduce itself—though some life manages to resist the urge, and a great deal more just can't get any. But even within monks and steers, individual cells still reproduce with wanton abandon.

Viruses give biologists intellectual headaches, because they hover right on the edge of life. A virus is a collection of proteins that cannot reproduce itself, but can commandeer the cells of other life forms to replicate it.

A technovirus, similarly, is a mechanical thing that takes over life forms to reproduce itself. Cars, for instance, enslave huge populations to labor every day in factories producing them. Sometimes technoviruses become malignant, devouring their hosts. Crystal Methamphetamine is a malignant technovirus. Cars have been hovering on the edge of malignancy for decades. But most technoviruses are symbiotic, giving something back to their hosts. Road reflectors, as Gregor pointed out, serve the very useful function of keeping even semiconscious humans within their lanes. Therefore humans want more of them, and reproduce them in vast numbers, and even replace them when they break or wander off. Thus do road reflectors become fruitful and multiply?

Jokes and stories and ideas represent a similar phenomenon. Leonardo DiCaprio speeches notwithstanding, most ideas aren't really "the most resilient parasite." They're symbiopsychoviruses. They can't reproduce themselves, but if they're of any value, we copy them and share them. They embed themselves in each mind that experiences them, forever altering, if only slightly, the experience of their host. They live on in our thought processes, experienced over and over, and sometimes give birth to wild hybrid offspring.

This story has been—and is, and shall be—a figment of your imagination. You cannot get rid of it now. It is part of you. Somewhere in your mind, for the rest of your life, a little armadillo will live, awaiting its chance.

Be good to it. It loves you.

Thank you for reading my book! I really appreciate all of your feedback, and I love hearing what you have to say. Please leave me a REVIEW on Amazon.

— *Alan D. McNarie*

About the Author

At various times, Alan D. McNarie's been a farm kid, a frozen yogurt salesman, a college professor, an award-winning poet and playwright, and, for many years, a freelance journalist on  the Island of Hawai'i, where he's published hundreds of articles and helped to foment several successful grassroots rebellions just by unearthing the facts. His first novel, Yeshua, won the Editor's Book Award over a quarter-century ago. His second has been a long time coming—but it's worth the wait.